# MEANT TO BE

First Edition

ISBN: 9780645415681

Formatting by Genicious

*https://laurenjacksonauthor.com*

# LAUREN JACKSON

# MEANT
*to be*

"You'll break my heart, Harley."

"Have you ever thought
you might break mine?"

*To everyone who's ever struggled with choosing what their heart*
*wants, over what others tell them to do.*

# Playlist

**Step Ahead** – DSARDY, Son Little
**I hate u, I love u** – Garrett Nash, Olivia O'Brien
**Look After You** – The Fray
**Love Me or Leave Me** – Little Mix
**Mad Love** – Mabel
**Everything I Wanted** – Billie Eilish
**Moonlight** – Gaullin
**Numb (Dubstep Remix)** – DJ RusLan
**Phases** - PRETTYMUCH
**Someone You Loved** – Lewis Capaldi
**I'm Yours** – Alessia Cara
**There For You** – Troye Sivan
**Breathe** – Lauv
**YOUTH** – Troye Sivan
**Without Me** - Halsey
**I Love You's** – Hailee Steinfeld
**Unsteady** – X Ambassador
**Somebody to You** – The Vamp, Demi Lovato
**Happier Than Ever (edit)** – Billie Eilish
**Colors** – Halsey
**Hurts Like Hell** – Madison Beer, Offset
**Apologize** – Timbaland, OneRepublic
**Bad Guy** – Billie Eilish
**Bad Liar** – Imagine Dragons
**Breakeven** – The Script
**Bruises** – Lewis Capaldi
**Don't Give Up On Me** – Andy Grammar
**Go F\*ck Yourself** – Two Feet
**Hate Me** – Ellie Goulding, Juice WRLD
**Middle of the Night** – Elley Duhe

# Chapter One

## Josie

Fern Grove. A place I longed to escape. A place I wish I never had to come back to.

I pull my car over near the *Welcome to Fern Grove* sign and spray my windows with windshield wiper fluid. The dust smears across it, making it harder to see out than before. Giving up, I continue on my way.

Peering out of the non-smudged section, I pass the sugar mill, the old petrol station, and the café that my mother used to take me to every Sunday morning. Everything looks the same. I follow the familiar route—one I couldn't forget, no matter how hard I tried—ending up at a long gravel road.

Dad's rust-spotted truck is parked where it always is, my mum's SUV and my brother's Subaru beside it. Sam's car is the only one to have changed in the four years I've been gone. He wrapped his last one around a telegraph pole—or so I read on Facebook.

It's only a moment after I cut the engine that humid air fills the car, causing my shirt to feel damp. I exhale, staring at the old, peeling house. If I'd taken a picture the day I left, not one thing in that picture would be different in the one I'd take now.

I really hate that.

My reflection in the side mirror catches my attention as I step outside the car. I flinch at the sight of it. I don't recognise myself. The roundness I used to get teased about at school is gone, replaced with a sharp jawline and gaunt cheeks.

Birds cry from the trees, and I hear Mum's radio blaring as I approach the front screen door, hanging on its final hinges, already partially open. I look at the gap between the door and the porch, thinking it would be far too easy for snakes to enter. Many times, I woke up to find one slithering across our lounge room floor or hiding in my bookshelves.

I knock once, then twice, before entering. The weathered floorboards groan under my weight. There was once a time I had memorised which ones squeaked and which didn't, in my attempts to sneak out uncaught …

*I barely take a breath as I tiptoe down the stairs, dancing over the floorboards as I reach the front door. Slowly, I swing it open. The warm night air washes over my skin before strong arms wrap around me, dragging me close.*

*He smells like cigarettes and whisky. Two scents a teenage boy shouldn't smell like, but it's a scent that's become familiar to me. A comforting smell that lingers on my hoodies and stains my pillow after we spend hours together.*

*"Did you wear that for me?" he asks.*

*A shiver rolls down my spine. My eyes dart down to the spaghetti-strap white dress that hugs my waist and shows off my legs. "Yes," I whisper.*

*His lips curve. He leans in close, his breath warm against my earlobe. "Good."*

The smell of baked goods guides me to the kitchen, and I mentally shake off the memories that are threatening to take over. I eye the walls, the faded wallpaper, the hanging photo frames. Everything feels too familiar, too small, too cluttered.

I pause. It looks like one thing has changed after all. My photographs on the walls. They're gone. I trail my finger down one of the dusty frames, seeing my mum, dad, and brother smiling back at me. My finger drifts to the empty spot beside them, where I should have been.

Sweat drips down the side of my face and I wipe it away. The heat is almost unbearable. I begged for years for air-conditioning or even ceiling fans. I glance to the ceilings, seeing nothing but accumulated dust and cobwebs.

Mum is humming under her breath, bent at the knees, inspecting something inside the oven. She slams the door shut and spins on her heel.

Our eyes lock.

The glass of water in her hand slips, shattering on the floor. "Josephine," she whispers. She blinks. Her eyes dart over me.

I'm much thinner than I used to be. My skin washed out, hair flat on my shoulders.

Mum creeps closer to me as if scared to make any sudden movements. "Is this real?"

My eyes feel watery as I nod.

Her gaze roams my face, focusing on my black eye. "Oh, honey," she whispers. "You're okay. You're safe now."

I fall into her arms and cry all the tears I've held in for so long.

# Chapter Two

## Harley

The hammer slams one, two, three times before the nail is all the way in. The sun is unrelenting as it beats down on my back. I drag the back of my hand over my forehead and stand, my legs protesting from being in one position too long.

"Kid," my supervisor roars over the sound of whirring machinery. "Take a break."

*Kid.* I've worked for his construction company for almost four years, only a few months shy of finishing my apprenticeship. I work the longest hours, carry the most weight, and climb the highest cranes. And he still calls me *kid.*

Cupping my hand in a half-moon shape over my eyes, my gaze settles on a familiar ute parked in the lot. My father's car. He must be inside the break room. Exhaling, I shake my head and throw a sloppy wave towards George, indicating I'm not taking a break.

"Suit yourself!" he shouts, shaking his head before disappearing inside.

My throat screams for water, but I'd rather pass out from dehydration than be in close proximity with my father. It's been hard enough earning respect from these guys just from sharing his last name, let alone them overhearing the way he speaks to me.

It's not like they don't know. Everyone knows. But I'd rather not have one of our fights happen with a front-row audience.

Turning my back to the shed they've established as the break room, I continue working. Sweat drips into my eyes, and the sting makes me wince. I rub them heavily and sigh deeply through my nose. I glance down at my watch.

Only six hours to go.

An hour and a half after my shift has ended, the sun is slowly sinking into the horizon.

Slinging my arms over the handles of my bike, I turn the lighter over in my fingers, watching the glint off the gunmetal-grey shell. I strike my thumb against it and light the end of my cigarette. Settling it between my teeth, I suck in a deep breath and tilt my head back, letting the smoke pour from my lips and fade into the breeze.

My phone beeps. Brennon, most likely. My best friend of fourteen years, roommate of three.

**Brennon:** Drinks tonight?

Pushing my hand through my hair, I let my head hang forward. I should want to do this. Be social. Interact. But everything is so *dull* here. The people. This place. Everything that is Fern Grove. Nothing interests me anymore.

It's time to move on. But to where? To do what?

*A few more months*, a voice whispers. *Your apprenticeship is almost finished. Just hang in there a little longer.*

I've been telling myself this for two years now. After a few too many beers and a breakdown yesterday, I packed my bags. They're stuffed inside my closet, hiding from Brennon's peering eyes. I'm so close to walking away from this place. I just don't have anywhere to go.

**Harley:** Working at the pub.

**Brennon:** Call in sick.

I shove my phone back in my pocket. Brennon's lack of work ethic frustrates the hell out of me. He's grown up in the safety net of wealth. He's never had to work to survive, and it shows.

Every muscle in my body hurts. Working 6:00 AM to 4:00 PM in construction and then 6:00 PM to 10:00 PM at the pub makes my body ache like it never has before. On days like this, it doesn't seem worth it. But it is. The more financially independent I am, the sooner I can get the hell out of here. And never come back.

The bike rumbles to life, and I ride directly to work. Shrugging out of my leather jacket, I swing it over a chair in the break room before grabbing my key tag. I swipe the tag over the sensor and punch in my code.

"Evening," Graham, the owner of the bar, greets me. Crow's feet wrinkles sit on the corners of his eyes and his beard has grown longer and scruffier in the past six months than I've ever seen before.

"Hey," I reply.

He looks tired as he passes me, clapping me on the shoulder before going out the back to clock off. My eyes settle on the bar, near-empty except for a couple of locals in the pokies room.

The pub is small and rundown, but that goes for basically all places in this town. It doesn't make much sense to renovate when the town doesn't get any tourists.

Robotically, I wipe down the tables, restock the fridges, and empty the dishwasher. When no more people have entered in the last hour, I rest against the bar and pull out my phone. I search for rooms to rent, making the radius a minimum of four hours from here. My thumb slides over the screen as I scroll, and I feel deflated when I see the prices of rentals.

Fern Grove is affordable and I halve the rent with Brennon, but when I move on my own, it will all be on me. As daunting as it is, it's a goal I'm committed to achieving. I can't stand to be here any longer, and I'm willing to make just about any sacrifice to get out. My loyalty to Brennon has been a big reason for me staying, but honestly, it's not enough anymore.

The bell dings, indicating the arrival of customers, and I glance up to see Nick. Sighing, I slide my phone into my back pocket and move towards the register. Even after all these years, Nick and I have never comfortably met eyes.

My gaze dips over his neat button-up shirt and beige slacks. I don't really have a valid reason for hating him, but I do.

"Your usual?" I ask.

"Yeah."

Curling my hand around the schooner glass, I place it under the tap and hold it. I push it across the counter. He slides his card into the machine—which doesn't have PayWave because Graham refuses to modernise even in the most basic form—and it takes several moments to flash approval. Without a word, Nick slinks over to the table furthest from the bar, where his father is already seated.

My gaze drifts towards the wet floor sign, and I'm half tempted to race past it so I fall and bang my head so hard I go into a coma for a few days. Or a year.

# Chapter Three

## Josie

I sleep soundlessly for the first night in what feels like months, and when I wake the next morning I feel like I've been run over by a truck. Heavy limbs, swollen eyes, hair sticking to my skin.

Slithers of sunlight beam through the blinds, and I wince, flinging my arm over my face. Birds outside the window shriek. I haven't heard those sounds since I left for the city. The mattress is hard and lumpy, the blankets are itchy and the room stuffy—but it's home.

The walls groan and sigh. Every movement of my family carries into my room. Voices. Footsteps. Pipes humming. Pots banging. The sounds are so foreign and yet so familiar.

When I was here last, I was a completely different person. It hurts to think about it all now—all the choices I made.

Rolling over, I curl into a ball. My eyes roam over the walls. My chest tightens as my gaze skims across the photographs. Handwritten song lyrics, poems, and quotes are draped unevenly across the walls.

My head hurts. So many thoughts and memories I've refused to let creep in, washing over me in tidal waves.

My gaze drifts to my bedside table. Reaching over, I open the drawer. I rummage through it until I get to a small bundle wrapped in tissue paper with a bow on it. Holding my breath, I unravel it. The necklace has rusted a little over the years. Pressing my thumb over the patterns, I flick open the locket. I stare down at the photograph of myself and the boy smiling next to me. My heart squeezes and I snap the locket shut and throw it back into the drawer as if it burned me.

*It was all a lie.*

I fling myself back across the mattress and wince. The pain in my face is worse than yesterday.

I turn my phone on. It takes a few moments to start back up, and for a second, I think it's dead. The screen eventually lights up, and when the vibrating starts, I place it down and wait it out.

Twenty-four missed calls from Elliot, twelve voice messages, nine texts.

I get through one text before I'm rushing to the bathroom, where I empty my stomach into the toilet bowl. Sitting back on my haunches, my arms tremble.

The door bangs open, and a foot kicks my leg. A manly scream fills the room, and I scamper to my feet, wiping my mouth.

My younger brother stands before me, open-mouthed, eyes wide.

"Are you a ghost?" he sputters.

"I wish."

He's silent as his eyes take in the bruises and scratches littering my skin. He swallows.

"Fuck … what happened to you?"

Sam's hair is longer now, falling in his eyes. He sweeps it back, only for it to fall in the same place again. He's tall now, a lot taller, and filled out too.

Words are stuck in my throat. I might be sick again.

"When did you get back?" he asks.

"Last night."

"You look like shit."

"I feel like shit."

Silence again. He surveys me, like I'm cattle he's fattening up to sell at the next auction. He places his hands on his hips, a frown tugging his lips down.

"Well. Shit." He shakes his head.

"Yeah."

His eyes haven't stopped roaming over me, inspecting every inch, frowning deeper with each passing moment.

"Want to go for a drive?" he asks.

"Okay."

I'm dressed, teeth brushed, and half-presentable when I climb into my brother's inappropriate-for-the-farm car. It has more dings in it than our tin roof after the 2011 hailstorm.

It's a dry heat out here, one I haven't missed. I brush my hair back and flip the visor up, unable to stand the sight of my black and purple eyes staring back at me.

"Your friends know you're back?" he questions, adjusting the radio, which is hardly audible over the clunking car.

"What friends?"

He makes a sound in his throat. They're not the only ones I never spoke to after I left.

"Your hair is long," observes Sam, side-eyeing me.

"So is yours."

He remembers me as a bubbly, talkative girl with an uneven haircut and crooked teeth. I whitened and straightened my teeth the moment I hit the city. My hair is now to my ribs and a platinum blonde, not the yellow straw-like hair I had previously. I swapped the curves for a diet of protein shakes, dropping the weight faster than I dropped my friends.

Eyelash extensions, lip fillers, and a bottle of fake tan have transformed me into someone unrecognisable.

Now I'm washed out, thin, and beat up. Damaged goods.

The car clatters and clangs across the gravel road, making me feel nauseous again. He winds up a hill, stopping at the old water tanks. We wordlessly exit the car and climb the tanks. The steel ladder is savagely hot as I mount it.

We dangle our legs off the side like we did as kids. Sam's skin has darkened from too many hours in the sun. Red dirt clings to him and kneads through his hair. He must have been out on the farm this morning. His thumb runs up the side of his hand, a nervous habit he's had for years.

"You just left," he says. His voice is a lot deeper now. "No goodbye. No explanation."

"No explanation was needed."

"And the goodbye?"

I stare out at the brown grass and endless paddocks. Sweat drips down the back of my neck. Dust settles in my eyelashes.

I fucking hate it here.

"I get why you left," he says after a few moments.

"I'm sorry."

"It's a little late for that."

I stare down at my bare thighs. Black, blue, purple. Some fading to yellow. Bruises. All over me.

"How long was it happening?" Sam asks with a lethargic gesture to my legs. I blink at him for a few moments, unable to comprehend how grown up he is. He looks a lot more like our father now. Dirt is caked under his nails, and it appears he hasn't shaved for quite a few days. The rugged look suits him.

"Long enough."

"A while, then?"

I don't answer.

"Christ," he curses, shaking his head. "You could have told someone."

"I could have done a lot of things differently."

"I don't even know you." He sounds angry this time, frustration and betrayal leaking into his voice. His hands bunch into fists, his knuckles growing white. "We were best friends. And now I don't know a damn thing about you."

I turn to face him with a sad smile. "I don't even know myself."

I don't leave the house for a week.

My arrival back in town is going to be newspaper-worthy gossip. I need to look my best. And for that, these damn bruises need to fade.

I slept, mostly. Ate a little. Cried a lot. Slept some more.

Dad's not speaking to me. Sam is trying to find out everything that has happened in my life since I left. Mum won't stop trying to fatten me up. Despite the constant sleeping, I feel exhausted.

Being back here is mentally draining. Everything I fought so hard to ignore and forget has caught up with me and doesn't look like it's letting go anytime soon. I would have gone anywhere else—if there *was* anywhere else.

It's noon, and I'm a little more than tipsy. I'm cruising around the house in a bikini top and denim shorts that leave "little to the imagination." Mum scoffed when she saw me. She didn't make a comment about my breast implants, but the disapproval is radiating off her.

"Do you need to walk around in that little of clothing?" she barks in annoyance when I fling myself beside her on the back chair, an iced tea clutched in my palm. My mother has a timeless beauty about her. Sun-kissed skin, pretty golden hair, and pale blue eyes.

"It's, like, forty fucking degrees," I argue.

She flinches at the profanity as if I'm still a child who's not allowed to say a naughty word. I want to snort at her expression, but I don't. She let me back in after everything. I appreciate that.

"Have you spoken to him?"

She wanted to ask this all week. I was wondering when she would finally build the courage.

"Who?"

She gives me a flat look. "You know who."

"Voldemort?"

Mum scowls, shaking her head. She's never appreciated sarcasm.

"Elliot," she hisses. "Has he tried to contact you?"

"Sure."

"Sure?" she counters, furrowing her eyebrows.

"Yes," I grind out. "He calls. Texts. Leaves voicemails. Threats. All that garbage."

A pitying look falls across my mother's face. I look away and slurp loudly on my drink, keeping my expression as blank as possible.

"Are you afraid?"

"No."

"You looked terrified, hon. When you arrived." Her voice is low now as if scared I might overreact. It's a possibility.

"I'm not."

Disbelief is clear in her eyes. "You drove five hours in the middle of the night."

I take a long sip of my iced tea, which is partly filled with vodka— okay, *mostly* filled with vodka.

Mum sighs as she stands, her knees cracking. "You want a cup of tea?"

I wrinkle my nose, unsure how she could possibly suggest a hot drink on a day like this.

"No thanks."

Resting my head back in the chair, I stare around the back porch. I used to spend hours out here, working on projects, reading, drawing. Drawing was something I loved to do, but I stopped when I moved to the city.

It's the coolest part of the house. Somewhere I feel like I can actually breathe. I take a long inhale, folding one leg over the other.

"What's on for the weekend?" I ask once she's returned.

The mug clips against the metal table, and the chair groans as she sits. She blows on the top of it for longer than necessary, before taking a tentative sip.

"There's a rodeo on."

I resist the urge to roll my eyes. "Great."

"You should come," she offers.

I finish my drink and stare at it for a moment, wishing it would miraculously refill. I twirl the straw around, and the ice clinks against the glass.

"What's your plan, Josephine?" she eventually asks after sitting in an awkward silence for several minutes.

"It's Josie, and I have no idea."

She sighs again. This time, the silence stretches. I settle into my chair and watch the sky. The clouds drift slowly, with birds ducking and weaving, the sun unyielding, beating down on the dying grass paddocks.

"I might need to stay a while." She glances at me. "I'm looking for a place, though. I won't be a burden."

Mum tsks. "We just got you back, Josephine. You're not a burden."

"Josie."

"Hmm?" she asks.

"It's Josie now," I tell her. I'd dropped the name Josephine the moment I drove past the Fern Grove sign all those years ago. Hearing my full name on Mum's lips makes me cringe. I'm not her anymore. I will never be her again.

*"You're my forever, Josie."*

Squeezing my eyes shut, I exhale. As much as I longed to forget *him*, the nickname he gave me ended up being the name I chose to go by. I've tried to convince myself it has nothing to do with him, but it's a lie. I've always been a great liar.

Mum's eyebrows draw together. "Josie. Sure. Okay. Why the name change?"

"I just needed something different."

Mum chews her lip. For as long as I remember, that's something she's done when she's thinking. She's dressed in cut-off denim shorts she cut herself. Threads hang down her thighs. Her leather boots are covered in dust, thick charcoal grey socks peeking out. She really is beautiful. Not that she makes any effort to show it.

"How did you meet him?" she asks.

"Elliot?"

"Yes."

Breathing out, I sink further into my chair and throw my legs out, crossing them at the ankles.

"I met him at a bar."

"What was he like?" she questions.

My stomach churns just thinking about it. Slowly, I shift the glass in my hand, watching the ice melt.

"Charismatic. Strong-headed. Stubborn." I laugh quietly. "Controlling."

"Did you love him?"

"We're getting deep here," I joke.

"It's a simple question."

"No," I reply. "I didn't."

"Have you ever loved someone?" she murmurs.

We meet eyes. I stare back unflinchingly. She already knows the answer to that. Slowly, she nods, looking out across the grass.

"Not Nick," she says. "Right?"

"I don't want to talk about this."

"I just don't understand, Josephine."

"It's *Josie*," I snap. "*Josie* Goddamn Mayor."

Mum blinks, jolting a little in surprise at my tone. "Right. I'll get used to it."

"There's a studio apartment close to town that I'm going to apply for."

"You'll stay here," she says firmly.

"Leaving already?" a deep voice says from behind us.

I startle, not having heard Dad return home. I swivel my gaze to where he is leaning against the kitchen doorway, his skin flushed red from the heat and slick with sweat.

"Lasted five minutes," he says. "Should have put money on it."

"Bruce." Mum frowns.

Resentment built up from the last four years plagues him. He hasn't met my eyes in three days.

"Leave." Dad shrugs, pushing off the frame. "It's what you're best at. Don't let the door hit you on the way out."

I stare after him, a retort hot on my tongue, but I swallow it.

"He doesn't mean it, hon," my mother murmurs.

Not taking my eyes off the doorway, I offer a half-shrug.

"Yeah. He does."

# Chapter Four

## Harley

The bullet slices through the metal with a distinct clang. The sound echoes around the valley. Inching the gun to the right, I squeeze the trigger again.

*Bang, bang, bang.*

This sound has become somewhat therapeutic for me. I prefer to come out here alone. I like the quietness and the stark contrast of the explosion from the gun.

I lower the gun and turn, yanking down my earmuffs so that they rest around my neck as Brennon lets out a low whistle.

"Have you ever once missed your target?" he asks.

I tilt my head, thinking. "Not for a while."

Brennon wears an impressed expression as he lines up his row of cans. I step back and rotate my shoulder; the kickback of the gun always leaves a slight jolt in my arm when I hit that many in a row.

His aim is sloppy, and he doesn't take the time to focus. He never does. Patience and concentration are something Brennon has never gotten the hang of. Brennon has high-range ADHD. It's never been addressed. There are many things that Brennon does that I don't agree with, but he is family. More loyal to me than my own blood. When things got hard, he took me in. Always. And for that, I will always stand by him…

*My father's foot slams into my ribs. Coughing, I half-roll, throwing my arms around my head. His heavy foot collides against my side over and over until I'm wheezing and spitting blood.*

*"Jamie!" my mother sobs. She stumbles towards him, her thin fingers wrapping around his bicep, attempting to pull him away.*

*He shoves her back effortlessly, causing her to crash to the floor.*

*"You're a piece of shit," my father growls, dropping down low. His fingers twist around my shirt as he drags me from the floor so that I'm sitting up. My eyes are heavy and swollen as I peer up at him. "Nothing but a waste of fucking space." His face lowers, so close that I can smell the stench of his stale, bourbon-laced breath. "You ever lay a hand on me again, I'll kill you."*

*My breath is raspy as he drops me onto the hard floor. The sound of Mum wailing fills the room. He stomps from the room, slamming the door shut behind him so hard that it rattles the walls.*

*"Baby!" she sobs, falling to her knees, her hands flitting over me. "Talk to me. Where does it hurt?"*

*"Everywhere," I choke out.*

*Tears stream down her cheeks as she gathers me in her arms, holding me to her. The door is kicked open, and she's pulled away from me. She cries out as he yanks her to her feet and pulls her from the room.*

*"Leave him," he demands, swivelling his narrowed eyes to me. "He deserves to be alone."*

*They leave the room and the sound of my mum screaming for me rings in my ears. After a long moment, I slowly push to my feet, barely able to support myself as I lean against the wall.*

*Sucking in as much air as I can through my teeth, I push off the wall and slip out through the side door. I limp slowly and quietly out through the gate. The trek to Brennon's seems twice as long and unbearable. The hot sun burns through my clothing, making sweat drip into all my cuts. They sting like a motherfucker.*

*I shove through the tall gate of Brennon's backyard, stumbling to my knees. With extreme effort, I scramble to my feet and keep walking until I'm in the back area that was once a garage, but Brennon has transformed into his room.*

*Gun-shots from the TV blast through the window, and I push through the door. Brennon is seated on the lounge, his legs propped up on the coffee table in front of him, his headset on. His eyes almost pop out of his skull when he sees me.*

*He's on his feet, rushing towards me. His arms take on most of my weight as I stumble, hardly able to see anymore. The swelling is the worst it's been in a while.*

*"Jesus Christ," Brennon mutters, stepping back, his hands on my shoulders as he quickly assesses my injuries.*

*He guides me towards the lounge, and I collapse heavily onto it, leaning my head back. Brennon moves on autopilot. He gathers the first-aid kit, which may as well be the Harley Repair Kit.*

*"You know the drill," he says. "It's going to hurt."*

*The stinging and burning is something I'm used to. I barely flinch anymore. I grit my molars and stay still as Brennon wipes and dabs, cleaning my cuts.*

*"Stay here," he says. "For as long as you need."*

*"Thank you," I hiss through the pain, screwing my eyes tightly shut.*

*"Anything for you, brother," he says, squeezing my arm. "You're family."*

"When are you going to come hunting with us?" Brennon asks, snapping me back to reality. He shoots, hitting two of the five of his targets.

*Us.* Brennon and his brothers. I barely have it in me to stand being around Brennon anymore, let alone with two others just like him. All of them together are chaotic, especially doing something as inhumane as that.

I used to go away a lot with Brennon and his family. I would have gone anywhere—with anyone—to escape this place for a while. His family has a farm even further west than here. We would go for a week or so. It was basically a week of drinking and hunting—and only one of those things I half-enjoyed. It's been years since I've agreed to go, and Brennon has yet to take the hint.

Shaking my head, I reload. "Not interested."

Brennon opens his mouth to argue—like we have many times about this—but he exhales and drops it. For the first time in his life.

"Next, you'll become a fucking vegetarian," he mutters.

"If you spent as much time focusing on the job at hand as giving me a hard time, you might be better at this."

Brennon's eyes swivel to mine as he glowers at me. "Fuck you, Harley."

I grin. "Try not to miss this time."

He scowls. He aims, and this time, he hits the two targets with ease. I clap my hand on his shoulder.

"Better."

Stalking back to the esky, I cup my hand over my eyes before I withdraw two cans of beer. I toss one at him and crack the other before taking a long sip. The alcohol is cold and crisp on my tongue. I swallow it down in greedy gulps.

"Christ, it's hot," I complain, blinking away the sweat threatening to leak into my eyes. Reaching into the bag, I pull out my cap and fling it over my head, shielding my eyes from the harsh sun rays filtering through the trees.

"Let's go to the dam after this," Brennon suggests. "Could use a swim."

"Sounds good."

When I finish my drink, I set up another five cans. Standing in my usual spot, I slide my earmuffs back over my ears and shoot. After Brennon has finished, we gather the cans up and tie the bag onto the back of the quad. Brennon loads the esky onto the back of the other before we rev the engines to life.

We take off, zigzagging and cutting each other off as we make our way across the fields. I let out a loud laugh as Brennon narrowly avoids a ditch that would have sent him tumbling.

The engine has barely turned off before I'm diving into the dam. The water glides over my skin and through my hair, relieving me from the piercing sun overhead. I shake my head when I emerge, water droplets spraying everywhere.

As I tread water, I stare down at my arms. Scars litter the skin of my left elbow.

"You ever going to ride again?"

I glance a Brennon for a moment before looking back down at my arm. A patch of skin is off-colour, where I had to get a skin graft. Sometimes, when I close my eyes, I feel it happen all over again.

The bull's head ducking, his back vertical. Being slingshot into the air. Hitting the ground so hard, it seemed like every bit of oxygen in my body was sucked up into a vacuum. Hooves digging into my body. Bones shattering. People screaming. Blood soaking my clothes, dripping over the dirt ground. Darkness.

I haven't ridden since it happened over a year ago. I only started riding to have something to do around here. To try to fit *somewhere* here. I hated every minute of it.

Tearing my eyes away from the scars, I look forward, out to the grass paddocks. A cow canters across the glade, stirred up from the sounds of the motorbikes.

"I don't know."

"You should," he replies. "You were great at it."

Every time I think about settling onto a bull's back, a sickening sensation grips my stomach. I've never felt anything like it. I've always been adventurous, getting myself into all sorts of trouble. I'm no stranger at the hospital, but something about this has shaken me to my core. Maybe it's because I really did, for a few moments, think I was going to die.

"Yeah. Maybe."

"Your number one spot has been taken," Brennon continues, oblivious to the fact that this is the last thing I want to be talking about. "Sam Mayor has gotten good. Really good."

"Good for him."

I can't look at Sam Mayor without thinking of his sister. And that makes my head hurt.

So much pain. Heartache. Regret. I think back to what I did and feel sick to my stomach. The way I acted. The things I did to Nick. I hate myself for it.

Seeing Brennon's lips part—ready to continue talking—I dive under the water. The thick silence fills my head, and my body relaxes. I swim far from him and deeper until my lungs burn, begging for relief. Finally, when I'm close to pushing the limit, I kick up to the top. Brennon's back on land now, fishing for another beer. He clearly didn't notice how long I stayed under. He never does.

After going under one more time, I also retire to the bank, pulling my clothes back on. I grab the can from his outstretched hand and finish it in one sip. My throat burns, and my head spins. It was too much, too quick.

"Let's head back," I say when it looks like Brennon is about to sit down. "I have to work this afternoon."

Brennon nods. "Sure. Let me finish this first."

I settle onto the bike, resting my leg on the wooden stump I parked next to. My gaze drifts over the grass. The bull incident was over a year ago, but I still think about it daily. It makes me wonder.

What am I doing here? What am I doing with my life? If I had died, what would they say about me?

There's no point saying any of this out loud. No one cares, especially not Brennon. He would tell me to shut the fuck up. Or punch me. Perhaps both.

"Let's hit it," Brennon says.

He swings his leg over the bike, then lurches forward, dust flying behind him. I dart around the dust cloud and speed up until we are neck and neck. I propel forward, leaving him behind.

Like I should have long ago.

That night at the pub, my phone sends vibrations down my leg as I'm refilling the ice bucket. Pausing, I pull it out, seeing *Louise* across the screen. A curse leaves my lips. We are meant to be hanging out tonight. I totally forgot about it. I never wanted to in the first place, but Brennon set it up, and I couldn't turn it down without seeming rude. He's 'concerned' about my lack of dating the past couple of years.

I don't have any interest in anything anymore, or so it seems.

Sighing, I decline the call and push my phone back into my pocket. There are a dozen unread messages on my phone from girls I've met at parties. I need to stop kissing girls when I'm drunk and expecting it not to have any consequences.

I pull on the handle and carry the bucket back out to the bar. Gary, the one guy who is here more than me, is lined up, an empty schooner glass in his hands.

"How've you been keeping?" he asks when I take the glass from him wordlessly.

I place it in the rack, ready to go into the dishwasher and pull out a new one, placing it under the tap.

"Not bad, Gary. Yourself?"

"Can't complain," the man says as I slide the glass over the bench. He offers me a wrinkled smile. "Put it on my tab?"

I chuckle—a forced one, to be polite—and take the ten-dollar note from him.

"I think you'd abuse that tab if we set one up." I smile.

"You might be right about that," he says gruffly with a wink before he moves back to his seat.

Huffing, I lean back on the counter, sweeping my gaze around the room. The outdated floors are scratched and worn down, needing to have been replaced at least a decade ago. The same faces that are here every day blink back at me as they pass, taking seats at their usual spots. Low rumblings of conversations fill my head.

Today is no different from any other day. Work, sleep, repeat.

A stale stench of cheap beer and old tobacco fills the air. Old men move around the tables, most barely glancing in my direction. I have nothing here. Sure, there's Brennon and the other guys that I associate with at parties, but it's not enough. Loneliness gnaws at me. And something else—something unnerving and unsettling—itching under my skin, making me restless.

Unlocking my phone, I stare at the time, wishing my deadpan stare would somehow quicken the speed of it. But I know the sooner I go home, the sooner this whole process repeats. My stomach cramps thinking about it.

The rest of the night inches by, and then I'm clocking off and striding out to my truck, the loose gravel of the carpark crunching under my boots. My lips press on the end of a cigarette, and I inhale sharply through my teeth. I lean against the truck, propping my foot up on the foot mount.

A text comes through.

**Louise:** Hey handsome, are you still at work? Are we still catching up? X

I finish the cigarette and stare up at the sky for a few moments before sliding into the driver's seat. The text remains unanswered as I cruise back home. Two cars I don't recognise are parked near our driveway. I sigh. *Great.*

When I step inside, there're voices murmuring and music playing from the lounge room. Quietly, I slink into my room and beeline for the shower.

I shower off the day, leaning heavily on the glass. The water running over the cuts I got from work stings, and I welcome the pain. Exhaustion burns my eyes, but I know Brennon won't let me simply go to bed when we have guests over. If I weren't madly saving every penny I earned, I would pay the extra rent to have my own place. But I can't make that sacrifice when escaping this place is what I ultimately want. Swinging the door of my closet open, I stare down at the packed bags. I must stand there for five minutes, my mind turning over the thought of doing it. With a heavy sigh, I close the door. I need a plan.

I dress in unintentionally ripped shorts—I honestly don't think any of my shorts have survived without some sort of wear and tear—and throw on the first shirt I see. I emerge from my room to see Brennon strolling towards me, a pretty blonde on one side of him, Louise flanking the other.

"Hi, Harley!" Louise perks up, her eyes raking over me.

I offer a tight-lipped smile in return. "Hey."

"We were just about to make another drink," Brennon says, his eyes boring into mine as if warning me not to be a 'soft-cock', like he usually calls me when I don't want to entertain all hours of the night like he does. Unlike him, I have a job. *Two.* I'm barely running on any battery by the time I make it back home, and the last thing I feel like doing is this.

"Sure."

He looks relieved as he nods at me, removing his arms from the girls and loping into the kitchen, followed closely by the blonde that I know I've met before but can't recall her name.

I shouldn't agree, but the numerous times he's looked after me makes me feel like I'm indebted to him. And it feels like I'll be repaying him forever.

"How was work? I texted you," Louise says. She's a tall, thin girl with dainty freckles scattered over her cheeks. Long, dark hair trails down her shoulders.

"It was okay. Yeah, sorry, phone was flat. It's on charge now."

Her smile brightens. "Oh. No problem."

In the kitchen, a glass of whisky is pushed into my hand, and I greedily down half the glass in one swig. Although I just showered and the air-conditioner is on, I'm beginning to feel sticky already. It's always so fucking humid here. I can appreciate Brennon's hotblooded nature, though, and his need to always have the air and fans on makes being at home much more bearable.

Brennon refills my glass when it gets low, smirking in my direction. He's grinning like a Cheshire cat, knowing he is getting laid tonight, even though he's been seeing another girl in town who probably thinks they're exclusive. Considering what happened in high school, it shouldn't bother me as much as it does. But things are different now. I'd like to think I wouldn't repeat my past.

We move to the dining table, where Brennon sets up a drinking game. I force myself to play along for three rounds before I admit how beat I am. For once, Brennon's eyes don't flare at me in annoyance. He must be ready to take the party back to his room, then. I've timed it well.

The other two disappear into his room, and I awkwardly ask Louise if she is planning to stay. She blinks at me, obviously having expected to hook up.

"I'll crash on the lounge," she says eventually, looking at the floor. I pass her a blanket and pillow before awkwardly leaving to go into my room. I've just drifted off to sleep when I hear my door creak open. Soft footfalls pad towards my bed, and a hint of lavender wafts over me.

"Hi," she whispers.

Exhaling, I peel the blanket back, allowing her to crawl in beside me.

"Were you asleep?"

"No," I lie.

"Good," she whispers.

When her hand moves to my thigh

When her hand moves to my thigh, I turn to face her, placing a hand on the side of her face. I touch her dark hair, twisting it around my finger, thinking about the blonde hair that I'd rather …

But that's a distant memory now.

I need to forget about her. It's all in the past now. And that's where it is going to stay.

# Chapter Five

## Josie

As I stroll into town, I feel like I've been transported back in time.

It doesn't take long to get to the café. I haven't been out and about since I got home, but now that my bruises have faded and I'm feeling semi-sane again, I thought it was time to venture out into the real world.

It's busy—as expected, considering there are few other options around here. The café is buzzing with voices, the clattering of utensils, and furniture scraping against the faded lino flooring. There's a collective intake of breath when I enter, the bell ringing like a foghorn announcement. With my tight-fitting top and mini skirt, I stand out like a sore thumb. My platinum hair shining under the lights is like a neon sign flashing above my head declaring *I don't belong here*.

The server behind the counter not-so-subtly eyes me up and down, a look of distaste on her puffy face. Her ginger hair piled on top of her head looks rigid as if it hasn't changed from that style in months.

"Visiting?" She chews gum obnoxiously. Bits of spit splatter onto the counter. "We don't get too many visitors here. Not enough touristy things to do." She says the word 'touristy' like it's a curse. She shakes her head as if annoyed, even though I haven't said anything yet.

"You don't remember me?" I ask.

It took a moment for me to realise it's Joanne Burnett under the puffy cheeks and dark freckles. She's changed a lot since we last knew each other. She babysat me once. I bit her thumb and made her cry. She was twelve years older than me. It scored me some cool points back in the day.

She offers me a confused expression, tilting her head. "We've met before?"

"Josie?" I offer. "Josie Mayor?"

"Josephine!" she half-shrieks, gaining even more attention. "I didn't … you look … wow," she concludes, dumbfounded. "Your hair … and your …" I don't know what body part she's referring to next. Everything, probably.

"Josie, yeah," I correct.

"Wow." She shakes her head. "You're back?"

"I guess so, yeah."

"Staying with the folks?" She leans against the counter. I notice she has little tattoos dotted up her left arm in all different shapes and patterns. Tattoos were very taboo here once, so I got at least three inked across my skin within the first year of having left this place behind.

"Yeah. For now."

"What have you been up to?"

"A lot."

She pauses at my dull response, waiting for more, before quickly realising that's all I am going to say.

"I married Angus," she announces. "You remember him?"

*Of course you did. In Fern Grove, you marry the first person you date because no one ever leaves.*

"Yes, Angus. I remember. You've been together for a long time."

"Got four little rugrats now too!"

"Four? Jesus." I raise my eyebrows.

She looks offended for a moment at my tone, but it fades quickly.

"Well, anyway, great to see you." She beams, and I'm a little surprised at that. I didn't think anyone would say those words to me, especially not the first time they see that I've returned. Four years might seem like a lifetime, but in the world of small-town scandal, it's not long. No one would have forgotten what happened. And why I left. "What can I get for you?"

The shop fills a little more while I wait for my coffee. I lounge against the counter and let my eyes roam over the pastries in the cabinet. It's a pathetic display compared to what I'm used to, and I feel sad about all the great restaurants and bars I no longer have access to. I watch as a fly enters through the crack in the door and lands on one of the brownies. I cringe, turning away from it. I'm definitely not in the city.

Two girls I remember from school notice me. Or rather, I notice them *gawking* at me. Their necks are bent, mouths whispering furiously, another girl craning to get a better look. Two boys are also sitting at the table, their backs to me.

I exhale, turning back to the cabinet. The fly has moved to one of the blueberry muffins. I had been thinking about ordering one and now quickly dismiss the thought.

"Is that really you?"

Hearing his voice causes my heart to drop into my stomach. Slowly, I turn.

Shock registers on his face when our eyes meet. His eyes travel over me quickly and hungrily, drinking in every detail, making my skin flare as if I were seventeen again.

Nicholas Schneider. High school sweetheart. Heartthrob. My

first boyfriend.

God. He is still handsome. Very, very handsome.

His skin is darker now, with freckles painted across his nose. His hair is lighter, sun-bleached, and clipped short. Maybe a little too short. His warm, leaf-green eyes are still as gentle, and as gorgeous as ever.

I remember pining after him. The flush deepens. Heat rises up my neck, and I smile charmingly, hoping I appear more aloof than I feel.

"Nick. Hi. Been a while."

He's speechless, eyes still searching. The stunned expression hasn't left his face. I must seem like a ghost. I feel like one. It's been so long.

He pulls me to him suddenly, and I stiffen in surprise. His big arms engulf me in a bear hug. I hate that I curl into him and hug him back harder than I have hugged anyone in a long time, excluding my lapse the first day I blew back into town.

When he steps back, his heavy hands are still on my shoulders.

"You look fantastic," he tells me, and I know he means every word. He loved me when I was ugly. "Very different. Like. So different." His eyes are wide. "But great. Wow. I can't believe you're here."

I've thought of this moment many times. I never pictured him to be so happy to see me. But of course he is. He's Nick.

"You too, Nick. You've aged well." We're only twenty-one years old—Nick actually twenty-two—but I feel like I've aged a lifetime since I was last here. "Is it weird to say you look a lot like your dad?"

"I don't think so."

"Good. Because I always thought your dad was pretty hot."

He exhales a breathy laugh, shaking his head. "Good to see your sense of humour hasn't changed." He smiles then. His wide, friendly smile. "Can we have dinner? Catch up?"

My mind automatically scrambles to think of a hundred excuses not to. I have none. Because I would love to have dinner with Nick. I also can't wrap my head around the fact that he is *happy* to see me.

It's also really nice of him to ask. Now I know for sure he doesn't hate me. That's a bonus.

"Are you asking me out, Nick?" I give him a catlike grin.

He turns pink.

"Yes, Josephine." He nods, smiling. "I'm asking you out. As old friends."

I roll my eyes. "That's boring. And it's Josie now."

He inches a little closer to me, enjoying the flirting. "Would you like it to not be as old friends?"

I offer a one-shoulder shrug.

His grin widens. "Then sure. I'm asking you out, Josie. What do you say?"

"I'll think about it," I say breezily.

Joanne slides my coffee over the counter. I thank her with a nod before turning to leave.

"That's it?" Nick presses, standing in front of me.

"What's it?"

He shakes his head at me, trying not to smile. "You're going to make me work for it all over again, aren't you?"

"I don't know what you're talking about," I say innocently.

"You. Me. The pub. Tonight. Seven."

I shake my head. "No."

"No?" He's incredulous.

"My house, six forty-five," I negotiate. "So you can give me a ride to the pub."

His gaze is on my mouth, exactly where I want it to be. I offer him a little smirk.

"Six forty-five. Your house." He nods. "I'll be there."

"Don't be late," I tease, brushing past him.

"Trust me, I wouldn't miss it."

The rumble of Nick's truck clattering down the gravel road sends a swooping sensation through my stomach.

The click of my heels resonates around the small house as I strut down the hall. My brother takes one look at my outfit and shakes his head, choosing not to comment. When I fling the door open, Nick is jogging up the porch steps, the floorboards creaking.

He's dressed in a button-up shirt and jeans, a typical 'going out' style for around here. He could pull off anything. It's hard—if not impossible—to believe he hasn't settled down with a nice girl or even married yet. Everyone around here settles quickly and starts families young.

His eyes roam over me, taking in my curve-hugging black dress with its plunging neckline. The girls around here do *not* dress like this. The thought of the dust and dirt in this house ruining my dress almost made me bail on the idea, but I decided the shocked faces and gossip swirling would make it worth it.

"You look …" He swallows. "Fantastic."

"Thanks." I smile, the first genuine one in a while. A compliment from Nick was something my world revolved around once.

As we make our way to the ute, a panicked look falls over his face.

"Wait!" he bursts, flinging the door open and frantically swiping at his dust-ridden front seat. He begins wiping a towel over it, which only smears the dirt.

"Man," he sighs, shoulders sagging in defeat. "Your dress."

I place a hand on his back. "You're sweet, Nick. It's fine."

He flips the towel, spreading it neatly across the passenger seats and shooting me an apologetic look. I gently lower myself onto the seat, not leaning into anything, and give him another smile. He closes the door after me.

The drive to the pub is short, bumpy, and hot. Nick speaks a lot, bursting to tell me everything that has been going on.

He is co-running his parents' farm with his dad; his mum having taken a step back to help his older sister with her three children. Elizabeth, his sister, married Doug (that was obvious since about the fifth grade), and they have three girls named May, June, and July. I thought he was kidding. He wasn't.

There are a few trucks spotted out the front of the pub. Nick pulls up at the entrance. It's not as busy as I expected, or maybe this is busy for this place, considering the population. It's easy to forget how small Fern Grove is.

It's instantaneous; the moment we walk inside, heads turn, eyes widen. Some recognise me, some don't.

Nick waves, smiles, murmurs 'g'day' to people as we make our way to a vacant table. I lean on my forearms once I've sat and regret it when my skin sticks to the tabletop. It's sweltering in here. I glance up at a ceiling fan weakly whirring above us, barely generating enough breeze to reach our table directly underneath it, let alone anyone else's.

Sweat dots Nick's forehead when he joins me, and he dabs at it with a napkin that was sitting in a steel bucket with a set of knives and forks.

"Enough about me." He smiles, continuing our conversation from earlier. "How are you? What have you been up to?"

"The city was busy." I shrug. "Lots of dinners, cocktails, rooftop parties."

"Sounds luxurious," Nick says, those soft eyes giving me his utmost attention. "What did you do for work there?"

"I'm an OHT."

"A what?"

"Oral Health Therapist," I explain, suppressing a smile at his adorable clueless expression. Frustrating on anyone else, but adorable on Nick.

"Sorry, I don't know what that is."

"I'm a dentist for children up to the age of eighteen, basically."

"Oh." He nods, his dark eyebrows dipping for a moment. "Cool. Do you enjoy that?"

"Yeah, I do. It pays well, and I'm always meeting new people."

"Good for you, Josie." He pronounces 'Josie' slow and a little strange, as if testing the word out on his tongue for the first time.

"I tried to become a professional makeup artist, but there is a lot of competition for that, so I tried this and stuck with it."

"Right," he says. He scratches the back of his neck, suddenly looking a little awkward. Both of those career choices aren't really career choices in Fern Grove.

"I'll get us some drinks. Black fish?" I stand so abruptly, the chair behind me screeches against the floor.

"I'll get them," he insists.

"Next round." I wave him off and saunter to the bar, feeling the eyes of almost every person in the pub on me.

I tap my fingers along the bar as I wait. A tall boy has appeared, with long hair pulled back into a messy low bun. His dark-washed jeans cling tightly to his legs, and a series of dark, swirling tattoos litter his arms. He doesn't look country enough to be in a place like this. Too trendy, too … *shit*. My heart flops into my stomach with a sickening *splat*.

It's him.

He laughs as he serves an old man with puffs of white hair covering his face and a round belly barely contained under his thin shirt. My eyes travel back to Harley.

*Harley freaking Caldwell. The boy of my dreams. Or rather, nightmares.*

Perfect olive skin. Stunning blue eyes. Razor-sharp jawline. God damn it. Why is he still so beautiful?

He finishes his conversation with the man and absently drags a too-used cloth across the bench before his eyes settle on me. Or my chest, to be more specific. I tilt my head to the side as his eyes travel everywhere I want them to.

"Sex on the beach," I say.

He startles as if caught doing something he shouldn't. "What?"

"Sex on the beach?" I drawl, leaning over and pushing myself onto the benchtop, watching his eyes drift lower once more. "Are you capable of making me one?"

He finally pulls his gaze to my eyes and blanches. Because he realises who I am. And he looks like he's been shot in the foot.

I nod, confirming the question behind his eyes.

"You …"

"Remember me?" I ask.

He hasn't blinked in about thirty seconds.

"I sure remember you, you piece of shit," I murmur, leaning further in, my fingernails pressing into the palms of my hand as I fist them. "You ruined my life, and I will never forget that. You're a selfish asshole, and I prayed I'd never have to see your face again."

With that, I straighten, the aloof expression finding my face again as I survey the basic alcohol selection.

"Two beers. Black fish will do." My gaze drifts around the room, and several people dart their eyes away.

Harley hasn't moved and doesn't until I look back. He slowly goes about obtaining the drinks, having grown paler in the last few moments. He slides the drinks across the counter, and I wave my card at him.

"So, no sex on the beach?" I ask when he stares at the machine, as if willing it to say approved faster than it wants to. It finally clears, the machine buzzing so loud, it sounds like it might take off. "Shame," I say. "That's my favourite."

He breathes hard for a moment, appearing speechless.

Good. *You bastard.*

When I'm back at the table, Nick is in deep discussion with the couple behind us, not having noticed the commotion at the bar, thankfully. It's a serious sore spot between us. I'd rather not rehash that piece of history, considering it's the first time I've seen Nick in four years. Since *it* happened.

"Eleanor, Charlie—you remember Josephine Mayor? My…"

"Heartbreaker, childhood sweetheart, girl of his dreams," I casually fill in as I slide back into my seat.

Both of their faces change when they see me. Most definitely because of my outfit and new appearance, but mostly shock over my return. I'm guessing, anyway.

"Sure, of course." It's Eleanor who speaks first. "Hi, Josephine. It's been a long time. How are you?"

"It's Josie now, and never been better." I smile sweetly. "And you?"

"Good," she chirps, glancing at Charlie.

Eleanor and Charlie were two years above us at school, and good family friends of Nick's, so I did a lot with them when I was here.

The small talk between us is strained and awkward, and they soon make an excuse to leave. We order our food, and I try to keep the distaste off my face when I see the limited options on the menu.

"There'll just be a twenty-five-minute wait tonight," the girl twangs, chewing her gum obnoxiously. "Possibly thirty."

"Why?" I deadpan, lazily looking towards the tables. "There is hardly anyone here."

"That's fine," Nick says at the same time. Always the polite, nice guy. "Thanks, Ainsley."

I glance to the bar, sinking a little lower in my seat, and notice Harley has disappeared. Good. I hope my arrival back in town has shaken him.

Mentally disregarding those haunting blue eyes of his, I shift in my seat, hating how my thighs sweat against the hardwood instantly.

"This heat is unbearable," I whine in exasperation. "Has no one ever heard of air-conditioning around here?"

"Air-cons exhaust the generators," he points out. "Remember?"

*Oh, I remember.* Continuous blackouts. Unable to move from the sticky, humid heat. Why anyone *chooses* to live here is beyond me.

"How's co-running the farm going? Is your dad driving you insane?"

"He's been good," he answers. "The drought was stressful on everyone, but we've bounced back. We always do."

Nick's thumb caresses the side of his beer glass. Condensation drips in a ring around the glass, warming the liquid inside to the point our beers are almost undrinkable. He takes another long sip regardless, obviously used to the taste by now.

"What's your deal, Nicholas?" I tease. "No fiancée, no wife? A catch like you?"

He cracks a smile—a forced, strained smile. "In case you forgot, my heart was splintered into a million pieces by a certain someone."

His words cut into me. *Very* deep, but we both force casual smiles on our faces, trying not to think too hard about the past.

"Little old me? Surely not." I wave off breezily. "I was a nobody."

"You were never a nobody. Not to me."

I drain the rest of my glass and clink it down a little too aggressively.

"Another?" he prompts, standing and reaching for my glass before I can answer, obviously wanting to escape the tension-building-by-the-minute air around us as much as I do.

The loud groan of a wooden door draws my attention. Harley reappears, looking a little dishevelled but more composed than earlier. When our eyes lock, I lean back in my chair, challenging him to make the next move. He looks to his feet, scuttling away like the coward he is. Long lost is the cocky bravado he once oozed.

Nick, Harley, and myself—all under one roof—with an audience watching our every move. Perfect.

"Where are you living now?" I ask Nick.

"At the farm."

"You still live at home?" The words are out before I can stop them. I couldn't imagine anything worse.

"Yes and no. I'm at the same place but in the granny flat out the back."

"Oh."

"It's fine." He shrugs. "Has everything I need. And Mum still cooks and does my washing."

I fake a smile. "Great."

Placing the glass against my lips, I take a long drink.

"You really never settled down in the four years I was away?" I ask, my curiosity not satisfied.

Exhaling, he shifts in his seat.

"There was a girl. She lived a few towns over. We met at a fundraiser. I thought we wanted the same things. I proposed after six months of dating." I watch his throat move as he takes a long gulp of his beer. "Turns out, she wasn't ready to settle down. My forwardness freaked her out. The relationship wasn't really the same after that, so we decided to part ways. There was another before her, but when I wouldn't … she wanted to … well … let's just say that didn't last long."

"Oh, Nick," I murmur, realising he had the same problem with her as he did with me. Guilt swirls in my stomach at the thought. "I'm sorry."

He nods. "Thanks. I'm over it all now, but it took me a while. I don't take dealing with heartbreak very well."

"No one does."

There's a heavy tension between us that thankfully gets broken when the waitress places our food in front of us.

Our eyes meet fleetingly before I look down at my plate. I force myself to eat at least half of my meal—even though it tastes like rubber—before I push away my plate. Nick has barely swallowed the last of his dinner before I'm leaning close.

"Want to get out of here?"

He only looks surprised for a moment before he nods. Nick's hand rests on the small of my back as he guides me around the bodies and out the exit. I look over my shoulder to see Harley watching. I shoot him a withering stare before we disappear through the door.

I try to ignore the dust landing on my heels as we make our way back to his ute. The carpark is patchy and uneven. I squint in the dim lighting, trying to avoid holes that are long overdue to be filled in.

"What's next for you?" Nick asks me as we bounce along the road. He clears his throat and repeats his question louder.

"I have no idea. I need to move out. Re-evaluate some life decisions. Move on, I guess."

"You're planning to leave?" he questions, glancing at me. "Again?"

I half-shrug, meeting his gaze. "Unless I have a reason to stay."

Our eyes lock on each other for so long, I hear the tires spin into the gravel on the side of the road. Nick yanks the steering wheel to the right, pulling us back onto the road. He apologises about twenty times, but I wave him off. I've been through a lot worse than something as minor as that.

Nick removes his seatbelt but keeps the truck running when we pull up at the end of my driveway, the air-conditioning barely cool as it spurts through the vents. It makes a loud humming sound that would drive me mad if I was forced to be in here for a long time.

"Thank you for dinner," I say, wanting to lie and say it was great food, but I can't force myself to pretend. I truly can't hide how much I hate it here.

"Thank *you* for coming." He grins his wide, teeth-baring grin. "Honestly, seeing you walk into that café … I couldn't believe it. After all this time."

I'm staring ahead, the yellow glow of the headlights shining into the distance, only the peeling fence posts and browning grass in view. I don't let his words sink in. Instead, I turn, offering him a smirk.

"Did you miss me?"

"Yes." He nods more seriously than I was hoping for. "Of course, I did, Joseph—Josie."

Unclipping my seatbelt, I climb over onto his lap, straddling him. Innocent shock registers on his face, and I settle in deeply, grinding into him and pressing my palms onto his chest. His shirt feels slightly damp under my skin.

"How much?"

"What?" he croaks.

"How much did you miss me?"

"More than you'd ever know."

"Prove it," I whisper.

His warm hands find my back, searing me through the thin fabric of my dress. I lean into him. When he hesitates, I place my mouth over his. I haven't kissed anyone other than Elliot for over two years, and it feels strange, but also like old memories.

His mouth is hot and slippery, his tongue playfully clashing with mine as we work out a groove. God. Nicholas Schneider. The boy I adored. Obsessed over. The boy whose heart I pulled out of his chest and stepped on when I didn't get what I wanted. I don't deserve this. Him. A second chance.

And here I am, back in his arms, like I never left.

I fumble at his buttons, his shirt tearing open under my rushed hands.

"Hey, woah, hey," he flusters when my hands sink lower.

Like always, Nick stops it from getting too far. Which was the start of all our problems.

"Don't tell me you're still holding on to this virgin act." I roll my eyes at him. "We're not seventeen anymore."

Anger and disappointment flash in his eyes. "I just got you back. I don't want to rush anything. I don't even *know* you anymore."

"Who cares?" I huff, pulling his chin to me and kissing him.

"Josie!" he snaps, pushing my hand away. "Stop."

We glare at each other for a heated moment. Guilt slams hard into my gut, but instead of letting it consume me, I bolt from the car. He's right after me, reaching for my arm.

"Wait!" He exhales so deeply that I feel the heat of his breath on the back of my neck. "Can you just wait a damn minute?"

"What?"

"This." He throws his hand between us. "You and me. There's a lot here. You know me, you know my values. Why do you always push it?"

"Because I want more from you," I snap. "I've always wanted *more*."

"You can't expect everything to go back to how it was, Josie. Not after ..." There's a thick silence. He can't say it. "Look," he sighs, running a hand through his hair. "This was too much, too fast, okay? Can we just ... pretend these last five minutes didn't happen?"

I let out a half-laugh, half-scoff, folding my arms across my chest. "No. Not really."

"Why not?"

"Because it's infuriating and confusing and just like four fucking years ago!" I hiss. He flinches. Naïve Josie would never have spoken like this to him. "Don't worry. I'll do everyone a favour and disappear again."

"Why are you being like this?"

I hold my chin high and glare over his head at the dark sky. He sighs heavily once more.

"Josie." His voice is soft. "I just got you back. Please."

Something in me crumbles. My hands fall to my side. He lightly touches my arm.

"What happened to you?" he whispers. "Something ... something bad has happened. Worse than here."

At that, I retract from his hold, backing up as if he'd slapped me. I force a flippant smile onto my face.

"Thanks for dinner and the make-out sesh. A night to truly remember. See you around, Nicky." I mock-salute him and turn on my heel before stalking into the house.

I glare through the blinds and watch as he shakes his head, bewildered, before hopping back into his truck and reversing down the driveway.

"Yikes," my brother's voice floats down the stairs. He's clearly just walked up them after eavesdropping. He is standing in his pyjamas, a bowl of ice cream clutched in his hands. "No wonder you don't have any friends. You're a total bitch."

He strolls away, and I stare after him, feeling a lot worse than I did a few seconds ago.

# Chapter Six

## Harley

Seeing Josie again was like someone had run me over with a truck. And then reversed to finish the job.

Again, I'm stood in the doorway of my closet, staring at the packed bags. *Fuck*. I can't leave now. Not when …

I refuse to let myself think I even have a chance. It's been too long. There's too much history to work through. And yet, just as I was building the courage to walk out of this town and not look back, she shows up. I'm not one to believe in coincidences, but surely this can't have happened without a reason.

A little reluctantly, I begin to unpack. Without thinking, I hang my clothes up just the same as my mother always did. I smile when I think about her. We used to play a game called 'Where are we going today?'

We would sit at the dining table, write down the place we wanted to go, and we would research a bunch of fun things we wanted to do when we were there. It was a small escape, just for a moment, from the suffocating life of living with Jamie—or, as I call him, sperm-donor.

My mother did a lot of little things to try to make life a little more enjoyable for me. For the both of us. I never really understood why she didn't leave him. No money, no family to rely on, no work experience, is my guess. The thing was, he wasn't *always* bad. To her, anyway. It's twisted and fucked up, but she loved him. Despite everything. And honestly, I can't really forgive her for that.

The sound of the coat hanger hitting the rusted metal pole makes me think back to when I returned after my time away. I tried to move once before. The people I stayed with weren't a good influence, and I wasn't in a good state of mind at the time.

It was a blur of partying. Meeting strangers, staying out all night, spending the next day hungover in bed. It was an unhealthy cycle that only got worse and worse the more time I spent down there.

When a few too many drinks led me to the bed of a girl who I didn't know was dating one of the guys I had been hanging with, I was quickly kicked out and told never to come back. I couldn't believe I let myself get caught up in that fucking toxic drama again. I'm older now. I'm meant to be better. But if anything, I'm getting worse.

Brennon welcomed me back with open arms and a lecture for trying to get out. Maybe he's right. Maybe being a bartender/labourer in Fern Grove is all I'm ever going to be. I just wish it was something I was okay with.

Despite it almost being midnight, I throw off my shirt and head down to the makeshift gym I made out of old equipment Brennon no longer uses.

A warm feeling of comfort settles over me when I place my hands inside the boxing gloves. I'm most at peace when I'm here. I do a few warm-ups before launching my fist into the punching bag.

Flashes of memories slice through me. Drinking. Smoking. Fingers sliding through long hair. Lips kissing down my neck.

Grunting, I punch harder, thinking of Nick, and Josie, and everything in between.

*You're not good enough for her,* my father's sinister voice whispers in my mind. *You're nothing.*

My fist slams so hard into the punching bag, it dislodges from the hook, crashing to the ground with a loud bang. I stumble to my knees, hitting the ground over and over, letting tears and frustration pour out of me until I'm completely empty.

# Chapter Seven

## Josie

When I step inside the supermarket the next morning, I'm craving the cool splash of air-conditioned air, only for it never to come. I exhale and move down to the freezer section, hoping that will offer me some relief.

"So, he hasn't called you?" a voice floats from the next aisle over.

I lean against the glass pane, not able to peel myself away from the cooler temperature quite yet. I hear footsteps moving down the aisle across from me.

"No," another voice replies, and my head snaps up at the sound of it. "I know it's taken him a long time to heal, but he is so confusing," the girl continues, and a scatter of goosebumps spike over my skin. "We've been out so many times now. He knows I like him. I don't understand why he would suddenly go quiet again."

"You know why, right?" says the other girl, whose voice is much more obnoxious than the other. It takes me a moment to place her, and I internally cringe. I despise both girls, and here they are, together.

"No?"

"Apparently, she's back."

Silence.

"Who's back?" It's definitely Jessica Thompson speaking. The girl who loved Nick almost as much as me. Maybe even more. The girl who wanted everything I had and would have gladly taken my place when I left.

"Josephine." The other voice belongs to Rianna Seeds, the girl who told me once I was too fat to be in her dance group. I grimace at the memory. That's something I'll never forget. "It's Josie now, apparently. And ..."

"She's back?" Jessica squawks. "And what?"

"They had dinner together last night." Rianna doesn't sugar-coat the truth, and I almost feel sorry for Jess. It's like Rianna wants to rub it in her face that everything she's been working towards has basically collapsed underneath her. Still a bitch, then.

"Joseph—Josie is back?" Jessica's voice has dropped to a whisper, and I have to step closer to the shelving to hear her. "Of course she is. It all makes sense now." I hear the tremor in her voice, and my heart sinks.

I don't want to hear any more. Jessica and Nick. Dating. I shouldn't be surprised. It mustn't be too official if Nick took me out. He is Good Guy Nick, after all.

*"He loses all sense of rationale when it comes to you,"* his mother's harsh voice splinters through my mind. *"Leave this town and never come back. Do everyone a favour."*

The air is still and suffocating. I turn and exit the store, forgetting to grab the bottled water I went in there for. I swallow down greedy gulps of air once I'm outside. I drive to a secluded area and wait for the anxiety to settle. I press my fingers flat on the burning leather of the steering wheel and even out my breathing, until the pounding in my head fades, and I can think clearly again.

*Don't think about it*, I tell myself. *You have a plan. You're going to apply for a job. Get yourself together.*

I check my reflection. I blink at myself and fix my makeup. When I'm calm enough, I turn the car back on and head to Danny's Dental, the only dentist in town. Inhaling a steadying breath, I walk inside. A bell above me dings as the door opens. Small, old, and cluttered. Nothing like the places I've worked before.

Daniel Sherlock appears, dressed in a faded scrub top and half-moon spectacles perched low on his nose. He offers me a friendly smile, wrinkles appearing over his face like lines on a roadmap.

"Hello, can I help you?" he asks.

"Hi, Mr. Sherlock. Do you remember me? I'm Bruce Mayor's daughter."

His white eyebrows shoot up, and he stares at me in surprise. "Josephine? Goodness, I didn't recognise you!"

He asks the usual questions: where have I been, what have I been up to. I skim over my time away, highlighting my degree and work experience.

"That's why I'm here," I conclude. "I know Fern Grove is a small place, but could you offer me any days to work here? I can take all children off your hands, up to the age of eighteen, and any standard or periodontal cleans."

He ushers me to the back of the surgery, where his office is. It consists of a small wooden desk, a computer that looks like it was bought fifteen years ago, and a wall of filing cabinets overflowing with patient files. It looks like he still does most records on paper.

The interior is extremely outdated, and the furniture is shabby, but I try not to focus on that too much as I take a seat on the only other chair in the room. The cushioning is protruding out the side of it, and when I sit, bits of stuffing fall onto the floor.

As Danny is semi-retiring, we negotiate that I will work three days a week, taking on any patients under the age of eighteen, and cleans. The pay is much lower than in the city, but I have a lot of savings and the cost of living is much different here. I'm honestly stoked he has given me any work, let alone as many days as this.

His hand feels leathery as he shakes mine, as if he has spent too much time out in the sun.

"You decide what you'd like to wear in regard to a uniform and invoice me. I don't mind what it is, as long as it is scrubs and covers everything it needs to."

I nod. "Thank you so much, Mr. Sherlock."

"Danny, please," he insists as we head back to the front of the office. "Next Monday, can you start? I'll organise to run an advert in the local paper telling everyone you'll be joining the team."

My cheeks hurt as I force a smile. Great. The last thing I need is for my face to be splashed across the local newspaper. The gossip mill will be working overtime once it's released. I also don't want to cater the thought of it potentially hurting his business. But it's not like there's anywhere else to go around here.

"I'll be here. Sounds great! I also have a lot of administrative experience, so I'm happy to take over the front desk, phone calls, bookings," I rattle off. "Just let me know."

"Honestly, that would be a relief," he tells me with a bright smile. "I'm terrible with that kind of thing."

"Sure. No problem. I'll see you next week!"

There's a bounce to my step as I head back to my car. When I'm alone, I let out an excited squeal. I thought my reputation here might damage my chances of getting hired, but Mr. Sherlock—Danny—didn't bat an eye when he saw me. He didn't care about the past or the changes to my appearance. It was refreshing.

Next on the list of things to do today is to meet Lynne, the property manager of Fern Grove. I have thirty minutes until we have to meet, so I detour to get myself a coffee and browse online for a uniform while I wait. I pick out three sets of matching scrub tops and pants—baby pink, lilac, and turquoise blue. One for every day of my working week.

I swallow down the lukewarm coffee that somehow also tastes burnt. I grimace, placing it back down into the cupholder.

Gravel crunches underneath the tyres when I pull up in front of a small property. It looks like someone has cut a part of someone's house and dumped it onto this small block.

The windows aren't aligned, there are patchy paint jobs on the walls in different shades of paint, and the guttering has come off the side. Everything is unkempt and overgrown, with weeds sprouting through cracks in the pavement.

"Good morning," Lynne greets me with a clipped, professional tone, the corners of her mouth pinching as she looks me over. "How are you?"

"I'm good, thanks. Yourself?"

She doesn't answer and instead cups her hand over her eyes.

"Not much to look at, I'm afraid. It's small and old. But it's cheap and perfect for a solo renter." She glances at me. I see her eyes dart to my lips, to my chest, back to my eyes. She remembers me. She's good friends with Nick's mother. She doesn't like me. "Shall we have a look inside?"

"Sure."

The gate opens with an ear-piercing squeak, and I stumble over a loose pavement.

"A gardener will come and take care of the lawns once someone moves in. He comes once a fortnight."

It takes her a few moments of jiggling the key to get the door to unlock, and she rams her shoulder into it to get it to open wide enough for us to step inside. It has the smell of a place that hasn't breathed fresh air for months. Dust has settled on every surface, and the wallpaper is peeling.

Despite the flaws, I sort of love it. This would be *my* space.

"I'll take it."

Lynne is mid-sentence and stops short, peering at me in surprise. We haven't even looked at the bathroom or laundry yet. With the way she is speaking, she must have expected me to hate the place. It's basically one big room with everything jam-packed inside.

"Oh. Okay."

She draws her eyebrows together. She tells me she'll call when it's finalised. As I drive home, I expel a heavy breath.

I'm back, and this time, I will do things right.

# Chapter Eight

## Josie

A droplet of condensation slides down the side of my glass, moistening the tablecloth underneath. Sam obnoxiously scrapes his fork over his plate as he eats, the sound of his chewing floating down the table.

"You got a job? And a place?" my mother echoes, her hand frozen in mid-air as she blinks at me.

"Yeah."

"Why?" my father interrupts. No congratulations. Nothing. "What's the point? You won't stick around here for longer than five minutes."

We all ignore him. I don't let his words hurt me. He's always been a tough-love kind of guy, and I'm used to it now. I'm not weak anymore.

"That's fantastic news, Josie," Mum says. "I did say you didn't need to get your own place, though."

"I'm twenty-one. I think I *need* my own place," I reply. Dad makes a disgruntled sound but doesn't comment.

"Where is it?" Sam asks before shovelling a large mouthful of mashed potato into his mouth. Some of it spills down the front of his shirt. I bite the inside of my cheek. His eating habits haven't changed much in four years.

"It's Cheryl's old place. Near town."

"Oh, yeah. I know the one. Small."

"It's fine for me," I say.

"So, when I go to the dentist now, you'll be the one doing all that shit to my teeth?" Sam asks, always having a way with words, as he makes a barbaric gesture towards his mouth.

"Sort of, yeah."

"That'll go down well in town."

Mum's fork hits the table with a loud clang. She fumbles to pick it up, and I glower at Sam.

"Gee, thanks."

Dad has gone an unhealthy red, and he suddenly pushes from the table and stomps out of the room. The screen door bangs open. He's probably gone out to smoke. He has pretended our entire lives that he doesn't smoke, even though we all know he does.

Mum sighs, and Sam shakes his head in an innocent, 'what did I do?' way.

"They'll have to deal with it," I say eventually.

Sam shrugs, spooning a pile of steamed vegetables into his mouth, yet again spilling some, although onto the tablecloth this time. "It'll be entertaining, that's for sure."

Everyone finishes eating in silence, and by the end, I've lost my appetite.

As much as I've tried to outrun the past, it'll always catch up to me.

Tuesday, my application was approved, and Wednesday, I was unpacking.

Music is blaring from my speakers, most of my boxes now empty, and the place is starting to feel homey. With some inspiration from Pinterest, I feel like I've transformed the space around me. It still needs a few final touches, but overall, I'm quite satisfied with how it has turned out.

I flop onto my bed. I was lucky enough that Mum had a spare she gave me. I didn't bring anything with me, but all that I needed, I managed to grab at the local store or order online.

This is the first time a place is *mine*. I grew up in a small, overcrowded house with parents and a brother who didn't understand personal space. When I moved to Brisbane, I rushed straight into a tiny two-bedroom apartment with a girl named Frankie, who had a scarily large spike running through her earlobe and a spider tattoo painted across her neck. We didn't speak much.

Then, I met Elliot. And everything happened quickly after that. Although the apartment we shared was amazing, I still never had my own space. With cleaners, gardeners, and cooks coming and going, not to mention Elliot hovering over my shoulder, I didn't have many moments of peace.

I was out with a friend when I first met Elliot. The bar had been loud and bright. I was five drinks in, one leg folded over the other, leaning in close to the man who had bought my last one. Feeling eyes on me, I let my own drift over to a guy leaning on the bar, a glass of something dark coloured in his palm. He was dressed in a polished suit. Clean, neat, professional. He smiled and beckoned me over.

Leaving the man mid-sentence, I glided towards the pretty boy in his impressive suit.

He was smart. Charismatic. Generous.

After a lot of conversation and too many drinks, we ended up back in his apartment, rolling in his sheets, his tongue down my throat, giving me everything I had wanted for so long from Nick.

And that's when it went *really* wrong.

It seems ridiculous when I look back at how quickly things moved. How isolated I became. How many red flags I chose to ignore.

I stare at the roof of my new place. I can't believe I'm back here. *Living* here. All because of *him*.

A knock startles me back to reality. I wander to the door to see Nick standing there. His skin is streaked with dirt. I push open the screen door, and he wipes his palms on his jeans before thrusting a bunch of flowers at me.

"Heard about the new place," he says with a shy smile. "Congratulations."

"Thanks, Nick." I grin, stepping back. "How did you hear about it?"

"I overheard Lynne telling Mum."

Of course. Fucking small towns.

"Come on in." I step back, holding the door open.

"I shouldn't. I'm filthy. I'm just finishing work," he says regretfully. "What are you doing for dinner tonight? I could swing by with some Chinese food?"

"That sounds amazing," I say, nervously twisting my fingers at the hem of my shirt. "I'm … sorry. For the other night."

"Me too. Let's forget about it."

"Already forgotten."

"Great," he says, his smile lines shining between the streaks of soil. "I'll be back here then, about six?"

"Sounds like a plan."

I spend the next two hours rearranging and sorting my place, then get ready for dinner. I settle on a pair of denim shorts with a high-neck singlet tucked into the waistband. I've just finished lighting some candles when there's another knock at the door.

"Oh, it's you," I say flatly when my brother appears.

"Nice to see you too," he says, brushing past me and walking inside. He peers around at the candles and back to me. His hair is greasy and flattened from the hat he has clutched in his hand.

"Expecting someone?"

"Maybe."

"Which boy is it?" he asks with an irritating flash of his teeth. "Thanks for saying bye. Again."

Ignoring his jab, I shrug. "I haven't left."

"You left the house."

"I'm still here, though," I say. "You can come see me any time."

"We can hang out?" he asks, leaning against the wall, rubbing dirt on it. "Share secrets? Paint each other's nails?"

"Didn't know that was what you were into, but sure."

Sam presses his lips into a thin line, before nodding. Without another word, he pushes from the wall and strides out the door. I exhale, watching him go. I grab a cloth and am wiping down the smudge he left behind when Nick arrives.

"Was that Sam I just drove by?" he questions.

"Yeah."

There's a pause as if Nick is waiting for me to elaborate but I don't.

He swings the bag onto the counter, the delicious smell of food wafting towards me.

"Smells great!"

"Also," he says, producing a bottle from the bag. "I brought wine."

"You know me so well." I grin.

As soon as the words leave my lips, I regret them. Nick meets my eyes, and I dart away, trying to remember what cabinet I put glasses in. I pour us two very large glasses; Nick raises an eyebrow but doesn't comment.

We dish out our plates, and since I don't have the space for a dining table, we move to the lounge. I fold my legs beneath me, feeling oddly unsettled as I try to limit how much I fidget.

"I got a job."

"You did?" There's a hint of surprise in his voice. "Where?"

"Danny's Dental."

"That's great, Josie. Does that mean you're planning to stick around for a while?"

I stuff my mouth full, so I can take more time to answer. "Maybe."

I feel nauseous at the thought of packing and moving again. Starting all over again. The last experience aged me a lifetime. I'd gladly do it to be away from here, but the whole experience is exhausting.

My hair sticks to my forehead, and I sweep it back. When I stand, I feel my shirt sticking to my skin. I bought several fans, scattering them through the small place. I turn on a couple, pleading for them to cool the place down. The candles are making it worse, but at least the place smells nice.

"I can't handle this heat," I groan. "It's disgusting."

Nick smiles. "You get used to it."

I shake my head, frowning. "Nope. Never did."

I settle back down beside him and finish eating. Nick reaches over, and I flinch at the quick movement. He pauses, eyebrows drawing together, and takes my empty bowl, placing it on the coffee table at our feet. I exhale a shaky breath, flattening my fingers onto my thighs.

"Are you seeing Jess?"

He blanches at my words. I lean back into the lounge, staring at him. I know I've made him uncomfortable, but I don't look away.

He sighs. "How …? Never mind. No. Maybe. Sort of."

"Huh?"

"I don't know." He exhales, raking a hand through his hair. "She's been interested in me for a while. I know that. We went out for dinner a few times."

"Do you like her?"

"Sure. She's nice."

"Nice is boring." I smirk.

He shakes his head, smiling. "Is it? Am I boring?"

"No, Nicky. Not you." I smile. "Have you kissed her?"

"Josie!" he exclaims, flushing, as if we were twelve years old again.

"Have you?" I press.

He groans. "Once or twice."

"Which is it?"

"What?"

"Once?" I fold my leg over the other, leaning in. "Or twice?"

"Twice. Does it matter?"

I shrug. "Not really."

He gives me an exasperated look. "You are so confusing."

"I think you mean intriguing."

He laughs. It's a warm, delicious sound that wraps around me. I lean over, running my fingers down his arm. "Are you going to see her again?"

"Hmm?" he asks, his eyes on my fingers.

"Jess?" I persist. "Will you be taking her out again?"

"No." He reaches for my hand, tangling our fingers together. "I don't think so."

"Why's that?"

"You know why."

"Say it," I whisper, a grin stretching over my face at the power I have over him.

"Because you're back."

I move so that I'm on his lap. His hands rest on my hips as he gazes up at me. I lean down and kiss him. A soft, deep kiss. His tongue is warm as he lets me invade his mouth. He groans as I press into him.

"Josie," he mumbles.

"Yes?"

"Let's not have this conversation again."

This moment could have been copied and pasted from four years ago. His words from earlier swirl around my mind. *Mum still cooks and does my washing.* Still here. With the same people. Living where he always has. Working the place he always knew he would.

My insides coil.

"It's just kissing, Nick," I say against his lips.

"And then it's not just kissing," he states, pushing me back. He stares up at me, his expression relaxed and friendly. Like always. Good Guy Nick.

Frustration bubbles inside me. So much time has passed, and yet nothing has changed. Even Nick can't escape this trait. A stabbing sensation fills me as I realise the same could be said about me. I suddenly let go, dropping my hands.

"Oh my God," I whisper, staring down at my hands. "I'm sorry, Nick. I never … I never realised how uncomfortable I would be making you feel."

His gaze softens as he offers me a small smile. "It's okay, Josie. You're frustrated. I get it."

I climb off him, feeling confused, frustrated—like he said—and nauseous.

"Let's go for a walk," he suggests.

The night is dark and still. Gravel crunches under our feet with each step. I dab my fingers over my forehead, removing the sweat that has gathered. Cicadas sing loudly from the trees, and it makes me smile. That's a sound I haven't heard for a while.

"Remember when we used to go down to the lake?" he asks, and I glance at him, seeing how carefree his face is. "The whole gang was there. We'd been down there for hours."

I nod. That was our main hangout spot. "Yeah. That was fun."

"Maybe we could organise a day down there."

"Sure."

"Who would you want me to invite?" he asks. Our hands touch, and he captures mine in his. It's big and warm, easily enveloping mine.

Memories of us flash through my mind. Me, Elise, Eric, John. My best friends. Strangers now.

"No one," I tease, trying to keep my voice light even though my entire body aches when I think about their smiles, their laughter, and everything we once shared.

"Did you keep in touch with anyone?" he asks, ignoring my comment.

"No."

"Not one person?"

"No, Nick. No one."

*Elliot made sure of that.*

When I think back on it, I can't believe how much control I let him have over me.

A mixture of emotions flashes across his face. I know he has a lot he wants to say, but he doesn't. A slightly uncomfortable silence settles between us. I can practically hear the gears of his mind turning long.

"You were seeing someone in the city?" he asks eventually.

A rush of cold floods my veins. The person I've been trying so hard not to think about since I got back here.

"Yeah."

"It didn't work out?"

"No."

The conversation falls flat because I let it. I don't want to talk about Elliot, or the life I lived with him. I was in a bad place. Even though I hate it here, it's not like how things were in the city. I might have had the glamour and the picture-perfect life, but behind closed doors, it was anything but.

If I stay, and do all the things I was meant to do all those years ago, I could be happy again. I could live this life. Settle down with Nick. Have kids. Reignite old friendships. It would be better than when I was away.

*But would it be enough?*

"Are you okay? With how everything ended?" The deep hum of his voice draws me from my thoughts.

"No," I say softly. "But I will be."

He removes his hand from mine and gently rubs circles on my back as we walk. Guilt grips my stomach. I'm being selfish. Fern Grove is Nick's home. He won't leave, and I don't know if I plan to stay.

And yet when he turns, facing me, I don't stop him from leaning down and kissing me. It's warm and nice, reminding me of the only thing I truly enjoyed growing up here. *Before* Cyclone Harley took over and destroyed everything in his path.

Nick walks me back to my place. He touches my shoulder gently, and I hate how much of a brotherly gesture it is.

We say goodbye, and I watch Nick leave, a strange, restless feeling settling over me. I put the leftovers in the fridge and clean up.

I'm not used to this. This quiet life of dinner and walks. Shops being shut at 8:00 PM. Everyone settled in their houses by 9:00 PM.

Sliding on my boots, I fling my bag over my shoulder and stride downtown. It doesn't take me long to get to the local pub. There're a few stragglers inside. I hear whoops from the pokies room, and see a few men sitting in the TAB area. They all turn to stare when I enter. I'm the only female here, including the staff.

I see him. Harley. He's wiping down the bar. His biceps flex, and I stare at the dark, swirling tattoos on his skin. He stands out almost as much as me. The light above glints off his gold lip ring. I stare at it for a heartbeat too long.

Compared to the simple country boys in this town, he is practically the opposite. And yet the town didn't turn their back on him as they did me. Or perhaps they did, and he was simply stronger than me.

My heart seems to beat sideways. I hate how he makes me feel.

When I lean on the bar, he turns his attention to me and flinches. I ignore the heat that rises in my cheeks when those gorgeous eyes connect with mine.

"Bourbon and coke."

He nods. He pours it quickly and pushes it towards me. When I hand him a ten-dollar note, our fingers brush. He swallows, stepping back to the cash register. It whirrs and clunks before the drawer flings open. He retrieves my change, and looks anywhere but at me when he places it in my hand.

"You here long?" he eventually asks when I don't move.

"As in tonight, or in general?"

"Um." He scratches his head. "Both."

"I don't know, and I don't know."

"Listen …" he says. Every pair of eyes is glued to us. Watching. Waiting. "Can we talk?"

"We're talking right now."

He gives me a deadpan look. *There he is*, I think. *The Harley I remember.*

"You know what I mean," he mutters. "I clock off in half an hour."

"And you want me to wait?" I ask. "To talk?"

"Yeah."

"Well." I shrug, spinning the glass slowly in my fingertips. "I guess I have nothing better to do. Pour me another."

He glances at my full drink before turning his back to me. By the time he's poured the second, my glass is empty.

I move into the pokies room. The air is hot and stuffy, filled with smoke. The smoker's area is meant to be outside, but every second person in here has one in their hand.

I take a seat far from anyone else, as much as I can in the small room, and slide a five-dollar note into the machine. I watch the money go down and down until there isn't anything left. I half-laugh to myself as I sip. Just like Fern Grove. It takes everything you have.

I place a cigarette between my lips and light the end. I feel eyes watching me. I take a long drag and stare down at the cigarette, a red kiss mark painting it. I've wanted to kick the habit, given my profession and all, but it's something that has stuck with me when I drink.

"Hey."

I've just finished my drink and stubbed out the cigarette when Harley appears by me. His eyes flick to the ashtray curiously for a moment.

I sigh, getting to my feet. "Where are we going?"

"Where do you want to go?"

"Aren't you the one that wants to talk? You make the decision," I snap at him in a huff, tasting the smoke on my tongue as it escapes my mouth.

He blinks at my words. I resist a smile. I'm not the girl he remembers, that's for sure.

A few pairs of eyes blink at us as we pass through the main area, out to the front entrance. I hold my head high, not meeting anyone's gaze. They can stare and talk as much as they want.

Harley's truck is shiny and a lot flashier than I expected. I slide into the passenger seat, the leather cool on my skin. His dashboard is lit red when he turns the car on, and I glance at him, hating how good he looks in the dim lighting. Well. Any sort of lighting.

He drives to the skatepark, a place we all used to hang around. He leaves the engine running. I'm relieved as the air-conditioning cools my body.

I half-turn, facing him. He taps the steering wheel with his thumb.

"I really fucked up," he says.

"You think?"

Harley presses the back of his head into the seat. "I think about it every day."

"And you think I don't?" I gripe.

"Never said that you didn't," he says carefully. "I just want you to know you're not alone."

"Right."

He sighs. "I'm sorry."

"Cool."

"Seriously." He finally turns his head, eyes meeting mine. "I'm sorry."

My mouth is paper dry. I nod, picking at my fingers. "Good. I'm glad you are."

"Josie," he groans.

My stomach clenches as he says my name. He always called me that, even when no one else did.

"You did. And cool. You're sorry. But it doesn't take back what you did." I scramble to open the door and almost wheeze when I step into the stale, humid air. "And guess what? Apology *not* accepted."

"Josie!" He's out of the car, striding after me. "Where are you going? It's late."

"Anywhere that's away from you."

"Stop being stupid. I'll drive you home."

"I don't want you knowing where I live, you creep!"

"You live in Cheryl's old place," says Harley flatly.

I whirl to face him. "Are you stalking me?"

"No. It's Fern Grove," he says obviously.

True. But I don't admit that.

I glare up at him. "I think it would be in both our best interests if you left me the hell alone."

"Bit hard when you're going to be everywhere."

My cheeks burn red, and I feel too hot. I suddenly throw my hands out and push him.

"Hey!" he snaps, stumbling back a step. "What the fuck?"

I slam my palms into his chest once more, and his long fingers circle around my wrists. My skin burns from the contact, and I refuse to let myself acknowledge that.

"Josie. Calm down," he demands.

"You calm down!"

He looks down at me. "Get in the car."

"No."

"If you don't get in the car, I'll throw you over my shoulder and carry you there."

I blink at him. If Elliot were demanding this of me, my legs would be shaking in fear. But with Harley, I almost want to smile. Despite how much he *has* hurt me, he never would physically. I know that with my whole heart.

We're in a heated stare-off for several moments. I yank my hands from him and stomp towards his truck, aware I'm acting childish but unable to control it.

We drive in silence, and he idles out the front. He peers through the window, where the flowers from Nick are sitting on the kitchen bench.

"Nice flowers."

I glare at him, sliding out of the car.

"Gift from Nick?"

"Why do you care?"

"I don't." He shrugs, loosely dangling an arm over the steering wheel. "Didn't take long. For that to start again."

"You have something to say, Harley?" I growl, narrowing my eyes.

"Nope."

"Good." I slam the door shut with much more force than necessary, and stalk into the house without a backwards glance.

# Chapter Nine

## Harley

Slamming my hand into the wheel, I growl. "Fuck."

She's back. She's finally fucking back, and Nick has swooped in. Again. Doesn't he remember? Doesn't *she*? How could she think this time would be any different? She's lying to herself—and lying to me. Stubborn fucking brat.

I stomp on the accelerator, and the truck lurches forward, the tyres spinning in the gravel.

The rumbling engine does little to soothe the ache in my chest. I dig the heel of my hand into my chest as if that would stop it.

I think back to our first kiss. From the first taste, I knew once would never be enough. Everything about her drew me in. Her smile, her eyes, her laugh, her genuine kindness, her ability to overlook all flaws to see the best in people. And most importantly, her heart. It was warm and full but tainted with the same twisted darkness that plagued mine.

When I get home, the house is silent. Drifting in and out of the rooms, I realise Brennon must be out. I call him, and after a few rings, he answers.

"Hey, man." There's significant background noise and I wince, pulling the phone away from my ear.

"What are you doing?"

"Just over at Logan's house. You wanna come?"

"Yeah, be there in ten."

I shower and dress, grabbing a ten pack from the fridge before jogging back out to the truck. Every time I stop for a moment, I think of the flowers sitting on the bench. My hands tighten around the steering wheel. My fist slams into it once, then twice, before I yell out in frustration.

*Why him? Why is he always in the fucking way?*

Sitting still for a few moments longer, I blow out a hot breath and let the anger in me subside. It slowly oozes away, and I feel the tension leaving my shoulders.

I can't think about her. Not like that. Not anymore.

The street is packed with cars, and I'm surprised to see a lot more people than I expected for a weeknight. Cutting the engine, I grab my things and head straight inside. The music is loud, the air stale with cigarettes and marijuana. There must be a lot of out-of-towners here.

"Harley!" Louise squeals, causing several heads to turn in my direction. She bounces over to me, a radiant grin taking up her face. Everything about her is off. She doesn't have long blonde hair. She doesn't have deep, endless eyes. She doesn't have that cute twist in her smile. *Fuck.* "I didn't think you were coming!"

"Last minute decision," I reply and wince at the standoffish tone in my voice. I force a smile.

I wrap my arm around her and plant a kiss on her cheek as she flings herself at me. When she pulls back, I dive towards her mouth. She squeaks in alarm. I'm not usually one for public displays of affection, but I'm really, really pissed off right now and need to blow off steam.

She kisses me back for a long moment, and it's then I realise *this* is my second chance. To win Josie back. No girl has ever compared to her in my eyes, and I need to do everything I can to prove it to her.

I step back suddenly, feeling repulsed that I came to that decision with another girl's mouth on mine. Her lips are swollen, and she's breathless as she gazes up at me with innocent doe-eyes. I flinch, hating myself even more than I thought I could.

"I didn't hear from you after the other night," she says, staring down at the floor, her cheeks reddening.

"Sorry," I say distractedly, leaning around her and putting the ten-pack into the fridge and sliding a can out.

Turning, I face Brennon, who is smirking at me.

"Let's get drunk," I say.

He grins. "Already halfway there, brother."

# Chapter Ten

## *Josie*

When I wake the next morning, my sheets are stuck to my skin. I groan, peeling them off me, and beeline to the shower. I only turn the cold tap on and let the water run over me.

I spend the day at work, even though I don't start until next week. I clean every surface, rearrange the waiting room, and spruce up the surgery room I'll be using. Danny says he doesn't mind as he watches me change basically everything about the place. I try to remember to ask him before going ahead with any changes.

The nurse, Belle, that works for him, seems nice enough. She's been in town for about six months. Long enough to know everyone, not long enough to know my history here.

I help her shut down for the day. Everything is old-school here, so it takes longer than it should, but I don't mind. I like being here. The place has character.

"Thanks for all of your help." She beams at me. "It's so nice having someone else here! Another girl, especially."

"Sure. No worries."

"What are you up to now? Want to grab a drink?" She tucks a piece of dark hair behind her ear. She's pretty, in an understated kind of way.

"I'd love to. I'm going to run home and shower quickly. Meet you at the pub in thirty minutes?"

"Sounds good."

We say goodnight to a tired Danny, and I rush home. I'm excited to have drinks with someone who doesn't know me and everything that has happened. For one night, I might pretend I'm not Josie Mayor.

I slip into a dress and think about wearing heels but decide last minute to go with sandals. I get to the pub just as Belle does.

"Hey girl," she greets me, and I'm thrilled to see her in a nice dress too. She has a kind face and a warm smile. She would fit in well around here.

When we enter, I don't stare back at anyone. We head straight for the bar and order.

"Man, that guy is so hot," Belle says, jutting her chin to Harley as he strolls in. "I tried to get his attention when I first moved here, but he totally blew me off."

"He's an asshole."

She turns to me. "Oh?"

"The worst kind of asshole."

"The hot ones always are," she sighs, staring longingly at him with her dark, round eyes. "Did you used to be together?"

"It's a long story."

"Sounds juicy." She smirks, raising an eyebrow.

"It's something," I mutter, scoffing a little. "How do you like it here?"

"It's okay." She nods. "Bit dull. Not much to do."

"You can say that again."

"Cute boys, though." She grins.

I move my gaze to Harley. He's staring back at me. Slowly, I raise my middle finger at him. A shit-eating grin spreads across his face as he gives it back to me. I'm a little startled at the resemblance of how he used to be.

"Prick," I mutter.

She eyes me for a moment. "Uh-huh."

"Don't give me that look."

"What look?"

"As if there's something going on when there absolutely is not."

"You said it, not me." She shrugs.

"Besides, I'm sort of seeing someone. An old flame."

"Oh?" She smiles before her attention is pulled from me. "Hey!" Her arm snakes out as she beckons someone over.

I turn and grimace when I see Jess. She freezes when she sees me before awkwardly walking over, probably realising it's too late to stop now.

"Jess!" Belle grins. "Hi!"

"Hey," she replies, noticeably less cheerful than her friend. Jess is a tall girl with light hair and rosy cheeks. She looks a lot more mature than she did four years ago. She no longer wears glasses, and her hair is much longer. She looks well—not that I want to give her any compliments. That girl has always gotten under my skin. She was like a bad smell I could never get rid of.

"This is Josie!"

"I know," she replies a little flatly. "Hey, Josie."

"Jess." I smile sweetly.

"You two know each other?" Belle asks, oblivious to the tension.

"This is Josie," Jess says a little firmly. "The girl Nick is seeing again."

Realisation dawns on Belle's face. "Oh …"

I slurp obnoxiously, draining the last of my drink. "I'll get the next round." I leave the two staring after me as I saunter to the bar.

"Now who's stalking who?" Harley raises an eyebrow.

"Ugh." I roll my eyes. "This is the only place you can drink. Get over yourself."

"There's the RSL."

"What?"

He leans on the bar. "The RSL serves alcohol."

I stare at him.

"Fuck you. Get my drink."

He smirks, throwing the rag he was using over his shoulder. "Yes, boss. Bourbon and coke?"

"Yes. And a cider for Belle."

"Look at you." He pouts annoyingly, but adorably. "Making friends."

"Please don't do that. Your face makes me feel nauseous."

His eyes darken slightly. "Sure it does."

I scowl at him before carrying the drinks back to the table. Jess is nowhere in sight. She was probably eager to get away from me.

"Well. That was awkward," Belle comments with raised eyebrows, taking her drink. She takes a long gulp before gently placing it back down, then gives me a curious look as if studying me properly for the first time.

"Yep," I reply.

"I didn't make the connection."

"It's okay. They weren't dating or anything. It shouldn't be that awkward."

Belle looks at me with a small frown. "She's pretty serious about him, from the sound of it."

I shrug, eyes lowering to my drink. "Well. That sucks for her."

"Bitch," Belle snickers, a playful smile dancing on her lips. "You and Nick were together in high school, right?"

"Yeah."

"Do you know Brennon?"

"Ugh," I scoff. "Yes. I hate him."

"Oh." Her face falls.

"Why do you ask?"

"I've been sleeping with him for two months," she says casually.

"Is he any good?" I ask.

"He's pretty good."

"I hope he's a better person than he was four years ago," I say bitterly, running my tongue across my teeth.

"What happened four years ago?" Belle asks curiously, leaning forward, a crease denting her forehead.

I wave off her words. I walked into that one. "Another story for another time."

"I'm holding you to that." She points a finger at me, then takes a long drink. The ice clinks against the glass. "Are you going to the rodeo?"

"I guess. Nothing else to do."

"Okay. I'll pick you up."

"Come over early. We can have drinks?" I suggest.

Belle grins, her face lighting up. "Sounds good to me."

We spend another hour at the pub. I learn she's a traveller. She stays about a year at one place before moving on to the next. This is the furthest west she's been, and says it will be as far as she goes. I can't blame her for that; I feel the same.

When we part ways, I spot Harley leaning against the corner of the pub, hidden from the main street but still in view enough that I can see him. He blows out a cloud of smoke and tilts his head back. He looks thoughtful as he gazes at the sky. I drag my eyes from him and walk home, blocking out everything I've ever felt about him. Because none of it matters now.

The sound of my phone vibrating on my bedside table meets my ears when I walk through the front door. I almost forgot about my phone, which is laughable. I was so attached to it once. Now I don't take it anywhere with me. I stare down at the screen.

*Elliot.*

I watch it ring out, the screen eventually going black.

Memories plague my mind as I go about my nightly routine and step inside the shower …

The bright lights make me feel dizzy as Elsa drags me through the crowd. We have gone on the Gravity Spin four times in a row, almost throwing up on the last round. We stumble towards the boys. Elsa's boyfriend wraps his arms around her, showering her with kisses, before plucking a bit of cotton candy and placing it into her mouth.

"Where have you been?"

I tear my eyes from Elsa and Wayne—who remind me so much of myself and Nick—to Elliot's stormy eyes.

"With Elsa."

"I called you three times," he hisses, his voice low. Deep lines appear around the corners of his mouth. "I told you not to leave my side."

I side-eye him. "Sorry."

Elsa and Wayne shout something about going to the balloon-popping sideshow, and I go to follow, but Elliot's fingers sink into my arm, pulling me back.

"What?" I growl at him. "What is your problem?"

"I saw the messages."

"What messages?"

"The ones from your ex-boyfriend," Elliot sneers, towering over me.

Anger boils inside me. This isn't the first time Elliot has gone through my phone. He screamed at me about opening messages from people that reached out from my hometown. Friends. Apparently, I'm not allowed to have any.

I was so shaken and afraid at the time, I deleted them all. I had no choice. We lived together and I didn't have enough money to move out.

I have to keep him happy. I always have to keep him happy.

"You went through my phone?"

"You never told me about them," he continues, eyes narrowing.

"I never replied. Means nothing to me," I argue, even though it means everything to me. "Let go of me."

"Or you deleted them to make it look like you never replied."

"What?" I exclaim, trying to yank my arm free. "You're being ridiculous. Let me go."

I attempt to follow our friends, but Elliot drags me between two sideshows. I protest and stumble after him. He steers me somewhere secluded, the noise fading away.

"I do not tolerate cheating or lying, Josie. Ever."

"I have not done either. You're severely overreacting. Let's join our friends and have a good time."

"Not until we finish our conversation," he snarls, grip tightening.

My hand snakes out, and there's a loud crack as my palm hits his cheek. He staggers back in surprise, and I glare at him.

"When I say let go, I mean let go!" I say angrily. I whirl around, ready to stomp back into the fair when I feel his hands on me again.

He spins me around, and then suddenly, there's a fierce ache as Elliot's fist smacks into my nose. I slam back to the ground, dirt and blood spilling over my face.

I struggle to breathe. A thousand thoughts run through my head. Elliot has been angry before. He's yelled, thrown things, plunged his fists through walls—but he had never done this.

"Baby?" he says, his voice completely different now as he crouches down beside me. He nurses my head gently, touching the side of my face. "I'm sorry. That was an accident. You hit me, remember? It was a knee-jerk reaction." I swallow, pain radiating through to the back of my skull. "I'm sorry, baby." More stroking. "But maybe next time you'll think twice about lying to me."

The water running over me has turned icy cold, and I wonder how long I've been standing in the shower. I step out and towel off, shivering, but not from the water.

I stare into the mirror. Wet hair clings to my skin. Dark circles under my eyes. I lightly touch my face, remembering the hit. It was the first one. I remember all of them. The pain. And everything after.

Quietly, in the background, I hear my phone ringing.

And I know it's him.

When I breeze through the lounge room, Mum startles so violently that she spills her tea.

"Gosh, Josie!" she shrieks. "Ever heard of knocking?"

Casually, I lean over to the wall and rasp my knuckles against it. She purses her lips in a frown, shaking her head. She looks relaxed and comfortable in a flowy maxi dress with thin straps. I can't remember the last time I saw her in a loose dress like that. She looks lovely.

"You look like you've seen a ghost," I comment.

"I'm not used to you being around," she admits quietly, streaks of grey in her hair shining in the natural light from the window. "Sometimes, it seems like you *are* a ghost."

Her words hang between us for a few moments before I flop onto the lounge.

"How do you cope living inside this house with no fans?" I protest, opting to change the subject.

"You get used to it."

I flick my gaze to her. That sounds awfully a lot like what Nick would say.

"Are you going to the rodeo tonight?"

"Yes, we will all be going." The way she says it—*We*. Like they're a family. Without me. She seems to realise this as well and awkwardly clears her throat. "Are you coming with us?"

"No, I'm going with a friend."

"A friend?" she questions, raising an eyebrow. "Nick?"

"No. You don't know her."

"I know everyone."

"Belle Mathers."

Mum blinks. "Who?"

"She works at Danny's Dental. She's only been in town for a few months."

Mum sets her mug down. I eye her as she shuffles the magazines on the coffee table, looking a little nervous.

"Josie," she starts. "Have you thought about talking to someone? After what happened when you were away?"

Away. When I fled this town and hoped to never return, she means.

I bristle at her words, straightening in my seat. "No."

"It might be helpful to unload on someone."

I push to my feet, flipping my hair over my shoulder. "I'm good, thanks for the concern. See you tonight."

I don't miss Mum purse her lips in disappointment before I stalk from the house without a backwards glance.

With each step, a new cloud of dust layers my boots. I feel it cling to my skin and settle in my hair. I sweep it back from my face. Dirt and sweat. I can taste it. It's everywhere.

It seems like everyone in town is here. Belle and I weave through the tents set up and the small crowds gathered. I see Nick leaning against the fence, a friendly smile on his face as he talks to Jess. I stride up to him and pull on his shoulder. Giving him no chance to say hi, I cover my mouth with his.

I feel her eyes burning holes into the side of my head. Jess looks taken aback at the display in front of her. I wait for the roll of satisfaction to come, but it doesn't.

"Nick." I smile, looping my arm with his.

His cheeks blush a deep red, and he can't meet Jess' eyes. I turn and flash her a grin.

"Hey, Jess. How's it going?"

She offers a pained smile. "Great, thanks."

"I was just going to grab some food. Does anyone want anything?" Nick tugs at the collar of his shirt, looking flustered.

He hardly waits for a reply before he darts off. Jess throws out an excuse to leave and disappears into the crowd, not before throwing me a scowl. Belle shakes her head at me once it's back to the two of us.

"Was that necessary?" She quirks an eyebrow, folding her arms over her chest.

"I feel it was."

"Jess didn't deserve that."

My teeth press together, and for once, I don't have a comeback ready at my lips. Because she's right. And I don't feel good about it.

"Hey, look who it is!" Belle suddenly says, waving at someone.

I glance over my shoulder to see Brennon, Harley, and a blonde-haired girl leaning towards the two of them, a flirtatious smile curved across her face. I straighten, my lips spreading to a thin line. Belle clamps her hand over mine and drags me towards the group. I attempt to dig my heels in, but she tugs harder, ignoring my silent protest.

Brennon looks different. It's weird to see him so grown up. His fair hair has darkened, his body has filled out considerably, and he has crinkles around his eyes that weren't there before.

His eyes widen as he takes me in, realising who I am. Shock registers on his face as he drinks in all the changes, looking deliciously surprised and impressed at the same time. This moment of Brennon and the others seeing me for the first time since I've been back has played out in my head many times; I can't quite believe it is finally happening.

"Pick your jaw up off the floor, Brennon. You might catch a fly in that big trap of yours," I say snippily before swivelling my eyes to Harley. Heat travels down my spine. I feel my body react to him straight away, and God, I *hate* it. Those damn eyes. That beautiful smirk. The lip ring that makes me feel a swooping sensation between my thighs. I eye him up and down, artfully schooling my face to seem as stoic as I can. "Harley."

Finally, I look at the girl standing there, and she steps back. Her face is vaguely familiar, and I'm sure we went to school together, but I don't remember her well. Her eyes flick between Harley and me, connecting the dots, remembering all that has happened. That flirty smile twists into a frown as she glances back to Harley before stalking off.

Harley exhales, raking his hand through his hair. It's dark, contrasting with his skin almost too well. It's too long, falling into his eyes every few moments. "Happy with yourself?"

I smile. "Sort of, yeah."

Belle wraps her arms around Brennon's waist, pulling his stunned gaze to her. Distractedly, he hugs her back, looking like he's seen a ghost.

"There you are," Nick says, looking a little out of breath as he joins us. He turns, his warm smile automatically stretching over his face until he sees who is with us. The smile drops pretty damn quick.

"Nicholas." Harley sends him an arrogant smirk.

Brennon has a sinister curve to his lips, his eyes flitting between Nick, Harley, and I.

"Harley," Nick says tersely. "Brennon."

I've lost some of my bravado as memories begin to tornado through my mind. I latch on to Nick's arm.

"That hot dog looks fantastic. Let's go get me one," I suggest, basically shoving him. "You coming, Belle?"

"I'll catch up with you later?" she asks, glancing between the boys and me.

"Sure," I reply.

I don't inhale until we are almost on the other side of the show-ground. Nick hasn't said a word—which is very uncharacteristic of him—and his lips are tugging downward. I know what he's thinking about, and I'm trying desperately not to let my mind go there.

"I thought you wanted a hot dog."

"Huh?" I ask, pulling myself from my thoughts. I look around and see floats and trailers, realising I've steered us in the totally opposite direction of the food stalls. "Oh."

An awkward silence settles between us. We both look over each other's shoulders, not quite able to meet gazes yet.

There's a crackle and a loud static sound before a voice booms, announcing the start of the rodeo. We walk to the fence, and I loosely dangle my arms over it, leaning my forehead against the metal, thankful it isn't too hot.

"Our first rider of the night, a regular here, is Sam Mayor! Everyone make some noise!" the announcer yells, and I snap my head up. I look at Nick, who doesn't seem surprised that my brother is about to be flung into the ring on a bull's back. I had no idea he was a rider, but I suppose I don't know him at all anymore.

The gates crash open, and the bull tears out into the ring, dirt flying up in a cloud under its hooves. My fingers tighten over the railing, my knuckles stretching into a pale white. I flinch as the bull bucks and kicks, each movement gaining more momentum. My brother has an adrenaline-filled grin etched onto his face and one arm soaring in the air, looking like he's reaching for the sky.

He just makes it to eight seconds before he's diving through the air. He lands in a tumble on the ground, the bull charging after him. Two guys in red sprint in frantic, zig-zag motions, trying to distract the bull. Sam gets to his feet and makes a run for the fence, flinging himself over it.

I let out a wild scream and a loud whistle. Sam looks over to me and hooks two thumbs up, beaming.

"He's really good!" I say breathlessly to Nick.

Nick smiles, glancing at me. "He's the best, now."

"Of course he is. He's a Mayor."

I rush around to the side where Sam is and leap onto him. He laughs, staggering back, grunting under my weight.

"Awesome, right?"

"Totally! You killed it!"

He sets me down on my feet, and we exchange grins. A few of Sam's friends wander over, and soon he's swallowed into the group, whooping, laughing, and cheering. I head back to Nick, unable to wipe the smile from my face.

"Okay, I'm ready for the hot dog now," I say when I get back to Nick.

He reaches for my hand. "Maybe later we can go get ice cream."

"Sounds perfect."

Hands tightening, we head towards the stalls. For a moment, everything doesn't seem so bad.

# Chapter Eleven

## Harley

Being back here, at the rodeo, is making me feel agitated. My heart pangs in envy seeing Sam Mayor absolutely killing it out there, just like I used to, no fear weighing him down. Nothing holding him back. He truly enjoys the sport. More than I ever did.

"Princess Josie scrubs up all right." Brennon turns to me the moment Belle leaves his side. I could tell her reappearance rattled him. "You didn't tell me she was back."

"She's back."

"I see that, asshole."

I push back from the railing and glance around, scanning the crowd to see if I can spot her. She's impossible to miss.

"How do you feel, man?" Brennon asks, and if his gaze were a laser, I'd be disintegrated into dust by now.

"What do you mean?" I ask in the most nonchalant voice I can muster. I continue to glance around us before giving up. I don't know what I plan to do if I saw her again. She's here with Nick.

"Cut the bullshit," Brennon scoffs, rolling his eyes so hard that they might disappear into the back of his head. "I know you're hard for that bitch. Despite what you did."

I whip my head to face him, and his face grows slack for a moment. He holds up his hands.

"Woah, hey there, killer. I'm only stating the truth."

"Fuck off."

"Yeah, think I will," Brennon growls, throwing me a glare. "You're a fucking bore these days anyway."

My nails bite into my flesh as I fist my hands. Brennon stalks away from me. He finishes his can before tossing it to the ground and disappearing from view.

Asshole.

"Hey, handsome," a familiar voice greets me, and I try not to show my annoyance as Louise sidles up to me. I instantly feel terrible when I see her kind smile. "How are you?"

"Fine."

"What are you up to? Any plans now that the rodeo is finished?" she asks, giving me a flirtatious smile.

"I'm pretty tired," I say. "Maybe another time."

Her lips spread into a thin line before she suddenly smiles. "Sure. Of course. See you later."

I walk away, pulling out a cigarette. I lean against the fence and watch everyone stroll by. My heart lurches when I see Josie and Nick walking towards the exit.

Seeing them together makes my blood boil. She is kidding herself if she thinks she can waltz back into town and go back to how things were. Before everything got messy and fucked up. It doesn't work like that. It's not fucking *fair*.

I take my time finishing my cigarette, waiting for the crowd to disperse, before making my way to my truck. I've unlocked it and have my fingers curling around the handle when suddenly a hand shoves my head, slamming me into the window. A sharp pain explodes across my forehead, and I curse, stumbling.

"Hey, you piece of shit," the voice that plagues my nightmares grunts. "You got money on you?"

Throwing my elbow back, I hit him hard, a satisfying crunch filling my ears.

"If I did, I wouldn't give any to you, you slimy bastard," I spit at him with more venom than a king brown snake.

"Hey!" a man yells out, jogging over to us. "What the hell is going on here?"

"Nothing," I growl, sending a glare to the motherfucker who just laid hands on me before climbing into my car.

I need to get the hell out of this place. But first, I need Josie.

# Chapter Twelve

## Josie

### *Four years ago*

The sounds of shouting float up into my bedroom room, and I jump to my feet in excitement. I drape my towel over my shoulder and run down the stairs, sliding across the floor as the doormat flicks up behind me. I hit the doorframe and steady myself before barrelling down the steps.

Nick, John, Eric, and my best friend Elise, are piled in the car. Nick hangs out the window, beckoning me to him. I tear down the driveway and throw myself into the car.

Elise's long, bronze hair flaps in the wind. She leans back, her fingers scraping mine, hers littered with dainty silver rings.

We pull up at the local quarry, delighted to find we have the place to ourselves. The boys race towards the water while we girls start layering on sunscreen.

"Hey," Elise says, rummaging through her bag before holding something out to me.

"What's this?" I ask, taking it from her and unwrapping the

tissue paper.

She shrugs, tucking a piece of her long hair behind her ear. "Something I made. One for me, one for you."

Trailing my finger over it, I smile down at the bracelet. It's thin and delicate, feeling weightless in my hand. The word 'best friend' is engraved on it.

"I love it." I beam at her, reaching my arm around her and pulling her towards me for a brief hug. I used to make us all sorts of arts and crafts items that declared our close friendship. It warmed my heart to see her do it in return all these years later.

"We must always wear it," she points a finger at me, "to remind ourselves we will always have each other. Despite everything else that happens."

"Deal."

Our hands meet in our signature handshake and then we finish spreading the sunscreen over our skin.

The scorching sun beats down on my back as I rush over to the rocks, the grass blades tickling my feet. I toss my towel to the ground and yank my dress over my head.

Elise does the same with her shirt, and I stare in envy at her cut-off denim shorts hanging loosely on her hips, her bones sticking out. I wish I were that thin.

Nick's brawny arms fold around me, and I squeal when my feet lift off the ground. I hate that my immediate thought is that I would be heavier than her when the boys messed around with us, throwing us over their shoulders. I love Elise—so much—but I'm also extremely envious of basically everything about her.

He whirls me around, my hair sticking to my face from the sweat. I bounce over his shoulder with each step, and then suddenly, icy cold water explodes over my body. I inhale sharply and when I emerge, I'm spluttering, my chest burning. Nick laughs loudly, and I splash him with water.

John and Eric fight over Elise's attention. She has such an effort-lessness about her. A charm that lures everyone in. Peeling my eyes from her, I settle on Nick, who is watching his friends with a toothy grin on his face.

Nerves bubble in my stomach as I move towards him. Nick and I have been together for a while now. We'd kissed a lot, hugged, and held hands, but I wanted more. *Needed* more. Elise had lost her virginity a year ago to Brennon, one of the hottest guys in our school. It had led to a flirty on-and-off-again type relationship over the last year, and there have been others since. Then there's me, little old virgin, even though I'm the only one to have had a boyfriend this long.

I press my hip to his side and slide my hands around him. He smiles, letting me wrap my legs around his waist. I press my lips to his. The kiss is slippery and cold, and my heart is thundering. He pulls back after a moment—like always—but I move to kiss him again. I press my hips into him harder, my hand running down his chest.

My hand sinks lower. He pulls away from me sharply, and I stumble, my foot slipping. My head goes under the water and Nick quickly reaches for me, pulling me back up.

"What the hell?" he hisses, his eyes darting to our oblivious friends who are busy splashing and tackling each other.

A hot blush floods my cheeks, down my neck, and across my chest.

"Um," I stammer. "I thought … maybe you'd … like that."

Nick looks at me like I've lit a bible on fire. He shakes his head. "No. Not until we are married."

My mouth is dry as I stare at him. He has mentioned this before, but I pretend he didn't. I didn't want to be the only virgin left in Fern Grove.

"Nick—" I try to reach for him, but he shrugs me off and moves towards our friends. He is soon laughing and joining in, acting as though nothing happened between us just now.

I swim back to the rocks and climb up. In a huff, I collapse onto my towel and glare up at the clouds. I am humiliated. Nick rejected me. *Again.*

Loud revving of an engine pulls me from my thoughts, and soon, we aren't alone. There is loud hollering and deep, male laughter as a black truck pulls up.

I swallow a lump in my throat when the boys get out of the car.

"Damnnnn," Brennon yells out obnoxiously, wolf-whistling at Elise, who is striding towards us, water glistening on her silky skin, as if she's just walked out of a swimsuit commercial.

Brennon is a complete ass-hat, but the whole school knows he has a soft spot for Elise. Everyone does. She's perfect.

"You're not welcome here, boys," Eric says in a voice deeper than his naturally is. "Move along. We don't want any trouble."

Brennon's face splits into a sadistic grin. "This is a pretty big place, Eric. Can't we share?"

Nick's gaze meets mine awkwardly, and I burn in embarrassment. I turn and meet the icy eyes of Harley Caldwell. He's watching me as he leans against the truck, one leg resting on the step up, chewing the nail bed of his thumb. His gaze travels across my body, from my toes to my eyes once more. The corner of his mouth twitches, his lip ring tilting with the movement.

"Looking good, Josie." Harley bites his lip softly, and I can't look away from it. A deep flush ignites over my body. No one calls me that. *Josie.* I like it.

Nick appears at my side, his shoulder bumping into mine.

"Beat it, Harley," Nick snaps.

Harley pushes off the truck and strolls over to us.

"How about we stay, and you go?" he drawls, tilting his head to the side as he eyes Nick, definitely not wearing the expression he wore when looking at me. His blue orbs flicker to me once more. "Except you, sweetheart. You can stay as long as you'd like."

Nick lets out a soft growl at Harley's words. My heart catapults into my stomach. Harley's tongue snakes out, running over his lip ring. My mouth feels unusually dry as I watch his movements, and I'm embarrassed to admit I'm a little mesmerised by them.

Nick's fingers wrap around my arm, and he pulls me after him, swooping down and grabbing my towel. The boys mumble and complain but don't further protest about Harley and the others.

They're dangerous boys with a wild reputation. There are rumours that Harley and Brennon made a group of guys jump off the cliffs naked and then stole their clothes. They boasted about it later on Snapchat as they lit the clothes on fire. Nick and my other friends know better than to get mixed up with them.

Everyone piles into the car. I hover near the door, waiting my turn. I look over at the boys who are laughing and pointing at us retreating. I shift my gaze to Harley, who raises his hand, giving me a brief wave.

"See you soon, Josie." He smiles. "Real soon."

# Chapter Thirteen

## Josie

I stare down at the bracelet, running my fingers over it. It was once attached to me through rain, hail, or shine. Now, it took me over an hour to find it, dredging through many bags, boxes, and anything else that might have concealed it.

Elise. I haven't thought about her for a long time. Because she dropped me. Like everyone else. Then I left and never spoke to her again.

I haven't seen or heard about her since I've been back. I'm surprised. She was very popular when I left. Maybe she moved. Good on her if she did.

Pushing to my feet, I move around the small flat, beginning to tidy things. My breathing becomes laboured, and soon I give up with a groan, retiring back to the lounge. This damn heat is going to kill me.

I need something cold. And strong.

Dressing in a loose strapless dress, I head down to the pub. I order myself a six-pack takeaway. If my mind is planning on reminiscing down memory lane for the rest of the night, I'm going to need a drink. Or several.

I'm passing the hidden corner of the pub when I hear a loud groan and a thud. Pausing, I hold my breath, straining to hear what's going on. More groaning. The sound of skin hitting skin.

Slowly, I lower my carry bag and reach for the pepper spray I have in my clutch.

Holding my breath, I inch around the corner silently. A broad-shouldered man is sending his fist into the stomach of an equally tall person. My eyes zero in on his long, tattooed arms. I'd recognise those anywhere.

"You give me what you owe me," he spits into Harley's face, his fingers scrunched at the neck of his shirt. "Or I'll break every finger in your fucking hand." The man sneers down at him. He reaches for Harley as if to hit him again.

I shoot forward and aim. The spray slingshots out of the can, and directly into the man's eyes. He screeches, recoiling back, clawing at his eyes. Harley collapses to the ground, blood gushing from his face.

The man stumbles to his feet and makes a blind run for it. I wait until he's no longer in sight before I drop to my knees.

Harley groans, touching his face.

"Harley!" I exclaim, breathless. "What the hell?"

"Nothing to worry your pretty little head about," he growls, dark streaks of red running in blurry lines across his skin. "Go run back to your boyfriend." He spits the word *boyfriend* from his mouth like it's a dirty word.

"Come on, get up. I'll take you home to your parents," I insist, not having any clue where he lives or who with.

Harley barks out a sharp laugh that makes me wince.

"Yeah?" he asks. "Who do you think that was?" A splatter of blood lands on the pavement next to me. "That *was* my dad."

Harley collapses on my lounge, his arm over his stomach.

I rush into the kitchen to grab paper towels. I dampen them with water before fetching an empty ice cream container. I sit on my coffee table and begin to lightly dab his wounds. He hisses but stays still, letting me clean him up.

"That was your dad?" I eventually ask. Of course, I knew about Harley's dad—everyone did—but he has aged a lifetime since I last saw him. I honestly didn't recognise him at all. "That's … a fucked up family situation you have there."

"You think?" he snaps sarcastically, the heat in his eyes making me wither. His expression causes my stomach to tighten. He's furious—at himself, his dad, at me. For a moment, I recall some things I had seen and heard about his dad back in the day. Somehow, amongst the madness of everything, I'd actually forgotten. He's hurt. Because he can see it in my eyes that I had. He probably doesn't realise I spent four years trying to erase every memory I have of him.

"Hey, I'm the one here helping you, aren't I?" I snarl back.

"Didn't ask you to."

"Ungrateful twat," I mutter.

I press—hard—into a deep wound on his forehead and he growls at me, eyes flashing. I smile sweetly before continuing to clear his face.

Harley's hand suddenly reaches out, capturing my wrist. My skin flares from his touch, and I'm frozen, watching.

"You're wearing your bracelet again," he says.

I'm speechless. I never knew Harley to observe anything about me, let alone something like this. The fact that he knew I wore it then and haven't until now …

My breathing is far heavier than it should be when I speak next. "Found it today."

"Did you visit her?" he questions.

"Elise?" I ask.

"Yeah," he answers, and for a moment, I truly can't believe I'm sitting here, having a somewhat civil conversation with Harley Caldwell.

"No." I shake my head. "I haven't spoken to her since I left. We … didn't end on great terms."

Harley's fingers stop dancing over my bracelet. I stare up at him curiously, registering the unusual expression on his face.

"What?" I ask, my voice barely a whisper. "What is it?"

"You don't know."

Not a question. I lean back, placing one of the blood-soaked towels into the makeshift bin beside me.

"Know what?"

"Elise," he answers after a heartbeat. "She's dead."

My ears are ringing. I stare down at my hands, clutching the paper towels, suddenly feeling like I can't breathe. This house is suffocating. The air is clogging my nose and filling my throat.

*Elise is dead.*

"Josie?" Harley whispers.

We're so close that my knees are between his. I can smell him. An intoxicating blend of caffeine, citrus, and cigarettes. He leans close, capturing my small hands in his big ones.

I *hate* Harley Caldwell. I don't want him anywhere near me, let alone *comforting* me, but I'm frozen, hardly daring to blink.

"Josie, shit, I'm sorry," he says, his rough hands squeezing mine. Blood drips from his face onto our joined hands, and he curses again, rushing to clean it. "I shouldn't have said anything."

"How long?"

"Hmm?" He stops, his eyes burning into mine.

"How long ago did she die?"

"Ah ..." He thinks for a moment. "Two years ago, maybe."

My head feels thick. A couple of years ago, I had all these messages from family and friends. I deleted my account, not being allowed—and also not wanting—anything to do with my past. I blocked the numbers calling.

They would have been trying to tell me this. Elise. My best friend. Who died without me. *Buried* without me.

I stand so quick I almost knee Harley in the face. I stagger to the kitchen and empty my stomach into the sink, unable to make it to the bathroom in time. My knees knock together as I wretch.

"How?" I choke out. "How did she die?"

"A car accident," he answers cautiously as if fearing I might explode any moment. "Eric ... your friend ... was the driver of the other car."

*Eric. The boy who has loved Elise since we were children. Her friend, her companion ... her killer.*

"He's fine," Harley says, although I didn't ask. "Some cattle got out. He swerved to miss them. The sun was in his eyes. He didn't see the other car." Harley pauses. "Are you okay?"

I wash my face, not caring if I wash off my makeup. I'm clammy and too hot. I numbly walk back to the lounge and sink into it, practically on Harley's lap.

"I missed everything," I whisper. Slowly, I turn. "And it's all because of what *you* did."

Harley left shortly after that, and thank God he did. Because the moment the door shut, I curled into my pillow and screamed until my throat was raw.

I cry all the tears I've refused to release over the years. It feels fucking terrible.

When there are no more tears, I shower. My face feels swollen. I don't dare look at my reflection. I can't bear to see myself so broken.

I crawl back into bed, staring up at the ceiling, and let the memories roll in.

# Chapter Fourteen

## Harley

I stand outside her door, too shocked to move.

She really didn't know? I wasn't the only person she dropped and never spoke to again? Of course, I knew she never visited, and after the rumours died down, no one mentioned catching up with her. But I never realised how disconnected she really was from here.

My heart splinters when I hear her scream, her chest-racking sobs floating out to me, hitting me as hard as the punches from my father's fists.

Everything inside me is begging me to go back in and comfort her, but I force myself to turn and leave her house. Everything feels shaky as I replay the moment I told her over and over.

I walk back to the pub. I don't want to go home, but I have nowhere else to go. I hate everyone here except her. And I'm the last person she wants to see right now.

I head back inside the pub and gather the things I'd left there. On my way back out, my shoulder barges roughly into someone, and

I flinch, quickly turning to protect myself, when I see Sam Mayor standing there, glowering at me.

"Oh," I say. "Hey, Sam."

"Harley," he mutters, barely looking at me as he trudges past. The strong scent of alcohol wafts over me and I watch him stumble to his car before pulling the driver's side door open.

Striding up behind him, I slam it shut. He lets out a yelp of alarm, turning.

"What the fuck, dude?" he growls, throwing my hand off his door as if my touch was poisoning it.

"Do we need to have this conversation again, Sam?" I ask him, tilting my head to survey the glazed look in his eyes.

Sam is a nice guy. Not particularly to me, but he has good reason. The last few weeks, he's been here, drinking a lot more than usual, before attempting to drive back home. Of course, the drive isn't very long—but that's not the point.

"Stop being an asshole," Sam snaps at me. "You ever get sick of being such a dick?"

"If you get in that car, it's not only your life that you're endangering, but everyone else that might pass you. Never know, it could be your mum. Dad." I step closer. "Josie."

He flinches at that, glaring hard at the ground.

"I know," he softly mumbles.

Before this, the last time I spoke to Sam was when we were competing against each other at a rodeo. I'd never seen someone look like they wanted to punch anyone more than he wanted to hit me that day.

I tried to talk to him, but he wouldn't listen. That particular trait seems to run in the family, it seems.

He's not the only one who hasn't ever forgiven me for the past, despite my efforts to explain things. In the end, I gave up trying to convince people I cared for her.

"Give me your keys," I say.

His jaw clenches. He still won't meet my eyes.

"Now, Sam."

With a heavy sigh, he slaps the keys into my hand before stepping away from the car and slamming the door shut.

I've made speculations as to what brought Sam to this, but I wouldn't dare voice it. Because he really *might* hit me this time, and honestly, if I have one more concussion, I might not wake up again.

The car beeps as I lock it, then we walk silently to my truck. The drive to his house is short. All the lights in the house are off when I pull up.

Despite having been stopped for a few moments, Sam stays where he is, gazing forward.

"You hurt her again, and I'll kill you."

"Trust me, I'm prepared to spend the rest of my life making it up to her," I say, sagging back into the seat.

Sam glances at me in surprise, finally meeting my eyes for the first time in … years.

"What?"

"I mean it," I reply.

He chews his lip for a moment, then nods.

"Good. I hope so."

# Chapter Fifteen

## Josie

### Four years ago

I slide the strap of my school bag over my shoulder as I follow Elise out to the courtyard. My shirt clings to me, and I dab the back of my hand across my forehead, removing the sweat that has gathered.

Nick, John, and Eric are sprawled on top of the tables. Eric's arm is folded behind his head as he reads. John is scrolling on his phone, and Nick is doing homework. I can't imagine what homework he is doing, considering we mostly get time to do it in our free periods. That's the thing about Nick. He always has to be ahead. Organised. Neat. Prepared. Unlike me, who realises we have an assignment the night before it's due.

"Hi, friends," Elise says breezily, plopping down on the seat beside John.

All boys turn to her with smiles and waves. Nick turns his head to me and stands. He curls an arm around my waist and draws me to him. I lean in, expecting him to kiss my lips, but he gently grazes my cheek before releasing me.

I slide in beside him, absently picking at my chipped nail polish.

"That's an interesting colour choice," Nick comments, his soft brown hair a little longer than usual, with a few light wisps in it from the sun. I love it long, but he always clips it super short. His mum likes it that way.

Glancing at the black polish, I shrug. I've never worn this colour. I always opt for light colours, rarely straying from pink or nude.

"I wanted to change it up."

He frowns for a moment before looking back to his notebook. "I prefer what you usually do."

I slip my hands underneath my thighs and lean forward.

"Can we go eat?" John asks, not looking up from his phone. "All I had was an apple for lunch, and I'm starving."

"Why did you only have an apple?" Elise questions, tucking a piece of her long hair behind her ear, her multiple bracelets jingling with the movement. Every part of Elise is long and slender. She sweeps her hair back into a messy bun on the top of her head, the muscles in her arms dancing. I glance down at my own arms. Pale. Freckled. Chubby.

"I forgot my lunch money."

Exhaling, I rock side to side. "Well, let's go, then," I agree. "This is boring."

Eric groans as he reels into a sitting position, shaking his long hair out of his eyes. He stretches, bones cracking in his back, before he pushes to his feet, looming over us.

"Lessgo," he says.

Nick slams his notebook shut and places it in his bag before standing. He reaches for my hand, and I slip mine into his, curling my fingers to hide the dark polish, suddenly wishing I never painted them that dark.

We pile into Eric's grandfather's car. The heat washes over me in a stifling wave. I wind the window down and stick my head out of it, trying to capture a breeze. The trip is short and bumpy. The air-con is busted, and the radio won't turn on, so we are stuck listening to John recapping the latest TV show he's been watching.

Elise is more polite than me, asking the right questions and feigning just enough interest to keep him talking. I can't pretend to have any interest in what he talks about. It's quickly becoming this way with all my friends. I don't know why, but it's happening more and more.

We arrive at the diner, and I rush inside, seeking the coolness. It isn't much better, but anything would be better than being crammed inside that car with three teenage boys and Elise, who *always* shotguns the front seat.

"Hello." Mr. Brown, the owner of the diner that has been here since before any of us were born, smiles. Mr. Brown has grey hair that's almost white. His eyes are kind and his smile is welcoming as he passes out menus and gestures to one of the many vacant booths as if we don't sit at the same one each time.

We all take our seats, and Nick throws his arm around the back of the leather seat. I lean so that my head rubs his arm, and he smiles.

"Your usual?" he asks.

"Yes, please."

"Do you want to share wedges?"

"Sure do!" John replies before I have time to.

Elise is sitting between John and Eric, like always. Both of them are half-turned in her direction. It's almost comical how transparent they are with their feelings for her. She is either totally oblivious, or fantastic at faking that she doesn't notice. Maybe she does, and she simply doesn't care.

Mr. Brown appears with a notepad in his hand. "What can I get you folks today?"

"The usual milkshakes," Nick answers with his friendly smile.

"And two bowls of wedges to share."

"Too easy." Mr. Brown smiles. "Anything else?"

"Not at the moment."

He nods before collecting the menus and hobbling back to the kitchen.

Tracing patterns with my fingers, I drag my fingertip over the speckles of chipped paint and dents in the wood.

For as long as I remember, this has been what I wanted. A great group of friends, and Nick. It's all I could think about. And now that I have it, everything I once thought was the most important thing in the world suddenly feels like it's not enough.

This place. The people in it. It's so small. Boring. Repetitive.

I feel like I'm losing my mind.

"Would any of you ever leave this place?" I randomly blurt, cutting John off mid-sentence without realising. For the past few weeks, I have been zoning out to the point I have no idea what is going on. Elise joked that I might be getting early Alzheimer's disease.

Three sets of eyes swivel towards me.

"Leave Fern Grove?" Eric asks, placing his phone down in front of him.

"Yeah."

"Why would you want to?" Nick frowns. "Everything you need is here. Friends, family, dependable work. A safe place to raise your kids."

My mouth dries a little.

"It's such a small town, though. Everyone knows everyone. Don't you want to travel? See what else is out there?" Throwing my hair over my shoulders, I turn, leaning on my forearms. "We should all move to the city and share a house! We could go out every weekend and explore the city! Travel wherever we want!"

"That sounds expensive," Nick says. "And I'm planning to take over my family's business."

"You could go for a few years and come back?"

"Why would I want to move to an overcrowded expensive city, where I would pay triple to have a tiny apartment instead of a nice house with a backyard? And why would I want to move away from everyone I love?" There's a hint of anger in his voice—one of the rare moments Nick has shown anger—and I meet his eyes challengingly. This isn't the first time I've mentioned this in the past few weeks. I can see the frustration behind his eyes.

I open my mouth to retort when Mr. Brown wanders back with an armful of milkshakes. The glasses clang on the table as he places them down.

"Wedges won't be long," he promises, sending the group a friendly wink.

"Did you see the circus is coming to the Ag Show this year?" Eric interjects, reaching for his phone. "I saw a flyer about it downtown. You guys want to go?"

He turns so that we can see the picture on his phone. Everyone murmurs in agreement, and I force a smile onto my face, ignoring how easy it is to be dismissed by them all.

Mr. Brown returns a moment later with our order, and I realise the usual sauce he brings me isn't there.

"Happy with everything?" he asks.

"Sure are," Nick says before I can protest. I narrow my eyes when I see him glance at the gravy, where the cup of sauce I like is usually beside it, before looking away.

Mr. Brown nods before taking the table number in his hand. His diner is mostly quiet as he only opens limited hours. He and his wife used to run the shop together, but since she's passed, he can only handle so many days. People have offered to work for him, but he always claims he is happy with how it is.

The conversation continues, the earlier topic never mentioned again, and I stare at the faded clock on the wall, watching the hand slowly tick.

The bell above the front door chimes, and loud laughter and footsteps trickle in. I glance towards the sound, seeing Brennon and Harley strolling inside. Everyone collectively stiffens in their seats.

Brennon looks over at our table and grins, nudging Harley. Harley's eyes—those stunning baby blues—settle over me. My pulse jumps, a shiver rolling down my spine. I've often found my eyes being drawn to Harley, and recently, he's been staring right back.

"Oh, hey, it's the freaks," Brennon drawls, leaning across the table and swiping a wedge between his fingers. "And Elise."

My cheeks colour at the clear sign of his attention on Elise and his blatant insult to the rest of us.

Nick sighs, leaning back in his seat. "Bugger off, Brennon."

Brennon's smirk widens. "Hey there, Nicky."

He tussles Nick's hair, and Nick's nostrils flare as he swats his hand away.

"Don't you have anything better to do?" I roll my eyes.

Elise flashes me a warning look, but I ignore her. Brennon's beady eyes flicker to me, and he makes a sound mixed between a scoff and a laugh.

"Just saying hi to my fellow school peers," Brennon replies, rolling the wedge between his fingertips before he flicks it towards John. It hits his face, and he flinches.

My jaw clenches, and I glare at the table as they move to find their own booth.

"I'm going to the bathroom," I mutter, lightly pushing on Nick.

He grunts and slides across the seat, letting me out. I stalk towards the bathroom and lean on the sink, staring at my reflection. I hate everything about myself. My skin, my hair, my body. I want to change all of it.

Blowing out a breath, I rinse my hands and adjust my ponytail before heading back outside. With my head down, I don't see anyone there. I bump painfully into them and stagger back. Warm hands settle on my waist, and I drag my eyes to meet Harley's.

"Hey there, sweetheart." He smirks, his tongue playing with his lip ring.

I recoil, my heart somersaulting in my chest. His eyes travel over my bare thighs before inching up my torso.

"You don't have to be such an asshole, you know," I spit at him.

Harley tilts his head to the side, staring at me curiously. "Have I ever mistreated you?"

I blink up at him as I think. Well. No. He hasn't. But Brennon has, and Harley has stood idly by, letting him.

"Asshole by association," I grumble, folding my arms over my chest.

"I am," he says. "An asshole," he amends, seeing my frown. He walks over to me and lightly grazes my cheek with his finger as he pushes my hair back. "But not to you, sweetheart."

His thumb circles over my cheek before he breezes past me and down the hall, leaving me trembling. He looks back at me as he slips behind the door.

Staring after him, I wait until I'm alone once more. Breathing heavily, I lean against the wall, wondering why the hell I liked that so much.

# Chapter Sixteen

### Josie

Harley's blood from last night stains the carpet, and I stare down at the scattered droplets at my feet.

I soak the carpet and begin scrubbing in an attempt to avoid thinking about last night. About anything, really. When I run out of things to clean, I feel the burning sensation in my eyes. I blink furiously and then realise I don't have the strength to stop the tears.

For once, I let myself feel everything. Chest-wracking sobs tear from me so violently that I stumble. I collapse onto my bed, gripping the sheets for support as I cry. So much pain, so many memories, so much time. It's too much.

I cocoon myself in the blankets and turn the TV on. My eyes ache. Rummaging through my nightstand, I find some leftover Valium I used to take. I swallow the pill down and sink into my pillows, hoping that when I sleep, I dream of nothing.

Sweat slides down my back and into my eyes. I blink away the sting of it and drag the back of my hand across my brow. It's a hot, still day. My sneakers slap the pavement in a calming rhythm as I run.

A truck slows beside me, and I glance to see Harley behind the wheel. Wind ruffles his hair, and sunglasses shade his eyes.

"Can't complain when this is my view on the way to work," he calls out over the rumble of the engine.

"Kiss my ass."

"Gladly," he snickers before tearing from the curb in a cloud of dust.

I glower after the car. My body flushes and I refuse to believe it is from anything other than the unbearable heat. The humid air is suffocating, and I soon have to slow to a walk, feeling light-headed.

I throw my hair into a bun and walk to the swimming pool. If I can't run, laps of the pool will have to do. I grab my swimmers and towel as I pass my house on the way.

There are two cars in the lot when I arrive, but no one seems to be in the pool. I line up at the canteen to pay the entry fee. A tall woman with mousy brown hair is rearranging things on the shelf. She turns, a warm smile on her face. Once our eyes lock, the smile vanishes.

A slither of ice spikes through my spine as we stare at each other.

"Hello, Mrs. Schneider," I eventually choke out.

Mrs. Schneider. Nick's mother. The woman who *despises* me.

She blinks at me for a moment, her mouth twisting. "Josephine. I heard you were back."

"Yeah."

I shift my towel to my other arm, feeling immensely uncomfortable.

"Three dollars fifty," is all she says.

I swallow and quickly count my coins before handing the money over.

*"Leave this town and never come back. Do everyone a favour."* Her

words, even though said years ago, ring inside my head like it was only yesterday.

I gather my things and start walking when she speaks again.

"Why?" she asks. I turn, hating how dry my mouth feels and the sinking sensation in my stomach. "Why did you come back? After all this time?"

"Karma."

Her eyes narrow for a moment. I don't clarify. I push through the gate and head over to the pool, eager to continue my workout. I like the silence when I'm under the water. No one is watching me. No one is listening. It's just me.

The coldness of the water feels electrifying on my skin as I dive in. I relish in the peacefulness of it as I propel under the surface. I push the soft green eyes of Annabeth—eyes that are so similar to Nick's—from my mind and try my best to ignore her words.

When I step out of the pool thirty minutes later, I still feel rattled. The workout helped, but the entire time I was consumed with the past and all the anxiety that comes with it.

I towel off and exit, avoiding eye contact with Annabeth. My thongs squelch with each step, and my wet hair sticks to my back. When home, I lock the front door and the windows. I triple-check everything is secure before I sit down in my bathroom, my back against the glass, my knees hugged to my chest. I bury my face into my thighs, wishing my father was here. I don't know why I'd seek him now, after everything, but I wish for his comforting arms and words of wisdom.

The next morning, I wake heavy and slow, feeling like I delved through years of emotional trauma in one day, and my body hasn't recovered.

My scrubs arrived—I had to pay an extremely ridiculous price for them to be express posted—and I slide my lilac set on. I twist my hair into a low bun, loose strands framing my face.

I spent a good minute washing my eyes as they still felt sore and a little crusty from all the crying. When I walk into the café twenty minutes later, it feels like every head turns my way, but I'm too weary to enjoy the attention. I order myself an extra-large coffee, hoping it'll kick the tiredness out of my system.

"Wow, nice outfit," Joanne compliments with a curved, unplucked eyebrow. "Where are you working?"

"Danny's Dental," I answer.

"Oh." She nods, clearly trying to figure out what I actually do there.

I'm ten minutes early when I arrive, having beaten both Belle and Danny. I realise then that I don't have a key, so I sit out the front and sip my coffee while I wait.

Fern Grove is a quiet town, and it's sleepy this time of the morning. Very unlike the city, which seems to never sleep.

The front door of the surgery swings open with a loud creak.

"Hiya," Belle greets me with a grin, her dark cat-eyes pushed into her hair, her glittery keys in her hand. "We come in through the back. I'll show you where to park."

Belle and Danny move about at a leisurely pace, and I have to remind myself it's a completely different atmosphere here.

I only have a couple of patients, and I panic when I first look at the schedule, wondering how I'll fill the rest of my day. I'm used to working in a place where you have deadlines and targets to meet. I know it won't be like that here, but it's difficult to rewire my brain.

I only have clean, and they are all with elderly patients who either don't know me or don't know of my past, which is a relief. In between my patients, I tidy the surgery and organise the stock. I lose track of time and only realise it's the end of the day when I see Belle shutting down.

We say goodbye, the two both offering me a lift, but I dismiss them. I enjoy the walk home after work. It helps me unwind. Although the air is too humid to feel very fresh out here, it's still a little relaxing spending some time outdoors after being cooped inside all day.

I don't turn to acknowledge him when Harley's truck idles beside me. It was a peaceful walk until now.

"Want a lift?"

"No."

"You sure?"

"Yes."

Suddenly, the car has stopped, and he is outside of it. I keep walking, but he moves in front of me.

"Josie."

"What, Harley?" I snap at him. "What's your problem?"

"You look nice," he blurts, taking in my attire. "First day?"

"Yes."

"How was it?"

"What do you want, Harley?" I ask, exhaling.

His tongue runs over his lip piercing, and I can't help but stare. His eyes swivel to mine, and in the harsh light of the day, they're a brutal blue.

"Look," he starts. "I want to say thank you for the other night. You didn't need to step in and help, especially after everything …" There is a thick silence between us, and he clears his throat. "And I didn't know that you didn't know … about …"

"It's fine."

"Is it?" he asks. "It must have been a shock."

"Harley, we're not friends. You don't give a fuck about me, so why are you trying to act like the nice guy?"

He looks taken aback by my words. "You think I'd be here right now if I didn't give a fuck about you?"

"You never have before, so why would you now?"

"How can you say that?" he growls, looking angry now.

"Because if you ever cared for me, you wouldn't have done what you did."

His hands fall to his sides, and we stare at each for a long moment.

"Now, please, let me walk home in peace." I shoulder around him and march onwards.

I hate that his words are swirling around in my mind. He doesn't care, and I hate that he is getting under my skin.

"Are you with Nick?"

I throw my hands up in exasperation as I look back. "What?"

"Are you seeing Nick?"

I glower up at Harley, pushing my tongue into my cheek. "Yes."

"Why?"

"Because he is the one for me, Harley. He always has been."

He shakes his head, looking furious. "No. He isn't."

"You know nothing."

"I know you weren't happy, Josie. That's why we—"

I throw my hands out and shove him. I've never been a violent person, but Harley brings out the worst in me.

"You have no right to talk to me. About *anything*." I feel tired and unsettled. I don't want to have this conversation now. Or ever. "Leave me alone, Harley. I mean it."

"No, you don't."

Ignoring him, I turn and stride away.

This time, he lets me go.

# Chapter Seventeen

## Harley

*Four years ago*

The sun is unrelenting, and I scoot towards the shade that keeps moving. Sweat dots my forehead and upper lip. I use my shirt to wipe my face before lighting the end of the joint and taking a deep breath.

It's quiet down here. A few of the boys and I often come down to the agriculture shed and roll up. No teachers venture down here, except the ag teacher, who is often too busy being inside his own head to even notice us, although we do make an extra effort to be discreet.

The insistent buzzing of Brennon's phone is driving me mad. I stare at him. "Who are you texting?"

Brennon's lips curve upwards. "Rianna."

I tilt my head. "Aren't you seeing Elise?"

Brennon shrugs. "You know how it is with Elise. On and off. She only likes to sink down to my level every now and then."

I snort. That's sort of right, though. She's little miss Perfect with her goody-two-shoes friends. Elise only every now and then takes a walk on the wild side with Brennon. Little does she know, he has girls on the go every moment her attention is turned off him. Well. Even when it isn't.

When I think about Elise, my mind wanders to her pretty little friend, Josephine Mayor. I can't get that girl off my fucking mind. There's so much more to her than meets the surface. She first caught my attention looks-wise—her stunning blue eyes, that gorgeous blonde hair, her cute round face. But the moment I became … well … a little infatuated was when I overheard her father grilling her one afternoon in the supermarket. He was shredding into her, tearing little bit by bit off her.

She stood there, chin jutted out, taking every comment from him with a fierceness I admired. I could see it from a mile away. Father with high expectations that no child could ever meet. Although not the exact same situation as mine, I really felt for her. Not many people around here experience the harsh reality of life like me. And then I saw that. And it intrigued me. Because there was a fire in her eyes so similar to how I felt around my own father. With her bright smile, perfect hair, and prim clothes, you'd never have thought her life was anything other than picture-perfect.

That's not the only similarity between Josephine and myself.

We don't fit in here. We long for more. A taste of adventure. The thrill of change. The hunger for life. I've learned a lot about Josephine since I started taking more notice of her.

Fern Grove suddenly seems a little less torturous, knowing that I might have a kindred spirit here. Our paths are going to cross. Very soon.

She just doesn't know that yet.

# Chapter Eighteen

## Josie

The surrounding walls are a pale yellow. Small and suffocating. Being back here, in general, makes me feel like I haven't come up for air in weeks.

Swinging my legs off the bed, I slowly stand and pad towards the bathroom. My gaze wanders around the place as I brush my teeth. The house is small. And old. But now that I have my furniture, it seems so much like home. It's my place. I'm safe here.

After dressing, I head into the kitchen and withdraw a bottle of water. I take a long sip and lean on the counter, staring out the window. The air simmers, showing how hot it is outside. I take another drink.

I walk towards the bedside table, and then yank open the drawer and rummage inside it. My fingers snag across a photograph, and I pull it out. It's an old photograph of Elise and me. She's holding out the camera, and I'm leaning my head on her shoulder, a small, shy smile on my lips. Her smile is confident and wide, so big that you can almost see every tooth.

Swiping my thumb over her face, I stare down at her.

"Oh, Elise," I whisper.

Blinking away tears, I fetch my purse and jog to the car. I stop by the service station to fuel up my car and grab a bunch of flowers. I make tracks out to the cemetery. Glancing around, I see that it's deserted.

I sit in my car for a good ten minutes before I'm brave enough to step outside of it. I twist the flowers nervously in my hands, having never visited a cemetery before. Taking a steadying breath, I explore the pathways, my eyes searching.

It only takes me a few minutes to find her gravestone.

### IN LOVING MEMORY OF
### *Elise Porter*
### *2000-2019*

My heart sinks low in my chest. I find it hard to breathe as I read and reread the words in front of me. I drop to my knees and place a hand over the soft grass.

"Elise …" I whisper, hot tears burning my eyes. "I'm so fucking sorry."

Tears run down my cheeks as I place the flowers down. I hunch over, pressing my fingers into my eyelids.

"You were too young. Too fucking young." I sniffle, so many untamed emotions rearing up inside of me, tearing to break free and ruin everything I have fought so hard to build. "And I wasn't here."

My mouth is hot and sticky as I try to inhale evenly.

"It should have been me."

Slowly, I sit back up. I hover a hand over my heart and the other on the grass, just before the gravestone. The tears keep coming and for a moment, I fear they won't stop.

I cry until there are no tears left. Until my legs are numb and my throat hoarse.

"I loved you." I clear my throat. "I *love* you. You deserve better than this." I choke on my words, exhaling. "You deserve the world."

Pushing to my feet, I sway a few times, the pins and needles shooting down my legs making me feel unstable. I wait a few moments before I lean over and touch the top of the gravestone. Pressing my lips to my fingers, I trail them over the top of the gravestone.

"I'm sorry that I let you down."

Breathe—in, one, two, three. Out—one, two, three.

I'm barely focused on the road when I drive back into town. I call into the supermarket to grab a few things. I internally groan when I spot the shiny, golden hair of Jess. I duck between the aisles and shake my hair over my shoulder, attempting to shield my face.

"Josephine?" I hear her call.

I exhale. "It's Josie."

"Oh. Sorry. Josie." She says it just like Nick does. *Joe-see.* Like they're having trouble pronouncing it.

"What is it?" I ask, sniffling, not looking up.

"I just wanted to clear the air. About Nick."

I snatch at a packet of chips and drop it into the basket, gripping the handle a little too aggressively. A pulsing headache has formed behind my eyes and the last thing I want to do is to be here right now, let alone with *her*.

"Nothing to clear."

"Well. There is," she says awkwardly. "We were ... kind of ... seeing each other."

"Take it up with him if you have a problem," I huff, brushing around her. I don't look up the entire time, and I throw my items onto the conveyor belt before she can reply. I've paid, and I'm out the door within a minute. Guilt gnaws at me, for everything I've done, and I grit my molars, trying not to crack.

It's quiet. A startling, still quiet, at my tiny house. I pack the things away and throw myself onto the lounge, burying my face into the pillow. When my eyes close, I see him. Harley. I feel his hands cupping my face, those stunning eyes piercing into me. Those luscious lips tilting into a smile. His voice filters into my mind as if he's here right now, murmuring in my ear.

*"It won't always be like this,"* he whispers. *"Things will get better. You'll see."*

# Chapter Nineteen

## Josie

### *Four years ago*

Fairy lights are strung from wall to wall, hanging over us, appearing as though the stars have dropped from the sky.

Loud voices and laughter fill the room, with the music so loud the floor beneath my feet vibrates.

Elise's hot breath is on my neck, her long arms secured around me as we dance and laugh to the latest hits blaring from the speaker. I'm light and buzzed from the alcohol. I feel great, considering Nick and I got into one of our infamous fights. The same as usual. I want more from him than he will give. But tonight, I'm forgetting about Nick.

"Eric wants to go for a walk," she whispers into my ear, her lips lightly touching my earlobe. "Should I go?"

"Sure, if you want to," I reply. "Do you?"

Elise shrugs, stepping back from me so that we can face each other. She looks gorgeous in a loose dress that reveals more skin than she usually would. She glows underneath the soft lights.

"Brennon is here."

I raise an eyebrow. "Is that on again?"

She blows out a breath. "Yes. No. I don't know. It's nothing serious." She rolls her lips into her mouth, her gaze shifting over my shoulder. "With Eric, it's always going to be serious."

"Do whatever feels right, El," I say. "Just have fun. Don't think too hard."

"I could say the same to you." She smiles, prodding her finger into my forehead. "What's been going on with you? You're so tense. Is it Nick?"

I wave her off. I can't admit it to anyone. That my boyfriend doesn't want to have sex with me. It's a humiliation I can't handle.

"Everything is fine."

"Mmhmm …" She nods disbelievingly. "If you say so."

"He's just over there," I murmur, jutting my chin out. "Brennon. He's watching you."

Elise darts a look over her shoulder, and their eyes meet. I melt away into the shadows. She doesn't even notice I've left.

I break from the hall and push out into the dark night, needing air. My thoughts are whirling inside my head. I'm not happy. There, I admit it. Tears burn my eyes, and I find a swing to perch on at the park close to the hall. The music is quieter out here, and I feel some tenseness in my muscles ebb away.

Nick is a good guy. *The* Good Guy. The guy you settle down with. But I'm not happy. I want more from him. I love him, but I'm at a loss.

"A pretty girl like you shouldn't be out here all alone," a surly voice murmurs in the dark.

I startle, whipping around and peering up at the dark figure of Harley. He is sitting up higher in the playground, his long legs dangling over the edge. His eyes glow a piercing blue in the dim light, and I can see his signature handsome smirk on his lips.

"Harley," I breathe. "You frightened me."

"Come join me."

My heart slams into my ribcage. "What?"

"Come join me," he says patiently. "The view is better up here."

Exhaling a little shakily, I climb my way to where he is and sit beside him. Our arms touch, and I feel his body heat through his thin shirt. His scent washes over me, and I take in a long inhale, savouring it. God. Harley Caldwell is the hottest guy in Fern Grove. And he called me *pretty*.

"What's the matter?" he asked.

"Just have a lot on my mind."

"About your nice little boyfriend?" he mocks.

I narrow my eyes. "Nick is a nice guy."

"I just said that, didn't I?"

"You said it in a way that seemed like an insult."

Harley grins. "Okay. You got me. Nick is a bore."

My eyes widen. Everyone likes Nick.

"A bore?"

"A snooze, a yawn," he says, leaning close. I can smell the cigarette on his breath with a strange combination of mint toothpaste. It's sort of delicious. "You can't really think a guy like that could satisfy a girl like you."

"A girl like me?" I straighten. "What's that supposed to mean?"

Harley lifts the cigarette to his mouth and takes a long drag. He takes his time blowing it out before he combs his fingers through his unruly hair.

"Josie, I see you," he says simply. Again, with the nickname. Josie. I really, really like that he calls me that. "Right through you, actually."

"What do you mean?"

"You're not like this hick town." Another drag. "I don't belong here. I don't fit in. But you know what?" He shifts so that he's facing me, his knee leaning over my thigh. "Neither do you."

All the air leaves my lungs. This boy—this arrogant, *dangerous* boy—has just said everything that has been on my mind these last few months. He's nailed it exactly. I don't fit here. I don't belong. And Nick and I aren't working.

"Want some?" he whispers, waving the cigarette in front of me.

Swallowing, I stare down at it. Slowly, I reach out and take it.

"What do I do?" I ask quietly, expecting him to laugh or mock me, but he doesn't.

"Take it between your lips," he murmurs, his voice soft and smooth. "And inhale."

My heart is racing as I do what he says. My mouth fills up with smoke, and I inhale sharply. It fills my throat and I suddenly cough, smoke billowing out of my mouth.

"Ick!" I groan, shaking my head, resisting the urge to gag. "That's disgusting."

He grins. "Try it again."

My hands tremble slightly, and he circles his over mine, steadying them. Our gazes lock as I press my lips around the end of it and take another drag. He bites his lip softly as he watches, the tilt of his lip ring causing a swooping sensation in my stomach. This time, it's smoother. I still cough, but not as bad.

"Again," he whispers.

My lip quivers slightly at our proximity. I inhale longer this time before I turn my head to the side and exhale softly, watching it drift away in a hazy cloud.

"I've watched you a lot, Josie," he comments, transferring the cigarette from my hand to his. "You and me. We're more similar than you'd ever know."

"You've watched me?" My voice is low, hardly audible.

"Yes," he whispers.

He leans close. The heat from his body rolls over me in waves. He pauses for a moment, waiting for me to pull away. When I don't, he presses his lips to mine. They're soft and inviting, and soon, his tongue is brushing mine.

Strong hands grip my waist, transferring me onto his lap, his warm fingers trailing down my sides. His hands are on my thighs and mine on his chest. The kiss is intense and hungry and something I've never experienced before. Nick and I have barely made out, and our kisses are *nothing* like this.

Harley's thumb brushes my underwear line, and I almost choke on my breath. I grind my hips into him, and he groans softly, pushing his firm hands further up my dress. This kiss is so deep that it's overwhelming. Our limbs tangle as I push deeper into him, feeling every part of hard muscle he has to offer.

I moan into his mouth, and the kiss deepens into something desperate as a feeling of longing crashes through me like a tidal wave.

I've done more with this boy in seconds than I have with Nick in eight months.

*Nick.*

I suddenly backpedal, and before I know it, I'm mid-air. I hit the sandy ground with a hard thud, winding myself. A fierce ache echoes through my body as I wince.

"Fuck!" I hear Harley exclaim. His feet land beside my head. "Why on earth did you just leap off the edge?"

I'm dizzy as I blink, the stars blurring together. Harley helps me to my feet, and I brush the sand away.

"Sorry," I whisper. "I can't. I'm with Nick."

Harley is silent for a moment. Finally, he nods.

"Sure," he replies. "For now."

Grinning, he leans down and kisses me again. It's softer and more conservative this time. He slides his hand down my back, scrunching up the fabric against my backside.

"This can be our little secret."

# Chapter Twenty

## Josie

When Nick called this morning, inviting me to spend the day with him and a few others at the quarry, I expected to be thrilled. But instead, I've been trying to think of excuses not to go.

I'm now dressed, waiting for him to pick me up, having convinced myself this is what I'm staying in Fern Grove for. Nick. I'm doing things right this time. *Nick* is right.

I'm clad in a white bikini top, and a high-waisted denim skirt, with my towel slung over my arm. My sunglasses rest on the bridge of my nose as I lean on the kitchen bench, waiting for Nick's truck to appear in the slim opening of my window.

When it does, I gather everything I need and slip out the door. It bangs shut behind me.

I feel a little nauseated when I see John and Eric in the car. My old friends. I automatically look to the front, expecting to see Elise. Instead, a girl with round, brown eyes and dark freckles sits in Elise's old seat, an innocent but kind smile on her face.

"Oh my God!" John bursts, tearing out of the car. He wraps his arms around me and lifts me off my feet. We spin around until I'm dizzy. I let out a laugh, slapping his shoulder gently.

"I'm going to throw up on you!"

John places me down, grinning. "Jesus, Josephine. You scrub up all right. Look at you!"

"It's just Josie, but thanks! You look great yourself, John," I say and mean it.

Eric, who has always been the tamer of the two, strolls around the car, his long arms dangling by his sides. I do a double-take when I see his face. Dark circles coat his under eyes, and his midnight-black hair looks oily and unbrushed. He's ghostly pale, much more so than I remember him being as if he is recovering from some sort of illness.

His eyes … his eyes tell me all I need to know. It's not an illness that plagues him. It's guilt. I understand because I've had a similar look in my eyes since everything went down.

"Eric," I greet him, almost awkwardly. I want to ask him how he is, but I don't. We hug instead, and his hug feels lifeless compared to John's.

"Missed seeing you around here," he says. "How've you been?"

"Good!" I chirp, ignoring the brutal truth of my life and acting as though leaving was the best thing to ever happen to me. "I'm totally cultured and wiser now."

He finally cracks a smile. "Good to hear."

I throw my arm into the car and give Nick's shoulder a quick squeeze before piling into the car with the others.

"Hi, Josephine!" the girl greets me. For a moment, I'd completely forgotten about someone else being here. "Shannon! Remember me?"

"Oh, sure. Hi, Shannon. And everyone, please, it's just Josie," I answer, even though I don't really remember who she is. She must be younger than us. John reaches forward, touching her arm.

Despite everything, it seems traitorous to have someone else here instead of Elise. I can't help but turn my head to look at Eric. Thoughts run circles in my mind, thinking about how hard Eric's life must be after everything.

Shannon talks a lot. Too much, too loudly, and her words string together as one as she hardly draws a breath. John and Nick laugh and talk along with her, while Eric and I stare out the windows. The last time we were all together in this car, we were different people. I wish we could go back and rewrite history.

There are a few cars parked across the grass at the quarry when we arrive. I feel a nervous sensation of tingles on my skin when I recognise Harley's dark black truck amongst them.

I throw my towel down and kick off my shoes. My eyes roam over the clear, turquoise water. The sun is unrelenting as it beats down on me.

My eyes pause when I notice Belle and Brennon perched side by side on a couple of towels close to us. They narrow when I see Harley and Jess there too. Are they a thing now, since she lost her chance with Nick? My hands curl at my sides for no valid reason. A good girl like Jess would *hate* a boy like Harley. I'm baffled she is even seen within a metre of him, let alone *hanging out*. Is there any part of my life that girl doesn't want?

"You okay, Josie?" Shannon asks me.

"Yes," I say a little rudely as I tear my eyes from the group.

"Josie!"

Belle's voice is like a foghorn over the glade, and everyone in the radius of us turns their heads to stare.

Belle leaps to her feet and bounds over to me.

"Hey, girl! What are you doing here?" she asks.

"To swim," I deadpan.

She gives me a look. "Hey, don't be pissy at me. I wanted to ask you to come, but one, you hate Harley and Brennon, and two, Jess asked if she could."

"I'm not mad."

"You're mad." She rolls her eyes. "I'll make it up to you."

"Unnecessary."

"I'm coming over tonight for movies and wine."

"I'm busy."

"Yeah, with me. I'll see you at seven."

I roll my eyes, acting like I truly mean my words, but she just smiles.

When I see the others get to their feet, I march to the edge of the quarry. Nick is helping everyone safely get into the water, as the rocks are extremely slippery, coated in a thick moss. I wave him off when his hand extends to me.

He dives into the water from the rocks, and I watch the group swim out deeper. I look to my side, seeing the ghost of Elise beside me. Her long, bronze hair. Her stunning smile. I feel her hands over my shoulders.

She should be here. She deserves to be here. More than me.

With my head buzzing full of thoughts, I stride into the quarry, completely forgetting about the rocks. My foot slips from underneath me and suddenly, two warm hands settle on my waist, righting me.

I whip around, meeting Harley's eyes and that stupid, irresistible lip ring.

"Watch yourself," he murmurs, his gaze lowering to my lips momentarily, before meeting my eyes once more. "Don't want to get hurt, now, do we?"

"You've done a plenty good job of that on your own," I seethe.

We glare at each other for a moment before I realise we have an audience. And that his hands are still on my waist. I step out of his touch, his skin leaving a burning effect on mine. The way his eyes dip over me makes my insides feel like someone has trailblazed through them with a lit match.

I'm thankful for the coolness of the water when I sink into it. I avoid Nick's curious—and slightly suspicious—gaze and dip my head under. When I see Jess and Harley closer than I appreciate, I make a show of flirting with Nick. I hate that he brings this side out in me, but I have little control over it. Harley makes me crazy.

After an hour, I retire from the water, leaving the boys to their wrestling and cliff jumping. Harley is laid back on his towel, propped up on his elbows when he notices me. His blue orbs peer over his shades as I walk. I hate how my body flushes under his gaze.

Impulsively, I grab the sunscreen and walk over to them. Harley takes his bottom lip between his teeth, his gaze running all over me, a gesture wildly hot, affecting me in more ways than it should.

"Hey, Belle, do you mind giving me a top up?"

"Sure," she answers, pushing to her feet.

I turn, positioning my ass right in his view, and hand her the bottle. I undo the back of my bikini top, and my breasts spill over my arm, which is pressed against my chest. I gaze ahead as I feel her hands lather the sunscreen over my body.

"You need help with that?" Harley asks, and no one misses the slight hoarseness his tone has suddenly taken.

Jess pales slightly as she stares from Harley, to me, and then back to Harley. Without a word, she gets to her feet and strides away. No one seems to notice.

Belle re-ties my top and places the bottle in my palm.

"Thanks, girl," I say. "See you later tonight."

"You bet!" She smiles, oblivious to the entire show taking place in front of her.

I strut back to my towel and collapse onto my stomach. I glance towards the cars, seeing Jess disappear inside one, then drive away.

This time, I don't feel bad. Because honestly, I just did her a favour.

There's barely a hint of morning sunlight peering through my blinds when I hear the loud exhaust of a car. A door slams, and heavy footsteps climb the two steps up my porch before knuckles rasp against the glass of the front door, rattling the wall. I startle awake, my heart violently shuddering in my chest, before remembering where I am. Expelling a heavy breath, I groan and fling my arm over my head, hoping if I ignore the person, they will go away.

"Wake up."

Squeezing my eyes tighter shut, I dig into my pillow.

"Wake up, wake up, wake up." A loud voice calls from outside.

"Ugh!" I growl, flinging the pillow away and stomping through the room.

"What in fresh hell is this?" I snap at my grinning brother. "It's not even six in the morning!"

"Hi, sister. I need a favour."

"No."

"I brought you a toasted sandwich and a coffee." He raises his hands, and the aroma wafts towards me.

Snatching the brown paper bag from his hand, I step back into the kitchen and plop onto the seat.

"Why do you need a favour at this time of the morning?" I ask.

"It's best to get work done before it gets too hot," he answers.

"What kind of work?"

"I just need a second pair of hands to hold some things for me, and I thought of no one more willing or more helpful than my flesh and blood." He slaps a hand down onto my shoulder, and I grumble, greedily reaching for the takeaway coffee cup and taking a long sip.

"Right."

"If you could get dressed any day now, that would be great."

I glower at him before pushing up from the bench. Rummaging through my drawers, I yank out the darkest jeans I can find. I throw on a singlet and pull my hair back into a ponytail.

"You'll want to cover yourself up," he says, staring at my bare arms. "It gets boiling out there."

"I don't really have a jacket I want to sacrifice," I reply. "The red dirt gets everywhere."

Sam shrugs out of the flannel shirt he's wearing and tosses it towards me. It hits me in the chest, but I snake my arm out before it falls. When I slide my arms through, his scent washes over me, warmly giving me flashbacks to our childhood.

"I have another in the car I can use," he says. "Ready?"

"Yep."

I shove on my boots and we make the bumpy drive out to the farm. He pulls up at the stables and we get out, the fresh air billowing the loose bits of my hair around my cheeks.

"You can take Jamaica." Sam waves to the stable near the back door.

I nod and walk over to the wall where two lead ropes are dangling from horseshoes my dad has tacked to the wood. I clip the lead to Jamaica's halter and run my fingers down his nose.

"Hi there," I greet him.

He nuzzles my hand before I swing the door open with a loud creak. I lead him to the corner of the stable where the bailing twine is, like I have a hundred times before as if I haven't been removed from this life for years.

Sam and I unrug our horses in silence. The only sounds are metal clips clanging, Velcro unsticking, and the loud chirps from birds in neighbouring trees. Sam saddles my horse for me, and I nervously place my foot into the stirrup before swinging myself on.

"You remember how to ride?" He grins.

"Like riding a bike, I'm sure."

He smirks. "We'll see about that."

I squeeze my thighs, and Jamaica moves forward, his hooves clopping on the cement. I adjust the reins and pat his neck a few times, feeling a little unsteady. It's been a long time since I've ridden.

"Where are we going?" I ask.

"There are a few fences down that I need to fix over the back way."

I look at the bag he has strapped to his shoulders and wonder how it fits everything he would need in there.

Once we're out in the open, Sam swivels his body in my direction. "Let's go."

"What?" I squawk as he pushes his horse into an easy canter. My horse leaps forward, following the other's lead. I yelp, clambering onto the reins and squeezing tightly, hoping I don't fall.

Once I get used to the movement, I relax. My breathing is loud in my ears and the sound of hooves hitting the grass pounds the air. The warm air slides across my skin, and at this moment, I feel *free*. And that's something I haven't felt for a long, long time.

"Keep up, old girl!" Sam yells over his shoulder.

"Fuck you," I mutter with a laugh, urging Jamaica to go faster.

As we canter across the paddocks, the sun out in full sight now, I throw my head back and let go. My hands move in the breeze, and I inhale a lungful of air. Sam whoops and cheers, also throwing his hands up.

Suddenly, my horse stumbles, and I fling forward, my head smacking into his neck. I tumble and fall down his shoulder, his leg hitting me before I fall in a splat on the ground. I suck in a sharp breath, the fall winding me.

"Shit!" I hear Sam cry out.

Jamaica stands beside me, peering down as if to ask, "What the heck are you doing down there?"

"You all right?" Sam asks, pulling to a halt.

"Yeah." I shake my head, standing and brushing the grass from my jeans. "I'll be sore tomorrow, but I'll live."

"Thought you were being brave on your first ride back," he says with a chuckle.

I mount and collect the reins, glaring at Sam.

"Don't you tell anyone about this."

"I already filmed it to Snapchat it later when I have reception."

"You're a bastard."

He grins, tipping his hat. "Thank you. Ready to keep going?"

Sighing, I nod. We jet off again, and this time I keep my hands exactly where they should be. We ride for roughly thirty minutes or so before we get to the fence line that is lying flat across the grass.

Exchanging their bridles for halters, we tie the horses loosely to a tree, where they can be in the shade, and graze while we attend to the fence.

Sam laughs, pointing to me. "You have dirt all over your chin."

I wipe at my face and glower at him. "You be nice to me, or I'm turning around and heading home."

"Yeah? You remember the way?"

Turning, I peer out at the paddocks and trees that look endless and all the same.

"Yes," I lie.

"Uh huh."

Scowling, I reach into his bag and have a drink before shoving it back in. We move to the fence, and Sam instructs me on what he needs me to do and hold. I nod and do as he says. Within minutes, sweat dots my upper lip and drips into my eyes.

It takes two hours to fix all the fences, there being more damage than Sam initially realised.

"Thanks," he says as he puts all his tools back into his bag. "Let's go to the creek. I'm dying for a swim."

Climbing back onto the horses, we make the trek to the other side of the property, where the creek runs. We remove the saddles, and Sam hoists me onto Jamaica while he uses a rock to help him mount his own horse. I charge into the creek, and water splashes up my horse's neck, hitting my face.

I laugh as we move deeper into the water. Sam and I play tips, racing in and out of the water, the horses loving it just as much as us. I haven't had this much fun in years.

We lay in the sun to dry after we retire back to the bank.

"Thanks for coming with me today. I appreciate it."

I turn my head. My brother has his arm over his eyes, covering them from the sun.

"No problem. It was fun."

"Even though you went ass over?" He snorts.

I give him the finger before pushing to my feet. "We're not mentioning that again. I'm starving. Want to head back?"

We remount and start the trek back to the house. This time, we walk. Jamaica stretches his neck out long as he sniffs the ground, trying to sneak in bits of grass when he thinks I'm not paying attention. Sam's flannel is tied around my waist and my hair drips onto my singlet.

The soft leather of the saddle squeaks with the movement of Jamaica's strides. I lean forward, smiling, the scent reminding me of my childhood.

"You say you hate it here," Sam murmurs. "Do you mean the place or the people?"

I consider his words for a moment. "Both. I hate the heat and the claustrophobic feeling that plagues me when I'm here. But yes, also the people." I exhale. "Maybe this town hates *me*."

"You think you don't belong, but have you ever really tried?"

I glance at him, but he's gazing out over his horse's ears, looking thoughtful.

"I spent my entire life trying."

"Did you?" he asks.

He meets my eyes, and I look away. "I thought I did."

Seeing this serious side of my brother is unnerving. He's grown up a lot since I was here last.

"Don't make the mistakes you did last time."

Twisting my lips, I nod. "I know."

"I hope so." He leans over and lightly punches my arm. "Come on, last one to the stables has to wash up lunch."

His horse gallops forward, and my horse lurches to follow. I lean forward and try to catch him, but he is much more confident and experienced than I am, beating me easily.

I'm tired, sore, and famished by the time we get inside. I rub my eyes and feel the dirt smear across my cheeks.

"Goodness, I haven't seen you dressed like that for a long time." Mum smiles. "How was it?"

"Good! It was … kind of … fun?"

"I'll fix you some lunch. You still have some old clothes up in your room if you want to freshen up."

I bound up the stairs and am almost at my bedroom door when Dad steps into the hallway. He eyes my attire briefly.

"Hi, Dad."

He gives me a tight-lipped smile and steps around me before he stalks down the hall with heavy footsteps. Sighing, I let myself into the room and beeline to the cupboard. I screw my nose up in distaste at the few clothes hanging on rusted coat hangers.

I settle on a white off-the-shoulder tee and denim shorts. The shorts don't fit, so I borrow a belt from my brother, not that it goes with the outfit at all.

My eyes flit around the room, taking in the photos plastered on the wall. The memories of this room hang over me like a ghost. If I stand still long enough, I swear I can hear Elise's laughter floating down the hall. I shiver and rush from the room, not being able to stand it for another moment longer.

Lunch is ready when I return downstairs. Mum has used leftovers from the roast they had for dinner last night to make hamburgers. I load up my plate and take a seat, feeling the tension roll off my father in waves.

"How's everything going?" Mum asks, her cheeks rosy from the warmth of the kitchen. "How's work?"

"It's really good. I like it there. I've learned a lot from Danny. He works very old-school compared to what I've seen in the city, but he has some really great tips."

"That's great, hon."

I exhale, circling my hands around the burger and taking a bite. I've gained weight since returning home and not living the lifestyle I was, but I feel stronger and healthier.

"What have you been up to?" I ask her.

"Oh, you know, busy, busy! Me and the girls are organising Farmers Week, so that always has me running around the clock."

Farmers Week is an annual event to celebrate the local farmers and help raise funds in case of a drought, which is a regular occurrence being out this far west. It's quite possibly the biggest event on the social calendar, other than the agriculture show.

"Oh, right, yeah. When is it?"

"Next Saturday," she replies.

"Are you entering the cows in the parade?" I ask, turning my gaze to my father, who has been silent since I came downstairs.

"Yes," he answers.

I think for a moment about something else I could ask him to make conversation about, but I draw a blank. At least he answered me, even if it was in a frosty tone with no eye contact.

As I lost the race home, I wash up after lunch, before joining Sam on the lounge. He puts on a movie, and I rest back, my legs draping over the arm of the chair. My leg muscles hurt already from riding. I used to ride all the time, but since I haven't for a few years, everything feels achy and strained.

I only last a few minutes into the movie before my eyes grow heavy. Mum takes a seat on the same lounge as me. Quietly, she rakes her fingers through my hair softly, like she did when I was a little girl.

I've forgotten what it's like to feel truly safe.

To be home.

# Chapter Twenty-One

## Josie

### Four years ago

Slamming my locker shut, I turn on my heel, looping my arm with Elise, who hasn't paused for breath in almost two minutes. She has been gushing about her night with Brennon. For once, I had a bit of action in my own life. With the last person I expected ...

My stomach has been in knots for two days now. I feel so guilty. And I'm terribly confused. I've always found Harley to be attractive. In fact, I've been infatuated with him since I met him, back when his teeth were too big for his mouth, and his lanky arms were abnormally longer than anyone else's our age. I always thought he was the most beautiful boy I'd ever seen.

That was before Nicholas Schneider, the golden boy, showed me attention. He was dependable, realistic, what was *expected*. Besides, Harley hadn't shown interest in anything other than the occasional make out session at a party.

Except for that one time we did seven minutes in Heaven when we were thirteen, and he kissed my cheek and grabbed my boob. I basically fainted at the time and he had laughed at me, embarrassing me in front of everyone. He never seemed interested in girls. Or anything except causing trouble and talking back to teachers.

I see him leaning against his locker, that handsome smirk on his lips. Elise's rambling fades to the background as I focus on Harley, who pushes off the metal and walks towards us down the hall.

I take in his long, muscular arms, the sleeves of his school polo tightly spread over his biceps. His dark hair is so long that it's swept back with a hair tie. His fiercely blue eyes settle on me, and a hot flush plagues my body.

I hate that I straightened my hair today. I hate that I spent longer than usual on my makeup. I hate that my skirt is a little shorter than it should be. I hate that I subconsciously did this for him.

The people in the hallway fade around me as we stare at each other. The words pouring out of Elise's mouth become background noise. I think of those lips, his lip ring cold on my skin, his hands up my dress.

When we disappear around the corner, I inhale so sharply that I choke. Elise blinks at me, half in concern, half amused.

"Did you just choke on air?" She laughs, quirking an unnaturally bronzed eyebrow. "Now that is talent."

I wave at her, clearing my throat loudly. "You were saying?"

She needs no further encouragement to continue her long-winded story of every single detail of the other night. If only I could share my adventures too. Elise wouldn't understand my complicated feelings. She would be horrified to know I'd let things get this far.

My head is in a daze for the next two classes. I can't stop thinking about his tongue, his long fingers, his scent that wrapped around me. God. Harley Caldwell. Of all people. How did that even happen? Where did it come from?

I'm so absorbed in my own thoughts that when the classroom door to my right opens and a hand snakes around my wrist, I don't fight it as I stumble. The door is closed, and then I'm quickly pressed against it. I don't dare to breathe.

Harley's eyes fix on mine. A deep, ocean blue that stills me.

"Hi," he murmurs, his warm breath splashing over my lips. "How's your day going?"

I can't think or move. Because the hottest boy in the school has his hands on me. His steady gaze has my entire body burning.

"A little more exciting now," I get out, focusing on the lip ring that his tongue is playing with.

He offers me his arrogant, handsome smirk before he presses his lips to mine. One hand cups my face gently while the other scrunches up my skirt. His thumb grazes my thigh, and I might just die right then and there from the explosion of heat inside me—and also because I haven't breathed for a solid minute now.

"I've wanted to do that all day," he groans, pressing into me. "Meet me after school?"

His lips move across my jaw, slowly and teasingly. I softly moan when he sucks lightly on the skin on my neck.

"Harley, I-I can't do this."

"Tell me to stop, then," he whispers.

His lips travel further down, burrowing between the base of my throat and the collar of my uniform. His finger slips between the fabric of my underwear and my skin. I moan softly, feeling a pulsing ache between my legs that I've never experienced.

He palms me softly, and I throw my head back, knocking it against the door.

"Do you want this?" he murmurs breathlessly in my ear.

My underwear is completely soaked. He can *feel* how much I want this.

"Why me?" I basically wheeze, forcing my cloudy mind to think rationally. "Why now?"

"I've always noticed you, Josie," he answers. "And you've never been unhappy. Until now."

"Who says I'm unhappy?"

"Me," he replies simply before his finger moves further into a place I've longed to be touched. "Does he make you feel like this?"

My breaths are coming out short and fast.

"Does he touch you like I do?"

A gasp leaves me as his finger slides inside of me. Fast at first, then slow and deliberate a moment later.

"Harley," I groan, and he pushes again. I feel my underwear dampen even more. My eyes close as he inserts another finger.

"Say it again."

My head falls back against the door as he adds pressure to a part of my body only I've ever touched.

"Harley," I breathe, feeling my insides coil in pleasure.

"Good girl."

I moan as I relax into the feeling threatening to consume me. I forget that this is wrong. It feels too good to think about anything else right now.

Our breathing fills the air as he quickens his movement. Heat sears in my stomach, and I throw my face into his shoulder, biting him as I let out a whimper. Something I've never felt before crashes through my body, igniting me. Everything around me blurs into a blissful daze as I tighten around his fingers.

A few seconds later, I blink back to reality. My legs tense and tremble, barely holding me up.

Grinning as if he's won some sort of prize, Harley removes his fingers from me and steps back. Eyes locking on mine, he slowly raises his fingers to his mouth and sucks on them. I'm frozen, completely mesmerised by him.

Pressing my thighs together, I watch him lick my arousal from his skin. My cheeks flood with heat.

"You still got that boyfriend?" he asks me.

Without another word, he shoulders around me and opens the door. I stumble out of the way, my knees knocking together. My hand is on my chest, trying to stop my heart from leaping out of it.

I readjust myself and rake my fingers through my hair. I exit the classroom, still feeling flustered and extremely turned on.

I've dreamed—many times—about how that would feel. I never expected it to feel so fucking good. And so fucking bad.

"Hey, you," Elise greets me, flicking her long hair over her shoulder. She pauses, eyeing me. "Did you and Nick just have a little rendezvous? What's that on your neck?"

My fingers fly to my neck, where Harley's lips were moments ago. "What? Oh …"

Elise grins, nudging me. "So, you've sealed the deal, right?"

"Hmm?"

"With Nick?" She rolls her eyes. "You never give me any details!"

Just then, the bell overhead rings loudly, and relief washes over me. Students spill into the hallway, hurrying to get to class. Nick's head bobs through the crowd, his face lighting up when he sees me. Elise has drifted, talking to someone, and I'm again relieved that she hasn't noticed that I was not, in fact, with Nick moments ago.

"Hey." He plants a kiss on my cheek, curling his arm around me. "I feel like I haven't seen you all day."

Suddenly, I feel cold. I fold my arms around me, wishing I could be anyone else right now.

Because the arm around me isn't the arm I want anymore, and I have no idea what I'm going to do about it.

# Chapter Twenty-Two

## Harley

Today has been one of the hottest days of the year. Sweat has soaked through my hair so much, it looks like I've stepped out of the shower. I dig the shovel hard into the ground, a recently healed cut splitting open on impact. I wince as the blood mingles with the dirt on my hand before dripping onto the ground.

"Hey," one of the guys says, noticing the blood. "You really need to take a break, man. It's scorching today."

Swallowing, I glance at the break room, seeing my father's old ute there.

"I'm all right," I reply.

Joe's gaze follows mine, and his eyes soften in understanding.

"Come on, mate. No one cares your old man is there."

A dry laugh bubbles out of my mouth. "I care."

Nodding, he goes to walk away, but hesitates.

"Fuck it," he grumbles. "I'm insisting. It's a disgustingly hot today, you're dehydrated, and you're hurt. Go home."

Blinking away the sweat, I shake my head.

"Thanks for your concern, but it's fine."

"As one of your superiors, I insist."

Growling, I toss the shovel aside. I know he's doing it because he is concerned for my health, but sacrificing a few hours of pay isn't something I'm happy about.

"Go home and rest. You look like you need it," Joe says. "Look after yourself, mate."

Leaving all my belongings inside the break room, I throw off my hat and vest, sliding inside my truck. My head spins, and I blink away little black dots that dance across my vision. Shit. I really do feel weak now that I've stopped.

Instead of heading home, I go out to the dam. Kicking off my shoes and shrugging out of my clothes, I dive into it. The water streaking through my sweat-ridden hair and over my strained muscles feels soothing. I moan in relief at the coolness.

Coming back up for air, I float on my back, gazing up at the sky.

My head is all over the place. It was already—before Josie came back—but now everything is even more confusing. Everything I felt for Josie has come back stronger than ever. Hell, it never went away. That girl has weaved her way into my heart and no matter how much I pull, I can't snap the thread.

After spending over an hour swimming, floating, and diving deep, I head home for a shower, then change into my all-black clothes that I wear for the pub. I head in early and order myself dinner and a beer. I sit off in the corner, where hopefully I'm out of sight and will be left alone. I peer up at the TV and watch a repeat football game I've already seen.

The beer is cool and crisp, a welcome relief as I swallow it down.

The bell chimes, and I glance up, doing a double-take when I see Josie walk inside. She's dressed in her cute work outfit—lavender scrubs, with a little tooth badge clipped over her left breast.

Her long hair tumbles down her shoulders and back in thick waves as if she had it twisted in an up-do all day and pulled it out just before coming inside. Even after working a full day, she looks beautiful and fresh, like always. She peers around the room, and I wonder if she's searching for me. My heart thumps unrhythmically at the thought.

Ainsley, the girl working in the restaurant tonight, hands over Josie's order. My finger twitches. I want to call out to her, but I don't. She pays and thanks the girl, before disappearing back through the door.

For a long time now, I've had a plan. Save money, get out of here. But now when I think about what that will be like, I think about Josie being with me. It's a picture I can't rid my mind of, no matter how hard I try.

I'm so preoccupied with my thoughts I don't notice someone approaching the table. Liam—a friend, I guess—offers me a casual smile. He pushes a thick bit of hair off his forehead.

"Harley, hey," he says. "What's up?"

"Just having some dinner before my shift starts," I reply, before shovelling a forkful of food into my mouth. "What are you up to?"

"Um, I was just wondering if you had any bud you could sell me?" he asks, peering nervously over his shoulder.

Leaning back in my chair, I prop my elbow onto the chair. "Brennon sells, not me."

"Yeah, but you're the financial guy, right?" he asks.

Sure, I've helped Brennon from time to time with things, but I'm no drug dealer. Not that Brennon does it for the money. He likes the thrill of doing something bad, and loves the attention he gets from it.

"Like I said, Brennon sells, not me."

Liam looks a little mortified at the refusal, sweat breaking out over his forehead. He's always been a bit of a shy guy.

"Right. Okay then. Thanks anyway," he mumbles, hastily walking back out.

A few of the men glance over at me suspiciously, and I wonder if they overheard anything. Or perhaps they thought the exchange seemed unusual.

Rumours of Brennon and I being involved in all sorts of shit have circled around town over the years. I'm guessing it's from all those times we broke into old buildings and houses, marking the walls with profanities and symbols. When I think back to all the stupid things I let Brennon talk me into, I feel like stabbing myself in the eye.

Sighing, I finish my meal, then take it back to the kitchen and place it on the dirty pile before going out back to clock in.

"Another day, another dollar." Ainsley smiles, seeing my unenthusiastic look.

"Yeah," I mutter. "Another day in paradise."

# Chapter Twenty-Three

## Josie

"For fuck's sake," I mumble, inching the volume of my speaker up.

I've been working out for the past thirty minutes and keep being interrupted by a deafening bass. It sounded far enough to be out of town, but close enough to still be heard from my place.

After another ten minutes of my muscles groaning in complaint, I retire to the shower and dress quickly afterwards. I've barely got my shirt over my head when my front door bangs open obnoxiously.

"Hey, bitch," Belle greets me, wandering in as if she owns the place. She collapses onto the lounge, propping her feet on the coffee table. "There's a party."

"I can hear that."

"We're going."

I quirk an eyebrow as I release my hair from its clip. "We are?"

"Yeah."

"Who's party?"

Belle shrugs. "Cameron someone."

"Oh, I know Cameron," I say. "He's my brother's friend."

"Great, he won't mind you gatecrashing, then."

"I suppose not." I eye her outfit of worn denim shorts and a baggy t-shirt. "Are you wearing that?"

She scoffs. "Of course not, but I didn't want to waste my time getting ready if I couldn't convince you to go."

"What else would I do instead?" I question, moving my arms around the room. "The night life in this town is like watching paint dry."

"My thoughts exactly. Do you have something I can wear?"

I gesture to my closet that's against the wall, close to the bed. The space is so small you can basically see everything the moment you step through the front door.

"Help yourself. Pick me something while you're there."

"Happily." She beams.

Belle chooses possibly the most conservative dress I own. A white, lacey off-the-shoulder dress. For me, she chooses a daring emerald green dress that outlines every curve I have to offer, and then some. We dance around the room and drink wine while we get ready.

A part of me doesn't want to leave because we are having so much fun here. I haven't had a girlfriend like this since Elise. A harrowing stab of pain splinters through me each time I think her name. Last night, I sat by her grave for three hours, watching the moon glitter across the pale gravestones. I've been going out there every few nights. I will ever forgive myself for missing her funeral.

"Nick is going to shit himself when he sees you." Belle grins. "And Harley, for that matter."

"I don't care what Harley thinks."

"Right."

Running my fingers through my hair, I study my reflection, forcing all my dark and heavy thoughts from my mind. Despite the heat, I've curled my hair in loose, beachy waves. The dress is far too upscale for a town like this. I bought it after seeing a celebrity wear it in a high-end fashion magazine. It had cost me weeks' worth of my salary to afford it. It was one of the many items I stashed in my car, fearing Elliot might cut it up, like he did to one of my other favourite dresses when I "disrespected" him.

After pouring another glass, I fumble for my phone and swipe out of the hundreds of unread notifications sitting on my screen. I lazily dial my brother's number.

"Sister," he greets. "What a lovely surprise."

"Hello, brother," I say in a sing-song voice.

"You sound drunk."

"I am."

"I see," he says. "You don't happen to be pregaming for Cameron's party, are you?"

"Busted."

"Wow, partying with my big sis. That's something I haven't thought I'd do for a while. When are you heading there?"

I shrug, even though I'm aware he can't see me. "Not sure. When are you?"

"I'm heading out the door now. Who are you with?"

"Belle."

"Do you need a lift?"

I look at Belle and grin. "Yes please!"

I fly around the room, gathering lip gloss, spraying perfume, and fetching my house keys. I blow out all the candles and make sure all my appliances are unplugged from the wall. Mum has drilled that into my head since I was young. With the heat out here, she was always terrified something would catch on fire.

"I didn't realise Sam was your brother," Belle says as we step out onto the porch. "He's a sweetheart."

"He's a good boy," I say, and then realise I have no idea if that's true.

We hear Sam's car's exhaust before we see him pull into the street.

We pile inside, and he gives Belle a wave over his shoulder. Cameron only lives a few minutes from my house.

Music blasts through the open windows, the pale curtains flapping over the pane in the breeze.

Curious eyes follow us as we walk to the house. Several people wander over, greeting my brother mainly, and also Belle. I notice how standoffish people are when it comes to me, clearly not knowing how to handle me.

Heat blossoms over my skin as I try to ignore the stares. The house is unbearably hot and stuffy, with too many warm bodies packed inside the walls. We weave in and out of the small groups, the drinks in the bag we brought jostling with each step.

When we enter the kitchen, I see Nick, John, Eric, and a few others—including Jess—milling together, talking, plastic cups in their hands.

Belle squeals, running over to Jess, and they hug, gushing about each other's outfits. I roll my eyes and turn my back to them.

"Josie!" Nick startles. "I tried calling you a few times. I was going to see if you were coming to this." He swallows, tugging at his collar. "And here you are."

"Sorry, I'm useless with my phone these days," I reply honestly. "And I wasn't. Belle dragged me here with no notice."

His eyes flick to where Belle is standing, Jess throwing glances at us over Belle's shoulders.

"Oh. That's okay," he replies.

Linking our fingers together, I pull Nick after me and into the lounge room, where the furniture has been shoved against the walls to make space for a dance floor. The light is dim in here, with strobe lights splashing across the room wildly.

A prickling sensation rips through me, and I lift my eyes to see Harley leaning against the wall, twisting a cup around in his fingers. My pulse races when his eyes explore my body. I feel a strong sensation of butterflies stir between my legs and it takes all my willpower to drag my eyes from his.

Slinging my arms around Nick's neck, I push my body against his and begin dancing. His strong hands fumble at my sides, almost seeming like he's unsure of himself before he finally settles them on my hips. I hate how cautious he is; it feels like I'm a teenager again.

Everything around me vibrates, and my eyes—like magnets—are drawn to Harley. He's still watching me.

Bruises and cuts still litter his face, and my stomach tightens at the memory of his father's fist plunging into him.

His tongue moves his lip ring, and my eyes follow it. A hot flash burns through me as I think about Harley's mouth on my body, his tongue sliding against my skin. I feel wetness between my legs and curse. No other guy has ever made that happen, and it infuriates me that Harley gets a smirk on his face, as if knowing *exactly* what effect he has on my body.

"I'm glad you're here," Nick shouts into my ear, and I startle, having completely zoned out, momentarily forgetting where I am and what I was doing. *Who* I was with.

"Nick!" A gangly guy wearing a striped polo slaps Nick on the shoulder, saving me from replying. He turns to me and blinks in surprise for a moment.

"Hey, man!" Nick grins, going in for a one-armed hug. With his other hand, he makes a sweeping motion towards me. "This is Josie."

"Hey," he says casually. "You're not from here."

"I was. A while ago." I force a smile.

"Ah, apologies. Welcome back."

When his eyes move more than a couple of times to my chest, I push away from the pair and exit the room, forgetting that it would have been polite to at least make up an excuse. I dart upstairs and use the bathroom. When the door swings open, Harley stands outside of it, his forearms resting on the top of the frame. My eyes wander over his muscles, before sliding back to his eyes.

"Hey."

"What do you want?" I exhale.

"Simply came here to go to the bathroom."

"Uh-huh."

He offers me a wolfish grin, bits of his dark hair splaying across his forehead. "I've been a bit distracted tonight."

"Oh yeah?"

His eyes move south, soaking in my appearance, but not in the leering way the previous boy was. This was appreciation in its finest form. Heat explodes all over me.

"Yeah," he murmurs.

"Excuse me," I say, glaring off to the side, refusing to let him see me be bothered by him.

"You're excused," he says, removing his arms from the frame and stepping back.

Swallowing, I side-step around him. My feet feel heavy as I walk down the hall. When I reach the staircase, I glance over my shoulder to see Harley smirking at me as he disappears behind the door.

Thoughts and images bombard my mind with each step, reminding me of the last time Harley and I were alone at a party together. I mentally shake myself. I'm *not* going there tonight.

Pushing through the crowd, I pluck an empty plastic cup from the bench top and fill it from one of the bottles I brought. I drain the entire thing in one gulp, and refill it.

Belle is still hovering on the edge of the kitchen with Jess and Rianna by her hip. Annoyance flashes through me because *she* was the one who brought *me* here. Sighing, I move out of the room and into the next, feeling like I'm floating, my head is so light.

Nick is out the back, talking amongst a small group. I flock to his side. His face lights up when he sees me, and guilt tramples through my stomach. Nick introduces me to familiar and unfamiliar faces.

Some remember me, some have heard of me, some have no idea who I am. It's a rush of blurred faces and names.

When I escape to fill my drink again, a guy from one of the earlier groups joins me.

"Hey." He smiles. "Liam."

"Oh, yeah." I nod. "Hi Liam."

"You came here with Nick?" he questions, quite obviously attempting to be casual.

"Not really, no." I shake my head.

"But there's something there?"

I sigh. "There was before. Maybe again." I rake my fingers through my hair, the edges of my vision blurring.

Liam peers at me with a mixture of amusement and curiosity. "I've heard some rumours."

"About me?"

He nods. I smirk.

"Don't believe everything you hear," I say.

"Yeah?"

"Yeah." I lean in, my mouth close to his ear. "Because it's all true."

Gliding around him, I drift to the table, scanning the assortment of food. Footsteps follow me.

"You can't leave me with that," Liam says. "Now I want to know more."

I pluck a grape and play with it for a moment, meeting Liam's eyes before I take a bite out of it. He watches my mouth and grins.

"It's a boring story."

"Doesn't sound boring to me."

Liam's smile fades, and he takes a step back. I look to the side, seeing Harley appear. Shadows cast over his face, revealing a dark tilt of his lips.

"Trust me," Harley interjects, leaning forward. His teeth graze my skin as he takes the rest of the grape into his mouth. "It's not boring."

Two hours later, I exhale, watching the smoke wisp before my face, before I hand the joint to my brother. The air is thick in the room we're in.

I'm on my back, legs propped on the wall inside Cameron's bedroom. Cameron and two other friends of Sam's continue arguing their latest conspiracy theory. My brain tunes in and out as if I'm driving further from the radio tower and am on the verge of dropping out of range.

"Are you ever going to talk to Dad?"

It takes a moment to turn my head and stare at Sam, who is rolling a joint between his fingers lazily.

"He doesn't want to talk to me."

"You haven't tried very hard," he points out.

"Neither has he."

"He's a proud, stubborn man. You're going to have to make the first move."

The room glitches for a moment, but when I open my eyes, everything is as it was. I tangle my fingers into my hair and slide them through, hitting a couple of snags on my way.

"He's older. More mature."

Sam snorts. "He might be older, but certainly not more mature."

"How long are you back for?" Ethan, one of the other boys, asks, sweeping his hair back from his face and dangling over the arm of the Lazy Boy he's perched on.

"I'm not sure," I say, like I have ten other times tonight when people asked. "See what happens."

"So you, like, really didn't keep in touch with anyone? You just dropped off the face of the earth for four years and then showed back up?" Ethan's blinks are slow, and his mouth is slightly agape. I can tell he's feeling high, because he probably wouldn't have said anything if he wasn't.

"Yeah." I reach for the joint, and my brother passes it to me.

"That's pretty badass." Ethan grins. "And you got super hot too."

Sam groans dramatically, covering his ears. I smirk and tilt the joint towards Ethan in a 'thank you' gesture.

After another drag, I push off the wall and roll onto my feet. I salute the boys in the room, then make my way down the hall. The party is starting to fade now, but the music is still blaring from various speakers, the room a foggy haze.

Jess, Belle, Nick, John, and Shannon are standing around a pool table, talking and laughing with each other. They fit together, like someone designed them all to look similar.

"Hey!" Belle calls out. "Where have you been?" Their heads turn my way, and Belle frowns. "Whose jumper is that?"

"Sam's."

Their eyes linger on mine, and I can only imagine how glassy and red-ringed they are. The corners of Nick's mouth tug down. He despises smoking. He once did a nine-minute-long speech in class about the disastrous effects it has on the human body. I remember every word of it since he practised it to me about a hundred times.

"I'm beat, I'm going to head home."

"What?" Belle says. "No! Stay!"

"Nah." I wave her off. "You look like you're having plenty of fun without me."

Her frown deepens.

"I'll walk you home," Nick offers.

"I'm a big girl, Nick," I reply, pulling the sleeves of Sam's jumper over my hands. "And this is Fern Grove, the most boring town ever. I think I'm safe."

Everyone stares at me like I've personally insulted them. I'm too high to care. I see Nick reaching out for me, but I continue to walk away and out of the house. The fresh air slaps my cheeks harshly, and I gulp it in, not realising how flushed I felt until I was out of the room.

After a minute or so, footsteps crunch behind me, and I scowl.

"I said I'm fine," I snap.

"I heard you."

My foot stumbles and I right myself, turning to see Harley strolling towards me, his hands deep in his pockets. I swallow, watching a loose bit of hair fall from his beanie. I almost laugh out loud at the memory of my father seeing Harley in town all those years ago and wondering why the hell someone would be wearing a beanie in this heat. It flashes through my mind so quickly that it takes significant self-control not to let myself giggle.

"Great. My stalker."

Harley smirks. "Never been called that before."

"Maybe not to your face."

"Nah, there's only one girl I'd want to stalk."

Heat trails down my spine, and I refuse to return his stupidly hot smirk.

He falls in step with me. Our shoulders brush, and goosebumps splinter over my skin like I've had an electric shock. My heart squeezes as memories threaten to override me.

"This isn't you," he says, gesturing back to the house. "You don't fit with them. You never have."

His words sink into my brain, hitting closer to home than I liked.

"How about you stop psychoanalysing me and worry about yourself?"

"It's kind of hilarious, you know, watching all of this."

"Watching what?"

"You repeat all your mistakes." The arrogant smirk fades as he sighs. "You're fucking stubborn."

"You don't know a thing about me," I hiss, whirling around to face him. There's not much moonlight tonight, so his face is dark, cast in shadows as he stares back at me. "Stop following me. Stop trying to talk to me, and stop thinking you know me. Because you don't."

"I do fucking know you," he snaps, eyes narrowing into slits. "I know you a bit too well." He leans closer, and I can smell the memories of us washing over me. "And you hate that I do."

We're both breathing hard, glowering at the other, before I drag my eyes from his and start marching back towards my house. His hands circle around me and pull me back.

"I didn't fight for you last time and I lost you," he growls. "Four fucking years I've waited, hoping you'd come back." My heart sinks into my stomach as his words hit me like tiny razor blades, slitting my skin and opening me up. "And now that you are, I'm not letting it happen again."

"You caused this!" I scream at him, hot tears boiling over the edges of my eyes, spilling down my cheeks. "I left because of *you*! You destroyed me! You ruined *us*!" Something that burns clogs my throat, and I stagger away from him, wiping my face.

He grabs my wrists, his skin lighting mine on fire. "You think you know everything, but you don't—"

"I know enough!"

"—And you don't fucking listen!"

"I don't want to listen!" I cry out, anger spurting out of me in waves. "I don't *want* to hear you. I don't want to care. Just *leave me alone*."

"You're such a fucking brat!" he seethes, fists balling at his sides.

"And you're a Goddamn coward."

Wrenching my hands from his hold, I stomp away from him and this time, he lets me.

"Am I?" I hear him ask in a low, calm voice. So unlike the yelling match we just had. "You're the one walking away."

The tears fall harder and faster with each step, but I don't turn back.

# Chapter Twenty-Four

## Harley

Watching her walk away from me is like someone is slowly dragging out the stitches of my badly sewn heart.

"Fuck." I exhale.

Kicking the ground, I start walking. I light a cigarette and shove the packet back into my jeans. It's not until I reach the small park that I realise how far I've walked. I collapse onto a swing, leaning on the chain. It groans underneath my weight. I slowly push myself back and forth, watching the toe of my shoe drag a line in the dirt.

I pick at my thumbnail until it peels and starts bleeding. I don't stop. Guilt and anger gnaw at me. Fuck. I thought I was done thinking about her and everything that happened. Now it's all stirred back up again, and I can't seem to get my head straight.

It wasn't very solid, but I had a plan. Get the hell out of here. But she's back. Now, I have a reason to stay.

It didn't work with her last time. Why do I think it'll work this time?

*Because it would have* … a voice whispers in my mind. *You were so close to being together.*

My phone screen brightens under my touch. It's well after midnight, and still hot as fuck. Cooler, certainly, but still too hot for this time of night. When I finish my cigarette, I light another one.

My New Year's resolution was to quit. Another thing I've clearly succeeded at. A ding pulls my attention back to my phone.

**Brennon:** Where r u?

Sighing, I stare down at my phone, then look out to the darkness.

**Harley:** Coming home now.

Slowly, I start on my way back home. My feet drag, and I light a third cigarette, even though my stomach is rolling and my throat burning.

I'm at the street of my childhood home before I even realise where I was heading. A one-story, old brick building that looks like it could blow over if someone breathed too hard on it. The grass is overgrown, the fence broken, the gutters hanging loose.

Only a few days ago I called in here, after I heard rumblings at the pub that some people were going to call the police about the noise. That's not anything unusual when it comes to my father. I stopped by; most of them were passed out by the time I got there. Considering how much my father stole and took from me, when I saw cash sticking out of his wallet, I took it.

Gingerly, I touch my face where he savagely pummelled me. He probably would have cracked my nose open if Josie hadn't been there to intervene. I shouldn't have touched anything of his. I knew better. But I did anyway. And like always, I paid the price.

My number one reason for leaving is to never have to see this place again.

I scoff before spitting onto the lawn.

"Fuck you," I whisper. Clenching my jaw, I look down the street. "And fuck this town."

# Chapter Twenty-Five

## Josie

It's been nothing but clear blue skies all morning for the opening day of Farmer's Week. I've been here for a few hours, helping get all last-minute things organised. People have poured through the gate. Visitors from border towns have tripled our usual population, and I curiously watch the various groups wander through.

Mum has a stall set up selling cakes, pies, and other pastries that she made throughout the week. Sam is at his sponsor's tent, selling riding equipment and merchandise. My father is organising the parade, and that leaves me in the truck and car wash. When Dad suggested it, I think he was trying to insult me, but my mother thought it would be a good way to raise funds.

Yanking on the hose, I take a long drink, and almost spit it back out when it spurts out lukewarm.

"Ugh," I groan before wetting my hands and flicking the water droplets over my skin.

"Having fun?"

Turning, I face Nick, who is leaning on a pole, smiling at me. He's dressed in cut-off denim shorts and a singlet, with a flannel draped over the top. A weathered-looking straw hat is perched on his head, and I bite my lip to stop myself from smiling. He couldn't look more country if he tried.

My sleeveless white top tucked into my pants has basically become see-through. My shoulders have bronzed already, and I know I'm going to be red raw by the end of the day, even if I have multiple layers of sunscreen on.

"Loads." I sarcastically grin.

"Do you want some help? I have a shift now, but I can come by after?"

I shake my head. "Thanks heaps, but it's fine. I'll manage. You'll be wanted elsewhere, I'm sure."

"Okay." He nods, slipping his fingers into the pockets of his shorts.

Gosh, he is handsome. The type of handsome that doesn't know it, but it's glaringly obvious to everyone else. And so incredibly kind. And patient. I exhale, shifting my weight from one foot to the other.

"Do you want to do something tonight?" I blurt.

His eyes lift from the ground to meet mine. Those gentle green eyes. He smiles.

"Sure. What are you thinking?"

"Movies?"

"Sounds great. I'll pick you up?"

"Sure. I'll find out what's showing and text you later."

"Okay," he replies. He tips his hat. "See you then."

"See you, Nick."

My eyes remain on his back as he walks away. I want to try with Nick. I can't let myself fall into this terrible pattern again, like last time.

For the next two hours, I soap and wash truck after truck. My arms ache, and my skin burns. I throw myself onto a shady patch of grass and let my body rest for a moment. I've made a few hundred dollars just on this, which makes it all worth it, but still doesn't change the fact that I'm hungry, hot, and tired.

A deep rumble alerts me, and I lazily open one eye.

"Working hard, or hardly working?" Harley asks, peering down at me from his window.

"I'm taking a much-needed break, thank you very much."

"Looks like your break is over. My truck is filthy." He grins, showing his straight, white teeth, and I scowl at him.

"Wash it yourself, you lazy fuck."

"I hope you haven't been this hostile to other paying customers. This is for charity, right?"

Reeling into a sitting position, I glare at him. "Only to those deserving of it."

He places a hand over his heart. "Ouch."

"Don't act like you have a heart," I mutter. A groan leaves me as I get to my feet. "Okay. Pay up and piss off."

Harley chuckles, stepping out of the car. He's in all-black, with a backwards cap planted on his head. Fuck me. He looks edible.

"I was thinking of tipping you, but with this attitude, I think not."

My eyes narrow. He curls his lips into a smirk.

He digs in his pocket and withdraws a fifty-dollar note. I stare at his outstretched hand.

"That's a lot of money for a car wash."

"Can you put a price on charity?" he asks sweetly.

"Suppose not." I take the cash from him and stick it into the container beside me. I lock it and slip the key into my back pocket. "You can go for a walk. It'll be done when you get back."

"No thanks." He pulls out a camping chair from the back of his car and places it under the tree I was just lying under. He collapses onto it, leaning back, placing his hands on the back of his head. "I'm going to enjoy the view."

"You're a total prick."

He winks at me, and I turn my back to him. My skin flushes under his gaze, but I do my best to ignore him. I spray over the truck with water before I fill the bucket up with soap.

Soon enough, I get lost in my thoughts as I drag the sponge across his truck. It's been lifted so much that I struggle to reach the roof. I boost myself up on the step but still can't quite reach all the surfaces.

Hands touch my waist as Harley steps onto the truck with me. Heat flares under my skin, and I swallow, watching his muscled, tattooed arms lean over. His fingers sink between mine and extend my arm further, reaching the spot I was missing.

"I've got it," I mutter.

His fingers at my side tighten, scrunching the fabric so tight that it lifts, letting our skin connect. His breath blows past my ear, and I clench my thighs together.

"I've got it!" I snap and twist my head, facing him. Big mistake. He's close. Too close. I stare into his eyes, framed by pretty long lashes. My gaze drops to his lips.

My breathing is heavy. His hand is still on mine, his other still touching my side. His thumb slides over the skin there, and my body flushes at the feel of it. Licking my lips, I watch as he takes the movement in.

"Get off me," I whisper, not moving my eyes from his lips.

"Your mouth is saying one thing and your body another."

His hand tightens. I can't breathe. Stupid hormones.

"If you keep looking at me like this, I'm going to put you in the backseat of my car," he whispers.

"What would you do to me?" The words leave my mouth before I can stop them.

A deep groan emits from his throat. "Very bad things."

He leans in. So close our noses brush. I shove off the truck and stumble, almost falling over. He blows out a breath and steps down, clenching his jaw.

"I had it. I didn't need your help."

His jaw is ticking furiously as we stare at each other.

"Bitch."

"Asshole."

His eyes narrow before he steps back, far enough from me that I can finally breathe. He turns and stalks away.

I rest heavily on the truck, the soap soaking straight through my shirt, but I don't care. I douse myself with the hose, feeling like he's lit a match over my body.

Begrudgingly, I finish cleaning his truck and take the tin to Mum, who has been collecting all the money raised. I have something to eat and drain a bottle of water before I head back to my tent.

When I return, his truck is gone.

Exhaustion plagues my body as I wait out the front for Nick to pick me up. Today was long, but we made over six thousand dollars just today, with more to come tomorrow.

Climbing into his ute, I lean over and peck his cheek.

"Hey."

"Hi." He smiles. "Tired after today?"

"So tired," I admit. "I hope I don't fall asleep through the movie."

"Me too," he says with a laugh, pulling from the curb.

There's barely anyone at the cinema when we arrive, so there's no line to get our tickets and popcorn. As we left the timing a little fine to get here, we head straight in and take a seat. Only two other people are seated already.

"How's work been?" I ask.

"Can't complain. I've been babysitting a lot too. My sister's girls."

"That'll keep you busy."

"They sure do." He tilts the popcorn towards me, and I grab a handful. "And yourself?"

"Yeah, fine. Different to what I'm used to, but good all the same."

The adverts play, and I sit back into the seat, trying my hardest to keep my eyes open. I'm mid-yawn when Nick's hand finds mine and gently squeezes it, before linking our fingers. I stare down at it, waiting for some sort of reaction from my body. Something. *Anything.*

"Josie?"

I startle, blinking awake. The lights are on, and the credits are rolling. I mentally curse and give Nick a sheepish smile.

"It's okay," he says with a smile. "You've had a big day."

"Was it good?"

"It was all right," he replies, pulling me to my feet. We dispose of our rubbish, and Nick's hand rests on the small of my back as we walk back to the car. "I'd suggest going for a walk, but you look wrecked."

"Sorry, I'm a dull date tonight."

"I'm pretty wiped myself."

"Night, Nick. Thanks for the movies. It was good, what I saw of it." I softly laugh.

I clamber out of the car with a wave and am halfway to the door before realising I didn't even think to kiss him goodnight. I half-turn back to see him driving away. I groan and push the door open.

I stumble straight to my bed, and when my knees hit the edge, I fall into it.

The date should be on my mind, but it's the interaction with Harley at the car wash that I can't stop thinking about.

When my eyes close, I feel his hands over my body, his hot breath in my ear. Groaning, I toss and turn, glaring up at the ceiling, feeling confused and damn frustrated.

# Chapter Twenty-Six

## Josie

Hours later, darkness wraps around me as I stare up at the ceiling. I listen to the cicadas in the trees outside the window. The air is hot and thick, making me feel like I'm drawing in unnecessarily deep breaths.

I push myself onto my side and check for the third time that the pedestal fan at the foot of my bed is on as high as it can go. Groaning, I flop back down, feeling my shirt stick to me.

My phone vibrates from underneath my pillow, startling me. I blindly grope for it, not remembering the last time I even used it.

*Elliot.*

My heart jolts as I read the name flashing on my screen. My mind drifts, thinking about those dark eyes, his black hair, that devilish grin that used to make me do whatever he wanted.

*It's been three months since the incident at the carnival. Since then, Elliot had been everything a girl could hope for. Taking me out for dinners, surprising me with flowers, and even organised a weekend getaway. The incident—which is what I refer to as the time Elliot's fist ran into my face—seems less and less real. Sometimes I wonder if I imagined the entire thing.*

*Elliot strolls into the room and leans against the door frame.*

*"What are you wearing tonight?" he asks.*

*I swivel in my seat. The black suit looks almost too good on his tall, thin body. He has a way of pulling off suits in a way that actors do. So handsome that you wonder if he is famous. The old me could never have walked into a party by his side. Even with my enhancements, I still felt like it wasn't enough.*

*"There's a pink dress I bought a while ago that I haven't worn yet, so I think I'll go with that," I answer. "You look dashing, by the way."*

*"Thank you," he says in his clipped tone that always sounds like he doesn't mean it. But the arrogance that he usually possesses isn't here tonight. It has been absent for a while, and I've enjoyed it. "But no, that's not what you're wearing."*

*I place my makeup brush down with a clatter. Elliot dictating what I wear has been a topic of many arguments between us. Anger heats my cheeks.*

*"Because," he continues casually, a coy smile on his face, "I bought you something."*

*"What?"*

*I wince a little when I see the annoyance flash across his face. He hates when I say that.*

*"I mean, pardon?" I quickly amend.*

*"This is for you."*

*He steps into the closet and reappears with a garment bag. I get to my feet quickly and feel a little dizzy, the two glasses of wine having gone straight to my head.*

*"For me?" I whisper.*

*He smiles, enjoying my reaction. "For you."*

*He holds it steady as I unzip it. A stunning red gown is inside. A bright, fiery red. A red meant for someone special. This dress is too much.*

*Too gorgeous. I am not worthy.*

"Oh, Elliot," *I gush.* "This is ... I have no words to describe how incredible this is."

"Try it on." *He smirks.*

*The dress fits me like a glove. A red, silky glove. The neckline is poised so low that my boobs poke out a little too aggressively. Inside the garment bag was also a string of pearls that screams money. More money than my entire family would have combined.*

*When we walk through the front door of the event, I feel ecstatic at the turn of heads and dropped jaws. I've always wanted this. This moment.*

"Smile," *Elliot says through gritted teeth, his arm a little firm on mine.* "And suck in your stomach."

*My insides tighten. My smile widens, and I try to ignore his words, not wanting him to ruin this moment. This is the first time in my life I have finally been happy with my weight and appearance, and yet, Elliot undid it all with a few words.*

*Cameras flash in my face, making me go blind for a few moments.*

*Elliot kisses my cheek, and I pull away for a moment, not realising that I even had, until his fingers bite into my arm, holding me in place, and I blink into the faces and cameras, hoping my distress doesn't show. It has been so good these last couple months, and now all the things I dislike about Elliot are creeping back.*

"Don't pull away like that again."

*Again, he says it through his teeth, his smile never wavering. I wonder if he has practised doing that. Or maybe he has done it so much in his life that it comes naturally to him.*

*I long for the moment I can escape him, and after thirty minutes, it came. I stay in the bathroom far too long, leaning against the wall of the cubicle, reminding myself that this is what I wanted. I like the dresses, the jewellery, the rooftop parties, the cocktails. I like this life.*

Then why do you need to convince yourself? *A voice in my mind taunts me.*

*I step towards the sink and stare at myself. I am unrecognisable. Striking dress, brown skin, highlights in my hair and body parts that aren't naturally mine. I look like the girl I've strived to be for so long. Why doesn't it feel right?*

*Pushing out the door, I stumble over my gigantic shoes, my shoulder barging with someone else's.*

*"Oh, sorry!" A deep voice exclaims in alarm, steadying me. "Are you all right?"*

*"Yes," I answer breathlessly, my eyes settling on light brown eyes and a kind smile. "Fine. Sorry."*

*"It's me who needs to apologise, I wasn't looking."*

*"I basically catapulted out of there." I offer a nervous laugh.*

*"Well. We can both be sorry, then." He smiles. "Gordon."*

*"Josie."*

*"Nice to meet you, Josie. Can I offer you a drink?"*

*"I'd certainly love a drink," I admit. "But I'm here with someone."*

*"Does he not like you to drink?"*

*"Not with men who aren't him."*

*Gordon's lips stretch. "Ah. Yes. You make a good point."*

*"Have a good night."*

*"Josie?" His hand touches my arm. So gentle, so different to Elliot's possessive grip. "Are you sure you don't want a drink?"*

*"It's not the drink I'm not sure about," I try to joke, but the words come out too heavy and flat.*

*"Josie!" a voice slices through the air, startling me so violently I jump, feeling like I've been caught doing something I'm not supposed to be. "I've been looking for you for the past ten minutes." Elliot thunders down the small hallway, his long legs striding beneath him. His eyes land on Gordon's hand on my arm and our proximity, his nostrils flaring.*

*"See you around," Gordon blurts, letting me go and scuttling down the hallway. I want to yell out to him, tell him to stay. Because suddenly I fear what is about to happen. I can feel it bristling in the air around us.*

"*Who the fuck was that?*" Elliot gripes, his long fingers twisting around my wrist. "*This is where you've been? Hiding in the hallway with another guy?*"

"*We ran into each other when I was leaving the bathroom—*" I try to explain, but I knew there was no point. It was there. The anger. Simmering in his eyes, itching to be released. The same anger I saw three months ago.

*Those fingers that were at my wrist suddenly grip my neck. He squeezes so hard a winded, pathetic sound leaks from my mouth. I suck in a sharp inhale, trying to get as much air into my throat as I can, but he doesn't allow it.*

"*After everything I give you,*" he snarls, his voice low, the threat in his voice more suffocating than his hold on me. "*You treat me like this. Ungrateful little bitch.*" *I feel the coldness of the pearls tightening around me.* "*If you ever disrespect me like this again, you won't see another day.*"

I've sat in silence, wrapped in my own memories, for a long moment. I'm slingshot back to reality, when my phone rings again, brightening in my hand.

My eyes watch the word *Elliot* until the screen fades out once more. A message pings, telling me a voicemail was left. I haven't been checking them.

Slowly, I slide my finger across the screen.

"Josie." His voice sends a mass of goosebumps scattering across my skin. The hair on the back of my neck stands and I squeeze my eyes shut. "I've played nice for long enough now." I think back to the few messages I did listen to. It's all words I've heard before. He loves me. He misses me. He's just *so* sorry. He will never do it again. He really, really means it this time. "Come back. *Now*. I am not one to be humiliated. I am not to be *left*. This is your last chance to come back willingly on your own. You won't like the alternative."

When silence meets my ears, my throat is bone dry. I shouldn't have listened to it. I know how he is, why did I expose myself to it?

There's a rustle outside my window and everything inside me stills. I barely breathe as I hear footsteps. I scramble to my feet, turning on all the lights. I rush to the door, to check if it's locked, when I see the dark hair of Harley. His electric eyes peer at me through the glass, his lips wet, a near-empty bottle of whisky in his hand.

"Josie," he mumbles, pressing heavily into the door. "Did I scare you?"

"Yes," I hiss, unlocking the door and swinging it open, my heart jack-knifing painfully in my chest. Considering he was leaning on it, he topples over in a mess of long legs and dark clothing. He rolls onto his back, grinning.

"Hey."

"Harley, what the fuck?" I demand. "What are you doing here? And drunk, might I add?"

He holds up his thumb and pointer finger, holding them together so that they were only millimetres apart. "Just a wee bit tipsy."

I scoff. "Yeah, right. Get up."

Using the wall, he eventually gets to his feet. His eyes land on my bare legs, and I realise then that I'm only in a white t-shirt, which is clinging to me because of sweat.

He gulps. "You look fucking fantastic."

A flush burns through me, and I fold my arms over my breasts. Words like that from a boy like him would have consumed me with delight once upon a time.

*Yeah ...* a snide voice in my mind jabs at me. *Once upon a time.*

"What do you want?"

He reaches for my arm and steers me to the lounge. He lightly pushes me so that I collapse onto it. He moves my coffee table out of the way and drops to his knees.

"Why do you look like you're about to propose?" I deadpan.

"Josie," he says, one hand held dramatically in the air, his other over his chest. "I may have had to get roaring drunk to do this, but

I truly mean it."

"Thought you were a 'wee bit tipsy'?"

"Shh." He holds a finger over his lips. "Let me speak."

I press my lips together and lean back into the lounge.

"Josie Mayor." He hiccups my name and blinks a few times. "You were the best thing to happen to me, and I fucked it up." My breath catches in my throat as his eyes bore into mine. "You didn't deserve what happened to you. That part of the night is a blur … I don't remember … It doesn't matter now. It's all pathetic excuses. I just want you to not hate me."

I blink at him in silence.

"That's it," he says. "That's what I wanted to say."

"Well," I say, still not sure how to react. "Thank you. I appreciate that."

He moves closer to me, still on his knees, and places his hands on my bare thighs. My heart surges in my chest, and I clamp my knees together.

"Do you forgive me?" he asks. His eyes are desperate. His hands are warm. The stench of whisky fills the space between us.

"No," I whisper, casting my eyes down.

"Is there a chance you might not hate me forever?" he asks.

"I don't know."

He nods. His thumb caresses the side of my leg, and I watch it. I tell myself to push him off.

But I don't.

He captures my hand and looks at the half-moon on my wrist. He drags his finger over it. Slowly, he pulls it to his mouth and kisses it. My lips part as we stare at each other. I can feel my shirt dampening as my skin flushes with a fierce heat.

He wedges my knees apart, drawing closer. Warmth from his body sears through his shirt. I place my hands on his hard chest, feeling his breath over my lips.

"What can I do to make you forgive me?" he asks.

"Nothing," I murmur.

"Nothing?" he asks, moving his hand to the side of my face. I lean into it, and his thumb moves against my bottom lip. "At all?"

"I hate you," my voice is a whisper.

"How much?" he breathes. My eyes are no longer on his, but on the lip ring.

"A lot."

"Show me," he says. "Push me away." He leans in closer. "Tell me how much you hate me." His dark hair falls across his forehead. "Scream it so that everyone else knows it too."

In between my legs throbs, and I swallow, tilting my head back. His lips move to my throat, delicately pressing soft kisses onto the skin there. A moan escapes me, and he pushes against me. I feel his hardness and sigh softly, letting my hands sink down his stomach.

"I can't hear you," he mumbles on my skin.

"I hate you."

"Do you?"

"I fucking hate you." I want to yell it out, scream it—like he said to—but it comes out as a breathless groan.

His lips move across my jaw before they possessively take my lips. The kiss is furious and deep. I wrap my arms around his neck, tasting the whisky on his tongue. He throws me back into the lounge, his body pressing on top of mine. I hook my leg around his waist, and he presses his erection into me. Desire pulses through me with every movement he makes.

His hand palms my groin, and I break for air, inhaling sharply. I feel myself yearning for more.

His fingers push the fabric of my underwear to the side and slide inside me. I arch my back, needing to be closer to him. My pulse races as he bites down onto my shoulder. I let out a cry of shock, mixed with pleasure. He sucks on the skin between my throat and my collarbone. I feel a hot sensation roll in my stomach. A feeling I haven't felt for what feels like years.

His fingers glide over the apex between my thighs, and I let out a half-moan, half-yelp at the sensation rippling through me. His hips grind against my side, and my fingers scrunch his shirt. I throw my head back and let out a sound I don't recognise. A wicked look flares in his eyes, spurring me on.

His fingers slide in and out of me, and he presses his thumb harder into my clit, moving it in precise circles that have me writhing beneath his grip. Sweat beads on my forehead as he applies more pressure. His hardness stabs into my thigh, making hot liquid pool in my lower belly. I buck my hips shamelessly, urging his fingers to press harder.

My toes curl as I whimper, trying to fight the orgasm that's threatening to slice through my body. I don't want *him* to make me feel like this. I don't want to give him the satisfaction.

"Come for me, sweetheart," he whispers, his deep, drawling voice shoving me over the edge. "I know you want to."

I choke out a moan as the orgasm rips through me. I throw my head back into the armchair, dots dancing over my vision.

Harley dives towards me, and my legs clench when I feel his tongue snake over the most sensitive part of me.

"Oh. My. God," I pant. "Harley."

His tongue laps over me, savouring my taste, making me wriggle and squirm. His hands slam onto my thighs, holding me still. My heart pounds in my ears, and I glance down to see those eyes staring adoringly up at me as he devours me with his mouth. I choke out a moan. He is so fucking sexy.

He presses harder into me, eating me like he's starved, and I'm the first meal he's had in a year. I've hardly had a moment to keep up with his tongue when his fingers slide back in.

"Oh!" I cry.

I grip his hair as his tongue slides over my clit. His fingers slam into me, and I close my eyes, feeling the wave of another orgasm rising. His mouth moves off me as heat bursts through me. I whimper when suddenly his thumb is pressed back there in just the right place to send me over the edge.

A moan mixed with a cry escapes me, and my vision fuzzes out of focus. I slump back into the lounge, breathless. My breath is coming out in short and fast pants. After a moment, I blink back to reality, my surroundings slowly reappearing.

I look up through my lashes to see his lips and chin glistening under the dim light.

Harley leans back, removing himself, before sucking on his fingers, his lips swollen and red. It has the same effect, all these years later. I slowly feel the heat inside me ebb away, and I relax, my legs quivering.

He exhales, a satisfied expression on his face. I can hardly believe the genuine smile on his lips.

"I missed the taste of you."

I comb my hair back from my face, feeling hot and flustered. I wipe at the sweat with my shirt, and when I push my shirt back down, Harley is looking at me with a hungry, dangerous smile.

"Do that again."

I roll my eyes. "It's late, and you're drunk."

"Not that drunk."

"Drunk enough."

My body is unsteady as I go to walk by him, but he pulls me closer, wrapping his arms around my waist. He peers up at me.

"I'm sorry I showed up in the middle of the night."

"It's okay."

"Is it?" he asks.

"No," I say, but don't mean it.

"You still hate me?"

"Yes."

"I don't believe you."

For a moment, I forget that I do hate him. My fingers betray me. They push through his dark hair. His face looks perfect in my hands. Brilliant blue eyes. Tanned, unblemished skin.

His eyes close. I let the other run down the side of his face, much like he did to me before.

"Go to sleep," I say.

"Here?"

"Maybe."

"Maybe?"

"Yes."

I step back and search my cupboard for a spare pillow. I offer it to him, and he silently takes it. He throws his shoes onto the floor. I flick the lights off and pad over to my bed. I desperately feel like a shower but don't trust myself around Harley, naked, in such a cosy space. I tell myself to go to sleep and not think, but it doesn't work. I hear his soft breathing not far from me and it's killing me.

He should leave.

But God, I want him to stay.

Just as I'm drifting into sleep, I feel the side of the bed dip, and I say nothing when he crawls in beside me. I press my lips tightly together as I feel him nestle in behind me, his hand finding my waist.

"Night, Josie," he whispers.

"Goodnight, Harley."

# Chapter Twenty-Seven

## Josie

**W**here Harley's arm drapes over my stomach is sticky with sweat, but I don't want to move just yet. His soft breathing fills the room. I stare at his smooth skin and dark hair, such a beautiful contrast over the white sheets.

I trace my fingertip over the tattoos inked over his skin, and when he stirs, I pull my hand back immediately.

He peers around for a moment, taking in his surroundings. When his eyes, so painfully blue and bright in the morning light, fix on me, I hold my breath. A lazy smile stretches across his face.

"It wasn't a dream," he whispers.

"It wasn't a dream."

He rolls onto his back, the sheet slipping low. I stare at this stomach, the tight muscles, the smooth skin. He brings his hand to his hair, and it sinks into it.

"I need to shower."

"Me too," he replies casually.

I roll my lips into my mouth. "Are you going to be here when I get out?"

"Do you want me to be?"

"No," I lie.

"I guess not, then."

We both say nothing for a moment. His hand inches closer to me and our fingers graze.

The vibration of my phone startles us both and I'm filled with dread, thinking it might be Elliot. In the chaos that is Harley, I forgot for a little while. About him, his words, the threat.

*Nick.*

Harley and I stare at the screen. It feels just as it did four years ago. Me, between the two of them. It rings out and a few seconds later, I get a message alerting me he left me a voicemail.

"Hey, Josie. I hope you're awake. I'm on my way over. I was hoping to take you out for breakfast. See you soon."

"He's coming," I say, yanking my hand away from Harley. "Now."

Harley watches me, a little warily. "So, I guess that's you kicking me out?"

"I didn't realise you intended to stay."

Harley's jaws clenches. A muscle spasms in his cheek before he throws the sheets off his legs and stands. He stomps into his shoes and fumbles through the small space, trying to find his shirt. I silently watch, unable to peel my eyes from him.

"Well. I'm going," he says.

"Okay."

"That's it?" He barks, making the sound mixed between a scoff and a laugh. He throws his hands up.

I half-shrug. "Yeah."

"You're going out with Nick?" he demands. "For breakfast?"

"Yes."

"Great." He yanks his shirt over his head, sending me a withering look, before the door slams shut behind him.

I fling myself back onto my bed and sigh. My fingers trace over my lips. I can still feel the heat of him. His scent is all over me. *Shit.* I fly around the room, tidying things into place, before I launch into the shower. I'm still in my towel when Nick arrives.

"Oh, hi, sorry!" he blushes and looks to the floor, turning his back to me. I almost glare at him. I want him to look at me. I want him to have trouble tearing his eyes away. I want him to struggle to keep his hands off me.

"Won't be a second."

I throw on a floral dress and pull my hair into a high pony. Nick is dressed in pale shorts and a casual white polo shirt, looking like he might be about to attend a lunch at the country club. I think of Harley's black shirt and dark jeans, my eyes scanning the room once more as if he might have left something else here. I notice the empty bottle of whisky by the lounge and quickly kick it underneath on my way past.

Nick hovers near the door and for some reason, the space suddenly feels too small and I need to get out.

"Hi," he says again when I appear by his side. He curls an arm around me and gently kisses my cheek. Soft, fragile, friendly. Just like always. "How are you?"

"I'm good. Yourself?"

"Really great."

"Why really great?"

He shrugs. "I'm always really great."

"Where are you taking me?" I grab my bag and keys, before locking the front door behind me. "Oh wait. There's only one place." The bitterness drips from my voice before I can help myself. I don't miss the sideway frown I receive from Nick. I suck in a quick breath of air, trying to get my overthinking mind to relax.

"What did you get up to last night?" he asks.

I keep my face neutral. "Not much."

"How's work?"

"It's good. Steady. A little dull compared to what I'm used to." Like everything.

"I'm sure you will get used to it." He smiles.

"And you? How's work for you?"

"Can't complain."

When I sit in the passenger seat, I pick at my fingernails. I feel bored already and we technically haven't left my house. My mind drifts, wondering what Harley is up to. Is he working today? What does he do when he isn't working?

"Are you going to get that?"

"Hmm?" I ask and see Nick's eyes are looking at my lit-up phone screen. I'm so used to the vibrations now that it hardly registers. "Oh. No, I'm not." I lock the phone and gaze back out the window.

"Is someone bothering you?"

"No." I shake my head. "Well. Yeah. Sort of. But it's fine."

"Is it Harley?" Nick's voice has an edge to it and his fingers tighten on the steering wheel.

"What? No." I give him an odd look. "It's Elliot." The name feels strange on my tongue, like it doesn't belong there. "The guy I was seeing before I came back."

Technically, I never ended it. When he was out late at a work dinner, I packed my bags and left. *Like I always do.*

"That was him?" Nick asks, eyebrows flying up. "Just now?"

"Yeah. He calls a lot."

"Do you answer?"

I shake my head. "No. We haven't spoken since I left."

"Are you okay?" he asks in concern. "Are you safe?"

"Yeah. He doesn't know where I am."

Nick looks a little bewildered at my dismissiveness. "Is he threatening you?"

"A little."

"A little?" he echoes loudly, cutting the engine.

"Nick, it's fine." I open the door and step out, the heat blasting over my face.

"But—"

"I really don't want to talk about it."

When we walk inside, it's hot and busy, and almost every table is taken. There's one down the back, fortunately close to the small breeze coming through the window. I order a coffee on my way past the counter, needing the caffeine hit to revive me from my broken sleep last night.

We've barely sat for a minute when Harley wanders in, wearing the same outfit he was wearing when he left my place this morning. I swallow, my throat going dry.

He orders a coffee and leans on the counter, his eyes sweeping over the tables. When they land on Nick and me—thankfully Nick's back is to him—they narrow. He gives me a sarcastic wave and if Nick wasn't chatting away to me, I'd give him the finger in return.

Sensing my attention elsewhere, Nick looks over his shoulder. He grimaces.

"Suddenly that guy is everywhere," he mutters.

I drum my fingers on the table, wishing the service wasn't so slow here. I need something to occupy my hands.

Harley receives his coffee before I get mine. Our eyes are locked as he lifts it to his mouth. Heat rises inside me. I can't get enough of those eyes.

It took me four years to erase him. And now everything is rushing back.

He takes a long sip before he's back out the door. I watch as he slides into his truck and speeds off, disappearing out of view in a rain of dust.

"Have you spoken to him?"

I startle, having completely lost track of what Nick was talking about. His eyes are studying me, and it hits me that he would have realised who I was staring at.

"Harley?" I ask. "A little."

Nick's chair creaks as he leans back. "A little."

"Bit hard not to when he works at the only decent place to drink and eat dinner," I say.

"Right."

Joanne serves us our coffee and I'm grateful for the interruption. I stare down at the darkness, curling my fingers around the mug.

I think about last night. How it felt seeing those eyes peering at me through the window. How good his body felt. His piercing inside my mouth. His hands are strong and firm.

Everything about him feels insanely good, but hopelessly bad. I hadn't wanted him to stop.

My eyes flick to my hands. I picture his tanned skin on mine. His big hands covering my small ones.

Nick is talking again, his smile having returned. I don't know what about. I blink back to reality and try to focus. All I wanted was this. Nick taking me out, giving me his attention. Exactly like four years ago, over the course of a few days, I seem to care so much less about the boy in front of me. I don't understand how this can be happening again. Haven't I learned from my mistakes?

"I have a headache," I blurt.

Nick stops mid-sentence. "Oh. Are you all right?"

"Yeah. Fine. But I might head home after this."

Nick blinks before nodding. "Sure. That's fine."

I've lost my appetite and manage only a few mouthfuls, before I spend the rest of breakfast pushing food around my plate. Nick realises my mood drop and we finish breakfast quickly. He doesn't reach out to me when he drops me off, like he usually would.

"I'll call you later," he says.

"Thanks for breakfast. Talk soon."

"Feel better," he says as I shut the door.

I walk inside and fall into bed.

I wish I could erase last night, but I also wish it would happen again.

# Chapter Twenty-Eight

## Harley

My fist slams into the steering wheel and the horn blares, piercing the stale air.

"Fuck!" I exclaim, punching my fist into it another time. The skin over my knuckle splits and pain skitters up my hand. Growling and hissing simultaneously, I flex my hand and stare down at the blood. My knuckles had only just started to heal from their last assault.

I spill my heart to her, and she ditches me. Again. For fucking Nick. How is this happening again? Hasn't she learned *anything*? It's me and her. It has *always* been me and her.

Nick's warm smile flashes in my mind and I feel sick to my stomach. I hate what I did to him all those years ago, and now it's happening all over again.

Throwing my head back into the headrest, I think back to last night. Her slender body underneath me. Her smooth skin sliding against mine. So tight, so warm. Blood rushes to my groin and I groan.

Stomping on the accelerator, I race home. I stumble into the shower and only turn the cold nozzle on. I strip down and step inside. My palms press against the tiles and I glare down at the ground.

Those lips. Those curves. Those fingers running down my body.

I'm so hard it hurts. I grip myself and groan out in anger and frustration, sliding my hand over myself, imagining it's her. Heat pools in my stomach and I buck my hips forward, gritting my molars so hard it's possible one of them cracked.

There's so much built up and with my memories of last night, it's only moments later that I spill into my hand almost painfully and sag into sitting position. Water laps over my legs and I bury my head into my hands, my elbows digging into my thighs.

Since Josie has been back, I finally feel alive again. Like there's a purpose for me. *She* is my purpose. But God, she is fucking stubborn. My shoulders sag and my eyes sting. I fear I'm moments away from crying—something I haven't done in a *long* time—and push to my feet, shaking the water from my face.

Re-dressing, I throw on my joggers and go for a run. I sprint hard and fast, until my lungs swell and my chest heaves. In this heat, it doesn't take long for my clothes to be drenched in sweat. My vision blurs and I stagger to the side. Falling to my knees, I roll onto my back and stare up at the sky.

Why does everything fucking suck?

# Chapter Twenty-Nine

## Josie

When I started walking, I was meaning to do a lap of the main block and head back home, but I walk the familiar path to my parents' house. The screen door is propped open by a gumboot which has a crack down the side.

With one foot stepped inside, I knock, peering down the hallway, the heat of inside almost knocking me over backward.

"Hello?" I hear Mum call.

"It's me."

When I enter the lounge room, Mum is on her tiptoes dusting the shelves, Dad's on his knees digging something out of the fireplace, and Sam is lazily sprawled on the lounge, a book in his hand.

"Hi, hon." Mum smiles. "How are you?"

"I'm good, you?"

"Oh, you know. Busy, busy," she replies distractedly.

Dad stands, not meeting my eyes and excuses himself. It stings watching him retreat, not even glancing my way. There's an awkward silence which follows, before I walk over to the lounge and smack Sam's leg. He groans, lifting his foot so that I can sit. I lean over and tug out one of his ear buds.

"Hey!" he protests.

"Good book?" I ask.

"Pretty good," he answers, shaking his head so that his hair falls out of his eyes. "What are you up to? You must be bored."

"Can't I come visit my family without a motive?"

Mum looks over her shoulder, meeting Sam's eyes, and they both shrug.

"Gee, thanks." I turn to Sam. "What are you doing tonight? Let's hang out."

"So you *are* bored."

"I want to spend time with you."

He rolls his eyes, looking much like he did as a teenager. "Okay. Maybe we can grab dinner and play some pool later?"

"Sure. That sounds good."

"I'll swing by at 5:30?"

I hook two thumbs up. Mum hums to herself as she goes about tidying and Sam's earbuds are jammed back into his ears. I lean my head back and stare up at the ceiling.

It doesn't feel normal to be here with them.

Everything here is so *dull.*

It's a quarter to six before Sam strolls into my place, not announcing his arrival. I startle, almost spilling wine on myself and the lounge.

"Took your time," I say sarcastically.

"I was busy."

"Doing what? Wearing in the lounge a little more?"

"Something like that."

I've become so bored that I've enrolled in an online course to develop more skills as an OHT, not that I can probably practise what I learn much out here. I'm able to do most online, but I'll need to drive back to Brisbane for a three-day practical assessment. I feel a little less like I'm stuck in a standstill after enrolling, which has given me some peace of mind.

Sam is dressed in overworn, unintentionally ripped jeans and a faded shirt that looks two sizes too big for him. His hair is scruffy and unkempt, looking like he hasn't bothered to wash it in the last week, or maybe two.

I go to make a joke about it but close my mouth, not wanting to offend him. We pile into his car. I kick away the food wrappers littering the floor. The engine rumbles to life and his stereo is deafening. He quickly turns it down, giving me a sheepish look.

There are a few more people milling around the pub tonight. It's uncomfortably hot, so when we order drinks, I ask for a glass of ice.

My eyes roam around the space, searching for Harley automatically.

"What's new with you?" I ask as we take a seat. I glance around one more time, but it appears Harley either isn't working or he's out the back.

"Working. Riding. Sleeping." He smiles. "That's all I do."

"I never knew how good you were at bull riding," I say. "I was so impressed at the rodeo."

Sam's face brightens at this. "Thanks. It was one of my better rides."

I dip my fingers into the glass and grab a cube of ice. I dab it over my flushed skin. Sam observes me with an amused smile.

"Look at you, such a city girl now. Fern Grove doesn't know what to do with you."

"And me it," I sigh. "I'm lost, Sammy. I don't know what I'm doing."

"You don't seem lost to me."

"How so?"

"Got your own place, secured a great job, seeing someone. Hell, you've been back five minutes and you're doing better than me."

"Everything just feels so slow and boring out here. It's maddening."

"Once you take a breath and slow down, you'll realise there's more to this place than you think."

"I'll believe that when I see it." I take a long mouthful, draining half my cup. "No one interests you?"

Sam offers a half-shrug, not meeting my eyes. "Few here and there."

"I'm sure the right person will come along soon enough."

The glass that Sam has been spinning in his hand stops and he looks at me, a little startled. I take another sip and lean back in my chair, both of us waiting to see if the other is going to say anything more. We don't.

"Do you have any other rides coming up?"

He nods, leaning forward and clasping his fingers together. "Yeah, in two weeks, in Ewingsdale."

"Cool. That sounds fun."

A loud creak gains both of our attention. When we look to the door, Harley wanders in, carrying a carton of beer. He walks behind the bar and opens the fridge door, before he starts piling the stubbies onto the shelves.

"Have you …" Sam trails off, inclining his head. "Spoke to him?"

*My skin heats under his fingertips as they trail down my skin. His fingers touching and teasing me in all the right places.*

"Uh, yeah, a little," I answer.

"How is it?"

I fiddle with the coaster. This is quite possibly the *last* conversation I want to be having with my brother.

"I hate him."

"Well. That's understandable."

We both take a sip, holding our drinks the exact same—our pinky fingers lifted off from the cup. We grin at each other. If someone told me that me and my brother were alike, I'd laugh. But then we have moments like this where our mannerisms are the exact same and I think I may believe them.

"Why did you do it?" he asks.

I stiffen, my train of thought having swept away for a moment. "Do what?"

"Cheat on Nick." I swallow, my throat drying out. "You say you love him, but you weren't happy. I could see it then and I can see it now." He tilts his head, eyes scrutinising me. "So, why did you do it?"

Maybe I wasn't as transparent as I thought. I keep an aloof expression on my face as I shift in my seat.

"A bad decision on my behalf. That's all."

"Bullshit."

I quirk an eyebrow. "There isn't any more to it."

"I don't believe that."

"Why?"

"Because Harley has been eye fucking you the moment he realised you were here," Sam jabs a finger at me. "And you've been doing it right back."

I blink for a moment. Have I?

My eyes travel back to the bar. Harley's deep eyes are like two pools of water staring back at me. Just one look from him sends heat flaring over me.

"Have not."

"Have so." He grins. "Admit it. Nick doesn't rev your engine like Harley does."

"Oh my *God!*" I half-exclaim, half-guffaw. "*Sam!*"

I sink into my seat, feeling like my face is about to light on fire. I really hope Harley didn't hear that.

While Sam laughs, I excuse myself to the bathroom and slip in there to collect myself. I don't like how right he is. When I step back out, Harley is in the hall.

"Hey," he says.

My body does that thing where it feels like I've gone too fast down a hill and left my stomach behind.

"Hey."

The hallway is dark and I'm finding it hard to breathe.

"How are you?" he asks.

"Hot. I need ice." I blurt.

"Uh, okay," he says slowly, pushing off the wall. "I'll get you some."

I follow him into the kitchen. The chef is singing to himself and has no idea he's no longer alone. Harley grabs a cup of ice from the freezer and ushers us back into the dim hallway. When he passes it to me, our fingers brush, sending a jolt of electricity through me.

His eyes fix on the ice as I run it up my arm. I press it into my neck and push it low over my chest, before settling it between my breasts. Harley's lips part as he watches. Feeling suddenly bold, I pluck it into my fingers and press it into my mouth, before I lean towards him. His lips open and I push the ice cube inside his mouth with my tongue.

Our eyes are locked on each other as he sucks on the cube, before crunching it between his teeth.

"I feel better now," I tell him. "Thanks."

I turn from him, but he grips my wrist, stopping me.

"Josie."

"Hmm?"

"I'm going out with Jess tonight."

My back straightens as I face him, suddenly losing the flirty smile from my face.

"I did it because of this morning," he mutters, eyes on the ground. "Seeing you with Nick pissed me off."

"Do you want to go out with her?"

Harley exhales. "No."

"Then you shouldn't."

"Do you want to go out with Nick?" he questions.

It's my turn to lean against the wall. I think for a moment.

"I did."

"You did?"

I shrug. "Things have changed."

"Or they're the same as before," Harley says. "Nick isn't what you want."

"What do I want?"

"Me."

Suddenly he's right in front of me. I inhale his scent and feel the heat seeping into me through his shirt. He plants his palms against the wall, his arms caging me.

"It's always been me."

His eyes drop to my lips and I'm so heated, I could drip into a pool on the floor.

"But you don't want me," I whisper. "You don't care for me."

"Why do you keep saying that?" He growls, anger in his voice.

"You wouldn't have done what you did." I close my eyes. "You destroyed me, Harley. And I can't forgive you." I slip out from under his arms, forcing myself to create distance between us. I can't do this again. It's too little, too late. "Go out with Jess. She will be good for you."

"What's good for me is you."

I shake my head. "You don't know that."

"Neither do you," he says.

I'm flustered by the time I get back to the table, wondering how long I was gone for. Sam's face is a little pale as he stares at me.

"What?" I ask, wondering if he somehow saw what happened in the hallway, until I see my phone in his hand.

"Your phone rang." I go rigid in my seat, my breath ceasing. "I answered."

I'm frozen under his gaze.

Sam looks stricken as he nods. "What the *fuck* have you got yourself into?"

Sweat dots at my forehead and my upper lip. I glance around the pub, feeling like the walls are closing in.

Elliot called me. Sam answered.

Last night Elliot screamed in my face. He was drunk. He caught me talking to one of his co-workers when I stopped by to have lunch with him. Apparently answering a question is considered a betrayal.

His face reddened. He was so close, spit was flying from his mouth and hitting my face.

He grabs the glass of wine from my hand and hurls it at the wall. The glass shatters, raining onto the carpet. A blood-red stain covered the wall, dripping down it.

"Listen to yourself!" I yelled back. "Can you hear the words coming out of your mouth? You sound like an insecure jerk! And a childish one at that!"

He moves so fast it was like lightning. He cracks his hand against my face, my nose and eye soldiering most of the damage. I fling backwards, smashing into the glass coffee table behind me. Bits of glass stab into me as I blink up at the ceiling, my mind trying to catch up with everything that just happened.

Elliot's fingers sink into my neck and he pulls me to my feet. My knees knock together and he presses harder, keeping me upright.

"You ever speak to me like that again, I will kill you." His eyes look black in the reflection from the window. He glares at me, those eyes I'd stared into many times before, now glowing with fury.

Abruptly, his hand moves from my throat and I collapse onto the floor. My chest heaves and hot tears spill down my face. My face throbs from the hit and my skin stinging from the glass. I fumble, trying to dig out the glass but my hands shake violently.

The lock of our bedroom door clicks shut. I sit still for a few moments, gathering myself. I wash myself off as much as I can in the guest bathroom, before collapsing into the lounge, shivering and crying.

The next morning, a croissant and coffee greets me. Elliot's gaze rests on my face. It's so sore I can barely move my lips.

"Here," he says. "How did you sleep?"

My head pounds as I sit up. I want to yell. I want to cry. How does he think I fucking slept?

My eyes are crusted from crying. Everything hurt.

"I told your work you're not coming in. I've got Marie coming over to spend the day with you, she knows you had a fall." He adjusts his tie and runs his hands over his suit jacket, smoothing it. "I have that work dinner tonight, but I'll be home before it to check on you. And then we can spend the weekend together. I'll take you somewhere nice." He leans forward and kisses the side of my head. I'm frozen, last night's events spinning through my mind.

A fall.

He closes the door behind him but his scent lingers everywhere as if he is still here, hiding in the shadows. I wince as I stand. I shower and pull out the first-aid kit. As I dab over my cuts and bruises, I tell myself this was the last time. I need to get out.

Knowing I only had limited time, I slowly started to pack some of my things. Things that wouldn't be noticed missing. I stuff the bag right into the back of the closet when I hear Marie let herself into the apartment.

Marie is Elliot's cleaner, who also likes to spy on me and report back to him, not that I'm here often when she is.

She shrieks when she sees my face and pulls me into the kitchen to nurse me, although I had just done that myself. I put on a brave face. Laugh about my clumsiness. She even helped me pick out and order a new coffee table.

I lay on the lounge and read most of the day, taking it easy. We eat lunch together and watch an episode of a housewife show she is obsessed with.

When she starts vacuuming in the bedroom, I search for my car keys. Angry tears well in my eyes. The bastard has taken them. I have a spare in my work handbag, buried in a zipper compartment full of lipsticks. I'm hoping he never found it. I'll search later, when it's safe.

Elliot returns from work a little early, to get ready for his dinner. He's back to acting like the doting boyfriend. It's unnerving how caring he seemed. How last night isn't a blimp on his radar.

"Should I stay home?" he asks, gathering my hands in his.

I shake my head. "This is important for your work. You should go. I'm happy here with my book." I gesture to it. "I'm getting up to the plot twist." I force a smile. "And besides, Marie has got me hooked on one of her shows. We're going to try and finish the season tonight."

"You're sure?" he asks, searching my eyes so intently, I almost look away.

"Definitely."

He's organised for Marie to baby sit me while he's at dinner. He doesn't trust me not to run. So he shouldn't.

He kisses me tenderly before leaving. Marie gushes about how sweet he is. How I'm so lucky. I almost emptied my stomach on the carpet.

I stage it precisely. We share some wine. I trip over my feet, throwing it all over her. She rushes to the bathroom to scrub it off.

I throw anything into my bag that is important. I dig out my spare key. I am out the door and running within thirty seconds.

And I don't look back.

"It's complicated," I tell Sam, trying not to let my mind be consumed by all the things that pushed me back here. *Him.*

"It's psychotic! He sounded like he was going to kill me! He doesn't even know who I am!"

"It's a good thing he doesn't, nor does he know where I live. It's better for everyone that he doesn't. You didn't tell him, right?"

Sam pales. "I said you were home."

I swallow. "I never told him where I grew up. I hope he doesn't somehow find out."

Sam leans forward, eyes wide. "He was the one who hurt you?"

Biting my lip, I nod. "Yes."

"Badly?"

"Pretty bad."

Sam exhales. "Shit, Josie."

"He keeps calling, texting, leaving threatening voicemails. He's obsessive."

"How did you end it?"

"I ran away," I whisper. "I left in the night when he wasn't home."

Sam's mouth is in an 'O'. "This sounds like a movie."

"I wish it was a movie." I feel myself crack, tears brimming my eyes. "What do I do, Sam? What if he finds me?"

Sam covers my hands with his big, calloused ones. They're tan and slightly wrinkled, from being out in the sun too often. Warm and big, like our father's.

"Then we will deal with it." He tightens his hold. "Let's get out of here. We can watch a movie or something back at your place?"

"Sure." I nod, blinking back the tears and not having much success in keeping them from falling.

When we get to the door, I run into Jess. We both stumble back and apologise before realising who it was we ran into. She's in a dress, nicer than the ones she usually wears.

Right. The date with Harley.

I glance over my shoulder to see him watching us. When he sees my face, his own falls. I shove out the door and follow Sam to his car, wishing the night would be over with already.

I tell Sam I need to shower before the movie, just so I can let all the tears out. Once they're gone, I'll be able to put the smile back on my face and pretend everything is fine.

Throwing on grey sweats and a loose top, I emerge, as there's a loud knock on the door. We exchange a look and Sam strides to the door. When he swings it open, Harley is standing there. He looks alarmed seeing Sam before his eyes settle on me. I quickly push to my feet and start to walk closer, then stop.

"Sorry. I saw you … when you were leaving … I just wanted to check if you were okay."

Sam sends a smirk over his shoulder at me.

"I have to step out for a second anyway, left something in the car," he awkwardly lies before darting out the door. Harley walks inside. Sam leaves us standing there awkwardly near the door, staring at each other.

"Where's Jess?" I ask. "Aren't you meant to be on a date?"

"Cancelled it," he replies.

"Why?"

"Because you were crying."

"Not over that," I say defensively.

"Oh." He says, his face falling. "Right. Of course not."

His words hit me like a punch.

"Well. Regardless, I wanted to see you." He mutters, pinning me with his gaze.

I hear Sam's car rumble to life and he pulls out of my driveway. I gape at him and his grin is visible through the window as he disappears into the night.

"Sorry to gatecrash."

"It's fine. We were going to watch a movie, but I guess not."

"I'll watch a movie with you," he says, looking annoyingly adorable. "If you want."

"Okay," I whisper.

A message from Sam makes me look down at my phone. He said he left to give us some alone time but to let him know if I want him to come back. I smile down at it, my chest warming as I type out a quick reply.

Harley locks the door behind him. We push the TV around so it is more visible from my bed, and crawl into it. When he lays down beside me, I hardly dare to breathe. He's warm, and so close.

We pick a comedy and settle into the pillows. He curls an arm underneath my head. I lean on his chest, hearing the steady rhythm of his heart.

"Thank you," I whisper. "For coming."

He tightens his arm around me.

"There's nowhere else I'd rather be."

# Chapter Thirty

## Josie

### Four years ago

It is an unusually cool night. The wind sweeps over my legs, and I tuck them deeper underneath the rug.

John, Eric, Elise, Nick, and myself are spread amongst two of our dad's trucks, huddled in the back of the trays. The screen flickers to life, and the sound booms around us in a patchy echo. Once a month the residents of Fern Grove gather in the soccer fields for a drive-in movie, like they used to "back in the day," my dad often says.

I'm not particularly interested in the movie being shown, but it's a fun excuse to meet up with friends and hang out. There isn't all that much to do in this town, so we take anything we can get.

Elise and John are segregated in the other tray. Eric bounces between both groups, wanting to hang out with Nick and myself, but not wanting to leave John and Elise alone either, although neither boys realise her affections are solely on Brennon and their constant fight for her attention isn't getting them anywhere.

I rest my head on Nick's shoulder, a soft sigh leaving me, watching the screen, but not really seeing. For a week I blew off my hangouts with Nick. Guilt has my stomach in knots to the point I can't stand myself.

Every time we hang out, it feels stale and forced, not that I think Nick has picked up on this. Sometimes I feel like it's so obvious, there could be a sign flashing above my head, and other times I wonder if he notices my behaviour at all.

Every day I tell myself I'm happy. This is what I want. I love Nick.

I respect his decision to wait. I say it in my mind over and over. I've tried more than once this week to talk about our future. It's what *he* wants, always.

My eyes roam around us. I can see multiple couples making out, the movie long forgotten. I envy them. Isn't that normal? To explore? To push each other's boundaries?

With my heartbeat loud in my ears, I place my hand onto Nick's thigh. His hand strokes my arm gently, eyes not leaving the screen. Barely breathing, I move it up his leg.

"Josie," Nick snaps quietly. His voice is low and this time, his patience has run out. "We are not having this conversation again."

Heat slaps my cheeks, and I kick the blanket off.

"Josie," he sighs, but I pull my hand from his outstretched one. "Where are you going?"

"To get more popcorn," I hiss at him through my teeth.

I stomp past the lines of cars, feeling the familiar sting of rejection and embarrassment circulating inside of me. How many times am I going to put myself through this?

Hands find my waist, dragging me sideways. My breath gets trapped inside my lungs as I'm ushered to the back of a familiar black truck.

"Hey."

Fire spreads through my body as those icy eyes settle on me. Harley's trademark smirk is visible in the next-to-no light.

"Harley," I whisper.

He combs my hair back from my face, tilting my head back. His breath is hot and buttery over my lips.

"I've missed you."

A jolt of something I can't describe makes my knees knock together.

"I've missed you, too," I say back, surprised at my honesty. It's true, I really miss him when he's not with me. I'm constantly searching for him in the hallways, looking for his truck driving by, waiting for the next time he tugs me into a classroom.

"Have you broken up with that boyfriend yet, or are you still trying to kid yourself?"

It's hard to process his words when his thumb rubs like that over my lip. My head feels foggy.

"You don't want to date me," I whisper.

"Don't I?" he questions. "Why not?"

"Harley Caldwell doesn't date."

"Until now."

My eyes drift closed. I still can't comprehend that these words are coming from him. No girl has managed to tie him down. I'm not anything special. Why me?

"You'll get bored of me. Boys like you always do."

"You don't think much of me, do you?" His hands drop from my face and I miss their warmth immediately. "You have nothing nice to say about me. Ever."

"I'm sorry," I say, and I mean it. "I just can't believe someone like you could like someone like me. I'm trying to protect myself." I pull my lips inside my mouth. "You'll break my heart, Harley."

"Have you ever thought that you might break mine?"

I blink. That never, not for a moment, crossed my mind.

His mouth is on mine suddenly and I feel the deep craving inside me finally satisfy. I moan into the kiss, his hands heavy and firm on my body. I sink my fingers into his dark hair, and then loop them behind his neck.

"Choose me," he breathes into me, tasting like a pleasant mixture of cigarettes, whisky and popcorn. A combination I'd never imagined to taste. "Be mine."

I'm starting to wonder if I've ever been anyone else's.

He spins me so that I'm on my back in the tray. Adrenaline courses through me. The high of being with him, the fear of being seen, the panic of someone looking for me. It only makes me want this more.

My skirt is pushed up my waist. His hands sear against the cool skin of my thighs. My underwear dampens and I moan when he touches me.

"Oh, darling," he whispers.

*Darling.* Such a delicate word from a filthy mouth.

He inches my underwear down my thighs. My heart slams against my ribcage and the starry sky blurs in my vision. Harley's head hovers between my thighs, offering me a wicked smirk before his tongue slides over me.

"Oh *shit.*"

I feel his lips smirk against me at my words. His tongue continues to move and I feel my insides turn to scorching liquid. Harley blindly reaches up, covering my mouth with his hand.

Heat wells in every limb of my body. I shift and squirm, feeling intoxicatingly good but tremendously bad.

I whimper into his hand, feeling every part of me clench. As my insides explode, a loud gasp escapes me and everything blurs. He sits back, his lips wet, hair sticking up everywhere. He stands, pushing himself between my legs as I struggle to control the tidal wave of feelings my body is experiencing. He grins down at me, licking his lips.

"I bet farm boy can't make you feel like that."

My breathing is heavy as I sit, placing my hands on his chest.

"No," my voice is soft.

"Time's running out, Darling." He moves, kissing me, letting me taste everything he just had. "My offer has an expiration date."

When our eyes meet, I feel like his are endless.

"Run along now," says Harley, his eyes darting to my lips once more. "Don't want to get caught, now do we?"

He kisses my nose, steps back, and releases me. My legs are like jelly when I stand, yanking my underwear up and shoving my skirt back down.

I press my hand against his hard chest, feeling the thump of his heartbeat underneath. His eyes narrow slightly in curiosity as I slide my fingers down over his hard stomach.

"Sweetheart," he whispers, glancing over his shoulder. My fingers shake as I fumble to undo the button on his pants. He leans back, his fingers tightening around the edge of the tray. "You don't have to."

"I want to."

Tugging his pants down, my breath escapes me as I see all of him. Swallowing nervously, I lift my eyes so that we are looking straight at each other, when my lips wrap around the end of him.

A low hiss escapes him and his fingers tighten, the skin stretching across his knuckles turning white. The ground bites into my knees as I run my tongue over him. A low groan rumbles from his chest as I lick up and down his length, pushing myself to take him further.

With my eyes still on his, I wrap my fingers around him and move it up and down. He murmurs something incoherent as his eyes drift close. His head falls back, bits of his dark hair falling across his face as I move faster, loving that *I'm* doing this to *him*.

Blood rushes to my cheeks as I quicken my movements. My erratic heartbeat thunders in my ears, blocking out every other sound around me.

"I'm close." He releases a breathy groan, bucking his hips upwards, thrusting himself deeper down my throat to the point I'm gagging.

"Again," I tell him, although it's more of a mumble, considering my mouth is full.

He pushes himself into me again, his hand pressing to the back of my head, tangling my hair through his fingers. He tugs slightly and I moan. The mixture of the pain and his pleasure is a wicked combination that I can feel myself already growing addicted to.

"Now," he chokes out, just as an explosion of warmth spurts across my tongue. Closing my eyes, I swallow it all down.

Slowly, his fingers drag tenderly across my scalp as I do one final lick before rocking back onto my heels. Dragging my mouth across the back of my hand, I gaze up at him.

"That was better than I could have imagined, sweetheart," he whispers, cupping my face gently and guiding me to meet his lips. We kiss and this time it's gentle and warm.

"I have to go," I whisper, the taste of him still on my tongue. "Call me later?"

"Yes."

He gives me a soft smile, stroking his thumb over my cheek. I step back. I touch his arm gently before I rush to the van, refilling the popcorn bowl I'd long forgotten about on the ground.

My breath still isn't back when I climb into the tray.

"Where did you run off to?" Eric questions, the faded light from the screen flashing a few times, casting a pale glow over my friends. I hope they can't see how flushed my skin is.

I wave the bucket. "Refill."

"Must have been a long line," he comments, more to himself than me as he drifts back to the other truck.

I feel Nick's eyes searing holes into the side of my head as I get comfortable. I sneak a glance over my shoulder.

Blue eyes stare back at me before they sink into the shadows.

# Chapter Thirty-One

## *Josie*

When I wake, I'm bundled up in Harley's arms. It's hot, a little too hot, but I don't move. I enjoy being back in his embrace after years of trying to forget how good it feels.

His deep breathing fans over my ear. I twist so that I gaze up at him. He has a razor-sharp jawline that my fingers are begging to graze over. His hair is messy, covering his closed lids, his lips softly parted. He looks so calm. So innocent. So good.

Harley Caldwell has never been good. Not good for me, not for himself.

When I think back to all those times we snuck around together, it still makes my pulse quicken. No one has made me feel half of what Harley used to. I sigh. There's no point using past tense. It's still the same now.

Eventually, I detach myself from Harley's grip. He groans softly as I get to my feet, stretching. Several bones crack and I shake out my limbs. I feel like I'm waking from a coma. I haven't slept that well or deep for a long time.

"Come back," Harley mumbles.

Despite myself, I smile. "I need to shower. It's fucking hot."

He makes an incoherent sound, rolling onto his back.

My nerves are on high-alert when I shower, feeling flustered and confused.

I throw on shorts and a singlet, tucking it in and piling my hair messily on top of my head. When I was with Elliot, I would look like I'm about to step inside a cocktail party—even if I was just in the apartment all day—and it feels nice not to worry about that. To not be *expected* to do that.

Harley and I stay inside my little house the entire day. We lounge in bed, eating, talking, watching movies. I never realised it was so *easy* with him. Effortless and endless conversations about everything and nothing.

After Nick tries to ring me, I switch my phone off, grimacing at all the unread messages and unanswered calls blinking at me, the red notifications a reminder of all the things in my life I've been ignoring. It's easy to forget about my problems when Harley is with me. Ironic, since he was the number one source of all my problems before.

We're sprawled on my bed, the fan's buzzing beside the bed, legs tangled.

"What was it like getting out?" he asks.

"Hmm?"

"Getting away from here," he clarifies.

"Like a breath of fresh air," I answer. "At first."

"At first?"

"Living and working in the city isn't like this. No one knows who you are. No one cares." I lace our fingers together, even though it's too hot to be touching. I should be resisting this. Putting up more of a fight. But having him here has been the first time my mind has eased in a long while, and I'm getting sick of pretending not to want this. To want him. It's tiring. I want to let go, even if it's just for today. "That's what I loved about the place. No one knew me, or my history."

Harley winces a little, reminding him of our past and all the ways we wronged each other. As much as I hate him for what he did, I'm not innocent in it, either. I didn't break it off with Nick when I should have. I strung them both along, keeping Harley as my little secret, and Nick as my protector.

I was a foolish girl, and I wish I could take it all back.

"It's so busy there. People care too much about what others think. They're all fake." I sigh. "I was the fakest of them all."

He touches my hair. "You changed a lot about yourself."

"I didn't want to be Josephine Mayor anymore," I whisper.

I hated so much about myself, and my body, so I altered everything I could.

"Who did you want to be?"

"Someone better." I watch his fingers thread through my blonde strands.

"Josie," he murmurs. "I used to be the only one who called you Josie."

My stomach clenches. That is true. As much as I hate to admit it, that's why I went by that now.

"Why didn't you leave?"

"I stayed with some mates down south for a while but it wasn't for me. I was in a pretty dark place for a while. I burnt some bridges." He clenches his jaw. "I've made a lot of mistakes."

"I think we all have."

"Some more than others." He comments. "What did you do while you were away?"

"I got a degree. Partied a lot. Made bad decisions."

"Did you make a lot of friends?"

I shake my head. "I met a lot of people who I spent time with. They weren't my friends."

"Why did you come back?" he asks.

Exhaling, I shift, pulling my legs out from underneath his. "I got involved with a dangerous guy. I ran away."

Harley stiffens. "You ran away?"

"Escaped"—I let out a bitter laugh—"is probably a better term. He was fucking mental, and I shouldn't have stuck around as long as I did."

"At least you're out of it now."

"I just don't know what's next for me. Should I stay, should I go? If I move on, where?" I sigh, feeling the pulse of a headache threatening to make an appearance. "It makes my head hurt thinking about it. I just need everything to stop for a while."

"This town is the perfect place for that." He smiles. "Nothing much happens here. Perfect rest stop."

I laugh softly. "That's a good point."

"Are you enjoying your new job?"

"It's fine." I nod. "More relaxed than what I'm used to, but I'm enjoying it."

"That's good."

"Do you like working behind the bar?"

"No," he laughs. "Not at all. I've been spending most of my days doing construction. Apprenticeship wages suck, so I have to work at the pub for extra cash. I'm in my final year though."

"Oh, great. Then you're a qualified builder?"

"Yeah. Thank fuck. Sick of being the one stuck with the shit jobs and the shit pay. The pay rise I get once the certificate is finished will make it all worth it."

"That's how I felt studying. I wanted to pull my hair out. But now that I'm done and have my degree, all the sweat and tears have paid off."

"I'll have to come see you at work. I never go to the dentist. I was terrified of them as a kid," he admits.

"A lot of people are."

He grins. "Go easy on me, yeah? No pulling out my teeth or anything."

I laugh. "It's not in my scope to pull adult teeth, so you're safe."

"Phew," he teases with a carefree smile that makes my heart ache. He looks at his phone and his face falls. "I have to go. I start work in an hour."

I bite my lip, surprised at the disappointment filling me. "Oh, okay."

Harley places his finger under my chin, tilting my head back. "I had a good time with you."

"Me too," I whisper.

His lips press against mine and I sigh into them. We kiss for a few moments and when he gets to his feet, my lips are still tingling.

"I'll call you," he says before he disappears out the door.

I blink, staring after him. I have no idea how I went from not being able to stand him in the room with me, to spending all night and day with him.

It's always been a whirlwind with Harley and this time, it's no different.

I spend the rest of the night mapping out the new course I'm taking. I watch my first lecture, take notes, and complete all the activity questions. By the time I'm finished, it's almost eleven p.m. I've only turned my phone back on for a few minutes, when a text comes through. I dread checking it, but am surprised when I see Harley's name on the screen.

**Harley:** Are you awake?

**Josie:** Yes.

*Harley is calling*

"Hey," he says and a strange thrill spikes through me.

"Harley," I greet him. "Hey. What's up?"

"I just finished work," he replies. "I can't stop thinking about you."

The pen I was using to take notes twirls ferociously in my fingers as I try to control my breathing. A huge smile takes over my face and I don't fight it. No one is here, I can let myself feel whatever I want to feel.

"I can't stop thinking about you either."

I told myself once he left that I had a moment of weakness and that was that. One phone call from him and I'm melting, eager to see him again, admitting the very thing I told myself never to say out loud.

"I want to see you," he breathes into the phone. "Can I come over?"

"Yes," I say.

"I'll see you soon."

I spring to my feet and clear any mess I've made through the day. I rinse the sweat off and dress in an oversized shirt, combing my hair up into a semi-neat ponytail. I'm contemplating putting on a bra, when I hear footsteps bound up the porch steps.

My body glides to the door and I'm opening it before I've let myself gather my thoughts.

"Hi," I whisper.

"Hi."

He leans down and kisses me, pushing me gently inside, kicking the door shut. He bends his knees and scoops me up, lifting my feet from the ground. I wrap my legs around his waist. He stumbles over to the lounge before lowering me onto it, never breaking the kiss.

My lips leave trails down his jaw, his neck, and back up again. His hand slides up my side, underneath my shirt. My stomach sucks in as his fingertips graze along the sensitive parts of my skin.

217

"How was your night?" he asks me, palming my breast. I softly moan, arching my back so that I'm pushing myself closer to him.

"Great thanks," I reply breathlessly. "I've started a new dental course. It's kicking my ass already."

He chuckles, nuzzling my earlobe before taking it between his teeth.

"You're a smart girl, Darling, I'm sure you will smash it."

*Darling.* I feel my toes curl with giddiness at the nickname he often used on me. I haven't heard him say it for so long. It's one of the things I often remember when I recall our nightly rendezvous'.

A blaring alarm suddenly pierces the air and I almost kink my neck from jolting. I laugh and wince simultaneously, rubbing my neck.

"My bad," he says.

"What is the alarm for?"

He reluctantly sits back and reaches for his phone, clicking it off. He moves to sit at the other end of the lounge and I'm glad I have time to gather myself. Things were getting hot and heavy very quickly.

"I'm feeding the neighbour's cat while she's away. I have to set an alarm so I don't kill it." He rubs at his face, looking weary. "You remember Ethel? The old lady who used to always give us lollies when we went past her house?"

"Oh yeah!" I brighten as I nestle into the cushions, making myself comfortable. I drape my legs over Harley's lap and his fingers walk over my thighs. "Wow, I forgot all about her."

"Yeah, well, she owns both the units off Crosswell Lane. She lives in one and Brennon and I are in the other. She visits her kids a lot, so I feed her cat when she's away."

"Aw, that's kind of you."

"Well, she never complains when we have the music up or people over." He shrugs. "She is super deaf though. Probably doesn't even hear us."

"That probably works out for the best." I laugh. "You're still close with Brennon, then?"

Harley's face sobers for a moment and he nods. "I suppose, yeah. There aren't many choices around here." It's meant to be a joke but it falls flatly. I've always despised Brennon.

"He was such an asshole," I say. "Still is, I'm sure."

"He's better."

"I'll believe that when I see it."

Harley stays quiet, watching his fingers make patterns on my leg.

"Elise's death shook him pretty bad." He blows out a breath. "He loved her."

"And yet fucked around with her all those years, when they could have been together."

As soon as the words leave my mouth, I regret it. Although not over such a great time span, I did much the same to Harley. I tried living the best of both worlds, too scared to take a risk on him.

He nods. "We were all dumb kids."

I nod, agreeing. I'm sure I'm not the only one to wish I could rewrite history.

"I better go," Harley says regretfully. "Otherwise Mr. Tuppins will be very cross with me."

I laugh. "Don't want to get on the bad side of a cat."

"I've learned that the hard way." He kisses the side of my head, pushing to his feet. He's halfway across the room, before he turns. "Can I come back here? And stay?"

*Absolutely not. Say no. Tell him this was fun while it lasted, but it's done now.*

"Thought you'd never ask."

He grins and handsome smile lines curve around his mouth. "I'll be back soon."

"I'll be waiting." I smile.

He's back within half an hour, showered, and dressed in a black V-neck shirt and shorts. I'm laying in bed, reading over my study notes, when he crawls in beside me.

"Is Mr. Tuppins happy?"

"Mr. Tuppins is happy." He grins.

He drags me across the mattress so that I'm pressed into him. I throw my notes off to the side, and snuggle into him.

This town suddenly feels a lot less lonely.

# Chapter Thirty-Two

## Harley

### Four years ago

My hand hovers over the page. *Write about a memory when you truly felt you belonged.* I stare out the window, watching a small bird land on a branch beside another bird. They chirp at each other and touch beaks. Exhaling, my eyes drift to where Josie is sitting.

Nick's arm swings around the back of his chair and his thumb rubs her shoulder. She smiles and laughs at something he says. My grip on the pen tightens as I glare at them.

The thing about Josie is that she is all smiles and laughs when they're watching her. But *I* watch her, when they're not. And it's not the same girl.

Pressing down onto the paper, I watch the ink bleed across it.

*It's hard to write about a memory, when the only time I feel like I belong, is with a person. Someone who sees me, like I see them, who doesn't fit in here, like me. Someone who wants more.* Needs *more.*

I see the way she looks at me. It's the same way I look at her.

Blowing out a frustrated breath, I throw the pen down. I've never felt like this. No girl occupies my mind. No one gets under my skin.

Seeing her with him fucking hurts. It's my fault. I went after her, knowing she isn't available, but I couldn't hold back anymore. And she feels it too. She's just afraid.

Anger and sadness swirl inside me. My mind is forever in argument. *Fight for her. Don't let her go. She's worth it.* I stare down at my words. *She's not yours to take. Leave her be.*

Josie Mayor makes me feel fucking ugly. Angry, possessive, jealous. Heat slithers through my veins when she folds one leg over the other, her skirt riding up her thighs. Pressing her full lips together, she turns her eyes to me. A ripple of awareness slides down my spine.

After a long few moments, her eyes face forward again. Clenching my jaw, I slide down into my seat. Fuck. This can't go on. She needs to make a choice. Me, or him.

Nick's fingers stroke her shoulder. She tenses, knowing I'm watching. Good. I hope she feels guilty, like I do. Do thoughts of the things we are doing keep her up at night, like they do to me?

Pulling my lip ring with my tongue, I narrow my eyes, watching the heat rise in her cheeks. She's uncomfortable.

The bell rings and I don't move as I watch her jump to her feet, sliding her bag over her shoulders. The classroom empties and I quietly follow. I see her break away from her friends, heading over to get a drink. As the last stragglers leave the hallway, I curl my fingers around her bicep and drag her into a shadowy spot underneath the stairs.

Her breath hitches as she stumbles in surprise.

"Harley," she whispers, her eyes darting to my mouth briefly before moving back to my eyes.

Grabbing each side of her face, I dive towards her mouth. She moans into me as we kiss. She opens for me instantly, my tongue sliding against hers. Her delicate fingers press into my chest.

Wrapping her arms around my neck, she pulls me closer. Her uniform rides up and I trace the lines of her stomach. She shudders, eyes fluttering closed. *This* is what I fucking wake up for of a morning.

"Meet me tonight," I whisper.

She moans softly as I kiss down her neck.

"I can't."

"Why not?"

"Plans."

"What plans?" I demand, biting into the soft flesh at the base of her throat.

She gasps against my ear and pushes her hips into mine, grinding softly. I groan at the feel of her and slide my hands around her to grip her ass.

"I'm going to the movies."

"Yeah, with me."

Her breathing deepens. "With the others."

"The others," I sigh, stepping back so that I'm looking into her soft eyes.

"Yes."

"Cancel your plans."

"I can't."

"You can."

Her teeth sink into her lower lip as we look at each other. Slowly, she nods.

"Okay."

A grin stretches across my face. "Yeah?"

"Yes." She smiles, flushing.

Trailing my hand down her hair, I pick up a strand of it and rub it between my thumb and pointer finger.

"See you there."

⁓

After school, the blaring music isn't enough to drown out my thoughts when I get to the gate in front of my house. Well, it once was a gate. Now it's strips of rusted metal hanging off its hinges.

If it wasn't for the music, I'm positive I'd hear the yelling. Walking down the side of the house, I yank out one of my ear buds. The yelling is coming from the kitchen. Inching the door open, I slip inside and head straight to my room.

When I hear glass shattering, I stride down the hall. Mum is sitting in her armchair, lower lip trembling as my father stands over her, shouting. I can't stand how she sits there and lets him do this. I don't bother bringing it up anymore, I'm too exhausted to argue.

"Get the fuck away from her," I snap. "She gets it. Pour another bourbon down your throat and leave everyone the fuck alone."

He whirls around to face me. Unshaved face. Glossy eyes. Long hair messily swept back.

"Don't you come in here and tell me what to do. Under my own roof," he snarls, his upper lip curling like it always does when he's had one too many. Or ten.

How many times does this need to happen before I learn to let it go?

Shaking my head, I turn away from him. I've barely turned my back to him when his hand slams into my shoulder and I stumble, jamming painfully into the wall. Photo frames crash to the floor, glass splintering at my feet.

My elbow flies back and connects with the side of his head. A scream floods my ears as my father's hand cracks against my cheek. My jaw dislodges for a moment and my knee gives way. I feel glass stab into my leg and I stagger to my feet, blood rushing to my head.

Blindly, I stumble for the door and leave, not looking back. This is usually the time I go to Brennon's but instead, I pull up Josie's contact.

"Hello?" she asks in a low voice.

"Josie," I breathe. "Can we meet? Like right now?"

She's silent for a moment. "Yes."

Pain pulses behind my eyes. I hear the front door swing open as I push my bike forward. I'm down the street and gone, but I can still hear him roaring my name. I ride as fast as my legs will take me. It's a trek out to the dam, but the more distance between me and him, the better.

Sweat drips into the cut on my cheek as I step off the bike and throw it down. I hiss with each movement. The sun is slowly sinking, but the heat is still unbearable.

I fucking hate this place.

A tire crunches on the loose gravel, and I look up. Her hair blows back from the breeze as she skids to a stop. She wanders cautiously over to me. She cups a hand over her eyes and stares at me. I push to my feet and reach for her hands.

"Christ." She gulps. "What happened to you?"

Dust circles us and lands in a soft layer over our skins. I shake it out of my eyes and look down at my feet.

"Fell off my bike. Being an idiot."

Her finger presses underneath my chin, forcing our gazes to meet.

"That's not what happened."

"Is it okay if we don't talk about it?"

Her thumb drags across my lip, touching the ring.

"Yes. But any time you want to, I'm here."

"Are you?" I ask softly. Her eyebrows furrow, head tilting. "You're never here. You're always with them. *With him.*"

She pulls her hand away and I feel a slight breeze pass over my skin at the lack of contact.

"My head is a mess. Everything is complicated."

"Do you like me?"

"Yes."

"Then it's not complicated."

She rolls her lips into her mouth, bits of her hair sliding out from behind her ear.

"If the roles were reversed, I would have made my decision long ago," I tell her. My hands twitch to sweep her hair back, but I leave them at my side. "I want to be with you. I can't be any fucking clearer. You want to be with me. What are you waiting for?"

"I don't know."

Breathing heavily, I step back, rubbing my hand down my face.

"Look, I really need to just not think for a while," I say. I yank my shirt over my head and throw it on the ground. Her eyes roam over my torso before sinking low over my stomach. "Swim with me."

Shyly, she steps out of her shoes and slides her cut-off denim shorts down her thighs. Heat rushes to my groin when she pulls her top off. I drink all of her in. Every beautiful inch of her.

After I throw my shorts off, she takes my hand, and leads me to the water. The water isn't as cold as I hoped, but it's still a relief from the dry heat.

Josie slides her arms over my shoulders and wraps her legs around my waist. Her breath fans over my lips as I grip her hips, pulling her closer.

"We can't stay like this," I say. "Not forever."

"No," she murmurs, pressing her forehead to mine. "But you will be."

"I will be what?"

"My forever."

# Chapter Thirty-Three

## Josie

The smell of coffee makes my eyes flutter open.

Harley waves the takeaway cup under my nose for a moment longer before standing, a grin stretched over his face.

"Morning sunshine, I bought us some coffees." He places them on the bedside table and retrieves two brown paper bags. "And some muffins."

"Yum!"

"I thought we could go for a drive and sit somewhere," he says.

I like that he hasn't suggested to do something in town. We both don't need the scrutiny. Especially since I haven't returned any of Nick's calls or texts.

Throwing a dress over my head and sliding into my sandals, I settle behind the wheel of my car, while Harley folds himself into the passenger seat.

We drive out of town, up into one of the sandy hills. I park close to the edge and wind the windows down, letting the warm air spill inside the car. I take a sip of my coffee and Harley hands the bag to me.

"Thanks for breakfast." I smile.

"No problem." He takes a sip. "I have to get going soon. Working today, and then tonight."

"Oh," I say.

Today is one of my days off. I've already divided my day into organising my weekly grocery shop, going over my study notes, and to check if next week's lecture has been recorded. I'm also going to buy myself a canvas and paint–something I haven't done for many years. It used to be a favourite pastime of mine and I'm looking forward to getting back into it.

"I like coming up here," Harley says. "It's peaceful."

I make a sound of agreement as I stare out at the vast blue sky and the red dirt. For such a plain view, it really is pretty. We grow quiet for a moment as we eat. It's so quiet, I think I can hear the place breathe. A quiet whoosh in and out, wafting through the windows, blowing my hair across my face.

"We should get out of here," Harley says. "Leave this town and never look back."

This is happening quickly, but perhaps, not quickly at all. This was what we should have done all those years ago.

I chew my food quietly for a moment, pondering his suggestion. Leaving is always on the cards for me, I truly do hate it here. Although the last two days have been a lot more bearable. But he is the reason for that.

I need more than this place. Adventure. The thrill. Excitement. But also, I want someone to do all that with.

"You're either the reason I'll stay, or the reason I'll go," I tell him truthfully.

"Could very well be the same for me, you know," he says quietly. "Once I've done my apprenticeship, there isn't anything holding me here." His icy eyes turn their attention to me. "Other than you."

I try to imagine my life with Harley. Letting go, being happy. Is that what has been missing all this time? Him?

A sigh fills the car and I side-eye him.

"I have to get going."

I fold the bag and tuck it into my cup holder. Harley inches the volume of the radio up as we drive back to town. When I idle in front of his house, he leans over and kisses me. I forget that we're in town, in front of people. I forget it all and kiss him back. It's not until I'm pulling from the curb that I see her walking down the street, shopping bags in her hands.

Jess.

She saw the whole thing.

Panic swells in my throat, making it hard to breathe. I'm rigid in my seat as I drive past her, not sparing her a glance. My hands shake as I change gears.

She saw. She saw. She saw.

I can't think about this right now. I need to organise my groceries, get home, and then I can have a meltdown. When I'm in town, around *these* people, I'm strong. Josie Mayor doesn't show cracks. She saves her tears for her pillow.

It's not until I'm inside the supermarket that I come back to the present. I blink, staring around me. I was so absorbed in my thoughts; I don't even remember parking the car. I mentally shake myself and pull a trolley from the bay.

I'm halfway through my shop, when Shannon bounds down the aisle. She clutches at my hands and spins me around. One of the oranges that was balancing on top goes flying to the floor.

"Josie, guess what, guess what!" she shrieks and I wince when eyes turn to us.

"Hi Shannon," I say much less enthusiastically than her. We really don't know each other well enough to greet like this. "What's up?"

"Look!"

She waves her hand in my face, so close I stumble back, thinking she might clock me one. I blink at her finger, seeing a diamond ring sparkling under the fluorescent lights.

"Holy shit," I whisper. "John proposed?"

"Yes!" she squeals.

I thought they must have only recently got together, but I really had no idea. That was just an assumption.

"Wow, Shannon, that's amazing news!" I gush, pulling her hand closer. "Congratulations!"

"Thanks! Isn't it gorgeous?"

"Stunning!" I smile. "I'm really happy for you both."

"Thanks babe!" Her eyes well and for a moment, I think she might cry. Shannon's tan skin has splotches of reds on her cheeks. Her freckles are so prominent, it looks like she's drawn them on. "So, we have been talking about this forever, so naturally I already have everything planned!" She tells me, like I should know all of this. I nod along anyway. "For our engagement party, I'm organising for all our friends to take a bus out to the city where we will stay for a night or two and go clubbing! I've only been once before and I'd really love to go again! You'll come, right? Everyone is coming!"

"Sure." I shrug. "I've been dying to have some fun. Count me in."

"Fantastic!" she smiles. "I'm making an event on Facebook with all the details. Talk soon!"

She's gone as fast as she appeared, and I feel a little dazed. I pick up the orange and continue shopping. That actually sounds quite fun. It would probably be a big event for these guys, considering there is nothing like that here.

*Everyone is coming*, she said. I wonder if that includes Harley and Brennon? I have no idea where they fall in the social circuit around here. Shannon seems like the type to be friends with everyone, so they might be on the list, too.

A road trip, with Harley, Nick, my old friends, and all the girls who hate me.

Sounds like a night I won't forget.

Shannon's announcement only distracts me until I'm home. Then I remember Jess seeing everything. It's not until my jaw aches that I realise I'm grinding my teeth.

Pulling out the new paint and canvas I bought, I block everything out. I turn my music up loud, place the cloth over my floor and start to paint. I don't have a plan, or even an idea of what I want to paint, but my hand keeps moving, the brush seamlessly gliding across the canvas, like I've never stopped.

My stomach growls with hunger, and when I glance at the clock, I'm startled to see hours have passed.

Stepping back, I gaze at the canvas.

The background is a mixture of different shades of grey. It's the top half of a boy's head. He's peering up at the night sky, a cloud of smoke drifting over his face.

Through the smoke, a pair of ocean-blue eyes peer back at me.

# Chapter Thirty-Four

## Josie

### *Four years ago*

**M**y feet slap on the floor as I sprint down the hallway. My laces are untied, my hair is all over my face, and for a moment I fear I've put my shirt on backwards. I screech to a halt and look down, relieved to see it sitting how it's supposed to.

I *was* on time before I slipped under the bleachers with a certain someone, and lost myself in soft hands, and body-tingling kisses. It also didn't help that I was almost to class before I had to run back and get my textbooks.

With my hair blanketing my eyes, I don't see someone also entering class at the same time. I hit a hard chest and fly backwards. Warm hands grab my waist, stopping me from falling.

"You all right, Darling?" Harley smirks, his hands still on me.

I step out of his hold and smooth over my hair.

I don't know how he's beaten me here. When he strolls in, I realise he isn't holding textbooks. Nick's face brightens when he sees me. No hint of suspicion on his innocent face. It makes me feel even worse. He would never, for a moment, consider I was capable of doing what I've been doing.

"Hey, I thought you were meeting me this morning before class?" Nick asks and touches my arm gently. His favourite way of greeting. I feel a pang inside me. There's no passion or romance with Nick. It's like I'm a family friend. Or worse, his sister.

"I got held up."

I've gotten good at this. Lying. I don't have to think twice anymore, which is concerning. What's worse? I'm learning to live with the guilt, which is not okay. I need to make my mind up. Deep down, I know what is right, but it's making the jump that I'm afraid of. I'm afraid of everything going wrong. This is a small town, I don't want to hurt anyone, or have anyone hate me.

I can't concentrate in class, knowing Harley is behind me. Even though he's in the back row, I swear I can feel his breath on the back of my neck. I'm hyper-aware of every move I make, thinking he might be watching.

When the bell rings overhead, we clamber to our feet and pack our things.

"Hey," Elise says, bumping my shoulder as she sidles up to me. "What are you going to wear on the weekend?"

It's Rianna Seeds' birthday this weekend. I'm not close with her, if anything, I despise her, but the entire class was invited and, in this town, there aren't too many parties. I can't be picky.

"I'm not sure. I have a black dress my mum bought me. So probably that," I answer. I always try my hardest to dress up for parties. I have to, being friends with drop-dead-gorgeous Elise. "You?"

"A champagne-coloured top and a skirt. I'm thinking boots."

"That'll look great."

I spend every afternoon leading up to the party practising my hair and makeup. I want to look perfect. I try straightening my hair, curling it, half-up/half-down styles, braids. I take photos of all of them and decide half-up, half-down, with red lipstick and my mum's favourite diamond earrings.

Rianna's house is a large brick home with arched windows, fading wallpaper, and toffee-coloured floorboards. Music booms from the backyard as we approach. The front door rattles as we open it and step inside. The party is located out the back, with the dance floor situated on the patio. Along the side of the pool fence is a long table with punch bowls and nibbles.

I'm not sure if it's the dress, the lipstick, or perhaps both, but I'm feeling confident. I toss my hair over my shoulders and clasp Elise's hand, dragging her to the tables. We pour ourselves a generous cup of punch—a mix of Vodka and creaming soda—draining our entire cup while still at the table and refilling immediately.

Harley is off to the side, leaning on the wall, arms folded over his chest, his foot propped. I try not to show that I can tell he's watching me. I swipe at Elise, pulling her to the dance floor. It's been a while since we got to have fun and let loose.

I shimmy down her body and drop into a squat. I bounce a few times and slide back up her, so close our noses touch. She laughs, throwing her head back and winding her arms around me. We dance, sing, and laugh until we're red-faced and our feet hurt.

Nick has been seated on one of the lounges basically the entire time, talking with a group of socially awkward kids who don't mingle much. I tried to get him to dance, but he waved me off, a little impatiently, which pissed me off. Huffing, I storm inside to use the bathroom, when I lock eyes with the one boy I've been dying to see.

Harley slips up the stairs and disappears. I peer around to see if anyone noticed, to find myself alone with only a couple making out in the kitchen. I'm quiet as I mount the stairs and follow Harley into one of the upstairs bedrooms.

My eyes flit around the room, trying to find him, when I'm pushed against the door. Like every time we look at each other, I'm sucked into those gorgeous eyes.

His mouth is over mine, and I melt into him. He lifts me and we fall into the bed.

"You look stunning," he compliments. "I can't take my eyes off you."

"I noticed." I grin.

"I need to have you, Josie," he whispers. "I need all of you."

I knew this moment was coming. It's been building for a while now. I've been trying not to think too hard about it, because I always expected it to be with Nick.

"Yes," I whisper, staring into those gorgeous blue eyes I love so much, chills breaking over my body. "I'm ready."

His eyes search mine for a moment before his mouth slams back onto mine. His hands are everywhere, sliding, gripping, scrunching, squeezing. He buries his face in the side of my neck, kissing and leaving soft bites across my skin. My fingers twist in his shirt and I pull it over his head.

He hovers over me. He is God damn perfect. And he is about to be all mine.

He pushes my dress up my waist and reaches underneath it, gripping me in his hand. I push myself into him. My fingers scrape down his bare back and sink low, resting on his backside. I pull his pants and they slide down his thighs.

I whine at the ache between my legs. I've wanted this so much, for so long. I press his hand into me, trying to ease the throbbing. Harley has a dirty smirk on his mouth as he takes in how much I want this. He slides his fingers inside me, deep and slow. I moan, throwing myself back into the pillows, arching my back. My fingers drag through his hair and down his neck.

Harley reaches for his pants and pulls out a shiny packet. With one hand still inside me, he tears the packet open with his teeth. My breath feels trapped in my throat as I watch him roll it onto himself. My body aches for him as Harley's fingers slide out.

"Okay?" he whispers.

"Okay." I smile.

He lowers himself onto me and pushes the tip inside. I gasp at the searing pain. My breathing quickens as he pushes in a little further. My stomach erupts into flutters at how big he feels. I whimper as I feel myself clench around him.

"Relax, sweetheart," he murmurs.

I draw in a deep breath and feel myself adjust and stretch. He waits until I meet his eyes and nod, before he gently starts to thrust. I moan loudly, pushing my hips up to meet his movements. He makes an incoherent sound in my ear as he shudders. My hands explore everywhere—his chest, stomach, back, butt. Every part of him is so perfect.

Thoughts of guilt swirl in the back of mind. This is wrong. So fucking wrong. But if it was so bad, would it really feel this good?

With one hand gripping my hip, Harley's other hand reaches for my hand. I feel his fingers tremble.

"Are you okay?" I ask.

He nods, closing his eyes. "I've wanted this for so long. You have no idea."

"You're nervous."

He smiles and breathes a soft laugh. "Yeah, I guess I am."

"Nervous about what?" I squeak when he thrusts into me again, almost making me lose my train of thought.

"That this is somehow all going to end."

"Us?"

He nods again and I lose focus as his hips move in a circular motion, hitting me in a deeper angle.

"I feel like you're going to slip between my fingers."

"I wooooon't," I try to answer but it ends up being a loud moan. I lift my hips, trying to move with him. My nails dig into his shoulders and he lets out a sound, almost pushing me over the edge.

His mouth moves over mine briefly, before sliding down my neck. He takes my nipple into his mouth and I arch my back, pushing myself closer to him. His thrusts become deeper and faster. He pulls out and slams back into me, a lot harder than he has before and I yelp.

"Harder," I gasp out.

This angle is exactly where he needs to be. He plunges into me faster and his fingers dance over my clit. It tingles and I moan.

"Right there."

"Here?"

"Yes!" I practically scream as the most powerful orgasm I've ever experienced barrels through me, leaving me shaking and breathless. My eyes fly open to see him watching me, lips parted, eyes dark.

"Fuck," he groans as he comes undone as well, drilling into me once more. "You feel so fucking good. Better than I could have ever imagined."

"Harley?" I whisper.

"Sweetheart?" He stops, eyes pouring into mine.

"I choose you," I murmur. "It's you. It's always been you."

The look on his face brings tears to my eyes. He is so happy. I never in a million years expected this from him. Bad Boy Harley. Delinquent Harley. Asshole Harley.

I think he's in love with me.

And I'm in love with him.

He kisses the side of my face as he thrusts, harder and deeper, growing more confident with each passing moment.

"You're going to be mine?" he whispers, smiling into the kiss.

"I've always been yours."

We spend longer than we should have tangled in each other's limbs, the sheets twisted around us. Heated, sweaty, breathless. Harley can't keep his hands off me, despite everything. We kiss so much my lips hurt. In between my legs ache, but in a good way.

Harley and I reluctantly peel ourselves from the bed. He gives me a long, lingering kiss that has heat licking my core in the most delicious way.

"When will you tell him?" he asks. "I can't go another day seeing you two together."

"I'll tell him," I promise. "Tonight."

Harley's fingers pull through my hair. His eyes intently scan my face, as if he is drinking in every single one of my features.

"I'll call you tomorrow," he says.

"We're finally going to be together," I whisper. "It doesn't feel real."

He grazes his nose with mine. "I know."

Thinking about the aftermath of this is enough to send me into an anxiety attack. I have no idea what my friends will think. What will happen to our group? How will Nick ever be able to look me in the eyes again?

All of these things have circled inside my head and crushed my spirit for so long. But I need to be brave.

I squeeze his hand, before I unlock the door and slide out of the room. I beeline for the bathroom to freshen up. When I reappear downstairs, I'm shocked to find life is going on just as normal. Nick is still on the lounge, Elise is playing cards with a group, and there's a group of girls dancing on the patio.

My whole world has been rocked and here everyone is, without a clue.

Pouring myself a drink, I survey Nick for a moment. He's chatting away to the group. He probably has no idea I wasn't out here. I feel like I was gone for hours.

When Elise notices me, she springs to her feet and bounds over.

"Hey, where have you been? I was looking for you."

"Hey, um, I need to talk to you—" I stop when I see her tear-filled eyes. "Are you okay? What's wrong?"

"Brennon is being cagey and weird," she huffs. "We were meant to meet tonight. He said he had a special surprise for me. He asked me to meet him in one of the spare rooms but they were both locked, and he hasn't been seen anywhere." Her eyes are scanning the area. "Do you think he was with someone else?"

"Well. The spare room on the right was occupied," I admit. "I don't know about the other one. I haven't seen him."

"He got pissed off that I was hanging with Eric. He's always telling me I lead him on. I argued that I'm not. He stormed off … I assumed we were still meeting though … wait a second. Were you in one of the spare rooms?"

Mutely, I nod.

Her eyes narrow. "What's going on?"

"I have something to tell you."

Her eyes drift over my shoulder and her lips spread into a thin line. I turn my head, to see what has her attention, when I see Brennon and Rianna emerge from the house. Both of their hair is messy and she's no longer wearing shoes. Elise's face falls, before she turns and strides out of the room.

Once Rianna has disappeared into the small crowd, I stalk towards Brennon.

"You're a piece of shit," I snarl at him. "Elise is way too good for you. Everyone knows it." My hand flies forward and my drink splashes onto his face. He stumbles back in shock, swiping at his face. I don't wait to see what intelligent response he has. I hurry through the house.

I find her leaning against the mailbox, head in hands, sobbing.

"Oh, Elise," I say, gently rubbing circles into her back.

"Why would he do that?" she cries. "Each time we get serious, he does something to screw it all up!"

"He doesn't know a good thing when he has it," I tell her, refusing to compare myself to him in any way. "Also, I threw my drink at him."

She chokes on her breath and peers at me through her fingers. "You what?"

I grin. "It felt pretty great."

She's silent for a moment, before she bursts into laughter.

"You're the best friend I could ever ask for. Nick is damn lucky to have you."

I smile half-heartedly, pulling her to my chest.

If only that was true.

# Chapter Thirty-Five

## Josie

I'm restocking my fridge, when I hear a knock on the door. I jump, smacking my head against the edge of the freezer. Wincing, I rub my head. I've never been this jumpy. Another thing I can personally thank Elliot for.

"Josie? Hey."

Twisting, I see Nick hovering in the doorway and I feel my veins fill with dread. I think back to Jess seeing me earlier. Has she called him? I wouldn't be surprised. It's like four years ago all over again.

"Nick! What are you doing here?"

His brows furrow. "To see you?"

I straighten, shutting the fridge door. My hands fall to my sides, and we stare at each other for a few moments. I wait for the other shoe to drop. Is he going to shout at me? Plead? Cry? I don't know what response would be worse.

"I've tried calling," he says. "Are you avoiding me?"

"I've been busy."

His frown deepens. "Right … Okay."

"I've started a new course," I continue, studying him and deciding that he doesn't know. Not yet, anyway. "And working. It's been a lot. Sorry."

His face softens. He leans on the kitchen bench. His leaf-green eyes are wide and curious. I can't bear to stare at them any longer.

"How is it all going?"

"It's good, I might need to work on my time management though." I try to joke. "How have you been?"

"Yeah, busy as well," he says, rubbing a hand on the back of his neck. "Did you hear the good news?"

I rack my brain for a moment before I realise.

"Shannon and John?"

"Yeah." He smiles. "Isn't it great?"

"I'm really happy for them," I agree. "The engagement party sounds fun!"

"Yeah, it does. It's next weekend, which I think is really quick." He laughs. "She's just posted the event."

"Wow, she doesn't muck around." I comment. "I haven't had a chance to check my phone yet."

"I thought we could go together."

"Yeah, well, everyone is going."

He blinks at me. "Uh, right. Yeah. That's true."

I continue pulling items from my shopping bags, just to have something to do.

"Well. I'll see you later …"

It's so awkward, I want to slam my head into my cupboard and knock myself out, just to escape this conversation. His eyes fall to my hands. I look down at them, seeing paint speckled over my skin. When I glance back up, Nick's is staring at the canvas. My stomach sinks.

He continues staring at the canvas, and then turns back to me.

He stands there, as if waiting for me to say something.

"Nick …" I start to say before his phone begins to blare. I wince at the loudness and he sends me an apologetic look.

"I need it loud to hear over the machinery. I forget to turn it down when I'm not working," he explains. "See you, Josie."

The floorboards groan as he strides out. When I see his truck fade into the distance, I blow out a breath of relief, sagging to the floor. That would have been a great moment to clear the air with him.

I have to do it right this time. I just need to figure out how that is going to be.

The week leading up to Shannon and John's engagement party became a methodical routine of working, studying, and Harley slipping into my bed at ten p.m., once his shift was finished.

Waiting for the sound of my front door creaking open and the right side of my bed dipping as Harley crawled into it quickly became a favourite moment of my day. Some nights we would stay awake talking until the early hours of the morning, and others were spent quietly, laying in each other's arms.

I haven't spoken to Nick all week. I am exceptionally great at avoiding people, and my problems. I try not to think about how terrible of a person I am for doing this.

My bags are packed and I'm sitting on the faded lounge chair on my porch, soaking up the sunrays, when I hear the sound of tires crunching over gravel. Belle's Mazda pulls into view. Her tanned arm flings out the window in a wave.

"Hey girl!"

I bounce down the steps and throw my bag into the back of her car before moving around to the passenger side.

"Hey," I say.

"Ready for a weekend of fun and excitement?" she asks me, her eyes covered with dark shades.

"Totally."

She sticks her tongue out at me before lurching us forward. My knees slam into the dashboard and she shoots me an apologetic stare.

"Still working out this whole manual thing," she admits, gesturing to the gearstick. "Never had one before."

I wave her off, but absently rub my knee, my skin now sashed with a red mark.

The bus is there when we arrive and I see many familiar faces hovering in the carpark of the R.S.L, duffel bags swung over their shoulders. Most of the people standing in the carpark I haven't seen since school.

A few people do double-takes as I walk close to where everyone is standing. I feel a little less like an outsider with Belle by my side.

"Are you listening?"

"Huh?" I drag myself back to reality, glancing at Belle.

Her hair is pulled back into a pretty French braid, trailing down her back, and she's wearing a white, cut-off top littered with an orange butterfly print.

She rolls her eyes. "I said, Brennon and I are getting serious. I think he might ask me out this weekend."

"What are you going to say?"

"Yes, obviously." She nudges me.

"And when you move away?" I ask.

She shrugs. "That's a problem for future me. Never know, he might move with me."

I chew my lip and don't respond. Belle is much better off to leave someone like Brennon behind when she moves on to her next place of residence, but I don't need to air my opinion. Plenty of people would think the same about me.

There's a layer of sweat over my skin already. I cup a hand over my eyes and use my other hand to fan myself, trying to minimise the damage the sweat will do to my makeup.

Nick, John, and Eric are off to the side, huddled in a small group, laughing and talking amongst themselves. I turn my back to them, half-hoping they won't notice me. I'm worried Nick might ask to sit with me on the bus.

In my mind, it made sense to *not* have the conversation I need to with Nick before this weekend, in an attempt to make the whole situation less awkward. Now I'm realising that was probably a dumb decision.

Jess is off to the side, standing with Rianna and a few other girls I remember from school. I avoid her stare and chew my thumb.

"What are you and Harley doing?" Belle asks.

I sigh, scuffing my shoe into the ground. "Good question."

"It doesn't have to be hard, you know," Belle says. "Just do what you want to do. Don't worry about anyone else."

"You make it sound easy."

"It can be."

"Last time I did that, my world got turned upside down." I adjust my hair and slide my glasses further up my nose. Belle and I have talked about this a lot this week. "It's not fair of me to turn Nick down again, after he stopped things with Jess for me."

"Because it's totally fair sneaking around behind his back."

I flinch at her tone and her face softens. She touches my arm, giving me a small, apologetic smile. I've been keeping Belle up to date with my life. It's nice to have someone to talk to. Usually, I bottle everything up to the point I explode. I'm trying not to do that anymore.

"Okay everyone!" Shannon calls out, waving her hand. "One minute before the bus leaves, make sure you have everything ready!"

Nick notices me and waves. I wave back and abruptly turn again, hoping he won't come talk to me. I'm feeling all kinds of anxious about him enough as it is.

I do a last-minute check that I have all my essential items. Everyone is shuffling into a line, when a truck pulls in. We all turn to stare as Brennon and Harley step out of it. There's a murmur amongst the girls in front of us and Belle breaks from me to greet them.

Harley's eyes shift to mine and my face breaks into a smile before I can stop it. I pull my attention away and when I face the front, Nick is watching me with a frown.

# Chapter Thirty-Six

## Josie

### Four years ago

I blink, reality sinking in.

My mind keeps replaying Harley's hands on me last night, his body on top of mine, kissing me all over, breathing in my ear. I had wanted it for so long and it had been everything I imagined and more.

I'm in love with Harley Caldwell. It's finally time to admit that and do something about it.

I've showered, dressed, and just plopped down onto the lounge with a hot chocolate in my hand, when I check my phone. My stomach drops when I see the number of notifications blowing up my screen.

Pulling up the Facebook app, I click on the latest comments, growing more nauseous with each moment.

**Harley and Josie!?!?!**
**Oh my God … isn't she dating Nick?**

**That's nasty … not even their bed**
**Dating two guys at once … slut much?**
**Girl, get some class**
**Dude … not cool, could have at least blurred faces**
**Here for the comments**
**Lmao, can't wait for her parents to see this**

I blink slowly down at the screen. I stare at my hands, count my fingers, and pinch myself. This has to be a nightmare. When everything stays as it is, my eyes swivel back to the phone. The room spins.

Rushing to the bathroom, I throw up. I'm shaky as I sit back, leaning on the wall for support. I pull up the video.

The room lighting isn't great, but you can clearly see who is in the video. I'm against the door and Harley collects me in his arms. We stumble onto the bed.

I throw up again.

No, no, no. This can't be happening.

I can't peel my eyes away. I watch in stunned horror, the moments I've been relishing, being aired all over social media.

Every kiss, every touch, broadcasted for all my classmates—and whoever else—to see.

The video plays twice before I force myself to exit it. I scroll to the top, to see what account it was posted from.

**Harley Caldwell:** *Posted Twelve Hours Ago*

**They call me Mr. Steal Your Girl for a reason, right @Nicholas Schneider? Shit was fun while it lasted. Hey @Josephine Mayor let's do it again sometime.**

*Twelve hours ago.*

This video was posted *twelve fucking hours* ago. And not only that, *my* account *and* Nick's were tagged in it. As fast as my fingers can move, I report the video. I don't know how it hasn't been taken down yet. Harley's body blocks the camera from seeing most of my private parts, which is probably why. It's still child pornography though, even if most of the bits are covered.

This isn't real. This isn't real. This isn't real.

I'm sick all over again.

# Chapter Thirty-Seven

## Josie

The trip was hot and long. There was a tension in the air. I'm not sure if anyone else felt it, but by the wandering eyes of Harley and the narrowed gaze of Nick, I'd guess I wasn't not the only one.

A swirling sense of nausea sat deep in my stomach the entire drive. I kept reliving old memories. I was so determined to come back here and make up for all my past mistakes. And yet, I've let myself fall into old habits. Habits I wanted so desperately to shake, but can't seem to.

Some days, I wonder what the hell I'm doing letting this boy into my heart again. And then others, I resign to the fact that I have no control over it.

Shannon tried her best to pump up the group by yelling out encouraging words and playing classic pop songs we all know and love. When we get to the hotel to check in, I suddenly feel like I'm on a school camp without the teachers.

Belle and I share a room. It's small, offering one double bed, a bathroom and a mini-fridge. It has plain décor, with a pale bedspread and a black and white framed painting hanging on the wall.

We split off into our own groups for the afternoon. Belle and I travel to the local shopping centre. We spend the first thirty minutes in Max Brenner, a café well-known for their amazing chocolate selection. We share half-a-dozen chocolate coated strawberries and a mocha each.

"God, I've missed good food." I grin. "You don't get this in Fern Grove."

"You do not," she agrees with a smile, running her tongue over her lips, getting every last bit of the chocolate dust covering them.

We move onto the shops. I breathe freely, the air-conditioning chilling over my bare skin. I haven't felt this nice of a temperature for what feels like months.

"I want to find a nice maxi dress," Belle says. "Something I can wear to, like, a nice lunch."

"I know just the place."

When I find the store I'm after, we both end up trying on several dresses, showing them off to each other on a makeshift runway in the dressing room, ignoring the other random shoppers who keep glancing at us.

"Ten out of ten, baby!" she claps and whistles as I strut past her.

I've never been one to wear long dresses, but I'm surprised to find myself loving the few I tried on. We exit the store, clutching half-filled bags. It feels so nice to be doing something so normal.

"I needed this," I tell her. "More than I realised."

She loops her arm with mine. "Me too."

"I'm so glad I met you," I blurt

She smiles, giving my arm a squeeze.

"I'm going to duck into the book shop really quickly. I'll just be a sec," she says before darting to the small, corner shop with stacks of books out the front. I used to read a lot, but haven't for quite some time now, not including study material. I make a mental note to pick that hobby back up.

I lean onto the wall and rummage through my bags, looking down at my new dresses.

"Hey stranger."

A shiver of excitement sails down my spine at his voice. When I look up, Harley is smiling at me. He has a Boost Juice clutched in his palm. He's dressed in a loose navy shirt and ripped denim shorts, his hair carelessly messy, as usual.

"Fancy seeing you here," I reply.

"Great minds think alike."

"Where's your sidekick?"

He shrugs. "Lost him about ten minutes ago. Yours?"

I jut my chin over his shoulder. "In the book store."

Harley's eyes sweep around him for a moment before he steps closer to me. I feel the heat from him brushing against my skin.

"I'm not sure I'll be able to stay away from you this weekend," he murmurs, tracing his fingertips down the side of my face.

"I'm not sure I'll be able to stay away from you, either," I whisper.

"Maybe we shouldn't."

"I don't want to hurt him."

Harley closes his eyes and exhales. The warmth of his breath feathers over my nose.

"You need to tell him."

"I will." I lean into his hand. "Soon."

"I've heard that before."

"Yeah, and I've been through this with you before, too," I say. "The last time I took a gamble on you, it cost me everything."

His eyes snap open, searching mine. "Josie, there's a lot you don't know about that night—"

"Hey Harley!"

I startle when Belle appears. Harley's hand retracts from my cheek, falling to his side.

He nods at her in greeting.

"Are you with Brennon?" she asks.

"I was. He's here somewhere." He replies. "I'll see you girls later, at the dinner thing."

We meet eyes again as he steps back.

*There's a lot you don't know about that night.*

I feel a little dazed as we finish shopping. My mind is on a continuous loop, thinking back to the night, mulling over details and trying to understand what he meant.

Once back at the hotel, Belle and I share a bottle of champagne as we get ready for dinner. Tonight, our plan is to go out for dinner, and then split off into mini-groups for putt-putt golf. When we gathered in the lobby of the hotel, Shannon called out names of who is in what group for golf. I hid my face in embarrassment. It really *is* like we are on an excursion.

"In Group C," Shannon continues. "We have Belle, Brennon, Harley, and Josie!"

Heads turn our way and I flush. Shannon insisted at the start that it was a random name generator that was sorting who into what groups, but I'm positive she made this one up. I can't help notice that Group A consists of Shannon, John, Nick, and Jess. If Shannon was trying to send me a message, I received it loud and clear.

"Yay!" Belle claps, grinning widely. "The gang is all together."

Nick's eyes narrow at that and I avoid his gaze. I see him from my peripheral vision, coming towards me, so I push through the bodies and slip out the door. I gulp in the cool air, trying to settle my erratic heartbeat.

I'm not ready for our confrontation. Not here, not while we're in this situation. I can't help but think it might be inevitable. And that makes me feel like I'm going to throw up my lunch.

Thankfully, dinner goes by quickly. The chef made our dinner in front of us, making a dramatic show of it, flipping and throwing the food around expertly. It's a performance I've seen many times, having lived in the city for a few years, but it had everyone who never left Fern Grove in awe.

"How was your dinner?" Belle asks the boys when we shuffle into our groups later in the evening.

"Pretty bloody good," Brennon answers.

Harley passes out the putters. His fingers graze mine as he passes the last one over. I want to grab him by the face and kiss him. Everywhere.

"Is it big enough for you?"

"What?" I blink, feeling myself getting lost in those pretty blue eyes.

"The stick." He grins.

I stare down at it, only then realising how small the putters are. "Oh. Sure. It's fine."

"My stick is pretty big. Do you want to try it?" His grin has transformed into a dirty smirk now.

"I've tried it before. I'll give it a pass." I smirk back.

Harley fake scoffs, placing a hand on his chest. "Ouch."

We move to the first hole. The first group has already moved on, with the second group having their last player go.

"Best to beat is two," a girl whose name I can't remember tells us over her shoulder as the group moves on.

"Watch and learn, kids," Brennon says.

I resist the urge to roll my eyes. It's gotten to the point that anything he says, even if it is completely normal, frustrates me. I've had to bite my tongue several times to not start an argument. I can't stand him. Never have, and probably never will. But for Belle's sake, I try to keep a lid on my anger.

Brennon lines himself up and swings, hitting the ball way too hard. It bounces across the green, and over the edge. He curses.

"Did you mean to teach us what *not* to do?" Harley drawls, striding up to the spot.

He readies himself before gently smacking the putter against the ball. Seamlessly, it rolls directly into the hole, with a definite *clink*.

He swings the stick and blows on the putter, as if it is a lit match.

"And that's how it's done."

"Beginner's luck," Brennon mutters.

Belle goes next. As she steps up to the spot, Harley falls back, standing so close our arms brush.

"How badly do you want to ditch this whole thing and go back to my room?" he whispers.

Every hair on my body stands, his smooth voice blasting a hot wave over me.

"Pretty fucking bad."

He makes a sound deep in his throat. "That can be arranged."

My body is on fire by the time I take my turn. I'm shocked that it only takes me two hits to get the ball in, considering my nerves are shot.

Once we've moved to the next hole, I fold my arms over my chest, watching Brennon. Harley lightly plays with the end of my hair. I try my hardest not to think about how close he is, and all the things I want to do to him. And him to me.

He grazes past me when it's his turn.

"The sexual tension between you and Harley is making me uncomfortable," Belle whispers. "It's hard to breathe around you two."

"I have no idea what you're talking about."

Getting through all eighteen holes seems to take the entire night, as there were so many people trying to get through. I'm relieved when we reach the end, calling it a night. I'm desperate to escape back to my room, to have a cold shower and sleep off this overwhelming feeling of lust that is trying to take over my body.

When I crawl into bed later that night, I feel exhausted. I pull the covers over me, sinking into the stiff pillows.

"You're going to fall in love with Harley," Belle whispers, rustling in the bed beside me. "I can see it."

Swallowing, I close my eyes.

I think it's already happened.

# Chapter Thirty-Eight

## Josie

### Four years ago

I can't breathe.

I need the ground to swallow me up. I can't exist anymore. How can I possibly face anyone again? The views and the shares made the walls close in around me.

My legs tremble with each step. Mum and Dad are in the backyard, Dad is whipper snipping the yard edges, and Mum is raking leaves that have dropped from our frangipani tree.

They don't know. God, I hope they never see it.

Heavy footsteps descend down the stairs. My face is a mess when I turn to see Sam staring at me, his phone in his hand.

"Josie," he says. "What the fuck …"

"How could he do that to me?" I whisper.

"Because he is Harley fucking Caldwell!" he shouts at me. "What the bloody hell were you thinking? That guy is the worst guy in town! You …" My face crumples and I collapse into the dining chair, sobs tearing from my body. "Shit, hey, shh …" Sam says awkwardly, taking the seat adjacent to me. "Look, sorry, I'm just shocked. I can't believe it."

My hands shield my face. I can't bring myself to see Sam's face.

"What about Nick?" he asks. "Nick is the best person I know. How could you …"

I cry harder.

"I've reported it. I assume you have. Facebook will have to take it down. It's …" He swallows, discontinuing his sentence. "They will. Soon, I'm sure."

Pulling from the table, I dash out the door. My eyes are full with heavy tears.

My first stop is Nick. A little manically, I drive over to his house, hardly able to suck in air the entire time. I rush up the stairs. The front door swings open before I get the chance to knock. Nick's mother steps outside, nostrils flared, her eyes in slits.

"Josie," Annabeth snarls. "Come to do more damage to my son?"

Everything inside me sinks.

"You were never enough for my Nick," she spits at me, her eyes blazing. "You've always been bad news. I knew it all along. How *could* you?" She steps closer, hands curled into fists. "We welcomed you into this family. Nick *adored* you."

"He will understand—"

"He loses all sense of rationale when it comes to you."

"I just need to talk to him—" my voice is pleading, but she cuts me off.

"You will *not* speak to him!" Her voice is sharp and I step back as if she has slapped me. "You will leave him alone." A vein throbs in her temple as she takes another step. I feel my heels reach the edge of the porch. "*Leave*. Leave this town and *never* come back. Do everyone a favour."

Her mousy hair whips around her shoulders as she turns. She steps inside and slams the door behind her. My entire body is shaking violently. I can't feel my legs as I stiffly walk back to the car.

Robotically, I open the door, but before I move to take a seat, my eyes travel up to Nick's window. He is staring back at me.

My hand flings to my mouth. I try to convey everything I'm feeling in my eyes. With a dark look, he shoves the curtains across the window and disappears behind it.

I'm cold as I slide behind the wheel, tears blurring my vision. I can barely see as I drive. In a dizzying panic, I drive to Elise's house. Elise is out the front by the time the car stops.

"Elise," I whisper. "I just went to—"

"You can't be here, Josie."

"What?"

Elise's face is hard. She hugs herself, taking in my tear-stained cheeks and ratty hair. I'm still in my pyjamas, I realise.

"My parents are here. They've seen it."

My eyes close. I feel my chest contracting, but there's no air inside my lungs.

"How could you do that to Nick?" She barks at me. "How long has this been going on?"

"A few months."

When I open my eyes, Elise's jaw is swinging. "*Months?*"

"I was going to break it off with Nick … Today, actually …" I drag the back of my hand across my nose. "I can't believe Harley would do this to me …"

"Well. It's Harley."

I scoff. "Yeah? And Brennon is a fucking angel, isn't he?"

Elise flinches. "Brennon might not be perfect, but he wouldn't do what Harley did. And I wouldn't do what you did." She shakes her head. My heart splinters when I see the look of disgust on her face. "What you have done to Nick is unforgivable."

There's a ringing in my ears. Her mouth is moving, but I can no longer hear her. Elise turns and walks away.

Everything is spinning. My head is light.

Little did I know, that was the last time I would see my best friend.

I must have left Harley fourteen voicemails. I drove to his house, but it seemed no one was home, not even his parents. I search everywhere for him. I call over and over, trying to get through. After over twenty missed calls, his phone ends up going to voicemail. He's either blocked my number, or switched off his phone.

When I get back to the house, my parents, and Sam are sitting at the dining table. There's a heavy, suffocating silence. The air is thick and when I enter, I see it on their faces.

They know.

# Chapter Thirty-Nine

## *Josie*

**B**elle and I lazed on the beach for the better part of the morning. Eric, John, and Nick joined us and thankfully, it wasn't awkward. We tanned, swam, and ran around, like we were teenagers again.

When Nick reached for my hand under the water, I felt a startling chill in my bones, reminding me that this is all going to come to an end soon. I'm going to hurt him, one way or the other.

After eating lunch by the water, Belle and I retired to the room to drink, dance, and get ready for the night out. I've had a blast. Escaping from my thoughts for a day has been refreshing.

The afternoon passes in a blur and soon, we're stumbling down the stairs to meet everyone in the lobby. It seems like we are the last to arrive. Our heels clip in a loud echo around the room as we descend the stairs.

I'm dressed in a red dress that is sticking to my body like second skin. It has a deep neckline, showing off a lot of my chest. I've matched it with nude heels and dangly, gold earrings. To finish the look, my hair is in waves down my shoulders and my lips are coated in a bright, red lipstick.

Belle had gone with a plainer look, a pale, sleeveless dress which is longer at the back than the front. Her hair is pulled into a high pony, showering off her slender neck and delicate collarbones.

It's starkly clear that we have lived in the city, considering none of the other girls are dressed up as much as we are and suddenly, I wonder if I've overdone it.

"Wow, you girls look incredible!" Shannon grins.

"As do you!" Belle smiles.

Nick and Harley both go to walk over to me at the same time, causing them to bump shoulders. They glower at each other and I sigh, exchanging a glance with Belle.

This is going to be a long night.

I feel good.

*Really* good.

The music is loud—so loud, my ears hurt—with the ground and the walls shaking around me. Belle and I jump around, lights flashing so bright there's dots across my eyes. We shout the lyrics so loud our throats turn raw.

Sweat gathers over my forehead as we loop arms, spinning each other around. I feel delirious. Drunk on life, drunk on this moment. I haven't had this much fun in … possibly ever. I've been out, I've partied a lot, but it hasn't ever been like this.

My eyes scan the dark club, looking for my favourite pair of eyes. The room spins and I blink slowly, trying to let the world right itself.

There.

Harley is leaning onto a table, slowly spinning a glass in his hand, his eyes drinking in every move my body makes.

My feet propel me forward. He meets me halfway and my fingers slide into his. He's dressed in a white shirt that is so thin, I can see his dark tattoos underneath it. The light flashes red over his skin, giving him a devilish glow.

The palms of my hands soak into his chest and run down his stomach, feeling every bit of hard muscle.

A slow smile spreads over his handsome face.

"Josie," he murmurs, and I somehow can hear him, despite the thundering music pulsing in the air. "Hey."

"Dance with me."

I pull him after me. There are bodies crammed on the dance floor, twisting and gyrating to the music. I slip my arms around his neck, flushing our bodies together. I feel the sweat through his shirt.

My body slides down his and I bounce on the floor, before shimmying back up. Every line of my body pressing into his. His hands find my waist before sinking over my backside, bunching up the fabric. I move my hips, loving the feel of his fingers catching the movement.

Right now, I forget about everything. I forget the eyes on us. It's Harley, me, and the music.

Harley's eyes devour my skin as I step back and spin, throwing my head back as he yanks me close again. His scent fills my nose, intoxicating me.

He is so beautiful. So warm. My head feels light as I gaze up at him.

"I need you, Josie," he says in a choked voice, eyes burning into mine, his breath stifling hot over my skin.

"Then take me."

Closing his hands around my face, he kisses me.

Harley kisses me so hard, my head dips back at the pressure. His tongue slides against mine, sending a fury of electric bolts through me. My entire body throbs to be closer to him. He gathers my dress in his hands, plastering me to his body, until we can't possibly be any closer.

My fingers sink into his thick hair. He smells, tastes, and feels so delicious and perfect. It's making me dizzy.

His hands tug and grip me, exploring expertly in all the right places. I moan into him, the desire to be alone, in a bed, somewhere far from here, consuming me.

And then I hear it.

*Her.*

Jess calling out to Nick.

Icy cold liquid bursts through me and I launch myself away from Harley. I'm hot everywhere, and disorientated. My eyes adjust to the flickering lights as I see Nick disappearing through the side door.

"Wait!" I try to shout, but it comes out as a slur. I fumble for my bag the strap having slipped off my shoulder.

"Josie," Harley says, fingers curling around my bicep. His skin burns mine and it takes all of my self-control to detach myself from him. "Don't."

"I said I didn't want to hurt him," I cry.

"If you go after him, then you're hurting me."

His eyes are pleading with mine. Those gorgeous, baby blues.

"I'm sorry."

I stumble, weaving between sweaty bodies, until I reach the exit. The cool night air slaps harshly at my face as I burst through the door.

Nick is striding away. I call out to him. At first, he kept walking, until I shouted his name again. He whirls around and suddenly, his face is right in front of mine.

"What!?" He snaps so viciously, I jump back a step. "What do you *want?*"

Words stick inside my throat as if I've just swallowed a tube of super glue. Nothing comes out when I open my mouth.

"Hmm?" he presses, stepping closer again. "What do you want, Josie? Because for the life of me, I can't figure it out."

"I'm sorry," I whisper. "I'm so sorry, Nick. It wasn't supposed to come out like that—"

His face blanches, his lips spreading into a thin line.

"Come out like that?" he demands. "As in, this has been going on beyond tonight?"

I feel small. So incredibly small. My insides sink slow and heavily.

"Jesus Christ." He runs a hand through his hair. "I'm not enough. I'm never fucking enough for you."

"Nick ..."

"Why him?" he growls. "Why that fucking prick?" I flinch. Nick never curses. Hell, I've barely heard him ever insult anyone. He's Good Guy Nick. "After what he did to you? How could you forgive him?"

"The same way you forgave me," I murmur.

He breathes hard for a moment. "Yeah. Well. Look where that got me."

"I'm sorry, Nick. I didn't want this to happen. I wanted to hate him ... I just ..."

"I can't believe I'm going down this road with you again. After all this time, you're still the same self-centred brat you always were."

The air leaves my lungs. I blink up at him with sodden lashes. My entire face is soaked from tears I didn't even know were falling.

"I wish you never came back," he snarls.

He spins, striding away from me. I try to breathe, but no air enters my mouth. I press a hand to my stomach, feeling everything twist painfully inside me.

"He's right, you know," a voice says. "You only want what you can't have and then when you get it, it's still not enough."

Jess steps in front of me, the light from the streetlamp casting a yellow glow over her. She looks taller, and I glance down at the gigantic heels she is in.

"Yeah?" I straighten, my eyes narrowing. "And how does it feel always being second best to me? Even when I was fucking *gone* you were second best."

As soon as the words leave my mouth, I feel disgusted with myself. Jess' jaw ticks for a moment, her fists clenched. She steps forward and jabs a finger so close to me, I feel the whoosh of air fan over my nose.

"You may have changed everything on the outside, but it doesn't change how ugly you are on the inside," she snaps, stomping past me, in the direction Nick disappeared.

I feel the venom of her insult slither through my veins, hitting a little too close to home. My stomach cramps painfully.

I still haven't caught my breath when I stagger back into the club, remembering at the last moment to wipe my face. As I slip inside the door, my heart stops.

A pair of dark eyes stare back at me. I blink a few times, trying to get the tall figure leaning on the bar to come into focus, but when my vision finally clears, he is no longer there.

It can't have been him.

Elliot.

My eyes roam wildly around the room, searching, but after a minute, I realise I must have imagined it.

"Are you okay?" Belle grips my shoulders, peering up at me.

"Where is he?"

She pauses for a moment before pointing over to a table. I hurry over to him and touch my hand to his back. He turns, glaring at me.

"Harley—"

"Nope."

"Please, Harley—"

"No, fuck this." He shakes me off. "You left me. Again. For him."

"Harley, I told you I didn't want to hurt him—"

"Who came over to who? Who pulled who onto the dance floor?"

"I know, I know." I cradle my head between my hands, a deep ache pulsing behind my eyes. "I just didn't want this to go down like this. I'm a fucking mess."

Harley's face softens slightly. He sighs.

"I need to get out of here. I need to think."

"About us?"

"About everything."

"Don't leave me."

Harley laughs and it's a sharp, flinching bark. I step back and he shakes his head, staring down at me.

"I asked you that exact thing. You looked me in the eyes and chased after another guy." He pulls away from me and stalks out the door.

My throat closes on itself. No air, in or out.

"What a shit show."

Brennon shoots me a wolfish grin over his drink before he takes a sip.

I glare back at him. Furious. Confused. Drunk. I take a steadying breath before speaking.

"This won't last long." I bite back. "You and Belle. She will realise what a piece of shit you are and then she will be gone. Just like Elise."

Brennon's grip tightens on his drink and he slams it onto the table. Liquid sloshes over the side, spilling across the table. In two strides, he is around the table, leaning close to me, his hot, stale breath plastering across my face.

"I've always hated you. You're a precious little bitch, and much more trouble than you're worth." Little bits of spit fly from the corner of his mouth. Involuntarily, I lean away from him. "I don't regret what I did to you. Not for a second."

"And what's that?"

"Leaked your sex tape."

Everything inside me freezes. The music is blaring, people are swerving around us, but everything else is in standstill. There's a ringing in my ears as I look up at his filthy smirk.

"That's right." He grins. "I filmed you. I posted it. It was all *me*."

Everything is slow, and stuck in time. My mind can't catch up with what he is saying.

"I had it set up. A little surprise I was doing for Elise. But then she pissed me off, and Rianna came to find me, and it all happened so fast. I forgot about the camera. When I found it later"—he lets out a dry cackle—"I couldn't believe it. Princess Josie, getting her hands dirty. I was going to show it to Harley, have a laugh about it, but then I remembered what you said to me that night." He leans in close, so close that I can smell the stale beer on his breath. "Do you remember what you said? Do you remember throwing that drink at me?"

I remember every fucking second of the night. Clearly. *Too* clearly.

"So I posted it. I went on Harley's phone after he fell asleep and shared it." He sends me a wicked gleam. "I hid it from his timeline. It was hilarious, watching him be so oblivious, when the internet was blowing up over the biggest scandal the town had ever seen." He rolls the sleeve of his shirt up, unable to resist showing the satisfied smirk on his face. "He was so drunk by the end of the night, I told him that we posted it together. He kept saying he wouldn't do that. Of course he didn't. Harley is a good guy." He shrugs. "I said the lie so many times, I even started to believe it. Hell, I think eventually he did too."

His words whirl around inside my mind.

*Harley didn't do it.*

"You ran me out of town." My voice is a mere whisper. "It was all *you*."

"All me." He leans onto the table, clasping his fingers together. "I told myself to never say it out loud, but God, seeing your face." A sadistic smile stretches across his face. "Definitely worth it."

Everything is too loud. It's all too much.

"I kept thinking … how am I going to be able to get rid of you this time?" he asks, lips tilting. "But it looks like you've done that all by yourself."

# Chapter Forty

## Josie

### *Four years ago*

It only takes me a day to pack my life into two suitcases and an overstuffed duffel bag. My car is filled, my first two weeks of rent have been paid for a small apartment located in the suburbs of Brisbane.

The house is silent and still when I creep down the stairs. I'm out the door and in my car in a blink.

When I pull out of my driveway, I watch my home shrink in the reflection of the rear-view mirror.

I am *never* coming back.

# Chapter Forty-One

### Harley

My throat burns as I gulp down drink after drink.

One step forward, three steps back. That seems to be how it is with Josie.

The music is so loud, it rattles the walls. I finish my drink and pick up my next one, having bought three at the same time. I watch the bodies move and weave against each other. I try to rid the taste of her from my mouth, but it doesn't work. She's intoxicating—having embedded herself into my body, mind, and soul.

When a pretty redhead saunters in my direction, I finish my drink, and leave the table. As much as I'd love to hurt Josie as much as she has hurt me, I can't even look at another woman. She's it for me. She always has been. My stomach feels sore and cramped from the alcohol and anxiety sizzling through my body.

The fresh air hits me with a blast as I stumble outside. I find somewhere quiet and pull out a cigarette.

When my phone rings, I wonder if it's Josie. Disappointment

sinks inside my chest when I see Brennon's name appear on the screen. Shoving the phone back into my pocket, I continue smoking, gazing out in front of me, watching people stumble past me in gigantic heels, flashy dresses, talking, and laughing. I wish I could share their joy.

After I finish, I head into a bar and order another drink before drifting over to the pool tables. I end up playing a few rounds with some random guys. After a while, I reluctantly return to the hotel.

Not being able to get our fight off my mind, I give in and dial her number. Straight to voicemail. Groaning, I toss my phone back into my pocket, and march up to her room. I bang on the door, not caring how loud I am.

A yawning Belle opens the door, rubbing her mascara-messed eyes.

"Harley?"

"Where is she?"

Belle shrugs. "Not here."

Everything inside me tenses.

"What do you mean she's not here?"

"She's gone."

All the air leaves my lungs. I've heard those words before. I can't go through that again.

"Gone?" I whisper. Her face softens at my panic-stricken face.

"She texted me saying Sam picked her up. He's taking her home."

Exhaling, I feel a little less sick. *Okay. That means she's safe and she's going home. She hasn't fled again. Not like last time.*

"Right. Okay …" I trail off. "That's great."

"I know," she sighs. "What a mess."

"Yeah."

"You really love her, huh?"

I stiffen. *Love.* Of course I've always known that's what this is. I've never experienced anything like this before. This overwhelming, soul-crushing feeling that is constantly threatening to destroy me.

"She's my girl."

Belle smiles sadly. "I hope it works out for you. She loves you, too. You're meant to be."

My heart squeezes painfully.

"Well. Thanks. Sorry I woke you."

"S'okay," she mumbles, sniffing, rubbing the back of her sleeve against her nose. "See you in the morning."

"Night."

The door shuts with a distinct click. Slowly, I make my way back to the room. Pushing a hand through my hair, I lean on the wall, not quite ready to deal with Brennon yet. I've dodged his calls and texts all night.

Exhaustion rolled through my body, but with this much on my mind, I doubt I'll get a moment of rest. Sighing, I open the door, filling with dread.

"Where the fuck have you been?" Brennon snaps.

Exhaling, my head pounds.

Here we go.

# Chapter Forty-Two

## Josie

**M**y forehead presses against the glass of the passenger side of my brother's car.

Without a word, I fled the night club and ran back to the hotel. I packed my things and called Sam, who begrudgingly agreed to come rescue me from this horror show of a trip, even though it's a very long drive for him. I didn't text Belle until I was on the road, in fear she might hunt me down and try to talk me out of it.

"Well. Sounds like a fun night." Sam grins.

I groan, pressing my head further into the glass, the vibrations from the glass hurting, but simultaneously seeming to sober me up.

"Why are you smiling like that?" I huff.

"So much drama. I love it."

I glare at him.

"What?" he asks innocently. "Can't I live vicariously through you?"

"You can, if you didn't enjoy it so much," I mutter.

His grin widens. "Come on, you knew this was coming. You needed to bite the bullet with Nick, but you wimped out."

"Aren't you supposed to be trying to make me feel better?"

"You denied me four years of bullying. I need to cram it all in now."

I roll my eyes, flinging my head back. "My life is so tragic."

"It's sort of exciting," he says. "People would do anything to have the kind of chemistry you and Harley have."

Shifting in my seat, I lean back on the door and face my brother. His long hair is unruly, falling over his face. He sweeps it back before placing his hand back on the wheel. I study his face for a moment.

"When am I going to meet him?"

Sam's hands tighten around the steering wheel. His eyes dart to me for a moment.

"What?"

"When am I going to meet your boyfriend?"

The silence feels thick between us and I clasp my hands together as I wait.

"H-how …" He clears his throat. "How did you know?"

"Please. When I forced you to watch *Gossip Girl*, you weren't watching it for the plot."

"Nate Archibald has a great ass," he agrees and when he smiles, it's the purest smile I've ever seen on his face.

I let out a snort. "Seriously though, I just knew. For ages. I waited for you to say something. You never did."

"Well. I can't imagine Dad will take it well. The whole thing has been eating me up."

"Sometimes we have to do things for ourselves, even if the ones we love don't agree with it."

Sam glances at me, a thoughtful expression on his face.

"Like you did."

I nod. He exhales, throwing another hand through his hair.

"His name is Kaleb. He lives a couple of towns over. We met at a rodeo one night. He's really great, Josie. You'd like him."

"I'd love to meet him," I say.

"Really?" he brightens at my words.

"Really. Name a time and a place, I'll be there."

Leaning over, Sam clutches my hand, giving it a gentle squeeze.

And just like that, those four years apart are forgotten. Dad might still not be talking to me, but at least things are right with my brother.

I don't leave my bed until well after lunch time the following day, and if I could, I would have stayed there permanently.

Anxiety has settled into my veins, making my mind painfully analyse every moment and word exchanged on Saturday night.

The bus is due to arrive back into town at four p.m. today. I've switched my phone off, since Belle has been trying to ring me over and over. I don't want to see if either Nick or Harley has reached out. I know they would have been alarmed when I didn't show up the next morning when the group regathered, but honestly, I can't even think about it all right now. I couldn't show my face there the next morning and sit on that bus with everyone staring and whispering.

Groaning, after I shower, I flop back onto my bed and throw my pillow over my face. I wish I could sleep for five years.

After spending the afternoon binge-watching Netflix, I force myself to order food and walk down town. The fresh air will do me good.

When I enter the pub, a heavy wave of muggy heat hits my face. When she notices me, the girl disappears to fetch my order. I lean on the counter, rifling through my bag for my debit card, when the door creaks open.

I feel his presence before I see him.

His eyes settle on me and we stare at each other. He must have gone straight to work after getting back home from the trip. He looks as bad as I feel.

275

"Here you go!" The girl chirps.

"Thanks."

I take the bag from her and turn my back to Harley. I don't release my breath until I'm a few metres away.

Once I'm home, I switch my phone back on. I sit on the lounge and listen to the vibrations as it turns back on. I numbly eat my food, staring at the wall. When the buzzing finally stops, I lean over and look at it.

Several missed calls from Belle. Texts from Harley asking me where I am and that he is worried.

And one more.

From Elliot. In the chaos that is my life, Elliot had honestly been at the back of my mind.

**Elliot:** See you soon, Josie.

# Chapter Forty-Three

## Josie

I lay in bed with the fan on full blast as I gaze up at the ceiling.

*See you soon, Josie*

*See you soon, Josie*

*See you soon, Josie*

Those words swirl violently in my mind, making me feel nauseous. What does he mean, *see you soon*? Panic wells inside me at the thought. Like I have all night, I repeat the moment I entered the club after the fight with Nick in my mind.

He was there. But he couldn't have been. The night club we went to was a very popular spot, one I *have* been to with Elliot on numerous occasions. But was he really there, the very night I was? If he was, surely, he would have flagged me down? Said something?

I was hysterical, drunk, with my eyes full of tears, when I thought I saw him. When I blinked, there was no one there.

I groan, throwing my arm across my face. My mind has been circling around this all night. I feel exhausted, but sleep won't come.

And it is way too fucking hot in here. Like always.

When there's a knock at my door, I startle so bad that I hit my head on my bedframe. Nervously, I get to my feet and pad through the room. My hands won't stop trembling.

Harley's face hovers outside the glass and I let out a shaky breath of relief.

I unlock the door, letting him inside. His eyes glance down to my bare legs.

"Hey."

"Hey," I say.

I reach up and curl my arms around him, pulling him to me. He sinks into my body, hugging me back.

"I'm sorry."

"I know," he says. "Me too."

"I'm so glad you're here."

When I release him, I stand on my tiptoes and kiss him, dragging him towards the bed. He kicks his shoes off and yanks his shirt over his head.

"You left."

"Yeah," I whisper. "I made such a mess of things."

"You can't do that."

"Do what?"

"Pack your things and leave without a word," he croaks. "That's the second time you've done that to me. When you disappear like that and don't reply …" He swallows, hands gripping my face tenderly. "You scared the shit out of me, Josie."

I push my body into his, lying my cheek on his chest.

"I'm always in flight mode," I murmur. "I never stop long enough to consider other people's feelings."

"You can't do that to me, Josie. Not anymore."

My finger draws patterns over his chest and I feel the steady rhythm of his chest rising and falling.

"Okay," I say. "I won't."

"Okay."

"Harley," I begin. "When you said there's a lot I don't know about *that night*, do you mean that Brennon was the one who posted the video?"

I feel him stiffen. "What?"

"He told me."

Harley stares into the darkness for a moment before he shifts so that we are facing each other.

"I don't remember the end part of that night very clearly. For years he insisted we posted it together, although I had no memory of it. I was sure I wouldn't have done that to you. But I couldn't remember." He blows out a breath. "He convinced me we did it together. But a few times he would say something about you. A passing comment, but it always stuck with me. The way he said it, *what* he said. It made me question a lot. But I had no way of fact-checking anything."

"I don't believe that you would have done that to me, Harley," I say. "I can honestly say that now. For years and years I did, but now ..." I move my hand so that I gently cup his face. "I know you. I know you couldn't have done that."

He kisses my hand softly.

"And I'm sorry for never hearing you out. I let myself be run out of this town."

"We both made mistakes."

"What do we do now?"

"Well." His hands slide over my hips and he pulls me onto him. "I want you to say yes."

"Say yes?"

"To being my girlfriend." He smiles. "My first ever."

I smile down at Harley, my bare thighs straddling his waist.

"Yes." I whisper. "I'll be your girlfriend."

"And Nick?" he questions.

"I will have to have a conversation with Nick," I sigh. "And apologise. Again."

His warm hands travel up my thighs.

"And you?" I press. "What are you going to do about Brennon?"

His grip on me tightens as he pulls me closer.

"I'll fucking kill him for what he did to you."

The next morning, when I wake up in Harley's arms, I realise that *this* is what is important and everything else is just background noise.

The soft rise and fall of his chest, his dark hair blanketing his eyes, his arm possessively wrapped over me. It's a comfort I'm quickly coming to crave. I feel safe. *Happy.*

"Good morning," he murmurs. "You're staring."

"Harley Caldwell," I whisper. "My boyfriend."

His eyes sleepily open and he gives me a lazy smile.

"Josie Mayor," his voice is deep and raspy from sleep. "My girl-friend."

"Who would ever have predicted it?" I smile.

"Me. In my dreams. For five fucking years."

An embarrassing, girlish giggle escapes me and his grin widens. He pinches my cheek and I nuzzle my face into his hand.

"I need to shower."

His eyes drift to my lips. "Hmm."

"Hmm?"

"A shower sounds nice."

His eyes travel down my neck, to my chest. I feel the air leaving my body as his eyes move further. Slowly, I push to my feet. I peel my shirt off and let it fall to the floor. Harley bites his bottom lip as he groans. Smiling sweetly, I slide out of my underwear and leave it also on the floor, as I strut towards the shower.

The pipes hum and groan as the shower starts up. I leave the door slightly ajar, my heart beating so hard I might collapse.

I'm inhaling hard and fast when a shadow falls over the door. It creaks open and I feel his presence fill the room. Clothes fall to the floor in soft thuds as the door opens. Harley steps in behind me. I feel his breath hot on my skin.

Goosebumps ripple over my skin and he steps closer, his hands falling to my waist. My head feels so light I fear it's going to detach from my body and float away. His lips press into my shoulder, warm and soft.

"You smell amazing," he whispers.

He pulls me into his chest and I feel all of him, hard and firm against my body. I suck in a sharp breath. He presses himself further into me as his lips travel down my back. His hands grip my backside, squeezing me in all the right places.

He turns me, icy eyes meeting mine way before dropping to my chest. His hands cup over my breasts and I softly moan, loving the feel of his strong hands on me. He cups them gently before taking one of them into his mouth. I lean into the cold tiles behind me, my eyes closing. His tongue laps over my nipple teasingly.

"Do you still hate me?" he asks teasingly, his smirk curving his lips.

"Yes," I whisper, smiling.

"How much?"

"So fucking much," I whimper.

His mouth moves down to my stomach. I widen my stance, allowing him access between my legs. The feel of his tongue is just as good as I remember and just as addictive. I throw my head back, smacking into the tiles so hard dots dance across my eyes.

"Oh," I groan.

"Sweetheart?"

A betraying whimper leaves me. I love hearing that word fall from his mouth. While that mouth is on *me*.

When Harley stands again, his mouth crashes onto mine. I snake my arms around the back of his hand, our chests sliding together, slippery from the water. I feel his hardness. I grip it in my hand and he hisses into my mouth. I grind myself over the tip and his hands tighten.

He kisses down my neck, across my chest, my hand moving faster and expertly over him. He groans into me. Heavy breathing fills the small space around us as I try to think. I want this so bad. I have for a long time.

I stand on my tiptoes and guide him between my legs. I push myself onto him and gasp as he fills me.

"Oh," I whisper, feeling my insides stretch.

Harley looks like he might physically be in pain. His face crumples in pleasure and agony.

"Oh, fuck, Josie," he moans, and he hasn't even started moving yet. "Are you on birth control?"

"Yes."

"Good, because it would be impossible for me to stop right now," he groans.

"I forgot how good this is," I whisper as he pushes inside me further. "How good *you* feel."

"I've dreamt of this, Josie," he pants. "Every night. This moment." He tenses, his hand softly gripping my neck. "I'm not going to last three seconds."

A loud bang startles us both so much we bump foreheads.

"Josie?" I hear Nick's voice float through the door. "You awake?"

My eyes widen in alarm.

"Oh my God," I whisper.

"Josie?" Nick's voice again.

Suddenly, a wicked smirk takes over Harley's face and he suddenly thrusts into me. I yelp in surprise—and pleasure—as he pushes further inside me.

"Harley!" I gasp as he thrusts harder into me.

"Josie?" Nick tries again. "You there?"

Nick knocks again and Harley pumps inside of me, hard, and fast. My eyes roll back into my head. It's just like before—exciting and scandalous.

My fingers scrape down Harley's back, biting into him, slipping every so often from the movements and the water. My phone starts to ring.

"I hear your phone," Nick says. "Look, I said things I regret the other night and I'm sorry. Please, just talk to me."

My fingernails bite viciously into his shoulders as my clit pulses. It's been far too long being deprived of this. Of him. The world spins, even after my eyes drift closed.

With one hand at my throat, he drags his thumb over my pelvic bone and swipes it over my clit. I bite my tongue in an attempt not to cry out at the sensation as he thrusts deeper into me, simultaneously pressing and circling my clit. He slams into me over and over, his grip on my throat tightening deliciously as his mouth moves messily across my lips and my jaw.

Almost aggressively, he pushes me against the wall and slides out of me. I feel his arm shaking as he steps back.

"What are you doing?" I almost want to cry at the lack of feeling.

"You know why it's always been me and you?" he whispers.

"Tell me," I whimper.

"Green lawns, white picket fences, and a big family," he grunts. "You don't want that. You don't want a gentleman who holds open the car door for you, who picks you up flowers before a date."

Gripping my hips, Harley spins me around and yanks me back towards him.

"You want someone to live an exciting life with you. To try new things. To travel. To *live*." His hands grip my hips. "You want someone to fuck you until you scream." My insides turn to scorching liquid at his words. "And that someone is me."

I bend forward, hands slipping against the tiles as he pushes back into me. A strange sound mixed between a moan, and a whimper escapes me as he relentlessly drills into me. His hand slips down the front of me. He slaps his finger onto my clit at the same time he rotates his hips, almost shattering my insides.

Breathing out hard, I try to remember that Nick is at the door, but the only thing I can hear is our bodies coming together.

I feel the orgasm rising. I clench my thighs together and he pants into my ear. "Ah, fuck."

It's the hottest thing I've ever heard.

My orgasm flares inside me, and I sink my teeth into my own arm to quieten the scream that bursts through me. Harley sinks further into me as a guttural groan rips through him. A blast of hot air blows by my ear as he thrusts into me hard one last time before sagging against me.

He kisses my shoulder, lazily inching up my neck, and lastly kissing my hairline. Slowly, he pulls out of me and I wince a little, knowing I will be sore—the best kind of sore—and turn to face him.

"Josie?" Nick's voice is so far away, so far in the back of my mind, I barely hear it.

Harley kisses me. It's soft and tender, nothing like the hungry, angry kisses we often share. I can see in his eyes how much he cares for me.

"Josie," Harley whispers. He kisses me again. I feel so light-headed and disorientated. "Please tell me."

"Tell you what?"

"That you don't hate me," he whispers. "Not truly. Not anymore."

His hands caress me and I struggle to focus on anything else.

"Okay. Well. If you're in there and ready to talk, call me." Nick's voice comes again and somehow in the last three seconds, I'd totally forgotten about him.

"No." I shake my head. "I don't hate you." I place a kiss on his head softly.

"Really?" he whispers.

"Really," I mumble into his mouth. "I don't think I ever really have."

# Chapter Forty-Four

## Harley

### *Four years ago*

A loud bang startles me from my sleep. Wearily, I rub my eyes and sit up, looking around the room. It's bright. Too bright. Wincing, I kick off the covers and scrape myself off the mattress.

I stumble into the shower. My head pulses. I drank too much. Rubbing my face, I lean back against the tiles and let the warm water run over my skin.

The next time I check my phone, the time reads well past lunch time. I sigh. I must have been totally out of it to sleep almost the whole day. Pausing outside the spare room, I listen for any sound of Brennon's parents before I make my way to the lounge room. Brennon is sprawled across the lounge, one leg draping over the arm of it, the television on.

"How ya feeling?" Brennon asks, briefly glancing at me as he reaches into the popcorn bag.

"Like I drank too many tequila shots last night," I groan. My limbs feel heavy and slow. "Why did you insist that was a good idea?"

Brennon grins, shrugging. "It felt right at the time. You were fucking wasted."

Throwing a hand through my hair, I collapse into the recliner. The leg rest flings up with a whoosh sound and I settle in. I didn't want last night to be hazy. I wanted to remember every moment.

Josie's lips kissing down my neck. Her tight body in my hands. How good she felt when I was inside her.

*"It's you. It's always been you."*

I go to send a message to Josie on messenger, but I'm logged out. I hope she isn't mad that it's taken me this long to text her. I go to log in to Facebook, to see that I'm signed out of that as well. Frowning, I enter in my details. It tells me three times that my details are incorrect.

Exhaling, I throw my phone back down. My head hurts too much to look at a screen right now anyway.

"How do you feel?" I ask.

Brennon is clad in baggy pants and a shirt that looks like it might be his Dad's. It has several stains down the front of it. He clears his throat and wipes his hand down his chest.

"Fine. Was a bit crook this morning, but better now that I've eaten."

"Want a coffee?"

"Would love one."

With a push, I get to my feet and pad into the kitchen. Brennon's house is about three times the size of mine. It's not anything too flashy, but it's a hell of a lot nicer than the walls I grew up in.

While I wait for the kettle to boil, I try logging into my other socials. All of them say the same thing. My details are incorrect.

"What the fuck?" I mutter, frowning.

"What?" I hear Brennon call.

Shoving my phone back into my pocket, I carry the two mugs of coffee back to the lounge room.

"Cheers mate," Brennon thanks as he takes it and places it down on the coffee table in front of him. "What's wrong?"

"My phone," I reply, throwing myself back into the chair after I've put my mug down. "It's not letting me log in to any of my accounts. Maybe I've been hacked?"

Brennon raises an eyebrow. "You were drunk as fuck, posting all sorts of weird shit. You might have got logged out for spam, or something."

"What?" I ask, glancing at him. "Posting weird shit? Like what?"

I pull out my phone again. That doesn't really sound like something I would do, but to be fair, I don't really remember the second half of the night. I remember the party, being with Josie, but after that, it's a mixed blur of tequila shots and a joint that clearly rocked me a little too hard.

"You don't remember?" Brennon shoots me a look and I send him a confused one in return. "And by the way, since when have you been fucking Princess Josephine?"

I blink at him. "How do you know about that?"

Brennon scoffs, lazily casting his eyes back towards the television. "You fucking sang it from the rooftop, mate. You really don't remember anything from last night? The thing you posted?"

Leaning forward, I dig my elbows into my thighs. "What the hell are you talking about?"

Brennon rolls his eyes. "Dude, you must have been really out of it."

"I told you about Josie?"

Brennon slowly nods. "Not just me, champ."

My stomach tightens painfully.

*Not just me.*

"I wouldn't have told anyone about it," I say quietly. "Not until she spoke to Nick."

"I can't believe you, man!" Brennon shakes his head. "You've been fucking Nick's girl and didn't even tell me!"

Anger boils inside me at his words. "Josie is not *Nick's girl*."

Brennon presses his lips together to attempt to stunt the smile trying to creep across his face.

"Right. Sorry. She's your girl, is she?"

I narrow my eyes. "What exactly happened?"

"You were saying all this stuff about how you two hooked up, and, by the way, score!" He grins, reaching over, holding his hand in the air for a high-five. "Not only did you bang the golden boy's girl, you filmed it?"

"What the *fuck* are you talking about?" I growl, fists clenching.

Brennon's eyes roll dramatically as he lowers his hand and repositions himself on the lounge.

"You filmed it and posted the video, rubbing it in Nick's face that you sealed the deal with Princess Josephine."

"Stop calling her that," I snap, the skin taught and white over my knuckles. "And I don't know if this is some sick joke, but I would never fucking do that."

He gives me a look. "Mate. I saw you do it. With my own eyes."

I put my hands over my face and press my fingers hard into my closed eyes. Fuck, fuck, fuck. This can't be true. I wouldn't ever do that. Not to anyone, but especially not her. Why would I risk everything, when I was so close to getting what I wanted?

Scrambling for my phone once more, I request a new password for my Facebook account. When I finally go through all the steps to get back in, my stomach sinks at the hundreds of notifications blowing up my feed.

I quickly bring the post up and I feel the colour drain from my face.

"What the fuck …" I whisper. "Someone filmed this?"

"Well. I set it up." Brennon says and instantly raises his hands when he sees my face. "With the intention of filming Elise and myself, not you. I had no idea you were fuck—I mean, *with* Josephine," he quickly amends when he sees my hand ball into a fist.

"But you're the one who posted it. Not me."

"I would never, *ever* do that."

"You did."

"And why the fuck were you planning to film yourself with Elise? Were you even going to tell her?"

Brennon shrugged. "Sure. Before it was going to happen. But things changed after I went downstairs. I actually hooked up with Rianna. We went to go into the spare room but it was locked. Never had a clue it was you, until we got back here."

Sighing, I tilt my head back and look up at the ceiling, trying to get my jumbled thoughts to make sense. This can't be true. It simply can't be.

I press call on Josie's contact.

*The person you are trying to call is unavailable.*

"Shit," I whisper, trying again. I try calling five times before coming to the conclusion that she has blocked my number.

I go back to my account and quickly hit delete on the post, but it's too late. It already has so many views, comments, and shares.

"Don't panic, bro," Brennon says, taking a long slurp of his coffee. "It'll all blow over. No one will care in a week or so."

"Yeah. Right." I ground out, staggering to my feet.

I would never do this to her. She has to know this.

I rush outside, not even bothering to get shoes, and drive over to her house. My heart sinks when her car isn't in the driveway.

I've barely put my foot out the door, when the screen door flings open and Sam strides out onto the porch, a murderous expression on his face.

"Sam," I quickly start, jogging over to him. "Where is she?"

"Gone."

My chest heaves. "What?"

"She packed up and left. Honestly? I don't blame her. After what you did." His face contorts into an expression of pure fury.

"I didn't *do* anything!" I shout.

"Yeah. That's exactly what it looks like." Sam nods sarcastically. "Do everyone a favour and *fuck off.*"

His hands shoot out in front of him and slam into me. I stumble back.

"Sam, wait—"

He shoves me harder and harder with each step, until my back is pressed against Brennon's truck.

"Don't ever speak to her again."

His lips twist around his words as he turns his back on me and stomps up the stairs.

My head is spinning.

Every part of me is shaking when I reverse out of their long driveway. I try again to reach her, but it sends me straight to voicemail.

# Chapter Forty-Five

## *Josie*

There are 172 lines in the ceiling. I know this, because I've sat here in Mr. Sherlock's surgery for the past couple of hours, and counted them three times. When I sit up, the muscles in my neck complain and I groan, rolling my head around, trying to loosen them.

I keep imagining what my future looks like. I see tattooed arms, ocean-blue eyes, and that pretty little lip ring. Nothing else matters.

No person in my position would ever have this kind of time at work spare, when working in the city. I've run out of things to do. I've cleaned every surface, reorganised every cupboard, finished a complete stocktake of all items, ordered our next three months' worth of supplies and also contacted all the recall lists.

Sighing, I slip out the side door and head to the reception desk. I pull up the schedule and see that Danny's book is filled from start to finish, whereas I only have three patients.

"Hey," I say to Belle, when I hear her head into the sterilising room. "Are there any patients I can see? To help reduce Danny's workload?"

Belle yanks off her gloves and tosses them into the bin before facing me. She draws her lower lip between her teeth for a moment.

"I don't think so, Josie."

I swallow, instantly my finger moving to pick at my nails.

"Why?"

Belle exhales. "Apparently Nick's mother has told all her friends that they shouldn't see you."

I blink long and slow, focusing on my breathing.

Belle offers me a sympathetic look. "Sorry, girl."

Sighing, I head back to my surgery and text Harley, asking what time he has lunch today. I reach into my bag and pull out my study material. I have to head into the city at the end of this week for a practical assessment, so I may as well use this time to study for it.

Two hours have passed before I hear the bell ding, indicating someone has entered the practice. I jump to my feet, excited to have something to do.

Harley is leaning on the desk, looking adorable in his fluoro shirt and work boots. Red dirt clings to his skin and the sunglasses that are sunken into his hair have a thick layer of dust settled on them.

"Hi." I smile.

"Hey," he says, pulling me to him and planting a soft, lingering kiss on my mouth. "I'm sorry you're having a shitty day. I know it's sort of my fault."

"What?" I ask, slinging my arms around his shoulders, not caring if his shirt is dirty.

"Nick's mum. She's only doing it because of everything that happened."

I shake my head. "It's all on me, Harley. I was the one who hurt Nick."

"So did I."

Years of guilt sits thick between us and I run my hand down the side of his face, wishing I could go back in time and undo all my mistakes.

I lean in and kiss him again. I could kiss him all day. I've held back for so long, it makes me feel a little delirious that I can now kiss him like this.

"Let's go eat."

We sit off to the side of the practice, underneath an awning. Harley pulls the burgers out of the bags and places them on the small table. It rocks unevenly each time we press onto it, so we have to put our drinks on the pavement.

"How's your day?" I ask.

"Hot. Long. But better now."

"I am so excited to get away from this hellhole for the weekend," I say.

Harley freezes mid-bite and blinks at me. "What?"

"I have that thing. Remember?"

"What thing?"

I finish chewing and take a sip of my drink before answering.

"I have my practical assessment. I'm heading there on Friday. I told you, didn't I?"

Harley pouts and I smile behind my hand. He looks terribly cute when he does that.

"I can't go that long."

"What do you mean?"

"Without seeing you." He shrugs, taking a massive bite of his burger. Sauce dribbles down his chin. "So, no, you can't go."

I laugh. "It's only a couple of days."

Harley has been staying every night, since he isn't on speaking terms with Brennon.

"A couple hours are too long," he replies with a serious face, but his smile is playful. The funny thing is—well, it's not funny at all, really—is that this was how Elliot acted, but instead of it being a joke, it was serious.

"I'm sure you'll survive." I tease. "Is Brennon still calling you nonstop?"

"Yep."

"Have you spoke to him?"

"Nope."

I sort of feel bad coming between two best friends, but Brennon did this to himself. He destroyed my life and I will never be able to forgive him for it, although in a way, I deserved it. I deserved everything he threw at me. Because I was a cheater and a liar. And honestly? If I can't forgive Brennon for the things he has done, how can I forgive myself?

My mind has been constantly looping since our conversation, wondering how different my life would be if that video was never created and leaked. I wouldn't have run away like I did. I wouldn't have met Elliot. Things would be so different.

"Wait, so not even when you go back to get your stuff?"

"I go when he's not there. I know his schedule," Harley points out.

"I'm sorry," I say, ducking my chin.

"Hey." He leans over, pressing his finger under my chin, forcing me to meet his gaze. "You don't have anything to be sorry about."

My heart squeezes. Harley has such a kind, soft side to him that no one has ever got to see before. In a way, it's sort of devastating.

We finish our lunch and I head back inside. I have two more patients before I head home for the day. I stay back and help Belle shut down before we say goodbye.

I stop at the supermarket on the way home and get supplies. As I'm standing in line, Jess wanders up beside me.

"Hey," I say quietly.

She looks over. "Hey."

"I'm really sorry. About everything that happened on the trip.

And everything before it." I run a hand over my face. "It was really shitty of me."

"Yeah," she replies. "It was." She steps in front of me, cutting me off, and places her items on the conveyor belt. "I'm just glad he's finally done with you. You've put him through more heartbreak than anyone deserves."

I feel like I've been sucker punched. Pressing my lips together, I step back from her and don't say another word. She's right. Everything she said is right.

When I get into my car, I'm taking the familiar route to Nick's house, without realising what I was doing. When I stop at the driveway, I feel drained and a headache is starting to form. I step outside and walk down the side of the house, hoping that I don't run into any of Nick's family.

I stop when I see Nick sitting on his front step, his head between his hands.

A mixture of guilt and sadness spreads through me. Just like Jess said, he didn't deserve this.

"Nick," I say. "Hey."

He looks up, saying nothing.

"I don't know what to say," I whisper, my lower lip trembling. "I'm a fucking terrible person."

He stares down at the ground before finally meeting my gaze.

"I know saying sorry doesn't undo all of the things I've done, but I truly am."

He nods. "I know."

My limbs feel heavy as I release a breath, stepping back.

"I'm sorry, Nick. For everything."

After our eyes linger on each other for a painful heartbeat too long, I turn and race to my car, trying to hold in all the emotions threatening to consume me. I'm not good at this. Confrontation. Apologies. I'd rather run away and leave it all behind. But that's not me anymore. Josie Mayor owns her mistakes.

On the way home, I stop by Elise's grave again. I sit in front of it, my fingers woven into the grass. I let myself feel everything. The pain, the hurt, and everything in between.

"I wish you were here," I whisper. "You'd know what to do. What to say."

When an elderly couple pulls up to the cemetery, I wipe my cheeks and return to my car. My heart stutters inside my chest, when I see Nick on my front porch.

I walk past him and unlock the door. I quickly unload the few things I bought before I head back to the door and lean on the frame.

"You coming in?"

Slowly, he stands, and brushes past me. He takes a seat on the lounge and I follow suit, tucking my legs underneath me. I don't know if it's because I'm nervous, or because the house has been locked up for the day, but it seems to double in temperature within minutes.

My fingers twist the bottom of my shirt. The tension between us makes it hard to breathe.

"It's always been him, hasn't it?" he asks.

I hang my head. "I'm so sorry, Nick."

"Did you ever love me?"

I lean my head back onto the lounge. "You know I did."

"But not as much as him."

"It's complicated."

"It really wasn't, but you made it complicated." Nick blows out a heavy breath, rubbing across his jaw, staring across the small living room. I follow his gaze, seeing his eyes resting on my recent painting.

"How could you be with him again, after everything?"

"It wasn't him." I lean onto my arm and rub my eyes. "It's a long story, but it was Brennon who posted the video. He got Harley wasted and convinced him that he did it. Harley always said he wouldn't have ever done it, but couldn't really remember. But Brennon admitted it to me that he was the one who posted it."

Nick is silent. "And you believe that?"

I nod. "Yes."

Nick shakes his head and stands. His eyes fill with unshed tears and my heart squeezes. I shove to my feet and place my hands on his shoulders.

"Look, I know I must seem like an idiot, but you don't know Harley like I do. No one does."

He barks out a dry laugh. "You don't say."

"I'm so sorry, Nick. I never wanted to hurt you. I lied to myself all this time, trying to convince myself I didn't want to be with him."

"Just stop," he whispers, eyes on the floor. "I don't want to hear about it."

"I don't want you to hate me."

"I can't hate you, Josephine. That's a part of the problem."

"You should be with Jess," I say. "She really cares for you."

"Now it's okay for me to be with Jess. Right. Because that would make you feel a whole lot less guilty, yeah?"

"Nick," I sigh and it comes deep from my chest.

The sound of my phone vibrating fills the room. We both stiffen, listening to it.

"That's him, isn't it?" Nick turns then, and looks around the room. I follow as his eyes travel over the two coffee cups by my bed, a black t-shirt strewn over a chair, Harley's shoes kicked off in the corner. "Oh my God," Nick says. "He's been staying here. You're together. Aren't you?"

I remind myself to inhale and exhale.

"Wow."

His soft, green eyes are round and sad as he stares at me before walking out. I will never forget the way he just looked.

"I'm sorry," I whisper, but when I look up, he's already gone.

# Chapter Forty-Six

## Josie

It's finally the day I get to leave. This entire week has been dragging. I already packed last night, but I'm gathering all the last-minute things I need before I head off. I've texted Harley a few times, he was meant to meet me here to say goodbye. I've been hanging around until he finishes work, but I haven't heard from him.

I look at the time on my phone again and sigh. I gather my things and make sure everything is unplugged and switched off before I head out the door.

"Hey there."

I spin quickly and see Harley leaning against the bonnet of my car, a duffle bag by his feet. He's dressed in a plain white t-shirt and dark jeans. His sleeves are slightly rolled, showcasing his delicious biceps. His hair is windblown, his sunglasses peeking out from the darkness of his hair.

"What are you doing?" I ask in shock.

"Coming with you."

"Really?" I ask.

"Yep."

I squeal and run down the steps, launching myself at him. He laughs as he picks me up, spinning me. I tighten my legs around his waist and he presses my back against the warm metal.

He covers my mouth with his, our tongues dancing, fighting the other for dominance. I run my thumbs softly over his ears and kiss his nose.

"I take it that you're happy with that?" He grins.

"Fuck yeah." I grin back.

"You driving, or me?" he asks once I'm safely lowered back to the ground.

"You can drive," I answer, tossing him the keys.

He slaps my butt as he rounds the car, sliding in behind the wheel. We stop by the diner, only getting there fifteen minutes before it's meant to shut, and grab ourselves coffees and snacks for the road.

Once we pass the *Welcome to Fern Grove* sign, I physically feel myself relax.

"I am so excited for this," I say. "You have no idea."

"Oh, I think I do." He smiles.

I scroll through my phone to find a playlist.

"What vibes are we feeling?" I ask.

"Energy booster, or road trip classics. Something fun."

"You got it," I reply.

I find just the one before I lock my phone and toss it back into my bag.

The sun is disgustingly hot, even at this time of the day. I crank the air con up higher and recline the seat back enough that I can comfortably rest my feet on the dash.

"I love that."

"What?" I ask.

"That you always have really dark nails. It suits you."

I glance at him in surprise, turning my attention back to my toes. They're a sparkling navy blue. I bite the inside of my cheek to stop smiling.

"I was thinking we could stop in for dinner before heading to the hotel? It's a pretty long drive."

"Good idea," Harley replies.

Inching the volume up, I rest my head back. Harley reaches over, placing a warm hand on my thigh. He grips it softly and I watch the veins protrude from his arm.

I must have dozed off because what seems like a few minutes later, we are pulling into a carpark and my eyes are drooping. I rub them and yawn. I stretch out and run my fingers along the base of Harley's neck.

"Hey sleepy," he says with a smile.

"Sorry," I say sheepishly. "I was going to drive halfway."

"Yeah, sure you were," he snickers, rolling his eyes. "Let's get some food."

I almost cry in relief when I step outside of the car. There's a cool breeze that washes over my skin.

"We're not in Fern Grove anymore." I grin, reaching for his hand.

"We certainly are not."

The neon sign flashes *Raise A Glass*, casting a purple glow across the carpark. It's bustling with people, but we manage to find a table near the back that's not too close to the speakers.

It's crowded and the music is so loud, it's hard to hear myself think. Empty cocktail glasses line the bar, with a few littering across the floor. Despite how many people are here, it doesn't feel stuffy or overcrowded.

"Drink?"

"I'd love one," I answer.

"Vodka?"

"Surprise me."

Harley disappears into the crowd as I plop down onto the cool leather seat. It's dark in here, the only lights are golden drop-down lightbulbs that swing over the top of our head.

I was worried about being underdressed in my yoga pants and high-neck white crop top, but it seems like it matches the vibe of everyone else here. I slide my leather jacket over my shoulders, loving the fact that it's cool enough to wear a jacket.

Browsing over the menu, I try to figure out what I feel like, when Harley slides into the booth sitting opposite me.

"Thank you." I smile, taking the drink and having a sip. It's cool and crisp on my tongue, making me dive back in for a second and third sip before I place the glass back down.

"This place is really cool," he says, nodding towards to the centre of the room. "Check it."

I glance over, seeing a band setting up. This, right here, is the type of bar I've always wanted to come to. There's nothing even remotely similar to this at Fern Grove, and when I was partying in the city with Elliot, it was much more upper class than this. I wouldn't even be allowed in, wearing what I am right now.

"What do you feel like eating?" I ask.

Harley's eyes darken slightly as they travel over my chest and down to my exposed stomach. The corner of his mouth twitches.

"You."

A blush burns its way across my cheeks and down my neck. I smirk back, leaning forward, tracing my finger around the rim of my glass.

"Oh yeah?"

"Yeah. Right now."

I clamp my thighs together. Shit. This boy sends me wild.

"I'm going to finish my drink," I say, slowly pulling my lip against my lower teeth. "Then I'm going to the bathroom."

He swallows as I drain the remainder of my drink. I push myself out of the booth and strut towards the dim light that has an arrow flashing towards the restrooms.

I hover near the door. My heart does a flip-flop sensation when Harley glides around the corner, his dark hair hanging over his eyes. I step inside the room. Not very often bars like this have their own bathroom, but I'm *really* glad this one does.

Only a moment has passed before the door opens. I lean on the bench and meet his eyes in the reflection.

"I have wanted to be inside you since the second I saw you today."

"Then do it."

He exhales a breathy laugh. He leans forward, leaving a trail of hot kisses down my neck. His hands possessively trace the curves of my body.

"I really like these pants," he whispers. "But right now, they'd look even better around your ankles."

His fingers tighten around the waistband before he yanks them down my thighs. He groans when he sees I'm in a thong. Lightly, he slaps my bare cheek and I gasp at the sting of it.

"Bend over."

"Yes sir."

He gives me a wicked grin, which I match, as I lean forward. His hand slides over the front of me and he pushes the fabric away. He clicks his tongue, moving his lips to my ear.

"You're soaked."

"I know," I whisper.

He chuckles, lightly teasing me with his fingers. I push back into him, making his fingers go deeper. He smirks at my neediness. Impatiently, I pull my underwear, shoving them down.

Lowering himself, his tongue drags across my folds and I moan loudly. His tongue moves quickly and precisely, making me grip the side of the sink hard.

"Just what I ordered." He smirks, standing once more. He grips my hips and when I think he's about to ease into my entrance, he slams into me instead. A shriek leaves my lips as he plunges deep inside me. His hand moves down my front, sliding right into the spot he knows will have me bucking against him in moments.

"Harley," I moan.

"Look at me, sweetheart."

With uneven breathing, I force my gaze to meet his. His stunning eyes are curiously watching me as his hand dances across me. He thrusts hard into me again and I whimper. It's extremely exotic *watching* him fuck me.

Colour splashes across my cheeks. Wisps of my hair fall over my forehead and little beads of sweat shine under the lights. He makes me feel … hot. In every single way.

"Josie," he grunts into my ear, his eyes expressing a deep, raw emotion that I've never seen on him before. "I've loved you for a long fucking time." He presses his finger harder into my clit and a scream escapes me as I climax.

I push hard back into him, trying to prolong my orgasm for as long as possible.

"Fuck," he mutters, a droplet of sweat sliding down his face, looking like he is a mere thread from losing control.

"I love you, too."

He lets out a shuddering breath as he comes, slamming into me harder than he ever has before. We both let out a moan at the same time, and I sag onto the bench, breathless.

"Jesus," he exhales, his hands dropping down beside me, caging me in his embrace. His heartbeat is fast and hard as it thuds against my back. His fingers lazily draw circles over my exposed skin.

"Is your appetite fulfilled?" I question innocently, licking my lips.

"Oh, sweetheart." He smirks wickedly. "That was just my entrée."

# Chapter Forty-Seven

## Harley

### Four years ago

Gone.

The word didn't completely process in my brain until days—weeks—dragged by and Josie never came back. It didn't truly sink in, until summer break came and went. The school formal. Senior exams. Graduation. Josie missed all of it. Because of *me*. Because of something I don't even remember doing.

Grazing my thumb over the rock in my hand, I throw it and watch it skip across the surface of the water. Flashes of a memory of me teaching Josie how to skip a rock threatens to bombard me, but I forcefully shove it out of my head.

It felt like someone stabbed my heart without stitching the wounds back up. I knew I loved her, but I didn't realise how much until she was gone.

I missed her. So fucking much. Meeting her gaze in the hallway. Watching her ponytail swish with each step. Her infectious laugh. Her warm smile. Our secret hook ups under stairs and in locked classrooms. Late night texting.

It's been a year and I still can't get her off my mind.

I call her every day. The number goes straight to voicemail, even if I try on someone else's phone.

After all this time, I still feel like someone is holding my head under water and I haven't come up for air. My chest aches. My lungs burn. Everything inside me hurts in ways I've never experienced.

I understand why she left. A scandal like that in a town like this can ruin even the highest people on the social ladder, let alone a young teenage girl. I just wish she would let me talk to her.

Even if I couldn't apologise enough for what has happened, I just want her to know I'm here and I always will be. Whenever—if ever—she is ready, I want to be together. I don't care what I need to do for that to happen. I'm willing to do just about anything.

I'll wait for her. However long it takes. I just want to know there *is* a chance.

For six months, there was nothing else anyone wanted to talk about. Guys whispered when I walked past their groups, girls shot me daggers with their eyes. Parents frowned down at me, elderly women shook their heads.

The bruises from my father's foot across my ribs and back didn't fade for a long time. I didn't fight back. I deserved every hit I got.

After Mike Johnston made a comment about Josie being a slut, I rammed my fist so hard into his nose that it broke in two places. That shut everyone up pretty quickly. A two-week suspension and a black mark on my record later, I'd do it again. A hundred times over. Because Josie deserves so much more than this.

In a way, I'm glad she got out. I wish I could.

I run my thumb across the crinkled piece of paper in my hand. It's a silhouette drawing of a guy with his arms wrapped around a girl as they stare up at a starry night sky. It's a drawing of us on one of the nights I needed to get out of the house and breathe fresh air.

She drew this for me. She loved me. She was going to choose me.

It's her birthday today. I tilt my head back and look up at the night sky. Hazy clouds cover most of the stars tonight, but there's one that shines brighter than all the others. I smile sadly up at it.

"Happy Birthday, Josie," I whisper. "Wherever you are, I hope you're happy."

# Chapter Forty-Eight

## Josie

The smell of coffee and a sizzling sound stirs me from my sleep. My eyes sting with tiredness for a moment as I rub them. Harley and I didn't get much sleep last night.

Rolling over, I wince at the ache between my legs. I glance down, seeing light bruises dotted over me. Smiling, I trace them with my fingers. Last night was a continuous high of Harley that I don't ever want to come down from.

Glancing briefly to the vacant side of the bed, I pull myself off the mattress and freshen up. I throw on Harley's t-shirt and stroll out to the kitchen.

Harley's muscled back is facing me. He's dressed in black briefs that sit snugly over his backside. Biting my lip, I grip him tightly before sliding my hands over his stomach.

"Good morning," he murmurs, his chest vibrating.

Leaving a kiss on his shoulder blade, I rest my cheek against his warm skin.

"You must have been up early. You went to the shops?"

"I got a few things," he replies, turning and leaning back onto the counter. My eyes slip across his body and back up again.

"It smells amazing."

"Sit," he demands. "Relax. You have a big day ahead."

"I'm happy to help!" I insist.

Shaking his head, he points the spatula towards the seat pulled up to the kitchen island. Nodding, I head over to it and sit down.

"How did you sleep?" Harley asks.

"Like a baby." I smile softly. "You know, when we eventually *did* sleep."

Harley sends a smirk over his shoulder.

"I didn't realise you could cook," I state, observing the efficiency of his hands as he glides around the kitchen.

A small bowl of fruit sits off to the side and I pluck a grape between my fingers, placing it onto my tongue. Harley saunters over and leans in, sucking it from my mouth. Heat flares inside me and I ache for him all over again. After last night, I'm positive I will never get enough of what that boy can do to me.

I place my hand to the back of his hand when he goes to move away. I lean in with a heated kiss. I taste the coffee on his warm tongue and moan into his mouth.

"I'm going to burn the pancakes," he murmurs. "But it would be worth it."

Grinning, I release him. His hair stands up at odd angles and his cheeks are flushed a delicious red. Planting my chin in my palm, I watch him.

"You like cooking?" I ask.

"Love it," he answers over his shoulder. "My mum was a great cook. She taught me a lot of things. She worked a lot and my father was a useless fuck who did nothing to help around the house. So, she taught me lots of things so that I could always cook dinner for myself when she wasn't around."

"Wow," I murmur.

"I used to spend hours watching cooking shows. If I put my headphones up as high as they could go and lay under my blankets, I couldn't hear them fighting. So. I watched a lot of shows."

My heart squeezes in my chest as I imagine a scared little boy, hiding from his father, trying to self-educate himself. It must have been hard learning he had to rely on himself so early on in life.

"You never talked about it much at the time," I say. "About your dad."

Harley is quiet for a long moment before he responds. "Yeah. It's pretty embarrassing. Having a father like that. Everyone knows he's a drunk. He's banned from basically everywhere in town. In a place like Fern Grove, everyone knows that kind of thing."

"You're not your father."

"We share the same last name. That's good enough for everyone to think I'm trash, too."

"I never thought of you like that."

Turning, he stares at me. "You had a pretty harsh opinion of me. You always have. Like everyone else."

"That was mainly because of Brennon and the things you guys used to do," I point out. "I never considered your father's behaviour a reflection on you."

His cheek moves as he bites his lower lip for a moment before he turns back around. My eyes flitter over the tiny scars across his back.

"Are they from him?" I ask. "Those scars?"

He twists, staring down at himself. They're not super noticeable—unless you've dragged your tongue over them, like I have—but if you squint hard enough, you can see tiny pink and white lines over his smooth skin. "Some. Mostly from accidents."

"What kind of accidents?"

"Falling out of trees, skateboarding, just being an energetic boy with no supervision." He smiles. "I was in and out of hospital my whole childhood. I was on a first name basis with everyone. Even recently, when I was doing the rodeos."

"I don't think I've ever broken a bone." I ponder, eyes drifting up to the ceiling, trying to recall.

"You never lived if you didn't break a bone!" He mock-gasps.

"I fell off horses all the time. Sam has broken his arm three times, but I always managed to come out okay after a fall." I shrug. "A few times I even landed on my feet."

"That's impressive. You used to compete, right?"

Nodding, I snag another grape from the bowl. "Yep. Dressage, jumping, camp drafting. The whole works."

"I went to one of your competitions once."

My eyebrows shoot up. "What?"

"Before anything started with us. I was walking by the fields. It must have been a home base one. I saw you riding around. Never imagined years later you'd be riding me." He grins wickedly as he says that last part and I blush, throwing a grape at his head. It bounces off his forehead and into his hand, which he throws easily into his mouth.

"You have a dirty mouth, Harley."

"You love my dirty mouth."

I roll my eyes. I can't disagree.

He slides the pancakes onto plates and artfully adds golden syrup over the top of them.

"These look amazing. I can't remember the last time I had pancakes."

He slides a glass of orange juice towards me before sitting beside me on the other stool.

"I used to make these for my mum all the time. After her and Dad would have a big fight. We'd sit in their bed and watch movies. It was called Pancake Day."

"That's sweet." I smile. "Are you and your mum close?"

"She died two years ago."

The fork slips from my hand, clattering onto the bench. I gape at him, wide-eyed.

"Your mum died two years ago?" I whisper.

"Aneurism. Three months or so after Elise died."

Placing my hand over my mouth, I blink at him. "Oh my God, Harley. I had no idea."

"How could you?" he asks quietly. "You weren't here."

He shovels a forkful of pancake into his mouth and I slowly lower my hand, suddenly feeling a little nauseous.

"I'm sorry."

"No one's fault," he says.

"For not being there."

His eyes lift to mine. "Things were different back then."

"I'm still sorry."

He nods, a muscle in his cheek clenching.

"I'm here now," I whisper.

"That's what counts." He gives me a small smile—one that doesn't meet his eyes before he continues chewing.

"What's it like with your dad now?"

"The same. He will never change. I avoid him as much as I can. He hangs around the construction site a bit. About the only place he can really socialise anymore. I stay out and work when he's around."

"You never go back to the house?"

"Nah. He's always drunk and looking for a fight. He isn't worth a moment of my time, honestly."

"That's awful," I say sadly. "I'm sorry."

Harley sighs, taking a long sip of his juice while simultaneously lifting his shoulder.

"Everyone has shit in their life. Some worse than others."

I chew thoughtfully, and we finish our breakfast in silence. I pack up the plates and wash everything before packing them away.

"Thank you for a great breakfast," I say, leaning up and kissing his nose.

"Any time." He leans back down, capturing my lips in his. "You're looking fantastic in my clothes, by the way."

"They're much more comfortable than my own."

"Maybe you should wear them more often." He smirks.

"I won't contest that." Stepping back, I grip the edge of his shirt, and peel it off my body. "But for now, I have to get ready."

The cool air nips at my exposed breast and I feel my nipples pebble at the feel of it. Harley stares at me in the most hot and possessive way. I feel myself turning to liquid.

His fingers graze over my skin as he takes my breasts into his hands and massages them softly.

"You have the most beautiful body." Leaning forward, he kisses along my shoulders. "Always have."

Warmth spreads through my chest. He loved me when I hated myself.

I moan softly as his lips move up my neck. His tongue circles over the ticklish part of my skin and I convulse slightly. He bites me softly and I slide my hands over him in delight.

"That is such a turn on when you do that," I whisper.

"Right here." He kisses and massages my neck with his lips. "Has always been your sweet spot." More pressure. "Other than …" Suddenly his hand is at my sex and his finger slides across my clit. "Here."

I shudder as he runs circles over me. I tilt my head back and he grips my hips, pushing me off my feet and onto the bench. He widens my legs, and sinks down between them. He slides his tongue over me and I gasp at how good it feels. My legs quiver with anticipation and I hook them over his shoulders.

His teeth lightly graze me and I whimper, gripping his hair with my fingers.

"Good luck today, sweetheart," he murmurs as he takes my clit between his lips and sucks. Hard. I cry out and shove his face harder against me. I feel him chuckle, sending delicious vibrations through me.

"Thank you," I whisper.

His tongue continues to slide efficiently in all the right places. My legs shake over his shoulders and I arch my back, pushing myself closer to him, deepening his tongue into me.

Heat surges everywhere and I feel the pressure building low in my stomach. My toes curl as his tongue quickens in pace. Just as I'm close, he suddenly pulls back and when I'm about to protest, his hand slaps over my sex in a short, sharp hit that has me reeling, sending me over the edge in hot, powerful waves.

I gasp out as he slaps me one more time before diving back in and tasting every bit of the orgasm he created.

"How am I going to focus on anything else today?" I moan, letting my body turn limp. "That is going to replay in my mind 1000 times."

Harley stands and drags the back of his hand across his mouth. He shrugs.

"Sounds like a you problem, not a me problem."

I lightly shove his shoulder. "I wish I could return the favour, but I'm going to be late if I don't get ready." Leaning up, I kiss him softly. "But I definitely will make it up to you later."

"Not necessary, sweetheart. Today is your day."

"Oh, trust me, I'll make it up to you," I murmur, slapping his backside as I saunter back into the bedroom.

Now, time to get my head straight.

I lean heavily against the wall of the elevator as it slowly inches up to the apartment Harley and I are staying in for the weekend. It was a long day of studying and assessments, but I passed. Today's assessment was the important one, so now that I've completed it and scored well, I feel like I can relax and enjoy my time away.

Hovering my card over the sensor, the door clicks open. Music is quietly playing when I step inside. A bouquet of flowers is perched beside champagne on ice.

"What's this?" I gasp as Harley strolls into the room, in nothing but faded jeans that hang low and loose on his hips.

"A congratulations on passing your assessment."

"How did you know I passed?"

"Because." He shrugs, wrapping his around my waist. He kisses my left temple. "You're brilliant." He kisses my right temple. "Smart." His lips move to my hairline. "And beautiful."

He steps back, grinning. "You did, right? Pass?"

"I did." I smile.

My heart swells inside my chest. To know someone thinks so highly of me. *Believes* in me, is something I haven't felt for a while. My eyes glisten with the threat of tears but I blink them away.

"Here, I got you this."

He shoves a small parcel, wrapped in tissue paper, into my hands. Curiously, I unwrap it. It's a simple silver bracelet with a tiny charm on it. Engraved on the inside, it has: *H & J* ♡

My jaw drops.

"Oh my God, Harley, this is beautiful."

"You like it?" he asks nervously.

"I *love* it!"

A wide grin splits across his face and he quickly takes it from my grasp. He tightly wraps it around my wrist and clicks it shut. I loop my arms around his neck and our lips collide.

He hooks his hands around the backs of my thighs and hoists me up so that my legs are securely around his waist.

"Where are you going?" I mumble against his lips as he bypasses the bed, heading into the bathroom.

"Bathtub."

I pull back enough to see that the bathtub is filled with water. It's adjacent to the long window, overlooking the beautiful sky-high buildings of the city. The sun is sinking into the horizon, casting a stunning orange glow across the sky in vibrant streaks. Gently, he lowers me. He kicks off his pants and I suck in a sharp breath at the sight of his bareness.

Tanned, smooth, and tightly packed with muscle. His body is a masterpiece.

I peel off my scrubs and twist my hair into a knot on the top of my head. His eyes possessively rake over my body as he drinks in every inch of me.

"Thank you," I whisper. "For making this weekend better than I could have ever imagined."

He strides forward and gathers my hands in his.

"You gave me a second chance. I won't mess it up this time."

Leaning forward, I press my chest against his as I kiss down the base of his throat. My mouth trails over his chest and down his abs. I kiss across his pelvic bone and I pause.

# VIII · X · MM

Softly, I trace my fingers over the letters.

"What is this?" I whisper.

"A date."

"What date?"

I sink onto my knees, peering up at him. He stares down at me. His Adam's Apple bobs up and down.

"I think you know."

"My birthdate."

Slowly, he nods. "Yes."

Liquid fire blazes through my veins as our gazes lock.

"You got my birth date tattooed on you."

"You're it for me, Josie. I've always told you that."

With my heart thundering in my chest, I keep my eyes on his as I move towards him, circling my lips around him. He hisses, his fingers sinking into my hair.

"That is so fucking hot," I murmur against him, my tongue sliding over his length.

"I won't last one more second if you do that with your tongue again," he pants. "And I have a whole lot planned for you."

Teasingly, I circle around the tip one final time before I stand.

He steps into the tub, pulling me with him. I can feel how ready I am and he hasn't even touched me. I place my knees either side of his thighs and slowly sink down onto him.

A deep, throaty groan emits from him as I take him deeper. One hand finds my waist, the other slides up my neck, bracketing my throat. Desire burns inside me as his fingers tighten. I never knew that would be such a turn on.

I grind against him, shifting my hips, feeling him plunge deep inside of me. He groans again, throwing his head back. He looks delicious as his eyes flutter closed. His lips part as he mouths filthy words. I ride him quicker now and water splashes over the sides of the tub. His hand squeezes against my throat, only making me go faster with need.

This feels so damn good.

"Keep–doing–that." He pants, slowly opening his eyes as he watches me. His eyes drift all over me and eventually down to where our bodies meet. His eyes darken, his grip tightening. I've never been looked at with so much desire in my life. It's a high I don't think I'll ever stop chasing.

His hand moves across my skin, sinking into the water. As soon as his finger touches me, it's like an electric pulse flares inside my body. I grind against him harder. His eyes brim with lust as he takes his lip ring between his teeth.

He thrusts hard upward into me and I shriek out his name, every piece of me detonating. He kisses everywhere. My face, my neck, my collarbones, my breasts, across my stomach.

Breathlessly, I slide off him and rest back against the tub. He leans forward, our foreheads pressing together.

"Holy fuck," he whispers.

"Yeah," I agree.

"I'm really glad I hijacked this trip."

I smile, breathless. "Me too."

When Harley stepped out of the bathroom, clad in a dark navy suit, and a turquoise button-up underneath, contrasting almost too perfectly with his eyes, my pulse jumped in desire.

It feels surreal being in this kind of lifestyle with Harley by my side. It's what I've always wanted. Me and Harley. Together. Away from Fern Grove and everyone in it.

We finished the bottle of champagne before we left and I was definitely tipsy through dinner. My head feels light as we dance. The lights dash erratically across the dance floor. We glide across it, deliriously drunk on this night. Being here. Together.

"This feels like a dream," I shout at him.

"It's better than a dream." He smiles.

His skin is warm as he draws me to him, flattening our bodies together. His hands slide through my hair, down the sides of my face and grip the material of my dress, bunching it at the sides.

"You look so beautiful."

Heat dances in my cheeks as I hold him to me tighter. We stay like this, embraced and swirling around the dance floor for so long, the straps of my heels have begun digging into my feet.

"Thirsty?" Harley asks.

Nodding. "Yes!"

Curling his fingers around mine, Harley pulls me after him, guiding us from the crowded dance floor. My head feels light and I stumble a few times trying to keep up with his long strides.

Turning, Harley faces me, a lazy smile on his face.

"I want this."

"What?"

"This." He waves his hand between us and then around the room. "This life. With you."

"What life?"

He shrugs. "Me and you. Living it up. Doing whatever we want. Away from that hellhole."

A wide smile stretches across my face. "Me too."

"Let's do it!" he says eagerly, circling his hands over mine, and pulling them to his chest. "I have one month left of my apprenticeship. Then we can go anywhere."

"Where do you want to go?" I ask him, excitement welling inside my chest.

*Yes, yes, yes.* This is everything I want and more.

He smiles. "I'll follow you wherever you want to go."

# Chapter Forty-Nine

## Harley

Rubbing my eyes, I wake with a smile on my face. I wince as the muscles in my legs complain as I stretch.

Last night, Josie and I danced for hours. Shouting lyrics, downing drinks, bouncing from one club to another, until all of them locked their doors, and turned their music off. We got ice cream and sat on a bench for a long time, talking, laughing, telling each other stories. It was one of the best—if not *the* best—night of my life.

Turning my head, my gaze lands on Josie. Her cheek is pressed to the pillow and her long blonde hair trailing in waves across the stark white sheet. It only covers a small part of her lower back, exposing the smooth skin of her shoulders and backside.

She is perfect.

Rolling over, I trail my fingers down the side of her body and squeeze her ass.

"Mm," she moans softly.

"Morning, sweetheart."

"Good morning," she mumbles sleepily.

She shifts so that she gazes up at me and my eyes focus on a couple of dark hickeys across the base of her throat. I wince. I must have been pretty drunk to do that. What am I, seventeen again?

Her palms press against my chest, flattening me onto my back. She straddles my hips and pure heat rushes to my groin as I feel all of her pressed against all of me. No fabric is between us and I feel how much she wants me, and she can feel how much *I* want her.

My hands rest on her bare waist and I stare at her stunning body. Blonde hair falls over her face as she shifts her hips sinfully against mine and I groan, pushing my erection hard into her.

This entire weekend has been something of a dream. I can't believe I'm here with her.

*Four fucking years* I waited for her to come back. To see her. To explain everything. I still can't quite comprehend that she finally *listened*.

The dazed smile on my face slowly dips into a frown. She pauses for a moment, staring.

"What's wrong?"

"This is the last day," I say, glancing at the clock on the bedside table. Eight o'clock. We have to be out of the hotel by ten. I don't want to leave. Reality sucks. This is way better. "I don't want this to end."

Her hands glide over my chest and down my stomach, making my insides coil and uncoil with each sensitive touch.

"This isn't going to end," she replies. "We've both wasted far too much time not being together to let this end now."

"I don't mean us. I mean this weekend. Returning back to that place. Back to our everyday life."

"Fern Grove is a much better place, now that we are together in it."

I open my mouth to reply but she slides unbearably slow onto me. I moan at the feel of how tight and wet she is. She grinds herself into me, pushing me deeper, and throws her hair lusciously over her shoulders.

She is a god damn fucking Goddess.

She rolls her hips and I thrust upward. She bites her lip, eyes fluttering closed briefly before they open and stare straight into mine.

"I love you," she whimpers.

I thrust hard, plunging myself as far into her as I can go.

"I love you more," I gasp, fingers tightening around her hip bones.

I'm my best self when I'm with her. It's always been like that. She's good, and it made me want to be good. I never felt I needed to prove myself for anyone, until I noticed her. She had always been there, but one day, everything changed.

She threw her head back and laughed. It caught my attention. I swivelled my eyes to her, seeing the golden sunlight glow across her pretty face. Pulling her hair behind her ear, she turned her head towards me. Our eyes met and it felt like I had been hit by a truck.

I blink back to the present. My fingers play with her as she rides me faster. Sweat slides down my forehead as I meet the rhythm of her hips. I feel her clench around me. I press harder into her at the same time I buck my hips.

A powerful orgasm crashes over her and she convulses, shouting my name so loudly, I wouldn't be surprised if the visitors down on the bottom level heard her. My own orgasm tingles through every limb.

She whimpers softly as she inches up and down my length. Everything loses focus for a moment as I release in the single most violent climax of my life. I collapse back onto the pillows with a gasp.

Josie stills, breathing heavy. She leans forward, laying down on top of me. We're both hot and slick with sweat, but I don't ask her to move. Her heartbeat drums against my chest. I slide my arms around her, pulling her closer.

"My God, Harley," she almost sobs. "I never imagined sex to feel like this."

"It's different when you love someone," I whisper.

She moves so that we're staring into each other's eyes. A smile finds her lips and she kisses my nose.

"That is so true."

Smiling in return, I slap her bare ass cheek. "As much as I'd love to be balls deep into you for the rest of the day, we need to get ready."

She pouts. "We have a little time."

"Yeah, and I'm planning to use it very, very wisely," I tell her, sitting us both up.

I wriggle to the end of the bed—as best as I can with me still inside her—and push to my feet. She clambers her legs around my waist as I stand and clings to me when she slips for a moment.

"Where are we going?" she asks.

"Shower time."

"Together?" She lights up.

"Together." I smirk, kicking the door shut behind us.

# Chapter Fifty

## *Josie*

It feels almost like stepping out of a fog when I slide behind the wheel of the car, ready for the trip home. I feel dazed and a little delirious. The whole trip was over in a blink. I feel giddy when I think back to it.

I can't wait to do it all over again. I'll have to think of some reason for another getaway.

*Or maybe a permanent getaway.*

Sliding my sunglasses up my nose, I angle the mirror so that it is easier for me to see and adjust the seat, considering my legs are certainly not as long as Harley's.

After two and half hours, my legs start feeling cramped and there's no longer a position that feels comfortable in the seat.

"Ready for a pit stop?" I ask.

"Sure."

When the next service centre comes along, we pull into it. Groaning, I step out of the car. Several bones crack as I stretch, using the car roof as support as I twist and turn my body.

"Sexy," Harley comments with a laugh.

"You weren't complaining this morning when I was twisting and turning." I smirk.

He two-finger solutes me. "Touché."

I slip the strap of my bag over my shoulder and when we start to walk towards the service centre, Harley's fingers slide in place between mine. I smile at him. This feels so *nice*. So *right*.

Everything that we have been through was heartbreaking and awful, but in this moment, it all feels worth it. *He* is worth it.

We grab coffees and lunch before hitting the road again.

Harley changes everything I did to the seat and I roll my eyes.

"Do you have to have the seat this damn high?" He huffs.

"Umm yeah. I need to see the road," I reply.

"And the top of every building we pass?"

I laugh, lightly shoving his shoulder. "Shut up."

He grins, turning the engine on. I adjust the volume and pick a new playlist as he crawls out of the carpark and back onto the highway.

The next hour of driving consists of me trying to keep my hands off Harley. With his crisp white t-shirt barely stretching over his biceps, those delicious tattoos and the wind blowing his dark hair back, my body is brimming with need.

"What?" he asks, giving me a side-eye look.

"You look so hot right now."

He quirks an eyebrow. "Yeah?"

"Hell yeah." I nod. "I think I need to do something about it."

"And what's that?"

Leaning over, I unzip his pants. He squirms in his seat, swallowing.

"I know very well what that mouth can do, sweetheart, and if you touch me with it right now, we are going to crash."

I smile sweetly.

"This may very well be the best road trip I've ever had." He grins, his hair sexily messy and cheeks flushed.

"There's going to be more where that came from, baby." I smile back. "Much, much more."

# Chapter Fifty-One

## Josie

O nce we were home, Harley left with a kiss to my temple and a promise he will be back later tonight, after his shift is finished. I feel a little lost after I've unpacked. I stare around the room, the walls surrounding me suddenly feeling less and less like home.

I experienced a taste of life outside Fern Grove—a very different experience to the last time I left—and I'm hungry for more.

After showering and changing into shorts and a strapless top, I head over to my family's house. The heat is sweltering, making me feel anxious and hot.

I stroll inside. Mum is sitting on the lounge with a book in her hand, sipping wine. Sam, as usual, has headphones jammed into his ears and some sort of device in his hands. Dad is fluffing around with something that's pulled apart and strewn across the dining table.

"Wow, look at you!" Mum's eyebrows shoot up as she eyes me up and down. "You're glowing!"

"Getting that D," I hear Sam mutter, and I throw him a warning glare before moving to sit on the edge of the lounge Mum is on. We have been texting a lot. I love that we are getting close again. I missed him while I was away.

"I had a really great weekend," I tell her.

"How lovely. Did you take your friend with you?"

"Yeah. Her friend." Sam grins wickedly.

I send him an irritated look before facing Mum again. "Friend?"

"The one you work with?"

"Oh." I shake my head. "No, uh, I went with Harley."

The book in her hands crashes to the ground with a startling thump as every pair of eyes turn in my direction. Swallowing uneasily, I force a smile onto my face.

"We worked things out."

"Worked things out?" Mum blinks.

"It was never him who did that to me. It was Brennon. You remember Brennon Michaelson?"

Sam scoffs. "How can anyone not remember that twat?"

I sneak a glance at my father, who is actually looking at me for the first time in a long time. He places the piece of metal onto the table wordlessly.

"It's a long story, but I promise you, he isn't the person you think he is."

Heavy silence fills the room. My chest constricts and suddenly it feels hard to breathe in here. Every part of my body feels tense and I furiously pick at my nail polish. There will be hardly any left at the rate I'm scratching at it.

"Oh," Mum eventually says. "So, what, you're together, then?"

I nod.

"About time," Sam comments.

"What about Nick?" she questions, looking a little pale.

"It was never Nick who had my heart."

A sound leaves my father and we all look over at him. His lips are pursed in a surly looking scowl.

"Something to say?" I ask, a bite in my tone.

"Looks like nothing has changed in the four years you abandoned your family," he answers.

I suck in a sharp breath. "You know what? I'm sick of doing this with you. If you don't want to be a part of my life anymore, then that's fine. I'll stop trying."

Shoving to my feet, I glower at him.

"You were the one who chose not to be in my life, Josephine. Not me."

With my fists curled, I march from the house. No one bothers to stop me.

I've spent the last hour sprawled across my lounge with the fan on high speed. Reaching for my phone, I bring up Belle's contact, calling her number. She answers immediately.

"I need a drink."

"Pub?"

"Yeah."

"Be there in twenty," Belle replies before the call ends.

After sitting down and breathing for a minute, I gather my things and walk to the pub. I feel some of the anxiety riddling in my chest fade as soon as I see those gorgeous smile lines and stunning blue eyes. His face splits into a genuine, warm smile when he sees me and suddenly I forget we have a front-row audience watching us.

I rush towards him and he gathers me in his arms, kissing me hard. I loop my arms around his neck, tightly clinging to him.

He leads me out the back and I lean onto the brick wall. He looks at me in concern. He pulls out a cigarette and offers it to me. I take it and he pulls one out for himself. He lights the end of mine and then uses it to light his own before stepping back.

"What's wrong?"

His lips close around the cigarette and the end glows orange in the dark. I do the same, taking a long drag, I fill him in. It wasn't that big of a deal, but not being in good graces with my family really unsettles me. Which sounds ridiculous after I left them without so much as a goodbye.

Harley moves so that he's standing close to me. He pushes a bit of hair back from my face and tilts my chin so that I'm forced to meet his eyes.

"He just needs time to process everything. He will come around."

"I've been home for months. He hasn't."

His hand sinks lower, his thumb grazing down my neck and rubbing circles just above my collarbone.

"It won't matter soon."

"How's that?"

"We'll be gone."

I smile. "I still want to be on good terms, regardless of where I live."

Nodding, he takes another long inhale before turning his head and exhaling the smoke downwind of me.

"I know, baby."

Standing on my tiptoes, I press my lips softly to his.

"I better get back out there, I'm meeting Belle here for a drink."

We hold hands right until we can't anymore. Harley moves around behind the bar and when I look up, Belle is watching us, eyebrows raised.

"Woah. What have I missed?" she asks.

I grin. "A lot. You better take a seat."

# Chapter Fifty-Two

## Josie

"Holy … shit."

"What?" I ask innocently.

"You look …" Harley blinks, eyes ravishing me. "Very beautiful."

"Really?" I smile, looking down at the dress.

It's a deep navy floor-length dress that is cinched at the waist and low-cut in the chest. I've paired it with dangly silver earrings and a pair of jewelled stilettos. Even with these gigantic shoes, I still only come to chin-height on Harley.

"Yes." He nods appreciatively.

Harley is in a dark suit with a navy long-sleeved top underneath, matching my dress. He looks devastatingly handsome. It's still so startling to see him dressed up like this and not in his usual black tee and ripped jeans. I love both looks, though. I don't think Harley could look unattractive if he tried.

It's been a week since the city trip and if I thought the high from being away together was going to fade, I thought wrong.

As much as I am loving how good things are going, I'm a little scared. Life has never been so good and I'm terrified something is going to ruin it.

Tonight, there is a Casino Night taking place at the town hall, as a fundraiser for the town. It's one of the biggest events of the year, as many bordering towns come over to support and celebrate.

The car park is full and people are milling outside of the hall when we arrive, some gathered in small groups. I don't recognise any faces for the first five minutes. Loud jazz music blares from the speakers. I survey the fancy flashing lights that have been strewn across the entryway. There's a water fountain display off to the side and an elegant tower of wine glasses perched on top of a table with pearl décor. Every year the town tries their best to make this event as high-class as possible and this year, it looks like they've succeeded.

Heads turn our way as we walk inside. Harley's hand finds the small of my back as we hand over our tickets.

Annabeth, Nick's mother, is the one sitting at the table alongside another woman who I've met before but can't recall her name. Her green eyes narrow at me before flitting to Harley. None of us say a word to each other.

Harley dips his chin, eyes meeting mine, then kissing me softly. I exhale, not realising how tightly I had grabbed his hand. This whole place makes me nauseatingly anxious.

"It's going to be fine," he says.

I've been dreading seeing Nick and the rest of the group. I imagine news about Harley and I has spread through the town by now. Eyes follow us as we walk inside. I don't know what they would be more shocked about—me having forgiven Harley and that we are here together, or the fact that Harley Caldwell is in a suit. Probably a combination of both.

Rows and rows of tables are plastered around the hall, with men and women in black suits behind them. Ladies in stunning gowns and men in fitted suits mill around, glasses of champagne in their hand, purses or wallets in the other.

Harley and I wander towards the bar and both get drinks. I take a generous gulp of mine and Harley flashes me a grin.

"Want to play some blackjack?"

"Sure," I reply.

We move towards one of the blackjack tables that doesn't have all the seats taken. I slide into the high chair and Harley does the same beside me. A young-looking man with rosy cheeks and messy brown curls smiles at us.

"Good evening," he greets politely.

We stay at this table for a few rounds. I feel safe and out of the way here, but I know we can't hide here all night. After winning forty dollars, I leave the table with a satisfied smile.

Harley and I take our time roaming around the hall, then circle back to the bar for a refill.

"I'm going to the ladies quickly," I say.

Harley's eyes flash before he smirks, leaning in. "You need company?"

My pulse jumps as heat splashes across my cheeks. I wonder if there will ever be a time that my stomach won't flip-flop when he smiles at me like that.

"I wouldn't want to ruin my dress."

"I can be very gentle," he assures me, grinning wickedly. "I can't say the same about your panties, though."

I tilt my head to the side, matching the lustful glee in his eyes.

"Who said I'm wearing any?"

His jaw clenches as his gaze travels over my body. He finishes his drink.

"You're making me feel very …" He clears his throat and adjusts his pants. "Inappropriate."

I smile sweetly. "That was never my intention."

He rolls his eyes. "Right."

"I'll be right back." I wink at him before I graze my left breast against his shoulder. I saunter away. By the time I reach the bathroom. I'm flustered, and I take a minute to calm down. That boy does crazy things to me.

The door swings open and I gasp, seeing Harley stride inside, a confident smirk on his face.

"We can't," I instantly say.

"And yet you went into this cubicle," he says, pointing at the unisex sign. "The only one on its own."

I press my lips together. "Okay. You got me."

Running his tongue across his teeth, he eyes the slit in my dress. My insides squirm underneath his gaze. He steps closer, his hands sliding over the smooth fabric and resting on my waist.

"Don't ruin my hair," I warn. "Or my makeup."

"Those are going to be the last things on your mind in a minute."

He puts pressure on my hips, turning me. I inhale sharply as he firmly bends me over and efficiently gathers my dress, pulling it out of the way. This has quickly become a little secret of ours. It's scandalous and extremely addictive.

Harley's hand disappears under the fabric, gripping my bare ass. He lets out a soft, throaty groan. His finger traces my entrance teasingly and I press myself into him, loving the feeling of his warm skin on the most sensitive part of my body. He sinks a finger into me and I moan softly.

"You're going to have to be quiet, sweetheart."

Closing my eyes, I nod.

Another finger enters and I gasp. His other hand travels up my stomach and grips my breast hard. I whimper softly as he fingers me slowly, ensuring I'm ready for him.

"I need you," I whisper.

"Now?" He smirks.

"Now!" I demand.

His fingers are replaced by his thick erection and I groan as he pushes in deep, stretching me. His thrusts are strong and slow at first before he circles his hips and slams into me, hitting me at the exact angle I needed. I moan his name over and over as he thrusts.

Arching my back, I push to meet his thrusts and he makes a guttural groan at the feel of it.

"Touch yourself," he murmurs.

My eyes pop open, meeting his. I'm immediately sucked into those blue eyes, breaking into chills. Swallowing, I move my hand to the front of me. He nods encouragingly and I bite my lip before pressing my finger onto my clit. It slips due to how wet I am, but I move it back to place and apply pressure. I push back into him, meeting his thrusts.

Every part of me is quivering and I bite down on my lip to stop myself crying out. My orgasm hits me like a wave and I let it crash over me. It takes all my self-control not to fall apart then. I push harder back into him and clamp my thighs together. His breath quickens and I watch intently as his eyes flutter closed. His lips part and his cheeks blossom a gorgeous red as he comes. He is so damn beautiful.

"Holy shit," he breathes, slowly stilling behind me and leaning heavily forward. His breath blows wisps of my hair forward as he tries to catch his breath.

Feeling a little light-headed—possibly from the wine—but most certainly from him, I turn to face him. We kiss for a few seconds, and I feel the cold tang of his lip ring press against my lower lip. The kiss is sweet and warm and delicate. He places my face between his hands, holding me as though I'm made of glass. His tongue slides against mine and I moan into him.

"I don't want to go back out there," he whispers.

"Me neither."

"But we have to."

"Kind of." I smile.

"You look so perfect," he whispers.

I kiss him again. "You do too."

I take a step and frown, staring down at myself.

"Uh, I'm going to need to clean up."

Harley chuckles, reaching for the paper towel. I take it from him and quickly clean myself.

"All night I'm going to be thinking about everything underneath that dress," he murmurs.

I smile coyly. "Oh yeah?"

"Hell yeah." His eyes don't stop roaming all over my body until we're stepping out the door. He steps back and gestures to the door. "After you."

I hope I don't look as flushed as I feel as we make our way back into the hall. People's stares don't go unnoticed, and I blush. We beeline to the bar and order another drink. I fan myself while I wait, feeling very hot all of a sudden.

When I turn back, we come face to face with Jess. I quickly pull my lips together and probably look like I've sucked on a lemon when I see that she is wearing the same hairstyle and makeup look I wore on the engagement trip.

Her eyes flit back and forth between Harley and me for a moment before settling on me.

"Have you seen Nick?"

"Hi to you too," I mutter.

"Have you?" she presses.

"Why the fuck would she have seen Nick?" Harley snarls at her. "She's here with me, isn't she?"

Jess bristles and the expression on her face is similar to many I've seen around Harley. His striking looks and harsh mouth make people fearful of him, although I haven't witnessed that side to him for a long time. He's always soft and sweet with me. It's something I honestly can say no one else has got to experience. That makes me selfishly happy.

Seeing Harley now with his jaw tense and scowling, I want to smile. Jealousy looks hot on him. *Very* hot.

"I'm worried."

Tearing my eyes from Harley and swinging them back to Jess, I frown.

"About Nick?" I question.

She nods, hugging her arms around herself. "He was meant to help set up but didn't show. No one has heard from him all day, and I went to his house before coming and he wasn't there. His parents haven't seen or heard from him either."

"Maybe take a hint." Harley shrugs and I dig my elbow into his side.

"That is definitely unusual," I reply, chewing my lip. "I'll keep a lookout and I'll let you know if we see him. Okay?"

Dipping her chin, she nods, staring at the ground. "Okay. Thanks."

Jess moves away from us, going back to her group, and Harley and I exchange a glance.

"I'm sure it's nothing."

"You might not care much about Nick, but there are a lot of people who do," I say, running my hands down my sides, smoothing my dress. "He's a good guy."

The words feel bitter on my tongue. There it is. Good Guy Nick. It's so automatic when I think of him.

Harley draws his brows together and we both take a sip, completely in sync.

"Sorry. I know he is. I just ..." He exhales. "He had you and didn't appreciate it."

I turn to him. "What?"

"I'm sure he loved you but he didn't worship you, not like you

337

deserve to be, and I hate him for it. I also hate that he turned his back on you after everything."

I stare open-mouthed at the boy in front of me. Well. He definitely isn't a boy anymore. A man. A stunningly handsome and thoughtful man. Who continues to surprise me every time I am around him.

A light punch to my arm hurtles me back to reality. I blink at my brother, who beams at me.

"Howdy there," he greets before turning to Harley. "Hey, man."

"Sam." Harley smiles politely, and I repress a giggle at the sight of him forcing a polite smile onto his face.

"You two know every single person here is talking about you, right?" he says casually.

"Yep," we both reply.

"It was getting really dull around here anyway." Sam offers a lopsided grin, clinking glasses with the both of us. "Want to have a go at whatever that thing is?" He points to a table off to the side that hasn't got anyone there.

Harley and I glance at each other and shrug. "Sure."

We spend the next half an hour following Sam around and mingling with his friends. They're nice enough, and easy to chat with.

"Sam, can you go grab some more ice, please?" Mum asks as she sidles up beside our group. "Oh—Josephine. You look gorgeous!"

"Josie," I automatically correct. "And thanks! You do as well."

My father remains silent as he stares steadily at Harley.

"Hi, Mr. Mayor." Harley clears his throat. "Nice to officially meet you."

Colour rises in my father's cheeks. With a clenched jaw, he takes Harley's hand and gives it a gruff shake before stepping back.

"Hello, Harley." My mum smiles kindly. "You look very handsome. I don't think I've ever seen you at one of the fundraisers before."

"No, I usually work," he replies, then clears his throat when he realises he might have sounded rude. "It's really great, though."

I rest a hand on his arm and smile at him. It's cute he is trying so hard. My parents move on after that and I turn to Harley.

"You little cutie," I tease.

The corner of his mouth lifts. "I am not."

"You are so."

"Need to use the bathroom yet?" he drawls, twisting his lip ring.

An ache builds between my legs and I press my thighs together, exhaling.

"I'd rather just leave this thing all together," I admit.

"Let's go."

"Really?" I ask.

"Why do you sound surprised?" He grins. "Do you think I *want* to be here?"

I raise an eyebrow and laugh softly. "No, I suppose not."

"Trust me, there are a lot of things I'd rather be doing." His eyes lower to my chest and back up.

"I'd like to know more about that."

"Oh. You will."

His arm snakes around me and guides us towards the exit. My feet falter when I notice Jess biting her nails and looking nervously around at the different groups. I scan the room. Still no Nick.

Brennon meets my eyes and I quickly look away. Thankfully, he hasn't approached us at all tonight, which I'm surprised about. His parents are one of the main organisers of this event though, which is probably why he is being on good behaviour.

"Hang on a second."

Grabbing Harley's hand, I drag him towards the group Jess is with. I waved to John and Eric earlier, but kept my distance since I know they haven't liked Harley in the past.

Jess jerks her head at the sight of us coming towards her.

"Have you seen him?" she immediately asks.

Shaking my head, I reply that we haven't. Her shoulders sag and she looks down at her phone, as if willing it to give her all the answers.

"Maybe you should try to call him."

Everyone turns to Jess, and she looks pained saying those words.

"I left my phone at home," I say.

Everyone gives me a weird look, obviously not realising how little I have to do with my phone anymore.

"We were thinking of heading off anyway. We will go look for him. I'll let you know if we find him," I say to her.

Sighing, she nods. "Okay. Thanks."

"Hey, Josie?" a voice asks.

I turn, seeing Shannon smiling at me. She looks stunning in a floor-length emerald dress. Her crazy curls are bundled into a neat bun on the top of her head, with ringlets cascading down her face.

"Did that guy ever catch up with you?"

I furrow my brows. "What guy?"

"There was a guy at the club, the other weekend, who said he knew you."

Icy dread fills my veins. I wait for her to laugh and say that she is kidding. Obliviously, she goes on.

"Handsome guy. Really tall. Dressed in a suuuuper expensive suit," she prattles away and I can feel the heated gaze of Harley staring into the side of my face.

"Did you tell him?" I whisper.

"Tell him what?"

My mouth is paper dry. "Did you tell him where I live?"

Shannon cocks her head, looking up at the ceiling. "Honestly? I don't remember. I was pretty drunk. He seemed really nice, I wouldn't be worried!"

The walls around me start closing in and I jerk my head as a nod. "Yeah … thanks."

I don't feel like I've breathed properly for a full minute until I stumble through the door and inhale a lungful of the night air.

"Jesus Christ," Harley explodes. "Is she talking about Elliot?"

I rake my hands through my hair, forgetting about how much effort went into styling it. The text he sent flashes before my eyes.

*See you soon, Josie.*

I blocked his number after that. I should have long before it.

"Who else would it be?"

Harley pulls me towards him. "It's been a couple weeks since we've been back. Nothing has happened. I'm sure it was nothing."

My breath is shaky and I nod. "Yeah … I hope so."

His nose grazes mine. "I won't let anything happen to you. We're together every night. You're safe."

I lean up and kiss him. My body relaxes at the feel of his warm, soft lips.

"Thank you."

"It's what I'm here for." He smiles. "Smoke?"

"Please."

He pulls out a cigarette and offers me the first puff. We're mostly quiet as we share the cigarette. My racing heart finally slows, and I feel my tense muscles unwind. I'm sure it's nothing. Elliot has impulse issues; if he knew where I was, I'd be aware of it by now.

"Are we really going to look for Nick?" Harley side-eyes me, taking one final drag before dropping the cigarette to the floor and stepping on it. He picks it up and throws it into the closest bin. Under the moonlight, his eyes have a silvery tint to them. The pale light highlights his high cheekbones and dark hair.

I give him a deadpan stare. "Yes."

"We are both over the limit."

"Oh shit," I curse, looking over at Harley's truck sitting in the carpark. "I sort of forgot about that fact."

"Yeah." He laughs. "We can check out some places in town on the walk home? See if he is there?"

"That sounds good."

I briefly glance at my tall heels and wonder how much pain I'll be in by the time we get home. Bending at the knees, I go to unbuckle the strap and flinch as a memory hits me. I got good at enduring long hours in heels when I was out with Elliot. I once took my shoes off and got a slap in the face for it.

A shiver rolls down my spine at the memory. I wonder if I will ever not have PTSD from the things he did to me. Deciding to leave the shoes on for now, I slide my hand into Harley's.

"Leaving so early?" a voice floats through the darkness.

We turn to see Brennon leaning against a car. He's dressed in all-black, his hands dug deep into his pockets.

Straightening my spine, I stare directly at him. Harley tenses beside me, his grip tightening on my hand.

"Come on, let's go," he says, turning to leave.

"Aw, now that you two have finally made it official, you don't have time for Brennon anymore?" His words slur together and he shakes his head, as if clearing his vision. "Only your best mate of *fourteen years.*"

"You know very well why I don't have *time* for you," Harley bites out, his jaw ticking furiously.

"You're going to throw away fourteen years of friendship? After everything I have done for you, for this fucking piece of trash?" he spits, jutting his chin towards me. My stomach tightens uncomfortably at his insult.

Harley yanks his hand from mine and strides towards Brennon.

"Say another fucking word about her."

"She is nothing but a useless slut who can't decide what she wants," Brennon growls, throwing a murderous look at me.

Harley launches forward. His fist smashes into Brennon's nose with a distinct crunch. I inhale so sharply I almost choke. Brennon flies back, hitting the ground with a painful-sounding thud.

"Harley!" I cry out when he drops to his knees. He bunches

Brennon's shirt and reefs him into sitting position. Blood drips down his nose, smearing over his lips.

"You're dead to me," he says coldly before releasing him.

Brennon falls back onto the grass in a sprawl. Harley pushes to his feet, and Brennon lets out a low, throaty chuckle.

"Don't come crawling back when she leaves again."

A muscle in Harley's cheek spasms but he doesn't turn back. He grips my hand harshly and pulls me after him. We walk for a long while before he slowly exhales. I touch his arm, and he hugs me to him.

"He is such an asshole."

"He is," I agree.

"I'm sorry."

"Don't be."

He kisses the side of my head, then releases me. His hand finds mine once more.

"Does it hurt?" I ask, bringing it to my lips, and gently kiss his knuckles.

"I'm used to bruised knuckles," he replies.

I softly trace them and kiss the top of his hand, dropping it back between us. We check the pub and the RSL, the only places that would still be open. When we still come up empty, we decide to look at the parks and popular walking tracks.

It's warm tonight but not stifling, which is nice.

"Hey, so, I've been doing some research," Harley casually says, swinging our arms, as if the last half hour didn't happen.

"On what?"

"Jobs, houses, rent prices."

"Where?"

"Lots of different places. I found a really beautiful town. It's small, not this kind of small though, right on the beach. Rent is a little pricey, but there's bordering towns that are more affordable that are only ten, fifteen minutes away." He sneaks a glance at me. "There's a new dental office going in. It's being built at the moment. There're several job openings there, and I also looked into getting my own ABN so that I can be a contract builder. Which means I pick how much I want to work and when. And the pay is really great. Also, it's only an hour drive to the city, so we could go out up there any time we wanted."

His hand tightens in mine and all of a sudden, my eyes are stinging.

Snippets of our future flash before my eyes. Laying on the beach, swimming every day, coming home from work, cooking dinner together.

Peaceful. Quiet. Happy.

"That sounds incredible," I whisper. "I want that, Harley."

"Then let's make it happen."

"When?"

"Whenever you're ready, sweetheart."

I tug him to a stop and slam into him, wrapping myself around his body. He hugs me back and kisses my hair.

"I'm serious about this, Harley. I want to apply for work there."

He nods. "Me too. I will, if you do."

"Tonight!" I say. "When we get home!"

Splatters of raindrops kiss my cheeks and I glance up at the sky in shock. Rain is rare out here. He thumbs away the water droplets.

He chuckles. "We are a little tipsy. And I can't write for shit. I might need some help with my resume."

"I got you." I smile, as the rain starts to get heavier.

"Do you even want to know where it is?" He arches an eyebrow, curling a hand over his eyes to keep out the water.

I shake my head. "As long as you're there, it doesn't really matter."

# Chapter Fifty-Three

## Josie

After walking around town for over an hour, we text Jess from Harley's phone to let her know we were unsuccessful in locating Nick. We decide to head back home. I'm starting to feel tired, and my feet are aching. The rain is coming in heavy now. I slide out of Harley's suit jacket and fling it over my arm.

The house is pitch-black when I step onto the porch, and I stop. Harley grunts as our shoulders collide.

"Ow," he mutters.

I stare ahead, blinking.

"What?" he asks.

"The door."

He looks at the door, noticing that it's open. I definitely locked it when I left. After everything, I've become quite OCD with locking the windows and doors.

Harley quickly moves in front of me and throws his arm out when I try to step around him. He pushes it open with his foot and steps inside. I walk in after him and try to find the light switch.

Suddenly, something hard pushes against me and I stumble. My ankle makes an awful sound as it bends in my heels. I fall to the floor with a shriek, hitting Harley on my way down.

"Jesus—fuck!" he cries out, trying to catch me, and we both end up in a tangle of limbs on the floor.

A *pop* echoes in the room. The door locking. Lights flood the room and I wince, blinking at the brightness. I moan, looking down at my ankle. It's either sprained or broken. Definitely *something* with the sound it made, and the pain pulsing through the lower part of my leg.

"Hi, Josie."

Goosebumps scatter across my skin. I swallow uneasily. I'd recognise that voice anywhere. He reaches over and slams something hard against the back of Harley's head. A crack fills the air, and a scream leaves my lips. Harley falls to the ground, going limp.

A slow, sadistic smile stretches across Elliot's face as he faces me.

"Did you miss me?"

# Chapter Fifty-Four

## *Josie*

I say nothing.

I'm too terrified to utter a word. Every part of my body trembles as I blink up at the man I ran away from all those months ago. He tilts his head to the side, his dark eyes narrowing.

"No?" he presses.

My heart slams so hard into my ribcage, I fear it'll bruise. Swallowing, I finally manage to choke out words.

"What the hell are you doing here?"

"I've been searching for you for months. Didn't you get my voicemails?"

*Oh, I got them all right.*

"Couldn't believe my eyes when I saw you out a few weeks ago. It took everything inside me not to throw you over my shoulder and leave with you." He leans back on the kitchen bench, crossing his ankles. "I asked a lovely girl for some details about you. She sold you out without a second thought." He peers out the window, using two fingers to part the blinds before letting them snap shut again. "Charming little town this is. Everyone is so trusting." He smiles. A cruel, cold smile. "Like old chap over there."

He dips his chin towards the other end of the small house and I quickly turn, seeing Nick tied to a chair. Blood streaks down his face and his head is hanging forward, as if he's lost consciousness. Duct tape covers his mouth, and his arms are restrained behind him.

"Nick!" I sob, a tear running down my cheek. I scramble to my feet, only to fall back down, my knee colliding with the floor. Pain skitters up my leg and my ankle throbs.

"Aw." Elliot smiles sadly. "You've hurt yourself."

"What the hell are you doing, Elliot?" I hiss. "What the fuck is going through your head?"

His gaze sinks low over me and my insides curl. Bitterness spreads through me like poison. I hate this man with every fibre of my being.

"You look ravishing, by the way."

The weariness I felt moments ago has vanished, replaced with spine-tingling adrenaline.

*Thud, thud, thud.* It's difficult to hear anything over my heavy heartbeat.

"Originally, I wanted to take you back home. Show you that it's me that you want. But I couldn't get past the fury I felt when I saw you again. You *left*. No one leaves Elliot Dawson and gets away with it."

"Do you hear yourself?" I seethe, my breath coming out in short, fast bursts. "You are psychotic!"

"You say psychotic. I say devoted."

"That's a twisted way to look at it."

Pushing his tongue into his cheek, he smiles. "Tell me, Josie, what sort of trouble have you gotten yourself into? See, Nick here, the one that sent you those messages that time—isn't he the old boyfriend? The one you were with the night of the club? I saw you run out after him. I thought you must have been having a lover's quarrel." He frowns. "I went to a lot of trouble to detain him, you know, only to find out *he* isn't the *right one*." His eyes land on Harley.

Rain batters against the window, and the wind howls outside. It hasn't rained since I've been back. A loud crack of thunder booms outside and I cringe. Pushing to my knees, I start to crawl to Harley.

"Uh, uh!" Elliot's voice is sharp. My heart sinks when I see a gun pointed at me.

Trembling, I sit back.

"Where the hell did you get that?" I whisper.

"I bought it."

"Where?"

"Is this really what you want to be discussing right now?" he asks, lowering to a squat so that we are eye level. He's so close that his familiar scent washes over me. Clean and crisp. His eyes are darker than the night sky.

Gritting my teeth, I glare at the front door. Elliot's cold fingers slam into my chin, forcing my gaze to his.

"You hurt my feelings, Josie. No one gets away with that."

The blood drains from my face as he pins me with a dark stare that makes my insides crawl.

"What are you going to do?" My voice is so weak, it doesn't even sound like me. Two men that have occupied my heart are bloody and unconscious. I can't focus on anything else but that fact.

"I'm going to take something from you, so you know how it feels." His fingers sink into my bicep, biting the flesh. I yelp as he drags me to my feet. My ankle screams, heat flaring down the sides. He shoves me into a chair. He presses the gun to my cheek, dragging it across my skin. It feels cold and slick. "Don't move."

He steps back and fumbles for the rope he has sitting there, then bounds my wrists to the chair. I hiss as the rope tightens, and the corners of his mouth twitch. He is enjoying this a little too much.

The legs of the chair drag across the floor and he places it about a metre from where Nick is still slumped over. My eyes follow the gun as he places it down and reaches for Harley. I tug at the ropes and they dig further into my skin.

With a groan, he hoists Harley's long frame over his shoulder and throws him down onto the chair, placing him in the same position as Nick. Harley's head bobs to the side, and I wince as I see blood run down his neck from the wound on the back of his head.

Elliot heaves a deep sigh, placing his hands on his hips, staring at the boys.

"They're heavier than they look." He dusts his hands and swipes the gun up before wandering over to where he was standing previously. He glances through the blinds again. Rain thunders down onto the tin roof, getting louder with each moment.

"We lived together," Elliot says tersely, coming back towards me. He sits on the coffee table and it groans under his weight. Neatly, he folds his ankles, staring at me with an unflinching gaze. "You told me you loved me. Was that all a lie?"

"I cared for you, Elliot, and you know how you repaid my loyalty? By bullying me, manipulating me, *hurting* me. Sending workers to spy on me in our own apartment. You're sick and twisted. You're not capable of love. You like to own people, and when you can't control them, you get upset and do crazy things." I seethe. "Like this."

He scoffs. "Yeah. Okay. Whatever helps you sleep at night, Josie." He tilts his head, eyes narrowing. "I'm not the one who abandoned you, without a word, into the night, never to be heard from again."

"You hit me! And threatened me. Constantly," I shout at him, hot tears brimming in my eyes. "If you call that love, then you're more delusional than I thought."

His nostrils flare. We glower at each other. He exhales, letting out a cold laugh.

"I didn't come here to argue with you, Josie. I came here to show you what happens when you hurt people."

"*You* hurt *me*," I hiss, my fingernails biting into the flesh of my palms. "I'm the one who deserves to get revenge. *Not* you."

I stare at him. I can't stop. I take in every bit of him. Long legs. Pale skin. Lanky arms. Gelled back hair. His collared shirt. His expensive watch. His leather shoes. Squeaky clean, like always.

"So." He faces forward and waves his gun at Harley, as if my last comment fell on deaf ears. "He's the new boyfriend?"

Despite the rain bringing a cooler temperature with it, the small house feels airless. I inhale and inhale, but nothing is getting to my lungs. Dots dance over my vision and I blink them away. *Focus, Josie.*

"The old flame versus the new flame." Elliot smiles. "Who will win?"

I say nothing. Heat rises in my cheeks and I pull relentlessly at the ropes. Elliot exhales a heavy breath, tapping the gun against the benchtop in a smooth, controlled rhythm.

"I'm a man of many things, but patience is not one of them."

I scoff. "Yeah. I don't need to be reminded of that."

"Now, now, don't be like that."

Tears of frustration well in my eyes when the ropes dig deeper into my wrists. This can't be really happening. This is some twisted nightmare or PTSD-attack, and my mind has tricked me into thinking it's real.

I squeeze my eyes shut.

*This isn't real. This isn't real. This isn't real.*

"Yes, it is," Elliot drawls, causing shivers to roll over me. I must have said those words out loud. "You know it is."

"What do you want?" I whisper.

"I've told you." He strides over to me, then leans down, pressing his face so close to mine that the tips of our noses touch. "Pick one."

"You're fucking crazy."

"Pick one to live and one to die," Elliot continues. His knuckles are an off-white as he flexes his fingers tauntingly over the gun.

"Those are the rules."

Rain drills into the windows and the awning slaps the side of the house. That paired with the metallic tap of the gun on the wall as Elliot walks down the lounge room is a nauseating combination.

Elliot walks away. I hear the quiet thud of his footsteps. I crane my neck as much as I can, trying to see him. Suddenly, the gun is pressed against my temple.

"Choose," he growls. "Or I will."

"I'd rather die than give you the satisfaction of making me choose between two people I love."

A frustrated grunt emits from his throat and he *tsks* at me, shaking his head. Elliot strolls unhurriedly towards Nick. He steps behind him and places his hands on his shoulders.

"You must love Nick a lot to throw him out like trash, yeah? Did you run away from him too? No goodbye? No note? No explanation?"

Sweat drips into my eye and I blink it away. Maybe I deserve this. After everything I've done, perhaps this is my reckoning.

"No, no, it's this one, right?" He glides towards Harley and playfully dances the tip of the gun down the side of his face. Everything inside me stops functioning. He notices and an evil, satisfied smile takes over his face. "Ah, yes, he is the one that must go."

"No!" I scream, thrashing wildly in the chair. It topples to the side and I wriggle and squirm, fighting against the rope as hard as I can. "I will do *anything*, Elliot. *Please.* Don't touch him."

"I wish I could let it go, Josie." He shrugs, looking at me sympathetically. "But I can't."

His thumb flicks off the safety switch and I scream so loud, my eardrums could have burst. Chest-racking sobs tear from me as Elliot places the gun neatly in the centre of Harley's temple.

"I hope you enjoyed yourself while it lasted," he says, his finger sliding over the trigger.

A loud burst of sound rockets through the room as glass shatters, raining down on the carpet. Brennon crawls through the window and suddenly stops, staring at the scene around him.

"Holy shit." His wide eyes take in everything. Nick and Harley slumped in their chairs, blood pooled at their feet. Me flailing on the floor, trying to get out of these ropes. Elliot holding a gun. Not aimed at Harley anymore, but at Brennon.

"Who the fuck is this?" Elliot barks, stomping closer to me and glaring. "Another boyfriend?" He screws his face up at me. "You really are a dumb slut, aren't you?"

"Woah, mate." Brennon raises his hands. Dried blood covers his face from when Harley landed one on him earlier. His eyes are glassy and bloodshot. I shiver again. He wasn't coming here to look out for us. He was coming to finish the fight. "Let's take it down a notch."

"I don't think so, *mate*." Elliot spits the last word and the gun tilts slightly in his hand. "You're just in time for the show."

Elliot raises the gun, pointing it straight at Harley's head.

Brennon launches forward, leaping somewhat athletically over me and tackling Elliot to the ground. The gun makes a sickening *pop* and the glass cabinet in the corner of the room shatters as the bullet slices through it.

Harley gasps, slowly raising his head. He winces and blinks, trying to process what is going on. Elliot and Brennon grapple with each other in a mixture of yelling and breathless grunts.

"Harley!" I whimper, ramming my fists into the chair and screaming, trying to get myself free. Harley starts to do the same. He manages to pivot the chair slightly and kicks his leg out, colliding with Elliot's back. Elliot yells out in anger before turning and facing the gun towards Harley again.

The same *pop* echoes as the gunshot splinters through the air. There's a ringing in my ears as I blink back into focus. Everything is dark.

Shakily, I open my eyes and stare at the blood soaking into the carpet.

# Chapter Fifty-Five

## Josie

### *Nine Days Later*

It's sweltering hot and my dress clings to my skin as I take my seat at the front row. Wearing black certainly makes this day even hotter. Rows and rows of white chairs are gathered at the edge of the church.

Somebody collapses into the chair beside me with a sigh. I glance at Nick. His face is still bruised from what happened, but they've faded significantly. He rests a hand on my knee briefly, glancing down at my strapped ankle.

"How are you holding up?" he asks.

Everything that has happened between us seems like a distant memory. He has been so kind and supportive through everything. For the first time in what feels like forever, we honestly are friends.

Jess fills the empty seat behind him. When she reaches for his hand, he takes it. I watch her thin fingers slide between his. I'm glad they're trying again. Guilt plagues me over what I did to sabotage them, but I can't think about that now. It's all worked out for the best. I just made some stupid mistakes along the way.

Everything that seemed so important before just doesn't anymore.

I looked around at the withdrawn faces and downward frowns of mourners gathered.

"I don't know," I say honestly. "I feel … numb."

"Might be the best thing, really."

I roll the funeral program between my fingers. That whole night is a blur in my mind. I remember everything, but weirdly none of it. Sweat slides down my neck and I collect it on my finger and wipe it on the skirt of my dress.

"And you?" I ask.

"I'm okay."

It's too bright. Everything feels off. I swallow and fold my leg over the other, my skin sticking to the seat.

"If everyone could please take their seats," a voice announces.

Warm tears slide down my cheeks.

*Let's get this over with.*

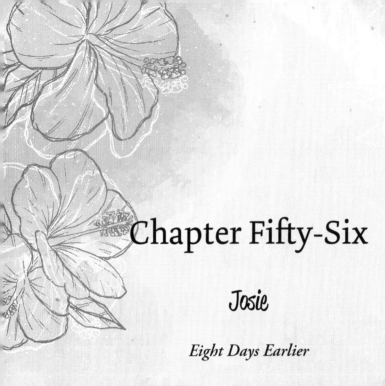

# Chapter Fifty-Six

## Josie

### *Eight Days Earlier*

Everything is white.

The walls. The sheets. The lights. The stiff gown wrapped around my body. Even the damn container filled with jelly that's stayed untouched on my tray. After being dosed up on pain relief, the throbbing in my ankle has finally subsided, but I still don't have an appetite.

My eyelids droop, but when I close them, flashes of that night tear through my mind, and suddenly, I can't breathe.

Elliot was detained a few hours after he left my house. He made it a few towns over before he had to stop for petrol. All police in the surrounding areas had been notified, and he was intercepted before he made it back onto the highway.

I do feel a little safer now, knowing he's gone and can't harm me anymore. But I'm still shaken to my core.

A knock brings me out of my thoughts. Mum, Dad, and Sam are hovering in the doorway.

"Hi, hon," Mum says. She has been in and out for the day, but this is the first time the others have visited. "How are you feeling?"

"Better." I smile weakly.

She waves the small bouquet of flowers that are clutched in her palm. They're pretty, filled with pastel pink, purple, and white flowers.

"I thought these might make the room look a little nicer." She places them on the table. "Do you need anything?"

I shake my head.

"I knew he was a scary dude, but I never thought ..." Sam shakes his head, his hair that is far too long falling into his eyes. "You're lucky to be alive."

"Some of us aren't so lucky," I say.

Chewing his bottom lip, Sam nods.

"I'm going to hit up the vending machine. Can I get you anything?"

"Water, please."

Sam gives Mum a look and they both walk back out the door, leaving my father and me alone. I shift in the bed, trying to get comfortable. His eyes rest on my ankle for a few moments before finding my face.

Tears brim in my eyes and I let them fall. He takes a seat on the bed, curling his arms around me. I rest my head on his shoulder and cry.

"I love you, pumpkin," he murmurs, kissing the top of my head. "I'm sorry I haven't been a great father these past few months."

I hiccup, sniffling, my tears leaving a wet stain on his flannel shirt.

"I haven't been much of a daughter, either."

"Hush now," he says, his voice more comforting than he could ever know. "None of that matters anymore."

I bury my face into his chest and his arms tighten around me.

"I'm thankful you're still here," he whispers. "My baby girl."

# Chapter Fifty-Seven

## Josie

### *Nine Days Later*

After Brennon's funeral, the whole town gathered in the hall for the wake. As much of a terrible person I thought he was, he saved my life that night. Harley and Nick's too. Elliot is completely unhinged—I don't think any of us were going to walk out alive if Brennon hadn't broken into the house when he did.

Not many people know what really happened, but I made sure to stand up and tell everyone Brennon saved all of us that night, and that act of heroism won't be forgotten anytime soon.

I rub circles over Harley's back. He's taken this hard, considering the two weren't on speaking terms and that the last time he spoke to him, he sent a fist into his face. He stayed at the apartment they shared for a week before he returned to me. I missed him terribly while he was away. I had gotten so used to falling asleep beside each other, in the other's arms. But he needed space and time to process everything that happened.

He packed up Brennon's things and took them to his family

before Harley put anything that didn't fit in my place into temporary storage until we move.

"He was my best mate," Harley murmurs, leaning forward, pressing his elbows into his thighs. "Took me in so many times when I couldn't be at home. I don't condone anything that he did to you—I will never be able to let that go—but I wish ..." He exhales. "I wish things had been different."

"I know, baby," I whisper. "Me too."

Harley looks haggard. He has a few days old stubble, and his hair is messy, but he still looks perfect to me. Dark circles hang under his eyes, and he rubs his face.

People move around the room, every so often coming up to us and expressing their condolences. I nod thanks for both of us, as Harley barely lifts his head the entire time we are at the hall.

A heavy sadness has settled behind those pretty eyes of his and I don't think it will be lifting any time soon. I can't even imagine the thoughts and feelings that would be whirling inside him right now.

We exchange a soft kiss.

"Let's get out of here."

Sniffling, he nods. "That sounds good."

The fresh air feels refreshing on my skin. It would be nice to walk all the way home, but my ankle is still too sore.

We drive in a comfortable silence. It's nice knowing we have each other to lean on. I still wake up in fits of nightmares, and Harley hasn't had much luck sleeping either. But knowing we have each other makes everything seem that bit better.

"Let's camp out at the dam tonight," he suddenly says.

We haven't been out to the dam since ... four years ago, when we used to sneak out there together and lay under the stars.

We shower and sleep the afternoon away, both of us exhausted and drained from the day. At about six, we pack a bag and throw some blankets into the back of my car, before we take the short trip out to the dam.

I place the blanket down and spread the pillows out. Harley lays down and I curl into his side, pressing my head into his chest, finally feeling peaceful.

# Chapter Fifty-Eight

## *Harley*

It's crazy how your perspective on things changes after someone you love dies.

Sure, there were many things about Brennon that I despised, but he was my brother. Obviously not by blood, but he was family. Nothing could ever change that.

He's always been there. From day one. It's going to be so strange not hearing from him every day. Not hearing his loud laugh, obnoxious jokes, always just being *there*.

Josie nestles into me, and I tighten my arm around her, pulling her closer, even though we can't physically be any closer. Pressing my lips against her hair, I run my hand down her back, trailing up and down.

Brennon was the last thing tying me to this place. Now, I can move on, and never have to look back.

I've wanted this for so long and now it's finally going to be my reality. I sigh into her, inhaling her scent.

My new life starts now and honestly, I've never been more ready for it.

# Chapter Fifty-Nine

## *Josie*

### *Two Months Later*

Warm, golden lights are strung across the roof of my family home. Soft music is playing in the background, and due to some recent fan purchases—courtesy of Mum—the house isn't as unbearably hot as it usually is.

I'm dressed in a simple pale blue strapless dress that stops mid-thigh. My long hair hangs loosely down my shoulders. I touch the bracelet on my wrist, the H & J engraving winkling underneath the lights. I smile, running my thumb over it. It sits next to my bracelet that Elise got for me.

I take a seat at the table. It's a farewell dinner for Harley and me, while simultaneously, our parents meet Sam's boyfriend for the first time. He finally came out to them about a month or so ago, and Mum thought this was a nice time for all of us to be together before I move away.

A warm hand slips across my thigh and I turn, seeing Harley's handsome face smiling back at me.

"Are you going to use that?" he asks, pointing to the pepper. Shaking my head, I pass it to him. He squeezes my thigh before gently releasing it.

"So, Kaleb, what do you do for work?" Mum asks.

Kaleb is a tall guy—almost as tall as Harley—with soft golden locks and gentle brown eyes. He's clad in a neat button-down top and dark-wash jeans. I noticed he also wore dress shoes and they squeak with each step he makes. His cheeks are touched with a hue of pink, broadcasting how nervous he is to be here.

My father, quite possibly the most opinionated man on the planet, took a while to wrap his head around the whole thing, but after my near-death experience, I honestly think he has taken a step back from things and has started to reconsider how he looks at life. Or maybe he realises that this life is short and he may as well use his time wisely. That's how I feel, anyway.

"I'm in accounting," he answers. "I work for my father."

"How lovely." Mum nods, reaching for the potatoes. "Do you enjoy it?"

"Yeah. It's good." He smiles shyly.

He hasn't told the parents yet, but Sam and Kaleb are going to be moving into my little house once I've gone. They've already signed the lease. I think Sam has been a little nervous about how Dad will go with dinner, let alone announcing that they are going to be living together. One step at a time.

"So, uh, where are you moving to?" Kaleb asks. Utensils scrape across plates and people murmur around the table. The music is calming, and I smile around at my family.

"A tiny little beach town called Kirra Bay," I reply as I continue to load up my plate. I pass the tongs to Sam. "It's about a nine-hour drive from here."

"Wow, that's a big move."

"We're excited for a change," I say. "I've only ever lived here and in the city, so it will be nice to experience something new. My friend who I work with is travelling to a town about an hour away from there, so it'll be great having someone I know semi-close."

"I'm planning to surf every day, once I know how," Harley interjects. "See if I can get this one out on the board."

I scoff. "I'll shred you any day."

"If you say so." Harley rolls his eyes. To be fair, Harley is naturally good at everything he does; he will pick up the sport in no time. He's closed the door on bull riding for good, and is keen to try something else. I think it will be a great new start for us both.

"You can teach me when I come to visit." Sam grins, swiping the saltshaker just as I reach for it, causing my hand to close around air. "And then we will see who the real shredder is."

"Uh huh." I nod seriously. "Totally."

"Your place is close to the water?" Dad asks.

"Yeah, about …?" I look at Harley for guidance.

"About a two-minute walk, or so it says on the property description," Harley finishes. We have been on the phone nonstop with the property manager and employers for the jobs we've applied for. It's finally all clicking into place now.

"Wow," he comments. "Imagine that."

"I can't." I laugh. "It's going to be incredible."

Mum raises her glass, her red wine sloshing dangerously close to the sides.

"To change and all the exciting opportunities that lie ahead." She smiles.

We each raise our own glasses and clink them together.

"Amen," Sam chirps.

# Chapter Sixty

## *Josie*

The boot of the car slams with a definite bang. I slide into the passenger seat and look over my shoulder, scanning the bulging bags stuffed across the back seat of Harley's truck.

I sold my car last week so that Harley and I could travel to our new town together. All of our stuff is already in transit. I was hoping to upgrade my car soon, so this seemed like the perfect time to do it.

Kirra Bay, our new home, is a nine-hour drive across an incredibly long, flat stretch of land. To break up the drive, we've planned a few pitstops along the way to visit popular tourist spots. We have three weeks until we start our new jobs, so we don't need to rush to get there.

In Fern Grove, I will always be That Girl. That Girl who cheated on Nick Schneider. That Girl who had her sex tape leaked. That Girl who was held at gunpoint. That Girl who was there the night Brennon Cooper was shot.

Harley has almost as dark of a history with the place as I do, with his teenage shenanigans, his family, his involvement in the scandalous sex tape that shook the town, and his close friendship to the boy who died.

Now we get to write a fresh, new story and honestly, the freedom of it couldn't taste any sweeter.

The warm breeze filters through the windows as we drive past the *Welcome to Fern Grove* sign. It's so layered in dust, you can barely read what it says.

"Goodbye, Fern Grove," I whisper. "You may not be missed, but you won't be forgotten."

"Cheers to that," Harley says, tipping his water bottle in the direction of mine before smiling at me. That gorgeous, genuine smile reserved only for me.

It can't get better than this.

Thank you so much for reading *Meant to Be*. I really hope you enjoyed Josie's story. I love writing romance stories with emotional, angsty characters that draw you in. I loved creating this world and I hope you enjoyed it as much as I enjoyed writing it.

**Thank you!**

# Acknowledgements

First and foremost, I'd like to thank the readers—thank you from the bottom of my heart for picking up this book and embracing Josie's story. Thank you for your love, support, encouragements, and reviews. I will be forever grateful for your support.

The idea of Meant to Be came from the song 'I hate u, I love u' by Garrett Nash & Olivia O'Brien. As I was listening to the song lyrics, it made me think about how much I love stories where people either shouldn't be together but fall for each other anyway, or those who walk the fine line of love and hate (and a pleasant mixture of hormones, passion, and drama). I wanted to create a story that shows this raw emotion and the struggles that one faces when their head says one thing, and their heart another.

Thank you to my friends, family, and partner, who have dealt with endless questions, ideas, and offering me much appreciated feedback.

A huge than you to Genicious – one of my closest friends who has helped me tirelessly throughout this journey. Thank you for helping me with all my questions, formatting, where to start, and teaching me so many things. I can never thank you enough!

My amazing 'Team No Sleep' girls who have given me feedback and crucial advice that has helped shape me as a writer and has motivated me to be where I am today—thank you Kenadee, Jess, SJ, Sydni, and Jordan.

Thank you to my amazing Book Club for supporting me endlessly—Chloe, Sam, Haley, Tamika, Liv, Lexi, Josie, Sarah, Erin, Libby, Beck, and Madyson. I love you ladies!

I'd also love to thank Georjette Mercer—a kind stranger who provided me with in-depth, helpful feedback that helped me so much. Thank you!

To Jane and Rachelle, my close friends who have always given me help when I've asked.

My editor, Emily Marquart for her incredible help. To Larissa Hage and Emily Wittig, my cover designers, for your amazing work. To Jordan Lynde, an amazing friend and supporter of mine, who did a final proofread for me.

To all the bloggers, reviewers, and BookTok accounts that have gone above and beyond to show their support. To anyone who has followed me on Wattpad and been a part of my writing journey. I can't ever tell you thank you enough.

Thank you!

**"Either write something worth reading or do something worth writing." – Benjamin Franklin**

# About the Author

Lauren Jackson lives in a small coastal town in Australia. Her hobby of writing stories developed into a passion when she discovered the website Wattpad at fourteen. Since 2012, she has garnered thousands of followers and millions of views on her stories, which helped her grow and develop her love for writing. She lives close to the beach with her partner and little dog, Ace. Lauren loves to write sweet, steamy romances, and is always writing a new book.

Stay tuned for more!

## Let's Be Social!

If you'd like to keep up to date with me, please follow me on social media!

**Instagram:** @laurenjacksonauthorr
**TikTok:** @laurenjacksonauthorr
**GoodReads:** https://www.goodreads.com/user/show/18315357-lauren

Made in United States
Orlando, FL
28 April 2023

32554620R00224